Kati Woronka

Mourning Sham

copyright 2016 Kati Woronka

Dedicated to all my friends who still know how to laugh.

For if you keep silent at this time, relief and deliverance will rise from another place, but you and your father's house will perish. And who knows whether you have not come to the kingdom for such a time as this?
(Zabur Book of Esther)

Mourning Sham,
By Kati Woronka

First Trimester

Chapter One

  Maha's hands rattled as she shook a cigarette out of the packet, then snapped the lighter half a dozen times before a flame held. She held it up and began to puff, then put the lighter back on the little metal table and attempted to make herself comfortable. The straw from her little wicker chair poked into her right leg, so she crossed it over the left, leaned back and finally inhaled deeply.

  Staring blankly at the birdcage hanging in the space between herself and the building behind her, Maha refused to think, simply breathing in of the warmth filling her lungs.

  After a few deep breaths, her hand dropped to her side. She continued to stare at the canary in the cage – endowed with the most impersonal name possible, Bird – for several long moments, ignoring the embers beginning to crumble to the ground.

  Bird stared back at her for a moment, then began to sing, jovially hopping back and forth on his little wooden log of a seat, alternately facing Maha and the neighbor's back window, which was mere inches from the cage. Maha's eyes were drawn to a flicker of light in the neighbor's window, and she muttered a curse under her breath. Houses in Beirut were built way too close together, and she hated the persistent lack of privacy. She had no idea who lived in the flat behind her, and yet there was no way of escaping their blunt participation in her world.

  Her mind easily began to list other things she hated about Beirut: the pollution and smog, the car horns, the disgusting tap water which created a greasy film on her sink every day, the frequent power cuts which seemed to remind the populace that the Lebanese war had never officially ended because no country in its right mind would choose not to prioritize establishing a dependable electric grid as a symbol of its new found stability. The aloof cockiness of the Lebanese, the constant fear of being exploited by a taxi driver, even the humble Syrian, Palestinian and Sri Lankan men who cleaned her street in their pristine Sukleen uniforms, epitomizing the hegemony of big business across this tiny country.

She missed Syria, so very much. Not the Syria of today. Today, she was glad that there were two mountain ranges between herself and the horrors causing her beloved land to disintegrate into a pile of rubble. She was not glad that there were two mountain ranges between herself and her mother, and she was not yet entirely able to fathom the two mountain ranges between herself and the funeral for her father and her youngest brother, happening this very afternoon.

But the Syria that she'd grown up in, studied in, the Syria where she'd met her husband and grown into womanhood. The Syria that she had left a few years ago, thinking she was accompanying her husband for a two-year training course and entirely unaware that she would never live in the real Syria, her Syria, again. Her thoughts turned to the broad verandas on the mountain overlooking the desert in her native town of Sednaya, and to the bright red moro oranges that grew in the mosaic tiled courtyard of her aunt's ancient Damascus home. She thought of the flowers that bloomed through much of spring and summer, the scent of jasmine and the purple and crimson blossoms on bushes in front of most every home, which stood in direct contrast with the crowded, filthy concrete streets of Beirut. She thought of how she could drive from one end of Damascus to the other in just over ten minutes. Even at the worst moment of rush hour, an hour before the fast was to be broken during Ramadan, Damascus traffic flowed better than Beirut traffic at any time of the day. She thought of the food her mother cooked and the sandwiches she sometimes bought on the street while out running errands. Every bite of food in Syria vibrated with a rich flavor which made any Lebanese meal feel as bland as the bread with which it was served.

As she neared the end of her now-familiar mental recitation of things-she-missed-about-Syria, she remembered the cigarette in her hand and put it up to her mouth.

Her mind began to drift to her father and thirteen-year-old Hani. Neither of them had ever held a gun, she was sure. Her father had no brothers, and so he had been exempt from military service, and, like most other Christians from her town, her family was determined to stay out of the conflict, keep their heads down and stay alive. But vengeance fell on them just as if they had been leaders of a militia. Every fighter in Syria had innocent blood on his hands now. And that blood now included blood from Maha's family. Her own blood.

As she sucked the last of the nicotine out of the tiny cigarette butt, she once again resolved to deaden her heart. With her husband Samir, Maha still traveled regularly back to Syria. To help. They would take food, clothes, bedding...anything they could rummage up to pass on to families fleeing the Damascus suburbs where the bombing was the worst. On these trips, Maha often sat with women who had lost everything: their children, their husbands, their homes. She listened to them, cried with them and prayed for them. But, now alone in Beirut, a world away from her own mother who had just become a widow, she felt no sympathy, no compassion for those widows in the shelters in Damascus. For months now she had just been going through the motions, aware that if she allowed herself to engage emotionally in what she was witnessing on her trips home, her heart would take a strong whack with each sob story she heard, and it would not withstand the beating. Instead, she was resolved to keep her heart out of it. And that was before the senseless destruction literally landed on her own doorstep. Now, no doorstep remained – though, apparently, the television had been left intact, with a little doily on top.

She shed no tears; instead, she smoked. Just as she was stamping out the cigarette, her phone, which lay beside the ashtray, began to vibrate.

Leila tapped her fingernails on the dark gray granite surface of the kitchen island as she held the phone to her ear and waited for her friend to pick up.

After four rings, Maha answered, "Darling Leila! How are you? I've missed you!"

"Oh, I've missed you too. What's new with you?" But rather than wait for an answer, Leila said what she had called to say: "I saw your Facebook post. May God have mercy on their souls."

Maha chuckled. "Do you know what they found in the rubble? The entire house destroyed, but the television still upright with that little doily crocheted by my grandma on top. My mom always wanted to throw that doily out because it was so old, and it's the only stupid thing that survived: that and a TV, of all things!"

Leila joined Maha in a few moments of hearty laughter, much more cheery than such a story should warrant.

Once the chuckles had faded, Leila asked Maha the practical questions: "What will your mother do? Will you go back to Syria for the funeral?"

"I have been trying to convince my parents to come to Lebanon for ages, since the beginning really. But Mama doesn't want to leave. She says it is her home and if the Christians all flee Syria, then we are just offering it to the Islamists. She will go to Damascus to stay with Auntie. Praise God, so far, the Bab Touma neighborhood is still safe."

"And you?" reminded Leila.

"Mama told me not to come, that it's too dangerous. It's silly because I go to Sham all the time with Samir, but Sednaya is now completely blocked off so I couldn't get back home anyway. Can you imagine? I'll never say goodbye to Baba, nor to my baby brother. He was about to start secondary school already, you know?" Those last words came out in gulps, as if Maha was forcing the tears back.

"*Masha'allah*. God creates, and man takes away."

Leila herself had not escaped loss. Praise God, her immediate family was safe, living in a camp in the Jordanian desert, in a couple of shelters that looked like shipping containers, donated by rich Arabian businessmen. As far as any of them knew, their village no longer existed, though no one had been able to cross the various frontlines to check for many months now. Two of her uncles and some her cousins had joined the Free Syrian Army early on, and most of them had been killed in the fighting. One of her cousins, though, had proved himself to be a natural at war and been promoted to an officer in the FSA. Leila made it a point not to talk to him, ever.

Sensing there was little more to say on the subject, Leila asked, "How is Samir?"

Over the phone line, Leila was convinced she felt Maha relaxing with the change of subject. "My husband is amazing. He's my hero. Everyone worries about me when I travel – and I worry too. But Samir, he has been detained a few times already! It doesn't stop him, though. He keeps traveling back and forth between Damascus and Beirut. He says he can't stop as long as there are people who don't have food to eat. He's here in Beirut right now, thank God. I'm going to keep traveling with him, because there are so many women in Damascus who need someone to listen and just spend time with them. And plus it's less scary to travel with your husband than it is to send him into harm's way. There's no way we could stop, not as long as there is need."

"So you're saying you've joined forces with a crazy man."

"I'm saying he is a man of God."

Leila nodded and smiled, then remembered Maha couldn't see her smiles over the phone. She didn't want her friend to get the wrong idea, so she repeated the phrase with which she ended most of her conversations with Maha, "You guys are amazing."

And Maha replied as she always did in these dark times, "May God have mercy on us all."

"*Ahmeen*," said Leila: a Christian word that Leila had learned from Maha, but she needed to borrow vocabulary from as many different traditions as possible to navigate a world in which everyone she knew had lost home and loved ones. "I love you, and tell your mother I love her. And please tell me if I can do anything."

To Leila's surprise, Maha responded, "Actually, there is."

"Really?" While Leila absolutely meant the offer, she had grown accustomed to its dismissal.

"Yes. There are so many wealthy people in Kuwait, and the Kuwaiti government itself has done a lot to help."

"For sure," Leila agreed. She was proud to be a resident of Kuwait, a great place to live.

"I know that you are doing everything you can to help your own family."

"Yes, darling. As I know are you."

"Well, Samir and I were talking the other day, and we were wondering if you could help us find some help. We don't want you to send us anything, but we wondered if you could ask around with your friends, and your husband's friends, if anyone can help Samir's project."

"Sure, I can ask."

"Tell them that he doesn't just serve Christians, ok? That's important. Yes, he's a pastor, and his work is in the church, but you know Sham. Christians and Muslims still get along in Damascus, it's not like the media keeps saying."

"Of course."

"The church helps everyone that they know who needs it, as much as they can help. But they want to do a bigger project, and they need help to do it."

"My dear friend, it would be an honor to help you. I don't know what I can do, but let me ask."

"Thank you."

"You inspire me. With your father and your brother...you have every right to run away, to complain. You should. But instead, you're thinking of others."

"What else can we do?"

Leila knew there was no good answer to a question like that. Too many conversations these days were filled with unanswered questions.

A moment of bloated silence later, Maha said, "I have to go. Thanks so much for calling. I love you. Please come visit soon!"

"I love you too. Bye."

Still on the veranda facing Bird, Maha puffed her way through another cigarette, wondering at the ironies of life. Talking about a fundraising campaign and the destruction of her house and the death of her brother and her husband's ministry to displaced families, as if such things were as normal as sharing a recipe for a new sweet or admiring the music videos of the newest pop star.

Why could she not explain her frustration to her dearest friend Leila? Why did she resort to laughter and words of inspiration? If she could not be honest with Leila, she could not be honest with anyone. Leila would understand! But instead, Maha allowed herself and her husband to sound like saints, subtly implying that Leila should feel guilty for living a life of comfort in a country that did not border Syria.

And she had laughed off her father's death. Of course. What else could someone with a limp heart do? She didn't want to, of course, but she had never known loss in her entire life. She'd grown up living a predictable and happy existence, with dependable friends, and an early marriage to a man who was the envy of all the other girls. A man she loved deeply. A religious man who stuck with her though he was surely embarrassed that his wife took to withdrawing into tobacco and alcohol.

So Maha too had been raised to expect everything to fall into place, and it had, so far. For this new chapter, she had no role models and no words of wisdom upon which to draw. She'd never read any books about suffering or loss or doubt or fear. She had no vocabulary for the disquiet she now began to feel as reality began to settle over her weakened heart, like a paperweight might land on a feather pillow. In films, people cried when a loved one died, but this was not her way. People screamed and wailed, but no tears came to Maha's eyes.

What she knew, though, was that this feeling was squeezing. Her heart was too weak, too soft, to withstand the heaviness. While she might be able to dodge the blows of others' loss, she could not dodge the cannonball that was her own loss.

She had laughed about it with Leila because she had no words. She did not even know what her own emotions were, only that they hurt. And the longer she sat on her little Beirut balcony facing Bird and the neighbor's window that was no more than two meters away, working her way slowly through an entire pack of cigarettes, the greater the pain.

She had to stop thinking about it. There was no other way. She refused the mental images of her father's embrace, or of the day he proudly drove her to the university to register, or of that precious moment when he walked her down the aisle. She refused the memories of playing hide-and-seek with Hani when he was only four and she already a teenager, of teasing him about his first crush, and most especially of his visit to Beirut just a month ago, when she had begged him to stay on in Beirut and register at a Lebanese high school, and he had insisted that he loved his school in Sednaya and that Mama and Baba would miss him too much.

Those and so many more memories threatened to overtake her mind, and squeeze their way into her heart, but she pushed them away. She went inside, turned on the television and pulled a beer from the fridge.

Chapter Two

Freedom. Such an important word.
For freedom the things we suffer.
I sit here in a tiny room in a nondescript building, anything but free. For the sake of freedom, I bear this confinement today.

How can I not? This morning, I spoke with a fellow blogger who told me about the daughter of a friend. This girl was not more than fifteen years old. She completed her middle school and was a bright student. She was particularly good at math and hoped to become an engineer. Then, two weeks before she was to begin her secondary school studies, war came to her neighborhood. So she has never even set foot in the big kids school; instead she saw her dream of being an engineer yanked out of her hands. They fled dodging bullets, to the soundtrack of bombs falling behind them, to go live with a relative. This girl arrived at her relative's home, surely hoping that at least she would be safe. Instead, I learned, her cousin fell in love with her, and when she said she was not ready to marry, he didn't take no for an answer. He raped her. She is pregnant. I weep for this girl. I weep for her lost dreams. I weep tears of bitterness against a government that would bomb her neighborhood, and against a young adult man who would take advantage of war to abuse his own cousin. Does he not have any idea of the value of freedom?

How can I not be willing to suffer anything for freedom? This afternoon, my Facebook timeline revealed a series of "RIP" messages to a friend of mine, someone with whom I had studied at university. A deeply talented man. He will get no eulogy or memorial. His brilliance and passion for perfection must accompany him to the grave for the sake of the safety of his friends. He was arrested two months ago and, yesterday, his body was dumped in front of his family home. He had suffered two months' worth of torture, limbs broken, face barely recognizable There were scars in unthinkable places. His crime? Loving things that are good. Like freedom. I am proud to be Syrian and deeply ashamed, mortified, by my government's hatred of us Syrians.

How can I not be willing to give up anything for the sake of freedom? This evening, I peek timidly out of the window in my tiny room in a nondescript building. I see the shelling not too far from where I sit. I know that men are killing each other, innocent civilians are being caught in the crossfire, and young boys will run around the neighborhood adding to their bullet collection when the battle ends. Boys who used to play football and smoke on street corners while watching the girls, now collect bullets for fun and learn violence from their role models. I mutter a curse against the men who have learned to kill so easily, but I scream a curse against a man who calls himself a President and a Lion, who nurtures the killing so freely.

Because at least those boys have role models who are fighting for freedom. What's your excuse?

The Mockingbird

Leila finished reading the blog entry. She had never for a moment doubted that the Syrian blog called The Mockingbird was in fact written by her old college friend Nisreen. Nisreen was a few years younger than Leila but was born smart and opinionated. Leila had always found Nisreen inspiring, and her spunk and attitude in person was roughly identical to what it was in these blogs. Leila took some pride in seeing The Mockingbird grow in fame because Leila had played a small part in introducing Nisreen to the novel To Kill a Mockingbird. A very small part – Nisreen danced to no one else's tune and would have read the book with or without encouragement from her friend – but a part nonetheless. And it had been in their joint analysis of the book that Nisreen had first put words to her own political leanings. Nisreen was a strong defender of truth, justice, and honesty. Freedom was no small jump from there. Leila wasn't sure she agreed with Nisreen's tendency to blame every single problem in Syria on the Assad government, but she did understand. And she wondered how many of The Mockingbird's readers understood the allusion to an American story about a man who had stood up courageously and against all odds for what was right.

Even though she was sure the Mockingbird was Nisreen, and even though she felt a degree of personal ownership in Nisreen's growing identity as a blogger, and even though she felt she had a special personal understanding of the nuances in this blog that was now read widely across the Arab world, and even though the Mockingbird loyally replied to all comments left on her blog... even so, Leila had no way of getting in touch with Nisreen. The thought of commenting as an anonymous fan was repugnant to Leila. She was not a random reader; she was Nisreen's old friend and sort-of-mentor Leila. And contacting Nisreen in any way that made their personal connection obvious could put her dear friend in danger.

Leila sat staring at her phone screen, studying the picture of the homely bird that Nisreen used as her profile image, wanting to scream. Leila had distanced herself from Nisreen – and to be fair, Nisreen from Leila – several years ago after Leila had had a romantic falling-out with Nisreen's brother. And back then no one in Syria had been on Facebook, and Leila had not yet been exposed to the now commonplace wonder that is email. So keeping in touch back then had required a focused effort, an effort Leila and Nisreen had understood would be at best awkward between would-be sisters-in-law.

But now she wished she had Nisreen's email address. She wished she could write her and tell her how much she still admired her. Nisreen was a beautiful writer, and her words were inevitably inspiring. She was a gorgeous, glamorous woman and she was one of the most courageous people Leila knew. She never feared for herself and was more likely to shout from the rooftops what she believed than consider herself for even a brief moment.

And then Leila would tell Nisreen how she had developed the habit of opening The Mockingbird first thing every single morning, anxious, nay desperate, to see a new post, but not because she loved Nisreen's writing – though she did – rather because she was absolutely terrified that something was going to happen to her friend, a lovely woman whom she had once called Sister. Leila would bolt awake each morning several hours ahead of the sun, and her gut would immediately begin to tighten.

Every day, she would try to keep herself in bed until a normal waking hour, usually to no avail as her mind would jump from one loved one to another, fretting and wondering what had become of them. Then when the sun came up, or when Leila gave up trying to sleep, she'd turn on her phone. She'd check her

Facebook newsfeed for news of her friends, and make sure there were no foreboding text messages from her mother. Then she would open up The Mockingbird. If there was a new post – which was roughly three times a week – Leila's entire body would begin to relax. One muscle at a time would let go its tight knot. Each complete thought in the blog translated to one more limb in Leila's body that would stop aching. Nisreen was ok. Nisreen was still alive and not in jail. She was most likely not at that moment being tortured since she had posted a blog in the last few hours.

Somehow, Nisreen's well-being had become a symbol for the well-being of all Leila's friends. Her family was mostly now safe in Jordan, or else fighting themselves. Sure, she worried about her uncles and cousins who had chosen to participate in the war, but she thought they were stupid as well. But her friends, the girls she had studied with in high school and then in university, especially her friends from the Medina Jamayea, the university dorms in Damascus, she had lost touch with almost all of them and had no way of contacting hardly any of them. She still called Maha regularly, and she had occasionally chatted with Roxy and Huda before the problems started, but that was it. All the other dozens of wonderful women who had passed through her life during the four years that she still considered to be the greatest years of her life had disappeared from her universe, each one to her own village or neighborhood, to her own husband and children and grown-up life.

That was all good and well when life in Syria had been normal and calm. She hadn't spent much time worrying about Nisreen, for example, assuming Nisreen had continued her university studies, graduated with stellar marks, found a job doing something interesting for an international company, then begun to consider marriage. Leila hadn't had to know how Nisreen was doing before and had given it little thought. But now she needed to know. Nisreen was the only one of her estranged university friends whom she had tracked down, and so Nisreen was the friend she worried about the most. If Nisreen was alive and well, then Leila could assume likewise about her other university friends. So Leila was alive and well.

Nisreen didn't blog on a daily basis, though. Two or three, maybe four times a week. Those days when Nisreen didn't post were difficult for Leila. She puttered around her cool marbled flat and listlessly watched her kids playing in the living room. For a day or two, though she fretted, at least, she could tell herself that Nisreen doesn't post on a daily basis, and she should give it just another day. Then, on the third day, Leila would start to lose control of her nerves.

Mercy on the day when a whole week might have passed with no updates from Leila's dear friend the Mockingbird.

Chapter Three

Oh, the pressure. Maha sometimes wished she never checked her email at all. Some invisible force seemed to always pull her to her laptop, but she could not explain why. Her email never had good news these days. Sometimes, like today, it was just irksome. Other times, it was tragic.

Today, it was an email from Leila. Bless her, that girl wanted to help. Married to a doctor who worked at a top hospital in Kuwait, living in a posh luxury flat, with her children attending the best schools: she clearly felt obligated. She had money to spare and was determined to spend every penny of it, and perhaps a bit more than she could actually afford, helping. Maha knew that Leila sent regular care packages to her family in Jordan and did everything in her power to make sure that, though refugees living in a shipping container in the desert, they were healthy and comfortable. Maha imagined that they did the same for Leila's husband's family.

They were not fabulously wealthy, but they still had a little bit left over each month. After all, the home they had been building for themselves in Damascus was no longer on their docket. Previously, Maha knew that they had been investing in purchasing a flat in an upscale part of town where Leila's husband could open a clinic. There was no future in Sham now, though, so Kuwait was as good as it was going to get for them.

But perhaps more interestingly, Leila had a slew of wealthy friends. American doctors, Saudi doctors, Pakistani doctors, Lebanese and Jordanians. Through the hospital, Leila and her husband came into contact with some people who could be rallied to help a good cause. And Leila had apparently taken Maha's request seriously and was determined that every single person she knew consider helping Syrians. Since Maha had broached the subject a few days ago, her friend had sent her, at least, a dozen emails or text messages with ideas or questions. She wanted lists of items needed, project budgets, success stories and photos to share with donors and potential donors.

It was all done with a good heart, but just opening those emails was exhausting for Maha.

The request of the hour was to calculate how many children Maha's networks could get coats and scarves and shoes to. And also, how much it would cost to send food for those children's families as well. Simple information, but information nonetheless.

Maha slammed the lid on her laptop shut, grabbed her wallet and keys, and walked down the stairs of her little building, then to the little shop down the road. Some chocolate might help.

She walked out of the building into Beirut's infamous smothering humidity. The smell of wet air lingered with the fug of pollution and the faint wafts of the salty sea just down past the port. As much as she hated Beirut, and as wearisome as she found Beirut's thick air, there was a soft comfort in its warm familiarity. Everything was collapsing, but she could always count on Beirut being sticky, smoggy and polluted.

The air in Sednaya, where Maha had grown up, where there now stood a bombed-out apartment building in which everything in her family home was reduced to rubble – except for a television and an ugly doily - and where her father and brother were now being buried, was always fresh and dry. Set on the side of a rocky mountain, Sednaya could always count on the dry desert winds passing through.

Maha trudged slowly up the street, preferring to avoid the minuscule creviced sidewalk. The shop was just at the end of her street, but it felt like a long, laborious walk as she stumbled on uneven pavement, weaved in and out of tightly-parked vehicles and tried to stay out of the way of moving cars.

She walked into the shop with its welcome air-conditioner filling the small space with a loud rattling sound and uneven gusts of cold air. She then greeted the elderly shopkeeper, a man who Maha knew full well had seen his own lifetime of war in Beirut a generation previously, who had lost his first wife and two sons to the bombing and who had himself fought for a few brief months in a Lebanese Christian Phalangist militia. Now he spent most of his time seated in his little shop, preferring to speak French over Arabic whenever possible, reading classic literature with his tiny reading glasses. Always civil and gracious to Maha, he nonetheless never seemed entirely content when his peace and quiet was disturbed by a customer.

Predictably, Mr. George looked up from his paper, lowered his reading glasses so he could address Maha from above them, and quietly welcomed her, saying, "*Ya Hala. Bonjourein, mon cherie*," a truly Beiruti linguistic mix. Then he went straight back to reading.

Restless, Maha wasn't so sure that chocolate was what she wanted anymore. She went over to the rack of chips and was trying to decide between Doritos and Salt 'n Vinegar when the bell over the shop door chimed. Out of reflex, she glanced up and positioned her body so as to avoid being taken by surprise. She had developed an uncanny fear of soldiers and police officers in the past months, subconsciously convinced that a moment like this might be the end.

It wasn't a soldier, though, nor a police officer. It wasn't a man with a gun. In fact, it wasn't a man at all. It was a woman, about her age, with flaming red curls, walking quickly up to the counter to address Mr. George.

By instinct, Maha averted her eyes and quickly turned back to the display of chips. That woman looked familiar. Very familiar. Though she couldn't place the familiarity, Maha felt a wave of memories rush over her. University, friends, happier days.

She inched around, to the chocolate display, where she could hide from the counter but hear the conversation.

The woman was asking the shopkeeper what kinds of cigarettes he had.

She was asking in Arabic – clearly she didn't speak a word of French.

That meant she must be Syrian. But these days, in Beirut, that was nothing new.

But to be in central Beirut, in a bedrock of Christian traditionalism, and to hear a Druze accent...that was unusual.

Maha didn't have many Druze friends, so it wasn't a surprise to her that this woman might be a memory from her university years. When she was a student, her friends had come from all over Syria, but except for Leila, she'd lost touch with almost all.

She dared to turn her head to the woman again, hoping to catch another glimpse of the woman unnoticed. But to no avail. The woman looked immediately at her.

Not more than a second of confused recognition was followed by, "Maha? Maha *habibty*? Wow, you haven't changed at all!"

Maha smiled hesitantly as the woman dropped the cigarette boxes in her hand and ran over and gave her a big hug.

Then she remembered. She gripped her old friend's back and screamed, "Roxy! I can't believe it! What are you doing here?"

The two women hugged as they hadn't since they'd been little more than girls at the University of Damascus half a decade ago. They stood there holding each other tightly, rocking back and forth, for a solid few minutes, with Mr. George looking on wordlessly. He would never let on that he, one of the few remaining stalwarts of the Christian-dominated French-speaking Lebanese Paris-of-the-Middle East that had reigned before the Lebanese civil war began in 1975, approved of a Syrian reunion in his little shop. He could not admit any pleasure in seeing a moment of intimacy between a good Christian lady married to a pastor living in his neighborhood, and a flaming red-headed Druze, who had descended, unasked, upon his shop. But these were dark days for all, and Maha felt she detected a glint of pleasure in the corner of his eye.

After a bit, Maha pulled away and grabbed Roxy's shoulders. "Let me see you. Red hair? Since when? It suits you anyway. Tell me everything."

Mr. George turned back to the tiny electric burner that he kept in his little alcove and put some coffee on to boil. He passed two little plastic stools over the counter and made the women sit. With these gestures, without saying a word, he turned his shop into a parlor.

Maha and Roxy sat down, still clinging to each other's arms as if to make up for lost time and ensure they'd not be separated again.

All but ignoring Mr. George, Maha asked, "What are you doing here?"

"I just wanted to get a cola. It's so hot outside."

"No, *habibty*. I mean, what are you doing in Gemayze? No one ever comes this way."

"Well..." began Roxy.

But Maha interrupted, aware that she was agitated. "What am I saying? That's a silly question for me to ask. I mean..." She paused while Roxy waited. "Oh. I'm such a fool. Seeing you brought back so many memories from university days. It's only five years ago since I graduated, but it feels like another life, doesn't it?"

Roxy nodded yes.

"But that's not the world we live in anymore, is it." Maha phrased it as a question but clearly didn't need an answer. After a few more moments she asked, tentatively, "How is your family? Are they..." Her voice dropped off.

"Praise God everyone is alive."

Maha's shoulders dropped. Her muscles had tensed up, as they usually did in similar conversations these days, in anticipation of more bad news. "Your husband?"

"Back in Sweida. He couldn't bear the thought of leaving our house. He's sure that if we leave the house empty, someone will steal it from us."

"Sadly, I guess he's probably right."

"But what is a bit of land or a pile of concrete, compared to the life he's living, if one might call it that?"

"Oh," Maha nodded as if in agreement. She supposed Roxy would know. Then, "Do you have children?"

Roxy looked like she had aged much more than the six years since Maha had last seen her, as she replied with a wizened smile, "Two. Leith is three, and Samar is just one year old." She looked down at her hand and smiled. Maha's next question must have been obvious, because Roxy soon added, "They're in Aley with my mother right now."

"You're living in Aley now?"

"Yes. Well, if you can call what we are doing living."

"How long have you been here in Lebanon?"

"Six months."

"So you haven't seen your husband for six months?"

"No." She offered no more information.

If it weren't for the fiery red hair and the sparkles running down the side of Roxy's jeans, Maha would be questioning whether this mature, sober, thoughtful woman was the same who had turned her dorm room into a festive jumble of adventure all those years past. Maha stared awkwardly at those sparkles on her old friend's jeans for a few moments.

Roxy broke the silence. "But what about you? What's your situation?"

"I live here, just down the street, actually. Oh, Roxy, what a terrible hostess I am, I should invite you to my home! Come, I'll make you coffee."

But Mr. George let out a well-timed cough. The women looked over at him and saw he was just now pouring out three cups of strong bitter cardamom-infused coffee.

"*Islamu Edeik*," thanked Roxy.

Maha muttered a soft "*Merci*" under her breath.

Mr. George went back to his crossword puzzle, barely acknowledging the two women's proffers of gratitude.

Fingering the little packets of Chiklettes and sore throat lozenges and Tic-tacs at her eye's level, Maha gazed at her old friend. There was so much to say, but she didn't want to actually say any of it. Thoughts of telling Roxy about Leila's humanitarian initiative, of opening her heart and revealing some of her own heartaches, or of admitting to her own fears, of asking for news about other mutual friends, all these thoughts made a vague appearance in Maha's consciousness. But none lasted long enough to shape into a complete thought. None seemed more important than preserving her own composure.

"Do you like my hair?" Roxy asked, breaking the silence in a way that made Maha feel like a student again.

A quick recovery. "I love it! But I hardly recognized you. How long have you been a redhead?"

"About half an hour!" Roxy grinned wide.

"Really?"

"Yes. You asked me what I was doing in Gemayze, and this is it. I came all the way down from Aley to get my hair done at a salon down the street."

"Which one?"

"Chez Jean. Do you know it?"

"I might have heard of it. I've never been. I get my hair done at the little salon right downstairs from where I live."

"Oh, I usually do, too. There's a little place in Aley I've been to a few times. But I needed a change in air, something different, you know?"

Maha grasped at Roxy's intimations of camaraderie. "Oh yes, I definitely know."

As Maha paused to put together a thought, Roxy leaned forward, opened her big round brown eyes wide, and took Maha's hands in hers. It was as if she knew.

"I don't know which is worse," started Maha. "Being stuck in this prison of a city – tell me, don't you feel like Beirut is a tightly wound circle of oppressive, polluted, crowded streets? You're so lucky to be in Aley. Anyway, I don't know whether Beirut is worse, or home. My father and my brother were killed. Just a few days ago. Our building in Sednaya was bombed. Not targeted or anything, just caught in the middle. We have no home, and I have no father. And my darling little brother, I'll see him no more. I should be grateful to be safe here away from them. It hurts so much to see what is happening to Bilad al-Sham. But it would be worse if I were there, wouldn't it? So I should be grateful to be here. But I hate it here."

And then she remembered Mr. George, who was copiously working his way through his crossword. He threw nary a glance their way, but he doubtless caught every word.

"I'm sorry, Mr. George. I didn't mean that," retracted Maha hurriedly.

Then he looked up and smiled. He understood.

Maha then felt a need to explain, "Mr. George has lived in Beirut his whole life, except for the months he fought with the Phalangists. He lost his family in the war. He is a good man who is kind to me. He treats me like a fellow Lebanese, even though I know it's hard on Lebanon to have all of us Syrians descending on them."

"I pray for Lebanon every day," commented Roxy.

Maha saw that Roxy's coffee cup was now empty. She took one last sip from hers then set the cup solidly back on the glass store counter that doubled as a display of mobile phone cards and little trinkets that an indulgent grandma might be persuaded to buy. "*Daiemeh*. Thank you, Mr. George."

She then stood up, and Roxy followed suit.

"Come back to my flat with me. You don't need to rush back up the mountain immediately, do you?"

In response, Roxy took Maha's arm, and they walked on down the street, occasionally stepping, still with arms linked, between parked cars to dodge a taxi swooping by.

As they walked, then as Maha made another pot of coffee, then as they drank the coffee and snacked on some stale baclava, then as they moved on to beer and sunflower seeds, then as the sky grew dark and Maha's little flat dimmed, then as they lit candles and cracked open another round of beers, then as their spirits began to relax and dull, they talked and talked. They spoke of loss, anger and bitterness. They spoke of the good old times. They caught each other up on the nuances of their news: marriages, babies, jobs and mutual friends. They timidly ventured into the virtual minefield of Syrian politics then quickly jumped out realizing they'd not last long before stepping on an explosive and blowing up their chat. They did find peaceful ground in the fields of hopes for a Syria that might be, a place of peace and freedom and cultural pride. They shared jokes and unbelievable stories that had become the legend of revolutions. Stories like that of the Islamic sheikh who had intervened on behalf of a Christian child. Stories like that of the man who lost both his legs and still somehow walked across the border into Lebanon. Stories like that of the couple who had met on the battlefield, married, and apparently still fought side-by-side. Stories like that of the doily and television in Maha's house that were left standing when everything else was destroyed.

Chapter Four

"Hello?"

"Leila?"

"Maha, is that you?"

"How are you, dear?"

"What's new with you, lovely?"

"Life goes on. What's new with you?"

"*Alhamdulillah.* How are you?

"Guess what!"

"What?"

"Guess. Or, to be exact, guess who is sitting in my living room right now!"

"Who?"

"Guess! Guess!"

"Ummm. Some famous sheikh?"

"No, better!"

"Some political leader?"

"Better! Come on. Who would you least expect, but be most excited to know is sitting here, right here in front of me, listening to our conversation!"

"I give up."

"You're no fun. Here."

Roxy took the phone in her hand, and said, "Leila *habibty*?"

"Yes. Who is this?"

"It's me. Do you know me yet?"

"Your voice sounds familiar. I apologize."

"Leila, it's me, Roxy!"

Silence.

"You don't remember me?"

"Roxy?"

"Yes! Roxy from the Medina."

"Roxy!"

"Yes! It's me, Roxy. I ran into Maha in the store yesterday!"

"Roxy, you're in Beirut?"

"I'm living in Aley now. Yesterday, I came down to Beirut and ran into Maha. I ended up spending the night."

"You're...you're alive!"
"Oh Leila, you were always so dramatic. Of course, I'm alive."
"But, you're in Lebanon. You're alive. You're talking to me!"
"Don't cry, Leila. God has protected us."
"He sure has."
No one spoke for a few moments.
"Leila," said Maha. "I have the phone on speaker."
"I want to know everything! Let's talk on Skype!"
"Alright. Just a minute. I'll log in."
"Ok."

Marble floors. Granite kitchen surfaces. A housekeeper. Leather sofas and a closet full of designer clothes. Organic vegetables, on God's life!

Leila looked around her living room, with her two beautiful sons playing and bickering with each other in the space set aside for their cornucopia of games and toys. She sighed. What was she doing here?

Her friends who were lucky, like Maha, had four hours of electricity and four hours off, pollution and unemployment to deal with. Leila had feared the worst for Roxy, with whom she'd lost touch a couple of years back, but now she knew that she could count Roxy in the ranks of the lucky ones. Alive and safe. But Roxy's husband was back home, facing daily risks. Roxy didn't say as much, but Leila was sure that she was barely making ends meet to care for her children in Lebanon. Roxy and Maha were the lucky ones. Leila knew of many unlucky people as well, people who had no electricity at all and never left their houses for fear of getting caught in crossfires. Not that their houses were very safe either since random shelling was always a possibility. People living in such fear included many of her own family members.

What was she doing in this posh, comfortable house, with enough space to fill maybe a dozen refugee families? She'd heard the stories of how they were piled into boiler rooms and cleaning closets throughout Beirut.

The boys were arguing, in their little boy voices, about whose turn it was to play with a toy. Today was the nanny's day off, and Leila supposed it was time to give them a time-out, but her thoughts took over.

On some level, she was aware that she should be as happy as a laughing baby right now. One of her dearest friends was alive and well, and Leila had imagined otherwise. This was fantastic news!

But that joy was eclipsed by the thought that Roxy was with Maha right now, and Leila was all alone in her Kuwaiti gilded palace, as good as a world away.

With this thought came guilt: guilt that she had fled nothing, that she had already been here, safe and sound, long before Syria became hell.

Leila's thoughts drifted back to her Mama, quickly becoming elderly, her Baba, who had been old for as long as she could remember, and her assortment of brothers and sisters-in-law and youngest sisters who had all fled to Jordan under shellfire. Why were they living in a refugee camp while Leila continued on with her simple and predictable life as though nothing had happened? She acted as if she had a home to go back to when their days in Kuwait ended or when holiday season came, but she didn't. This was sad, but her own flesh and blood had no home at all.

Today wasn't the first time that Leila felt this uncomfortable feeling in her gut. At least once a day, she wondered if there was a way to invite her entire family to come live with them in Kuwait. Or if she should ask Hassoun if they could send more back to Jordan, maybe rent them a real house to live in rather than relegate them to a shipping container in a fenced camp in the desert, eating the crap food that the World Food Program made her sisters-in-law queue up for once a month, in the dry heat like beggars.

But the emotion was stronger today for some reason. For some reason, Leila could barely bring herself to walk over to the play area and tell the boys to share. When she finally did, she grabbed her youngest, Saleh, in her arms and held him, tight.

The two-year-old could sense that his mother needed him, and gripped her neck tightly in his two chubby arms. Leila's eyes were dry, but her breath was heavy. She clung to her poor little boy, tried to imagine what life would be like if she and her little family were also in Za'atari camp in Jordan. Or making do in a shack on the roof of a building in Beirut that had never been fully repaired after the Lebanon war.

After a while, Saleh began to squiggle and asked for down. Leila reluctantly let go and watched as he ran back to play, eager to be with his big brother again, the previous disagreement conveniently forgotten.

Leila watched them play for a few minutes. Then a thought popped into her head. She gasped, and both boys looked up at her. "What happened?" asked Hammoudi.

She let out a giggle. "Nothing, Mama. Would you like to put on a video?"

Both boys squealed and ran over to the sofa for the rare treat. Leila queued up a YouTube video of a BBC cartoon then headed to the table where her laptop sat open, a half-composed email to her network of donors awaiting completion. She'd do that later. For now, she opened her browser and started searching for flights to Amman.

"But we don't have anyone there!" protested Hassoun.

"My family is there," pointed out Leila. The obvious.

"You know what I mean!"

"Do I?" Leila was shouting, even though she knew there was no reason to shout.

"What are you going to do, fly into the Amman airport with your Syrian passport, catch a taxi to Za'atari and ask to be admitted as a refugee?"

"Why not?"

"Who does that? You don't just volunteer to be a refugee."

"But they're my family," Leila repeated.

Hassoun reached for Leila and drew her into a deep embrace. She leaned her head against his shoulder, and he stroked her hair for a few moments. "I know you miss them. You're so full of love, *haiati*."

Finally, Leila's nose started to twitch. She felt the tears that hence had gone unshed beginning to gather behind her eyes. Soon, if she wasn't careful, they would burst out. Once the dam broke, she feared there was no reigning it in again. But she was safe here, wasn't she?

"Why do you want to go so bad?" Hassoun asked again.

Leila swallowed her tears for another day, pulled away, and looked him in the eyes. "Because I can't stay here anymore. I can't just pretend to do something. I need to be there, with my flesh and blood."

"We're your family, though."

"You are. But so are they. I don't know how to explain it, but I really, really need to be with them right now. I am going to go crazy if I stay here like this any longer. Your family is safe and doing fine in Turkey. Imagine if they had to live in some godforsaken camp in the desert?"

"*Istaghfar Allah!*" spat Hassoun.

"See?" Leila retorted. "I can't just go on with life as if everything were normal."

"What about Lebanon? Didn't you say you have some friends in Lebanon? Maybe you could visit them for a few days."

Leila's eyes lit up for a few seconds. To spend a day, just one brief afternoon even, with Maha and Roxy! What a dream! All that would be missing is...she pushed the tremulous thoughts of her former best friend away. No. She wasn't traveling to be with her friends. It was her family who needed her. It was her family who she needed. Who needed her.

Her husband really was a wonderful man. A few minutes later, he nodded without asking her to explain. He understood. He always understood. "I'll call the travel agent in the morning," he said simply.

Leila went into the kitchen to get his dinner, already mentally putting together a list of items to pack.

"How much longer do you think you'll stay there, *habiby*?" asked Maha over the crackling Skype connection.

"I don't know. It's like the needs never end; it's a bottomless ocean of tragedy here," replied Samir.

Maha kept silence. There are no niceties, even for one's own husband, to respond to that.

"Yesterday," Samir continued after a minute, "when we were in Qaboun--"

"Qaboun? I thought you said you were staying in Damascus!"

"Well, yes. Qaboun is in Damascus."

"But it's not the safe part of Damascus. Do you know what they are saying about Qaboun?"

Garble Silence Static. Perfect timing for Samir to get out of explaining himself.

A second later the connection was back. "Samir? Samir? Are you there? Can you hear me?"

"Yes, I can hear you. Can you hear me?"

The number of times they had said these words to each other may very well outnumber the number of times they'd said "I love you."

"Yes, *habiby*, I can hear you. So you went to Qaboun. Thank God you're safe."

"Yes, indeed. God is looking out for us, though. I really do believe that we are doing his work. Yesterday, when we went, all we had was a truck full of bread baked by that old man in Bab Touma, remember him where we used to buy our croissants?"

"Of course. He's still there? Wow."

"He promised to give us as much bread as he could find flour to bake. He thinks that we can do one truck delivery a week with his bread."

"Do greet him for me."

"And he greets you. He asked about you, actually."

"May God keep him."

"Indeed. So he gave us his first truckload of bread, and we took it to Qaboun. We had heard that there were a lot of families in Qaboun who couldn't leave and that no other help was getting to them. I know what you're thinking. Aren't there families in other, safer, neighborhoods, who also don't receive help? And you're right, but we heard that it was even worse in Qaboun. We went through the checkpoints--"

"Who was with you?"

"Well, my brother, of course, and then this guy Bassam who is a friend of my brother's from university. He's from a Sunni family with relatives in Qaboun, so we thought he'd help us get through the rebel checkpoints. And we had no trouble with the government checkpoints, of course."

"Whose car?"

"My father's."

"Good. I'm so glad you're safe."

"I love you, darling."

"I love you too."

"Now will you let me tell my story?" Samir reminded.

"Yes, yes, of course. Sorry."

"So then, we got there and..."

Static, garble, silence. Perfect timing.

After half a minute of waiting and calling out, "Samir, Samir! Can you hear me?" his voice came through again, clear as a bell, saying, "Isn't that amazing?"

"Oh, Samir, I'm so sorry. I missed the whole story. The connection is too weak."

"What was the last thing you heard?"

"You just started talking. Start over again, ok?"

"Ok. So it took us more than two hours to get there, but when we got there we still had all the bread – a miracle in itself, really – and we went to the mosque to ask where the neediest families were. The Imam was there, and we were able to talk to him. He seemed really shocked to see us, but he was very kind and grateful. So he called over two young men and told them to go tell Abu this and Abu that to come to the mosque because there was assistance. They did, and the Imam invited us to tea. He was a gentle old man; most of his family has left, but he refuses because he says his place is with his community, whom he serves. I don't understand who these people are who are ruining our country sometimes – the bakery guy, this Imam, my friends, none of us want this. But anyway, before we were half done our tea, people started coming in. Women, mothers with their children. Young men and old men. Teenagers. It must have been three hundred people! And the Imam told us that probably each household only sent one or two people."

Maha interrupted, "Samir? Wait. I don't understand. What are you saying?"

"Well, first, I'm saying that there was nowhere near enough bread. Maximum one piece of bread per person there, but they were so desperate for it, and they accepted it so gratefully."

"Oh, I'm sorry. And the poor baker thought he was doing something great."

"He was doing something great. Do you remember when we handed out those clothes at church last month? You know how it is – people don't really want used clothes. Probably hardly anyone even used what we gave them, and they stuck with their rags. They didn't come for the clothes."

"Right. Of course not. It was the big social event of the month. It was so fun pouring coffee and sitting around with the women."

"So I think that the people of Qaboun are very, very hungry. They really have nothing. They are all too scared to leave, and hardly anyone will enter. You know what they are? They're the forgotten of the earth. They've been left in a bombed-out neighborhood to die. On the main street, I didn't see a single building that was intact. But they're all hiding in their flats or in whatever spot they've carved out for themselves, and we gave them an excuse to get out. They are still hungry tonight, I'm sure. But we gave them an event to go to, you know?"

"Yes, I can see that. They must have loved seeing your kind face."

"Thank you. But do you see why I don't think I'm ready to come back yet?"

"Should I come to you then?"

"I would love to have you here with me. Do you want to?"

"Well, I do hate Lebanon."

"Who would you travel with?"

"I don't know. Maybe I'll just come by myself."

"No, don't do that. It's too dangerous. Maybe I'll come get you."

"Don't be silly. That's too expensive and, even more, dangerous."

"Ok. Well, let's see if someone is traveling soon. Or maybe I'll have to come back to Beirut to get more supplies anyway."

That night, Maha slept fitfully. She really did miss Samir. He had been gone two whole weeks this time. He was back in Syria, and her father's funeral had just taken place back in Syria, and her mother refused to leave Syria. Maha really wanted to be with her mother right now. And her husband. Why had she stayed behind this time? They had discussed the importance of Maha being in Beirut to raise funds that could be used to help Syrians in need, but she had only managed to garner a couple hundred dollars so far, hardly enough to make any notable difference in the lives of people who were living life essentially under siege.

She dreamed with pictures of the empty ruins of gray concrete buildings. She hadn't gone to bombed-out neighborhoods herself very many times, but YouTube had kept her updated. The images were clear and distinct. Lots of rubble and piles of concrete. Metal rods poking out here and there. Tilted angles everywhere. Hardly any construction existed in perpendicular right angles anymore. Speckles of pink tiled walls or blue kitchen sinks that had survived the wreckage. The dark gray of soot blanketing everything. And abandoned streets with no more than one or two figures walking down a wide road where before the crowds had been too thick for so much as a baby's stroller to navigate.

Piecing together what Samir had said with other stories she'd heard, her dreams conjured up images of families huddled together in the inner echelons of those buildings, as many as twenty people in a room, all on a floor carpeted with faded red and brown mattresses. Walls with cracks and peeling paint that could collapse at any minute. The ubiquitous television playing images of war, the only distraction these people had from themselves, each other or their hunger.

The smell of these rooms must be absolutely horrid, and in her half-awake state, Maha's nostrils filled with something pungent and nauseating.

So nauseating that she jerked upright in bed and felt bile in her throat.

She ran to the bathroom and was barely at the toilet when her dinner came up. For ten minutes she hovered over the toilet basin as the nausea returned and she vomited more, then felt more nausea and then vomited again. Images of a doily on a television surrounded by rubble kept alternating with that of a child walking down an abandoned street, the ruins of residential buildings on either side. She saw the child through a sniper's viewfinder and vomited again. The child walked up to the television and wiped her tears in the doily. Maha vomited again.

Finally, when she was sure there was nothing left in her system to expel, she walked into the kitchen to grab a cup of water. One little sip brought another wave of nausea, and she ran back to the bathroom to dry heave into the toilet.

The next hour continued like this, and finally, her stomach was settled enough to turn on her own television, a TV without a doily on top, and watch reruns of American sitcoms until she drifted into a black sleep. The sound of pre-recorded stale audience laughter drowned out the sounds of bombs and the deafening silence of abandoned streets.

Chapter Five

Maha spent the next week sick in bed. Every time she decided to go to a doctor, it got better, so she decided to wait and see; then, whatever this vicious bug was, it would attack again with a vengeance. For a week, her days were spent huddled on the mattress or in a lump on the sofa, and her nights were given to stumbling between the bathroom, the kitchen and her bed. She could barely get a bite down and consumed little but flower tea and cigarettes.

Late one night, when the streets were finally quiet, and the sky was still pitch black, as she sat in a ball on the bathroom floor, it occurred to Maha that her sickness might be more than just food poisoning mixed with disgust at what was destroying her country. There was another reason women her age sometimes took ill.

She slowly stood up and made a weary beeline for her phone, which sat on the little table by her bed. Opening the calendar app, Maha counted back one week, two weeks, three weeks...and when she reached six weeks and realized that it had been well longer than that, she dropped the phone and fell into bed. Gripping her pillow and staring at the wall, she told herself not to over-react. But deep her in her gut, she knew that numbers don't lie.

Realizing that sleep would not be joining her tonight, Maha eventually went to the living room and turned on rubbish late-night television. She watched three stupid comedies, during which she made three more trips to the toilet and reached for her pack of cigarettes at least a dozen times before telling herself to hold off until she was sure.

As soon as the sun had fully risen, Maha picked up the phone.

Roxy answered after five rings, with a groggy "*Aloh*?"

"Are you still sleeping?" Maha asked. "I'm sorry. I'll call back later."

"It's fine. The kids are up already, and I need to make them breakfast anyway." Maha could hear the sounds of Roxy shuffling through the house, with children's giggles in the background.

"I see," Maha hesitated.

"What's up?" asked Roxy. "You're the one who usually isn't awake this early. It's not like you have kids that jump out of bed with the sun each day!"

Maha couldn't muster up even a hint of a laugh.

After a moment, Roxy asked again, "What's up, dear?"

"Ummm... Well..." Maha tried to think. She had not planned this conversation; she just really wanted to talk to her friend. "Speaking of children..."

"What about them?" Roxy asked brightly. Maha could hear dishes rattling now.

Maha took a deep breath. "I've been sick all week. Pretty much from when you went back to Aley until now, I haven't been able to eat. It's really bad."

"Darling! Have you been to a doctor?"

"Not yet," hesitated Maha. "The thing is, I'm not sure that I'm actually sick."

"If you can't eat and you don't feel well, then..." Roxy's voice trailed off, went silent, then half a second later returned with something little short of a scream. "Are you pregnant?"

"I... I might be?"

"It's possible?" Roxy asked slowly, her excitement still leaking out.

"I never really thought about it. Samir and I never planned on... It really didn't seem the time, but I guess it's possible."

"When was your last period?"

"I can't remember. It has been a while."

"Girl! You march yourself down to the nearest pharmacy right now and buy yourself a pregnancy test. Call me as soon as you're done. Go. Now. Talk to you soon."

Roxy hung up. Maha glanced at the screen of her phone to see that the call had been deliberately disconnected, then let it drop to the sofa to her side as she pondered Roxy's reaction.

Less than a minute later, she felt the phone vibrate. Maha picked it up and saw a text message from Roxy. "Go. I'm waiting."

Obedience seemed like the easiest course of action, so Maha dressed herself and forced down a few sips of water. She picked up her wallet, phone, and keys, and headed out the door.

The pharmacy was just at the end of the street, next to Mr. George's little mini-mart, and to her surprise Maha found it already open.

Later she would question her wisdom in requesting a pregnancy test at her local pharmacy, where she could have no hope of anonymity at all, but at this moment, Maha simply did what Roxy said.

She walked home, went into the bathroom and followed the instructions. As she waited for the result to appear, two thoughts came to mind: that if she was pregnant she would have to give up tobacco and alcohol, and that she had absolutely no idea what she would do with a baby. Neither thought was very palatable, but at least the shock of possibly becoming a mother was obscured by her preoccupation with giving up her little vices.

By the time the little lines appeared on the stick, Maha already knew what to expect. The test was positive.

She walked straight to the kitchen and took all alcoholic beverages out of the refrigerator and threw out her cigarettes. Then she called Roxy again.

"Well? Well?"

"It was positive."

"*Mabrouk*! A thousand, a thousand thousands of congratulations!"

Maha wasn't sure that she wanted congratulations. But of course, this was the expected response. How often had she immediately congratulated someone upon learning that they were expecting a child...

A child?

"Maha?" Roxy interjected herself into Maha's thoughts. "Are you still there?"

"Yes. Yes. Sorry. Thank you, darling."

"It's quite a shock, huh?"

"A shock? Yes."

"I remember when I found out I was pregnant with Sahar. I just walked around the house all day carrying the little pregnancy test with me, looking at it every once in a while, and then just wandering more. That's really disgusting, that stick, you know, but I was so confused, like I couldn't believe it. So don't worry. You'll get used to the thought. Maybe it's good you're feeling ill, even. It will help it feel more real."

"Oh, I don't see anything good about being so nauseated, or losing a night's sleep."

"Be ready, honey, because many more sleepless nights are in your future."

"Ugh," groaned Maha. "But Roxy, I didn't really want to be pregnant."

"You didn't?" Roxy's shrill voice could hardly have sounded more incredulous.

"No. Not now."

"Now?"

"What kind of a world is this to bring a child into? This is not a time to be thinking of growing my own family. It's a time to be surviving and maybe trying to help some other families."

"Did you talk with Samir about that?"

"Yes, sure. He loves children, but all his attention is on the families he helps. It's like they are his children, and they are our family."

"Oh," Roxy paused, thoughtfully. "So how does that make you feel?"

"Well, sometimes I miss him and the life we might have had. But I agree with him, too, don't you?"

"What do you mean?"

"How can I want my own children when my father and brother were just bombed away?"

"You can't think that way. Maybe you should think of it as some kind of healing – bringing new life to challenge the death that surrounds us."

"That makes no sense at all!" laughed Maha.

"Of course it does." Roxy continued. "Think about it. All of the images we see on TV, even the images we remember because we lived through this, you and me. It's gray and black. It's smokey and full of fire. It sounds like explosions or eery silence. But a baby, well, a baby is clean, white, smooth. It's full of its mother's milk and it sounds like giggles and gurgles. When it cries its tears are innocent, and all it wants out of life is to be fed and clean and well-rested. These images and sounds may drown out all that awfulness a bit."

"Roxy, that's beautiful! You're becoming a poet!"

Roxy laughed that off and continued, "Think of your mother. What more can heal your grieving mother's heart right now than to cuddle a bundle of new life in her arms, to comfort a child's colic and to laugh with a baby?"

Maha thought of her mother, dressed all in black today, surrounded by her sisters and no doubt holding an embroidered handkerchief with which she could dab at her bitter tears in a dignified way. "Yes, my mother will be glad to have something to celebrate, once she gets over her anger that I didn't allow her a full year to grieve. You know, in our custom, no celebrations should happen within a year of a death in the family."

"But you must have already been pregnant when your father died, you just didn't know it, right?"

"You don't know my mother if you think that logic will make a difference."

Roxy laughed and now Maha was able to laugh with her.

Then Maha continued, "But that's not all. I just spoke to Samir and was planning on joining him in Damascus. He said that there were so many widows grieving, so many families that he visits. He'll never let me go now."

"You had better not think of traveling to Damascus, girl. You're living for your baby now."

"That's why I didn't think of getting pregnant now. How am I supposed to do my little bit to help the mothers who have lost their children when I'm busy making my own child?"

"That, my dear," said Roxy curtly, "is what faith is for."

Without giving it much thought, Maha said, "I could really use a friend right now. Can you come down to Beirut for a few days? Or, if not," she rushed to add, "Maybe I can come up to Aley?"

"I'm coming!" Impetuous Roxy needed no more urging than that. "Let me just talk to my mother-in-law."

Immediately after hanging up, Maha realized with a fair bit of irritation that she had told her old friend from university before she told the baby's own father. Even more irritating, that feeling led to a new wave of nausea and the expulsion of the flower tea she had downed an hour ago. As she wandered out of the bathroom, she decided she could really use a cup of coffee, but when she got to the kitchen stopped herself remembering that she had heard something about avoiding coffee when pregnant. She was going to have to research what she should and should not do. She knew about the alcohol and the cigarettes, but what about tea? What about going out for walks, was that dangerous? What about sweets, would she have to give those up? What should she start eating and doing to stay healthy? She should probably find a doctor.

And she really needed to tell Samir. She couldn't share the secret with Roxy and hide it from her own husband.

Could she? The moment she told him, life was going to change. Her husband loved her very much, but he could be a bit overprotective at times. She knew him: he was going to lay down the law on her the moment he found out. He would worry and maybe even cut his trip to Damascus short. Well, maybe there was a silver lining to this development after all.

She opened Viber and saw that he was online. Samir, with a photo taken of the two of them in the beautiful seaside port of Byblos, north of Beirut, taken at sunset a couple of months back.

She set the phone down and walked into the bathroom, where the stick lay in the garbage bin. The two lines were still solidly there. She wanted a cigarette. She needed to calm her nerves a bit before making this phone call.

Why is it sometimes so much easier to talk to friends than to one's own husband?

She went out on the veranda and took in a breath of fresh air. It wasn't quite the same thing as a smoke, but it would have to do. So as to avoid any further distraction, she walked as quickly as she could to the sofa, picked up the phone and rang Samir.

"Maha?" he answered after just a few seconds.

"Hi, Samir."

"How are you? I'm just about to leave to do another distribution. We're taking clothes to a community center in Barzeh."

"I'm... I'm..." she tried.

"Maha? Is something wrong?"

"No, I'm fine," she said. Well, maybe more than fine. Maybe not fine. Close enough.

"Are you sure?"

"Eh," she said, shortly. He understood her yes.

"Can we talk later? We're just heading out now, and you know how the checkpoints can be."

She was just about to say yes, that she'd call later, but she stopped herself. She couldn't put this off and lose her resolve. "I'm pregnant," she said simply.

Samir's side of the line sounded like it went dead.

"Are you there, *habiby*?" Maha asked. She didn't want to have to say it again.

After a moment, "Did I hear right?" he asked. "Did you say you're pregnant?"

"I did."

"Wow." She could detect no emotion in the way he said the word. Then again, with a bit more spring in his voice, he repeated, "Wow!" Then a third time, almost shouting, "WOW!"

"I'm sorry, Samir, I know this isn't what we talked about."

"We're having a baby? We're having a baby!"

"Well, yes, it looks that way."

"That's amazing! I don't even know what to say! No, wait. Obviously, you can't come here. Ok. I'll send the boys up to Barzeh, and I'm coming back."

"You don't need to come now, I'm not sick," protested Maha.

"No, you're not! You're going to have our baby."

"I didn't expect you to be so excited," Maha then admitted.

"What are you talking about? What a blessing."

"I'm glad you're happy."

"Aren't you?" he then asked.

"*Malish*. It doesn't matter. It's big news, that's all."

"I'll see you tonight, ok?" Samir continued.

"Are you sure? It takes nine months, you know."

"Yes, maybe I'll come back to Sham in a few weeks, but now we need to talk and plan, don't we?"

"I love you, Samir."

"And I love you very, very much."

She pressed the red button then sat staring at the phone. She had known that he would come back, but not that he would drop everything immediately. Maha quickly called Roxy and told her she probably shouldn't come after all, that Samir was on his way home. But Roxy insisted on coming just for the afternoon.

They spent the afternoon plotting and dreaming. Syria and war, for once in a very long time, was far from Maha's balcony, as they discussed what Maha should be eating, old wives' tales that would help her predict whether it was a boy or a girl, wardrobe decisions, and even some ideas of names. Maha sipped flower tea, what she anticipated might become her drink of choice during the coming nine months, and Roxy put a couple of beers back in the fridge for herself.

Before heading back to Aley, Roxy had helped Maha clean the flat. All surfaces were spotless and everything was in its place. Maha cooked Samir's favorite meal, lentil soup and baked kibbe mince with potatoes and tomatoes. When Roxy headed out to catch her bus Maha walked out with her – after confirming on the Internet that a walk down the street would not harm her baby – to pick up some of Samir's favorite bread from the bakery down the street. Oddly, she felt no nausea at all that entire afternoon, so on her way home from the bakery she picked up another pregnancy test just to make sure. It was still positive.

Pre-war, the journey from Damascus to Beirut took three hours, four on a terrible traffic day. Now, it could take double that. Sometimes it was still fast, but it just depended on the checkpoints. Samir had texted when he left Damascus, right around noon. He usually texted again once he crossed the border, but now it was 7 pm and Maha had still heard nothing. Seven hours from his door to the Lebanese side of the border was a bit longer than usual. No, as much as she didn't want to admit it, it was quite a bit longer than usual.

After feeding Bird and teasing her little pet for a few minutes, she began pacing the little flat, then began really craving a cigarette. How was she going to survive an entire pregnancy without smoking? Perhaps this would finally force her to give it up as she'd wanted to do for so long already. It really was a disgusting habit. But right now she was struggling not to rationalize that it would somehow not harm the baby, even though the Internet was quite clear on that particular point.

She turned on the TV and stared at a reality show for a while, but her mind was not interested in being entertained, and her thoughts kept drifting back and forth between ways in which her life was bound to change over the coming months, worrying about Samir and being angry at Samir for not calling.

Around 8 pm, Maha picked up her phone and tried calling her husband. His Lebanese phone was still off. So she tried his Syrian phone. Also off. He was not online on Viber, WhatsApp, Skype or Facebook. So she sent him a text message on both numbers: Is everything ok? When do you think you'll be home?

Then she texted Roxy: Samir not here yet. Hope you got home safely.

Immediately Roxy replied: Oh no? Should I be worried? Yes, just got home a few minutes ago.

Maha: I don't know. You never know. Of course, I'm worried.

Roxy: I should have stayed with you.

Maha: No, I'm sure it's fine. I'll let you know as soon as I hear. My love to your family.

Roxy: Kisses xoxoxo.

Then Maha opened her email. There was a message from Leila. Subject line: Change of Plans. Big surprise there – what didn't change these days? She quickly opened the email and read the brief message in which Leila apologized because she was not going to be able to do any more fundraising in Kuwait for a while because she was going to visit her family in Jordan.

Well, fair enough. Leila should be near her family in these days. They were her first obligation.

Maha wasn't actually upset with Leila, but Samir hadn't arrived yet, it was late evening, she was enjoying a respite from the nausea that she was fully aware would soon be back, and now Leila had abandoned their project. This added up to a very irritable Maha. She picked up her phone and dialed Samir again. His Syrian phone was off. His Lebanese phone was off. She did a few more laps around the apartment and flipped a few more channels.

But her hands were fidgety. Her legs were fidgety. She wanted a cigarette more than ever. And she wanted to go to the fridge and crack open a beer. She wanted to go for a walk. That she could do, she reasoned, as long as she stayed close to home and kept her phone closer. During the two years she and Samir had lived here, half a dozen new nightclubs had popped up just down the street, making for very noisy nights but for streets that were just as busy – and therefore safe – at night as they were in daytime. She grabbed her phone and her keys and, without so much as a glance in the mirror, wandered out the door and down the stairs. As soon as her feet hit the ground floor of the building, she could hear voices on the street, and felt a small comfort in the company of others, strangers though they were.

She went in the general direction of the nightclubs. The middle of the street was the best place to walk now: few cars passed, but the sidewalks were quickly filling up with youth, smoking their cigarettes and drinking their beer.

Bile began to gather in her throat even while the smells called out to her, beckoning, tempting.

She walked to the far side of the road to get away from the nasty, yet tantalizing, stench of stale beer and nicotine. She walked on ahead and picked up her pace. The fresh-ish air, as only Beirut could offer in its slightly cooler polluted evening, was refreshing.

Until she puked. About five hundred meters up from her house, the biscuits she had shared with Roxy that afternoon came up.

And so she stumbled home, the craving for a smoke and a pint well past. Now the smell just pushed her to the side of the road to vomit again.

She entered the foyer, out of breath and feeling more alone than ever. Before braving the stairs, she leaned on the railing with her left arm while she checked her phone with her right. Still nothing from Samir. She opened her text message app and scrolled through the messages just to make sure she'd not missed anything, and then fell onto the stairs. As she dialed his Lebanese number, then his Syrian number, confirming both were still out of service or turned off, she sank down onto the bottom step.

Feeling dizzy and desperate for some water, yet nauseated at the very thought of more liquid in her stomach, a tear came to her eye.

It was now 10 pm and she knew it was time to worry. She picked up the phone and dialed Samir's closest friend, a pastor at a nearby Lebanese church. He answered, thinking it was Samir, but when Maha blurted out that Samir had left Damascus 10 hours ago, and his phones were both off, he immediately swung into action. He promised to make some calls and get right back to her.

Then Maha dialed Samir's brother in Damascus, the one who had been planning on doing the distribution with Samir that day. At first he didn't believe what Maha was saying, kept repeating that Samir had left them – abandoned them, really, without explaining to them why – right before they left for Barzeh, saying he was needed in Lebanon. Maha kept trying to explain that she knew this already, that he was coming to see her, and that he had called her when he left Damascus. After repeating herself several times, she finally got him to understand what she was saying, and protests were replaced by a stunned silence.

Everyone knew that, at this point, the most likely scenario was also the worst case scenario.

There were only two real options, one more horrifying than the next. Either he was dead, caught in crossfires or riding in a taxi that had been targeted for some reason, or he was taken at a checkpoint, or at the border. He could have been arrested by anyone, but it was most likely the regime. And most likely at the border. And he was almost definitely at this moment, if not dead, being tortured.

Samir's brother's response was identical to that of their Lebanese friend: he told Maha he would make some calls and get back to her.

Then he hung up and Maha was alone in the hall. The tears welled up. Her body was exhausted from several sleepless nights in a row, a little bit of worry added to a massive amount of nausea. And her brain, already worn out from trying to wrap itself around the loss of her father and brother a few short weeks ago, was now struggling to grasp the concept of bringing a child into this world. She uttered a curse against God. This was more than she could bear, she thought, as she broke down in violent sobs.

No neighbor heard her, or if they did, they hid themselves in their flats and gave her privacy to mourn alone. Alone. She felt utterly abandoned, wishing the Beirutis could be just a little bit more like the Shamis, and lend a helping hand while asking her personal and inappropriate questions. Because at least then she wouldn't be alone. Her tears were bitter and sharp, but she refused to feel fear or worry or sadness. Instead, she chose anger. She sobbed and moaned and cursed in a whisper, as long as it took for her to once again catch her breath.

She had no idea how long she sat there, but eventually, she began to wonder why no one had called her yet. What would take longer to confirm? Death or torture? She suspected that an arrest would be easier to track down, which meant that her husband, the father of the baby now growing in her womb, was probably dead.

She stood up and walked up to her flat, one heavy step at a time.

When she finally walked into her own private space – not that the world out there had felt shared in any sense of the word – she dialed Roxy.

When Roxy picked up, she immediately asked, without any formalities, "Is he back yet?"

"No."

"Oh, honey, may God have mercy..." her voice faded off. When Roxy couldn't think of the right thing to say, Maha knew, the situation was indeed dire.

"His phones are both off," Maha decided to explain her feeble attempts at solving the mystery thus far. "So I called his friend here in Beirut, and I called his brother in Damascus. Neither of them had any news, but they promised to check. They haven't called."

"And you, you're all alone there in Beirut? I shouldn't have left."

"Don't be silly. You have children to care for."

"And a perfectly capable mother-in-law," Roxy pointed out.

Maha didn't reply. She was out of platitudes.

Silence hung on the expensive Lebanese phone line for several minutes until Roxy said, "I'm afraid I can't come back tonight, but I'll be there first thing tomorrow. You need to get some rest. Is there anyone there in Beirut you can stay with?"

Maha thought. She imagined that Samir's friend's wife would allow her to stay over for the night. "I can ask a friend," she said, tentatively. She didn't want to spend the next several hours being sociable, but she wasn't sure she could handle being alone either.

"Do that. You can't be alone. I'll come down as soon as the kids are off to school tomorrow morning. I'll call you when I'm near, and you can tell me where to come."

"I love you dear. Thank you."

"Many kisses. And we'll pray. It could still be nothing," Roxy reassured, with just enough confidence in her voice to give Maha an inkling of hope.

After hanging up, Maha thought for a moment and decided Roxy was right. She called Samir's friends and asked if she could come wait at their house. They, of course, agreed. She grabbed the minimum of personal items, and a big bottle of water and a box of tissues in case she fell ill on the way and walked down to the street where a taxi passed by seconds later.

Samir's friend was apologetic. None of his friends had been able to learn anything yet. He knew someone whose cousin used to work on the Lebanese side of the border and who still had some friends there. Through that connection, he had been able to confirm that Samir had never crossed into Lebanon, but no one had seriously suspected he had.

They made up a bed for Maha in their guest room and were just saying goodnight when Samir's brother phoned.

"Did you learn something?" Maha asked, forgetting to say hello.

"Yes."

"Is he...is he..." her voice trailed off.

"No!" exclaimed his brother. "He's alive! But he was stopped at the border. He is being held there."

"Why?"

"We don't know."

Of course, they didn't. There was generally no reason for anything these days.

He continued, "We have some friends who are going to go tomorrow to try to negotiate his release. He's not politically active, he's helping a lot of people, and we have distant relatives close to the government. We'll get him out, you'll see."

Maha noticed at this moment that she was no longer teary or weepy at all. Her eyes were dry, and her mind was clear. Her stomach was calm, as well. But she was worried. "Until then?"

"We pray," her brother-in-law replied simply. And what more could he say?

"We pray," she repeated. Then said, "Can you call my brother? Don't bother my mother, but I think my brother should know."

"Sure. Is there anything else I can do?"

"Just let me know as soon as you hear anything."

"Of course."

She hung up and relayed the conversation back to her hosts. Samir being a pastor, and her host being a pastor, the necessary next step was a prayer meeting. Maha had no interest in praying at this moment, but she played along, listening as her husband's seminary roommate implored to Jesus for his release, and then as his wife repeated the plea in even more soulful a tone. As they prayed, Maha's eyes kept coming back to the digital clock. 11:30 pm, then she thought, Today is his half-birthday, 17 April 2013. I wonder if he remembers. 11:31pm.

When they finished, they bade her a goodnight again, and she tried to go to sleep, but the nausea attacked again, and she spent much of the rest of the night in her husband's friend's guest bathroom.

The next day, Roxy came down the mountain again, in a show of solidarity which touched Maha to the core. Five years had passed but it might have been yesterday that Maha had taken Roxy in during the painful weeks of divorce from her first husband. Roxy gave no indication at all, though, that she was looking out for her friend because her friend had once looked out for her. It was a deeper sense of friendship, a sisterhood that could not ever be repaid, not by either of them.

And so perhaps it was natural that, as they awaited news from Syria, their conversation drifted to life in the dorms. Maha told Roxy about Leila's plans, and they speculated about how Leila would adapt to life in a refugee camp after several years of luxury in Kuwait.

Then the conversation drifted to another university friend, Huda. Neither had had any news of Huda in a very long time, and they had no idea where she was now. Maha had kept in touch with her for a while after university, but had not had any news of her since the problems began. They spoke with a candor they had never spoken with at university, commenting on the fact that Huda is Alawite and from a village near to the president's own hometown, and speculating whether Huda was now staunchly pro-regime. As members of Syria's minority groups, Maha and Roxy were also expected to be pro-regime, and Roxy admitted that she had no personal grievance against the government, but said that she also understood the need for change. Maha's extended relatives were all pro-regime, and she knew many people who still worked for the government today, though fortunately none of them were currently fighting in the army. The older of her two brothers had just finished military service a few months before the war started; her youngest brother, had he not been killed in the attack, would have been drafted in a few short years. Perhaps he was a marked man either way, Maha pondered. But she and Samir, after living in Lebanon then working in poor Muslim communities in both Lebanon and Syria, had reached a different conclusion. For the sake of their humanitarian work, they tried hard to stay out of politics, but the truth was that Samir was becoming quite desperate to see the end of Bashar al-Assad and was convinced that the regime's current brutality was the height of all evil. This was why his arrest was so frightening – if someone had caught wind of his heretofore privately-held views, the government may never let him go.

But Huda was Alawite, the sect whose entire position in society relied on the Assad government. If she was an open-minded woman, as she had been in their university years – indeed, she had suffered greatly at the hands of the so-called "system" – then she must be an outcast in her own village today. And if she sided with her ethnic loyalties, then her fate lay with the fate of the regime. In other words, by supporting the downfall of the regime, Maha realized, she would be supporting the demise of an old university friend.

"Did you have a Facebook account before the crisis?" asked Roxy, walking into the kitchen from the balcony where she had been making faces at Bird.

"Of course. But we lived in Lebanon before that," Maha replied as she picked up the boiling pot of water from the stove and poured it over the dried flowers in the teapot.

"Oh, that's right," nodded Roxy as she absentmindedly arranged two teacups and spoons and sugar on a tray.

"You didn't?" asked Maha, bringing the teapot over to the tray.

Roxy carried the tray out into the living room and set it on the coffee table and Maha sunk weakly into the sofa. "Nope. But I already have 200 friends."

"What kinds of friends?"

"Mostly friends from home. My cousins, family members, neighbors. But I've found many old friends from the Medina as well."

"Really?" asked Maha, perking up slightly. "Who from the university have you found?"

Roxy listed off a long list of names that were unfamiliar to Maha, then commented, "But I never saw you on Facebook!"

"I wonder why. I guess my privacy settings are a bit high... Are you friends with Leila?"

"No, not Leila either."

"I am," smiled Maha. "Here, let me add you." She opened her computer and typed in the name as Roxy spelled out the English letters for her, and send Roxy a friend request. Then she showed Roxy Leila's page.

Once they had scrolled through Leila's photos and some of the recent inspirational quotes she had posted, Roxy suggested, "Let's look for Huda."

Without comment, Maha started typing "Huda" into the search box.

But that turned up a thousand names. "Do you know her last name?" asked Maha.

"No idea. You?"

"If I knew it I can't remember."

Roxy suggested adding "University of Damascus," which cut it down to a few hundred, but none of the photos looked like their old friend. Roxy took over scrolling and searching while Maha poured the tea.

For the next half hour, they sipped their flower tea out of little glass teacups and perused the profiles of dozens of Huda's and other people affiliated with their alma mater.

In the process they found a handful of other old university friends, but no sign of Huda.

"This is sad," commented Maha after a while. "If someone doesn't have a Facebook account, do you know what that means?"

"Yes, yes," Roxy nodded. It meant that they were most likely either dead or in big trouble. "Let's keep looking!"

Another half hour later, their search paid off. They found that their old friend Huda was still living in Latakia, or, at least, her Facebook persona was.

"Well, at least, we know she's alive. I hope she stays safe," said Maha.

"Add her!" suggested Roxy. "I'm going to send her a friend request now. You know, just like a hello."

"I can't," Maha replied. "It would be too risky. Not with Samir..."

And, as if on cue, the phone rang right then. It was Samir's brother calling from Damascus.

"Talk!" Maha almost shouted into the phone.

"I'm afraid we don't have news yet," he answered, graciously avoiding pleasantries and getting right to the point.

"What?" Maha replied, less graciously.

"Well, we went to the office in Damascus, and they sent us to another office and, well, you know how it goes."

"Is he still being held at the border?"

"We believe so."

"So go to the border!"

"We're trying, but we need someone to go with us. Otherwise..." Otherwise, they might all be arrested, were his unspoken words.

"Keep trying."

"Of course. He's my brother, too."

"Yes, I know." Maha hung up the phone without any farewells or thank-you's. She immediately felt guilty but was too tired to try to make right with her brother-in-law.

Roxy leaned forward and took Maha's hand in her own. She just held it for a few minutes, and the two women sat side-by-side.

Finally, Roxy said, "It's not a problem for me to add Huda, is it? It will be good to be back in touch with her."

"I hope," Maha said, leaving so much unspoken. How could she be friends with someone helping her husband to be arrested and tortured? But then again, how could she be friends with someone helping the rebels who had most likely bombed her family? She was beginning to run out of friends, she thought, even as she sat next to a dear soul from a former life.

Chapter Six

Today I met an eight-year-old girl. She should be collecting dolls and filling coloring books with drawings and stickers. She should be practicing her reading and writing, learning about science and asking her older brother for help with her math homework.

But this girl only attended one year of school. She has no dolls, and she can't see. She lost her eyesight two years ago when her street was bombed. She was no one's target. She couldn't be anyone's target; she was too young, innocent of all deeds, an untainted soul, when a bomb hit the house across from where she was playing in the street. Shards of glass flew at her and cracked her porcelain face. Her face was filled with scars as the glass scrapings made their way under her skin.

The regime bombers, the face of evil, should not be able to wake up in the morning after doing such a deed. But instead of feeling the weight of the horrors they imposed on this sweet young child, they get up the next day and do it again.

I can't accept that they did it on purpose. I can't accept that any human soul is so dark, so dirty, so ugly, as to knowingly attack children. I refuse to accept that they did this on purpose.

But they went home, parked their tanks, ate their dinners, went to sleep in their beds, and got up the next day to do it again. And the day after, and the day after that. When do I have to accept that not only do they know that they are destroying innocent souls, but they are doing it with intent? Because when you know the extent of what you will do, and you still do it, how can it not be intentional?

I write these words, trying to rationalize something for which there is no rationale.

The truth is that the future of this sweet eight-year-old girl ended two years ago when those shards of glass hit her face. She has lost her sight and will never finish learning how to read. She tells me she had learned the alphabet and was beginning to put together simple words. That is where it ends for her. She tells me that she loved drawing and coloring, but now she sits at home listening. Listening to the grown-ups mourning kinder days, listening to bad news on the television, listening to the bombs that continue to fall in the distance.

Treatment exists for girls who have lost their eyesight at the age of six. A good doctor could have removed those tiny diamonds of glass from under her skin, and her face may have healed entirely; instead she is covered with tiny scars and tells me that she is always in pain. I even read of medical procedures that might have restored her eyesight.

But instead, after the bomb fell, her mother ran out and scooped up the bloodied child, carried her into the house where the family hurriedly packed some suitcases, and they fled. It was this event that convinced them that their home was no longer safe, so they went to live with relatives.

It was several hours yet before they knocked on the door of a health clinic, only to find that it had been shut down. Then the next day they made it past another series of checkpoints to a hospital, only to wait another full day to be seen. There were not enough doctors and too many patients. Once a doctor saw this little girl, he informed her mother that he had more urgent problems to deal with, and he faced a shortage of supplies even if he did have time to provide treatment. And so, too young to understand what her mother was struggling to grasp, the girl was turned away, destined to permanent blindness and lifelong scars for entirely avoidable reasons. But at least, she was still alive, the mother thought as she held her youngest tight in her arms.

She was a sweet girl. As I spoke with her, I stood in awe at the beauty of humanity, at how a girl could be so full of smiles, laughter and kind words, when she had suffered so much.

She understands now, two years later. She told me that it is as if it is always dark out. She giggled when she told me that she had been scared of the dark when she was a child, before the problems began. Now every day is dark. But in her dark universe, her other senses have become more acute, and stronger than any other is the sense of emotion. She can feel her mother's nervousness, my despair, her father's anger, her brother's determination. She can feel the changes in the world around her.

As we spoke, this little girl who had lost her face took my hand and patted it, telling me not to cry, because it would be alright.

Then I came home and sat down to write this blog. She is sensitive and has wisdom beyond her few years, but she is naïve. It will not be alright. Not until the dogs who destroyed this sweet child's future are themselves destroyed.

Nisreen was still alive and well. Leila had been concerned when several days had passed without a post from the Mockingbird. Now she could travel in peace.

The bags were packed and were now lined up by the door. Two big suitcases held clothing for herself, her two sons, and her sisters. She had spent much of the last few days shopping for her sisters. Two small suitcases held toys and some pieces of this and that, which she had picked up for her mother. Leila didn't know much about what to expect, but she knew that her family was living in a Caravan, nothing more elaborate than a shipping container, in a camp in the desert. So living was probably going to be sparse, and with that in mind, Leila had also stuffed as many sheets and towels into the luggage as would fit.

The boys were both freshly-bathed, in a new suit of clothes each, with their hair perfectly combed and parted to the side. Leila had also purchased herself a new traveling outfit, blue '*abaya* with a red floral headscarf.

She snapped the lid of the laptop shut for the last time. From here on out, her connection to the world would be her phone.

Hassoun had a cousin who lived in Amman, and that cousin had agreed for Leila to stay with him and his family while she investigated how to join her family. She had spoken to them on the phone, telling them she was coming to visit and that her family was in Za'atari Camp, but she had not wanted to share more. Plus, Hassoun's cousin had sounded dubious that it would work for Leila to get into the camp and had explained that most Syrian families looked for a Jordanian resident to vouch for them and get them out of the camp. Conspicuously, he had not offered to vouch for her family. He would house Leila and her boys for a few days, then she was on her own.

Laughter came from the boys' bedroom. They were playing with their daddy, making train tracks with a Thomas the Tank Engine kit that Hassoun had brought back from his last work trip to Dubai. She could hear Hammoudi making "choo-choo" and "chugga-chugga" sounds as Saleh apparently tried to keep the train on the track with help from Daddy. She wandered into the kitchen and poured herself a glass of water, wondering when she might be back in this home and when her boys might play with their toys again. Was she doing the right thing, she wondered, taking her children out of school three weeks early to travel to a refugee camp? Logic dictated that this was terribly wrong, the act of an irresponsible mother, but she was taking them to see their grandmother and to meet their cousins. Hammoudi had only vague memories from his last trips to Dera'a, and Saleh had been a babe in arms the last time it was safe to travel home. It was time for them to go home, and they were young enough that missing a few weeks of school would cost little. Their cousins, the ones they were hoping to visit, had missed a full school year and a half between when the problems started and when they arrived in Za'atari. Surely her own children were not above their cousins.

Hassoun's phone rang. Leila answered, not wanting to interrupt father-son time. "*Aloh?*"

"Abu Mohammed, please?"

"This is his wife," replied Leila.

"He ordered a car. I'm downstairs."

"We'll be right down." Leila pushed the little red button and went into the boys' room. "The car is here," she said, looking at the window rather than at any one of her boys.

Hassoun guided Saleh's hands as, together, they dragged the train to the station one last time. "We've arrived!" he shouted, and both boys cheered. Then he said, "Time to go. Let's run to the door." All three of Leila's men jumped up and hurried to the door where they began putting on their shoes. Leila slowly followed.

Hassoun grabbed the largest suitcase and headed down the stairs. Leila helped Saleh finish tying his shoes then took each boy's hand in one of her own, and they started down. Hassoun and the driver passed them on their way back up to fetch the rest of the bags.

Hassoun had hoped to take them to the airport, but he had to report to the hospital in an hour's time, so he had arranged this car.

There were no more words to be said. He gave each boy a big hug and a kiss and kissed Leila demurely on the cheeks. They promised to talk regularly, and she promised to text him to let him know when they took off and landed, and he promised to visit as soon as he could get a weekend off, hopefully in two weeks' time.

Then she stepped into the back seat, next to the boys, and Hassoun pushed the door shut. They were off. She took Saleh and pulled him onto her lap, and he wrapped his arms around her neck. Leila pulled Hammoudi to herself with her left arm, and he snuggled into an embrace. The three sat that way for several minutes until a tear began to form in the corner of her eye and the boys started wiggling. They went back to playing with some little plastic trinkets that Leila had packed into a small bag, and Leila leaned against the window watching the buildings pass by.

Five hours later, without a hitch, the plane touched Jordanian ground. Hammoudi's face was glued to the window, watching the gray and brown sands come into focus. Saleh was fast asleep.

They taxied, and the pilot gave them a lecture about the wonders of Amman's brand new airport, how much the King of Jordan had spent to build it and how it prepared Jordan to be a new travel hub for the region.

Once they had parked in the bay, everyone jumped up and immediately started unloading their bags from the storage bins above their heads. Hammoudi was ready to run off, too, but Leila held him back. Saleh was still sleeping, and it was a lot for her to carry on her own, even more so if competing with dozens of other travelers. They would wait.

She had no idea of what to expect once they were off the plane, passports stamped, baggage collected and customs cleared. Hassoun's cousin would hopefully be waiting for them, but would she even recognize him? She had only actually met him at their wedding festivities when she had sat in Hassoun's family home and entertained an endless blur of relatives and well-wishers. Plus, he was a reluctant host, and she doubted he would try very hard to be hospitable.

How far was the camp from Amman? How would she gain entry? What would be the reception of a Syrian at the airport, or anywhere else for that matter? Jordan had almost a million Syrians now living inside its borders, and for a country boasting only six million of its own citizens, this sudden population bump had wreaked havoc on the economy, on security, and on just about every aspect of everyday life. Would she be perceived as the enemy? When the Iraqis had fled to Syria during Leila's university years, she and her friends had either ignored or scorned them.

She couldn't wait to sit in her mother's living room, even if that living room was a flimsy mattress on the floor of a shipping container. Mama would make tea and hold her hand.

Now the plane was nearly empty, and Leila stood up. There was nowhere to go but off the plane and into Jordan. With the assistance of a very kind young male flight attendant, she collected her carry-on and the boys' two bags. She took Saleh into one arm and the handle of her suitcase in her free hand. Hammoudi proudly slung his little backpack over his shoulders and set off in front.

Passports were stamped within minutes, and then after nearly an hour's wait in the massive baggage hall, their luggage came rolling by, and by the time they approached the customs official, Leila was exhausted. Hammoudi and Saleh had run around in circles chasing each other during much of the hour they had waited for their luggage, and it was nearly impossible to secure them. But she had tried and was aware that her scarf was now lopsided and her lovely traveling coat rumpled. The boys looked no better as Leila pushed the baggage cart and they lagged behind her, hand-in-hand. The customs official took one look at them, smiled sympathetically and waved them through.

The cousin was waiting, with his wife. To her great relief, Leila recognized them easily, and they were friendly. They told her all about life in Jordan and pointed out landmarks as they drove the 45 minutes to their house. Leila and the boys were led to a spacious room with two single beds, filled with toys on which the boys immediately pounced. An hour later, dinner was served, in all pomp and circumstance, but as soon as it was polite to do so, Leila withdrew to the room. The boys were asleep soon enough, and Leila was left with her thoughts and her phone. She texted Hassoun with the update, and also dropped Maha a text. To her surprise, Maha replied quickly saying that she had news, lots of it, and asking if Leila could get on Skype. Leila apologized because she was already in Jordan with no phone, and so they began chatting on WhatsApp.

Maha: Roxy is here with me.
Leila: Oh, give her a big kiss from me!
Maha: Kisses back.
Maha: How are you?
Leila: What is new?
Leila: I'm fine, haven't really seen any of Jordan yet. Tomorrow the adventure begins. But I want to know what your news is!
Maha: Well, I have awful news, and I have strange news. Which do you want?
Leila: I want your news.
Leila: I guess the awful news first. If it needs to come.
Maha: Samir was arrested.
Maha: He was stopped at the border last night.
Leila: Whhhaaaaaaaat?
Leila: Nooo! How can that be?
Leila: How are you?
Maha: He was coming home because of my other news, but they took him. His brother is working to learn more and try to find someone who can get him out.
Leila: How are you?
Maha: We think he must be being tortured.
Maha: I don't have much news yet.
Leila: HOW ARE YOU?
Maha: Maybe I tell you my other news.
Leila: What is your other news?
Maha: I'm pregnant.
Maha: That's why Samir was coming back yesterday.
Leila: *Masha'allah*...congratulations!

Maha: I don't know if it's good news.

Leila: Of course it's good news! It's a new person God has created.

Maha: Whose father is in jail.

Leila: We will pray him back.

Leila: How are you feeling?

Maha: About the pregnancy?

Maha: I am sick a lot, I'm worried, I didn't plan on having a child. But little by little, I am getting used to it.

Leila: How long has Roxy been with you?

Maha: She was here yesterday after I found out I was pregnant.

Leila: You only found out yesterday?

Maha: Yes! Then I called Samir, and he wanted to come back. But then...

Leila: It's not your fault. If his name was on the list, it was on the list. It didn't matter when he traveled.

Maha: Even so.

Maha: Anyway, so Roxy came back again this morning. She is a great friend.

Leila: So are you.

Leila: Is there anything you can do?

Maha: I don't know. I want to go.

Leila: Don't! You can't! What can you do that your brother-in-law can't? Plus, you have a baby now.

Maha: I don't think it would hurt the baby, and maybe seeing a woman's plea...

Leila: Or you could be arrested, too.

Leila: Don't go. Please, don't go.

Maha: But I don't want to sit here and do nothing.

Leila: Aren't you a pastor's wife? Pray.

Leila: And I will pray.

Maha: I don't think I see any point in asking God's mercy right now.

Leila: And tell Roxy to take care of you.

Leila: And take care of yourself.

Leila: I wish I could be with you now.

Maha: How do you feel about being in Jordan?

Leila: I don't know. I guess we will find out.

Leila: Tomorrow I have to figure out how to get to the camp.
Maha: Does your family know you arrived?
Leila: No. I will call them tomorrow.
Maha: I hear most people are getting Jordanian family or friends to vouch for them to get out of Za'atari. Maybe you can do that.
Leila: Who can do that?
Maha: Aren't you staying with family?
Leila: Relatives of Hassoun. I can't ask them.
Maha: I think the camp must be horrible.
Leila: I don't know. We'll see. I'll try to keep WhatsApp open.
Maha: Take care of yourself, my dear.
Leila: You too. My love to Roxy.

After a fitful night's sleep, Leila emerged to the sound of breakfast plates and cups.

"Good morning!" Muna, Hassoun's cousin's wife, greeted her.

"Good morning to you."

"Are your boys still sleeping?"

"Yes, it seems they are. It was a tiring journey."

"Here, have some breakfast," and her hostess stood up and led Leila to a seat. Bread, labne, za'atar spices, olive oil, and olives awaited, alongside a cup of strong sweet sage tea. "Sage tea is a Jordanian specialty. I don't think you have it in Syria, do you?"

"No," admitted Leila. "But we have Jordanian friends in Kuwait."

"Good."

With the tea poured, the two women ate their breakfasts in relative silence. Leila knew she should be friendly, but her every thought was on the adventure that lay before her.

"The car is going to be here at ten," Muna broke the silence. "Do you want your sons to go with you? The Sri Lankan maid can take care of them here if you prefer."

"Thank you, that's very kind," murmured Leila. "They will come with me."

Muna nodded shortly. "Take sandwiches for them, then, since they won't have time for breakfast."

"May God bless your hands." Leila went ahead and grabbed two pieces of bread and silently put a piece of cheese on each, then rolled them into little wraps.

Muna banged her tea glass down hard on the tray and started shuffling plates.

"I'm sorry," added Leila. "I don't mean to be ungrateful. It's just…"

"Don't say anything. We all understand." Muna said this even as she picked up the tray and escaped into the kitchen.

How could she truly understand and yet create such strict barriers as to what kinds of help she was willing to offer? No one was going into the desert with her, and no one was willing to sign a little sheet of paper that would allow her parents' release from the camp. All they did was call a taxi driver, no doubt a friend of theirs, and arrange for Leila to pay for a lift.

Leila wandered into the bedroom and started nudging the boys, who were spooning on the single bed under the window. They moaned and rolled over several times until Leila managed to pull one, then the other, into a standing position. She dressed Saleh in her arms and pointed Hammoudi to his clothes.

She piled their belongings back into their suitcases and left them stacked along the room's one free wall. The suitcases were significantly less full now than they had been yesterday since Leila had pulled out the gifts for her family and loaded them into five large shopping bags that she now lay in the corridor outside the bedroom.

It was as she placed the black '*abaya* for her mother and sisters into a bag that it finally hit her: her family was a two-hour drive away. No more than a hundred or so kilometers separated her from them, and they were within the borders of the same country. Her own flesh and blood, the woman who gave her birth, so close she might soon touch them.

What would they be like? Would they look the same, or would they have lost a lot of weight? Were they healthy? On the phone, they always guaranteed her that they were fine, but she knew that such comforting words held little truth value. Was everyone there? If anyone else had died, they surely would have informed her. Were there any new babies, or neighbor children who had joined the household?

These questions could only be considered, really, after she found them. Would she even find them? Would she be allowed into the camp?

What would that one moment in which she caught her Mama's eyes...what would that feel like? The joy and the pain wrapped together into one moment of promise.

Pushing back the temptation to grow emotional, Leila took up her purse, told the boys it was time to go, and asked Muna's Sri Lankan housekeeper for help carrying the shopping bags down to the car.

She forgot to say goodbye to Muna.

Jordan was barren. Northern Jordan was not unlike Southern Syria, but it was drier. Scattered growths of brush and yellowing tundra broke up the otherwise sandy-grey stretches that extended as far as the eye could see. Various sets of rolling hills, the foothills of the mountains that separated Jordan from Palestine, kept the car swooping up and down on wide and smooth highways with a ridiculously low speed limit strictly enforced by police checkpoints every few miles. The car would drive 120 or 140 km per hour for a few minutes, then slow to the requisite 90 to pass through the checkpoint, then speed up again until the next. Occasional blue signs indicated exits for villages and towns, but very few houses were visible from the main road. Every once in a while, they would zoom past a shepherd with his herd of goats, or overtake a bus chugging up a hill. Otherwise, the highway and the wilderness belonged to Leila, the driver, Hammoudi, and Saleh alone.

Though Dera'a had fewer hills and was a fair bit more fertile, Leila's stomach tightened as she leaned against the window and stared. The little tufts of grass and the struggling farms reminded her so much of home that it hurt. Her cousins had worked on farms much like the ones they occasionally passed: tidy, and irrigated yet barely green. The sparse houses were built of a white concrete, just like the houses at home, all with flat roofs for summer evenings or for building a new flat when a son was ready to marry.

Kuwait, with its wide pure sandy desert, was a different world, but now she was close enough to Syria that she might see it from the top of a hill. Perhaps the driver would take her to such a hill and perhaps she might make out some Dera'a villages that she knew from her childhood. Perhaps she would see tanks rolling through, bombers in the air, militias in formation, or mules helping refugees escape across the border.

Or maybe she wouldn't see any such thing. Maybe that lovely village nestled into a little hill in the distance was a Syrian village, but from afar it looked so peaceful, so idyllic, so welcoming.

Home is where the heart is, according to one of Leila's favorite English sayings. If so, then today, home would be found in Za'atari Camp for Syrian refugees, near Jordan's northern border.

But wasn't home where the heart was formed, where child memories took shape, where relationships first developed, where one's family's sweat and tears and blood had worked the land? Surely she still had a home in Syria. Syria could not be gone. It would always be home.

"Madame? Madame?" The driver repeated this a few times until Leila broke out of her reverie.

She glanced over at the boys who were happily playing with their tablet. "Yes?"

"The exit for Za'atari is up ahead here. You can see the camp in the distance just yonder," and he pointed to what at first glance seemed to be a desert mirage. In the distance, the washed-out brown color that surrounded them in all directions was broken by a mass of white. It looked like an entire city of white cloth. "The tents, Madame," the driver explained.

Leila gasped softly. It was massive. She knew that Za'atari now ranked as Jordan's fifth-largest city, entirely occupied by Syrians, almost all of whom supported the opposition and who still traded in Syrian currency, and indeed many of whom still traveled back and forth to Syria in a bustling cross-border business. But to see the camp in person, from afar, to see how massive it was, fell on Leila's heart like a lump of lead. In those white tents and Caravanat dwelled as many as 100,000 people who had lost everything, fleeing horrors no one should witness.

And in one of those white shelters was her own family, just another family in the camp's mass of humanity. They were no different, no one special, except that they were hers.

"So, Madame?" the driver asked.

"What?" Leila pulled her eyes away from the window and leaned forward to hear the driver.

"I'm asking if you want to stop to pick up supplies or if we go straight to Za'atari."

"Can you buy food in the camp?" asked Leila.

"I have never been. If you want to take food, maybe we should buy it here."

Of course, a Jordanian would recommend buying food from a Jordanian market rather than whatever the Syrians in the camp might have to offer. But Leila agreed. Inside the camp, she wouldn't have the choice. And a good daughter must not show up to her mother's home empty handed. Or was it her mother who wasn't supposed to show up to her daughter's home empty handed? The world felt so very upside-down right now.

They stopped at a supermarket and Leila filled a few bags with vegetables, meat, fruit and nuts since Mama had told her that they received rations of dry goods from the World Food Program. Three bags were piled into the back of the car, alongside the bundles of gifts from Kuwait.

Then they pulled up to the gates of the camp. Hundreds of people sat on the sides of the road by the camp entrance. Leila asked the driver who they were, and he said they were people waiting for their relatives. She wondered if she would be sitting by the side of the road in a few minutes.

All of a sudden, with the exception of the Jordanian soldiers manning the checkpoints at the camp's gate, she felt like she was back in Syria. Elderly women dressed in all black, with little tattoos on their chins, walked alongside younger women in the types of outfits Leila had worn before moving to Damascus as a university student: cute but poor cuts that did not fit right, bright colors and lots of glitter, and white headscarves. Always white headscarves. Boys ran alongside them in tattered jeans or khakis and polo shirts. Their faces were brown and their hair spiky.

Yes, these were her people. Leila felt a shiver run up her spine.

Then they were at the checkpoint. The driver did the talking while Leila sat in the back, now holding her two sons, one on each side of her. She could barely hear the conversation, but Jordanian-to-Jordanian was likely to be much more effective than anything the addition of a Syrian woman's voice might contribute. She breathed the *shahada* under her breath. Her mother, her sisters, were right on the other side of this soldier in his navy blue uniform and insignia embroidered with silver Arabic letters.

After a few minutes, the driver turned back. "Madame, do you have their phone number?"

"Yes," she replied simply.

The soldier now leaned in and looked at Leila with her two sons. "Why do you want to come in here?" he asked Leila.

"I would like to visit my family," she replied. "I just arrived from Kuwait." Hopefully adding a bit more information would not prove counter-productive.

"Can I see your passports?"

Leila handed the driver her passport, copy of the family book with the boys' details, and a letter from Hassoun ensuring that it was right that her sons be with her at this moment. He passed them on to the soldier, who waved for the driver to pull over so other cars could pass through.

Wandering over to where the car was now stopped, the soldier read the papers slowly, then lazily handed them back. "You should call your family and they will come get you and take you in."

"I can't go in and surprise them?" Leila asked.

"That's difficult," the soldier said in the tone which meant, simply, no.

As overwhelming as was the thought of that moment when she caught her mother's eyes, walking up to her little Caravan, it never frightened her as much as the thought of picking up the phone, dialing it and telling her sister that she was waiting at the entrance to the camp. And yet this is what she had to do. Hands trembling, she pulled out her phone and scrolled down to Nuha's name.

On the third ring, her sister picked up. "Leila? Hi!"

"Hi, Nuha."

"How's Kuwait?"

"Well, actually..."

"What?"

"I'm...uh...well...um...I'm here."

Nuha hesitated, then said, "Here? Where?"

"Za'atari."

Another pause. Then, "You're here? What are you talking about? What are you doing here?"

"I came to visit." Then, before Nuha could start asking all the questions she was surely about to ask, Leila said, "Someone needs to come greet me. They won't let me enter the camp on my own. I'm at the main entrance."

"Of course! I'll send Mohammed. *Yallah*."

"Thank you," and Leila hung up the phone. There was too much to say, too many things to ask. Better not start quite yet.

They waited half an hour, but finally, two of Leila's nephews appeared at the main gate. They chatted briefly with a few different sets of soldiers, then climbed into the car with Leila, as if this was a normal affair. It was a fifteen-minute drive through the dusty camp roads to her family's little plot. And then she caught her mother's eyes.

Chapter Seven

The stories, oh the stories. Leila had heard many, on the news and in blogs, over the phone from her family, through friends. But the stories her mother and sisters told her, now that they were seated together drinking tea on the padded floor of a shipping container, still came to her as a shock. And they were made all the worse for the fact they had happened to Leila's own flesh and blood.

The fighting came to their village early in the war. Right on the outskirts of Dera'a, where it all began, theirs was a conservative Muslim community whose inhabitants had lived a simple but difficult existence. With each year over the past decades, life had grown a little bit more difficult. More young men looking for jobs, lower income from farms, prices rising, fewer opportunities. Men were frustrated because they couldn't afford to marry. Women were frustrated because their homes and the meals they were cooking were never nice enough. Freedom had always been limited, but the economic pressure made it even harder to live under the stronghold of a government watching every move. It's one thing to renounce the right to dream when bellies are full, homes are comfortable, family is nearby, and the wildflowers and hills of the countryside offer a regular escape. It's another thing to pretend to be happy when nothing is going as planned.

On top of that, it had never sat right with the Sunnis of Syria's southern villages that a Muslim country was being governed by an Alawite, a wannabe Muslim at best, who had strong allies with Christians and Druze. No one in their village had ever really liked the government.

So when protests and fighting broke out in Dera'a city, many of the young men in Leila's family joined the protests. At first, it was innocent and even in good fun. Protesters in Tunisia and Egypt had just two months before managed to topple their regimes of decades. The news swept through Syria like a wave of little electric shocks. A new day was dawning, and anything was possible. With just a little bit of gathering, shouting and face-painting, Syria could be free and prosperous again. All those years of pent-up frustration and bottled-up hope were now going to be released. It wasn't called Springtime in the Arab world for nothing. Fifty years of wintry oppression were finally ending, the sun poking through the clouds, the snow beginning to melt and the first little blossoms of hope budding.

Taking to the streets and shouting at the top of one's lungs for the downfall of the regime, then, was the most natural thing in the world. There was a lot of pent-up energy, anger and desire to release.

The eyes of the world were on the protests in the Middle East. The revolutions in Tunisia and Egypt had been almost entirely bloodless. The general expectation in Dera'a was that Syria would be freed with a similar dose of ease.

So when the protesters were met with tear gas, then rubber bullets, then clubs, then real bullets, the revolutionaries retreated and regrouped. Quitting was no longer an option. Pandora's box had opened and was not closing again.

One of the early victims of military brutality was from Leila's village, and this loss served to toss barrels of gasoline onto a spreading forest fire. Villagers organized themselves, collected rocks and learned the recipe for Molotov cocktails, then went back out to the streets.

When the Free Syrian Army formed a few months later, founded by a group of defectors from the Syrian Armed Forces who were unwilling to hunt and kill the protestors, dozens and dozens of youth from Dera'a region flocked to join their ranks. Many of them were Leila's own cousins and uncles.

They began militarizing the village, creating checkpoints and barricades, and arming youth. The underlying feeling of hope and optimism was as strong as ever. Little boys playing grown-up war, was what many of the women said to each other with chuckles as they tried as best they could to get on with the business of living their lives. But farms were left neglected while the men of the town spent their time training for volunteer militias. Financially, the villagers of Southern Syria went from struggling to destitute. Still, even the women, once they got their grumbling out of their systems, felt that growing nugget of hope that something new, something wonderful, was coming to their beloved villages and precious nation.

When the first bombs fell on Leila's village, everyone's enthusiasm took a bit of a hit. Three children were killed in seemingly random attacks. The regime would later defend such attacks as being directed to Free Syrian Army strongholds, and claim it was not their fault if the FSA used children as a decoy. The blood of those children was on the rebels, not the elected Syrian government, they would say. But no one was convinced. The mothers of those children cursed President Bashar al-Assad at the top of their lungs, calling him by the names of various filthy animals. Their fathers, brothers, and cousins vowed revenge. Enthusiasm was gradually replaced by anger. This was no longer just a fight for freedom, it was a war against a tyrannical regime whose day most certainly had passed.

Leila's brothers were the first of the family to leave Syria. Leila had always loved her mother, but the sheer determination with which she kept her sons out of the war made her into Leila's hero. In their village, all strong-bodied men were expected to join the struggle. How many of them actually wanted to do so was difficult to say, because everyone was assumed to believe in the cause and it was generally considered pure cowardice to believe but not fight. All men declared, with grit in their voices and a smile on their faces, their desire to do whatever it would take to bring victory.

Leila's brothers may have agreed with the cause, but they were all family men, and peace-loving. Leila had never appreciated how well she had been raised and had been prone to compare her fellahiyeh family with her cosmopolitan friends in Damascus and in Kuwait. But when war broke out, her brothers had the wisdom and strength of character to declare that, in their humble opinion, violence was not the answer to anything. They had done their military service for the government years earlier and were quite sure that their weapon-bearing days were ended. They were willing to join peaceful protests, help publish materials, or provide humanitarian assistance to victims of the fighting, just about anything, really, other than pick up a weapon and shoot it at another human being. But this was the only acceptable response in rural Dera'a during the early months of the Syrian conflict.

So Mama connived and plotted a way out for her boys. She used up her life savings to pay a mule to get them to Lebanon, where they found work as day laborers. One of her brothers owned a little shop in the village, and his wife stayed behind to keep the shop open. Another one of her brothers was a government employee. When he crossed the border into Lebanon, he lost his right to a salary, but Leila's Mama took his wife and children in under her roof. The third brother had been farming the land, but no one was farming these days anyway. Mama took his family in as well. She snuck the three men out in the middle of the night, aware that great as the risk from the regime may be, angry compatriots could be an even greater danger. The men resisted and insisted, saying that they needed to stay and care for their families, but all was arranged, and their mother would not take no for an answer. One does not defy one's mother.

The next day, she stood down an angry mob of cousins and distant relatives at the door, who claimed her grandsons, the sons of the men who had fled, as soldiers in their so-called division of the FSA. These four boys were aged 7, 9, 10 and 12. She replied that their division was little more than a militia mob, disorganized and uncommitted, and more interested in getting backing from a rich Saudi businessman than in gaining freedom for Syria. They tried to push their way into the house, and she refused with the force of will of a mother bear protecting her cubs: shame on them for recruiting children as soldiers, and over her dead body and under threat of God's wrath would they send her children to die.

The oldest boy, the oldest grandson of the family, the jewel in the eye of his father, mother, grandfather and grandmother, ran out from under his grandmother's big black '*abaya* and offered to serve. He couldn't be stopped. Not yet a teenager, he confused an eagerness to serve his country, with pain at losing his father and being told that his dad was a coward. Appeased, his self-offering was enough for the militia to walk away with their recruit, a child who had barely encountered puberty.

One month later the boy was back. His leg had been blown off in a mortar attack, and his stomach was badly scarred. He was dumped outside their house one day with an FSA flag draped over his body. Thus was he honored for his sacrifice, though he was not compensated in any way. After that, no one tried to conscript the younger cousins. The wails of his mother echoed through the village that afternoon.

Since then, Leila's oldest nephew has never spoken. Not a word. No one knows what he saw, what he did, or where he went during that month.

For nearly a year, Leila's Mama and sisters and sisters-in-law scraped together enough to ensure the family's survival. The land lay fallow, and a regime-imposed blockade ensured that hardly any food could enter the region. Most of the customers at the little store down the street that Leila's sister-in-law Rana operated in her husband's absence were worse off even than Leila's own family. Unable to turn hungry neighbors away, she gave out credit liberally. As long as items were on the shelves, she sold them, exchanging goods for an entry in a ledger. When there was no food left to sell, she used the store as a repository for clothing donations sent in by FSA supporters in the Gulf, or barring any tangible products at all, hosted Qur'an meetings in the tiny space.

The meetings were widely popular, with every available space in the little shop occupied and bodies spilling out on the street. In these difficult times, the desire to be near God was stronger than ever. The fighters spoke less and less of freedom and more and more of religious struggle. Women, desperate to care for their families, thronged together to feel a little touch of the divine, a little whisper that their fight was for a noble cause. For God.

The little shop became a hub for the destitute. It was a place where people would come for help or for hope. They could count on, at minimum, a smiling face from the women who worked there – Leila's two sisters had joined their sister-in-law in running the busy but entirely unprofitable operation. They helped whenever they could, and they also became a repository of information. They kept track of who was providing assistance where, which roads were safe for civilian travel, which hospitals were still operational, which buildings had space for families who had been displaced from their homes and had no means of fleeing the region, and who was providing classes for schoolchildren in their homes since the school was now closed. They pointed people in the right direction and made introductions. In these activities, they provided a type of hope that the FSA militia was not providing, and that the regime had never provided. They even began arts and crafts activities for teenage girls, who produced colorful embroidered scarves and bags that brightened life in a village otherwise gone gray.

One day, two young local fighters wandered into the shop. They wore tattered jeans and the same shirts they had surely one day not too long ago worn to school, with camouflage hunting vests covered in bulging pockets. Tied across their foreheads were green headbands with freedom slogans written in white, and slung over their shoulders were the now-ubiquitous AK-47s.

It was not unusual for soldiers to wander and help themselves to whatever on the shelves they wanted. There was no questioning fighters' urge to eat.

On this occasion, these two men wandered slowly around the shop, grabbing a can of tuna here, a pack of biscuits there. They took several cigarette packs and stuffed them quickly into a few of their vest pockets. Rana and Nuha stood behind the little wooden desk with cracked paint that served as the shop counter, observant but avoiding eye contact and saying nothing.

Instead of walking out and back to their makeshift barracks or whatever checkpoint they were supposed to be manning, the fighters lingered in the store. The women kept their eyes down or on each other, making a point of ignoring the soldiers. Soldiers had free reign. They could take whatever they wanted, and there was no fuss to be made. Furthermore, Rana and Nuha were two young women in a store with two even younger men carrying guns and in a conservative village, the general consensus was that it would be better if the women were not there – even if it was their store.

Pockets stuffed, there was no reason for the men to stay, but they kept circling the little space over and over and over again. Nuha allowed herself a glance in their direction and immediately realized her mistake. Her eyes caught those of one of the young men, who had apparently been staring at her for several minutes already. He walked up to the table behind which the women stood, hand-in-hand.

"You're Abu Muhammad's daughter, aren't you?" He asked, leaning his arms on the table and leaning into her.

She could smell his breath, and it was not a pleasant smell. Nuha nodded quickly and looked to Rana.

The other fighter then walked up and joined his friend. Both then sat on the table and leaned in, far in, to the two women. The second then said, "You! You're the one whose husband deserted the cause, aren't you?"

Rana, dressed in a bright blue *galabiya* that barely masked the curves of her hips and breasts, and a pink floral headscarf covering her thick black hair, took half a step back until her backside was pressed against the little shelf on the back wall.

"What a shame, to be married to a man with no honor," he continued.

Rana glanced at Nuha, who gripped her hand more tightly. The two women looked at obscure spots in the distance as they leaned back against the wall behind them.

"Then again, I suppose he abandoned you, too, didn't he?" Then he laughed and slapped his mate on the back. He sized Rana up very slowly and deliberately. "I don't think it was because you weren't pleasing him, no. Maybe it's because he wasn't pleasing you. You need a real man."

"What a joke!" Nuha exclaimed, then clamped her hand over her mouth. Now she was staring straight into the eyes of the soldier who had done all the talking. "I'm sorry. I didn't mean. I just, well, you're really young, aren't you?"

The AK-47 clanged against the desk as the young man lifted his legs over the desk. "I'm 21. Old enough."

Nuha opened her mouth, then closed it again, then started pulling Rana away from behind the desk. The boy was now centimeters away from them.

But Rana drew Nuha's arm tight and stood her ground. She stomped on the floor and grabbed the young man by his shirt collar. "I may not be old enough to be your mother, but you would do well to think of me as your big sister. Your very big sister. You are too young to know what you are talking about. My husband is the most honorable of men who is doing the right thing by not getting caught in a meaningless killing game like you. You're too young to know the difference. How dare you tarnish the name of the father of my children?"

The young soldier's eyes widened, and he slowly inched away, but his friend was not deterred. He hopped over the desk and grabbed Nuha by her shoulders, staring deeply into her eyes from so close that Nuha couldn't look anywhere other than back at him. "Your sister-in-law talks a lot. My friend talks a lot." Then he planted his lips right on hers.

Nuha wriggled, but he pulled her away from Rana, breaking their hand grip, and pinned her against the wall. She tried to scream but could barely get out a grunt.

It sounded like Rana wasn't faring much better with his friend, and Nuha tried to reach out to help her sister-in-law, but while the soldier may have been young, he was also spry. And he was a trained fighter. It was no match for Nuha as he began feeling her up and fiddling with her clothes.

Then, just when Nuha was getting her head around the fact that she was about to be raped, shots rang out right outside the store, and a man was heard shouting at the top of his lungs. She couldn't tell what was being said, but it was enough for the soldier to hesitate just long enough for her to pull her face away from his grip and scream.

There was more shooting in the street and then a man came running into the store. He grabbed the two soldiers' necks, one with each hand, and pulled them away. In the scuffle, Nuha felt Rana grab her arm and pull her to the door. They peered out. There was no sign of any fighting on the street, so they tiptoed out and leaned against the outer wall of the store, gripping each other and panting.

They heard the voices of men still inside the store, arguing.

Seconds later, it was over. The two young soldiers stumbled out the door and ran down the street. Each threw a rapid panicked glance in the direction of the two women but otherwise didn't stop. They just jogged away.

Then an older man appeared at the door. It was Rana's uncle, a man in his mid-forties who was himself an officer in the militia.

He walked up to the two women, holding one another in an embrace. "I apologize for the soldiers. They will be disciplined for this."

Rana and Nuha just looked at him.

"It was God's mercy that had me outside your shop just now. You shouldn't stay in the shop alone. The soldiers are young and hungry – hungry in many ways. They don't understand the important work that you do for the cause, I don't even know if they always understand their own role or the meaning of what they fight for. But I try to teach them. I try..."

"Thank you, Uncle," said Rana.

"Yes, thank you so much," echoed Nuha.

There was not much more to say. One day, when she was alone with Leila, Nuha would whisper to her older sister that she saw no mercy in a God who rewarded their good deeds and their religious devotion with such treatment. But Rana had not stopped saying *Alhamdulillah* – praise God – over and over.

By the time the uncle left, a handful of neighbors had gathered on the street. The officer's decision to let out shots in order to stop the soldiers may have been effective in stopping the violation, but it nonetheless proved disastrous for the two women. What the neighbors saw were two women who had been taken advantage of by two soldiers. They saw two women who had allowed two soldiers to enter their private space. As a result, those two women were to blame, every bit as guilty for what happened inside the shop as the attackers. Their reputation was ruined.

So that evening, the family began plotting their move to Jordan.

The first thing they did was find out who could help them move and how much it would cost. The women had to sell most of the gold from their weddings to pay the mule. They called Leila and asked for help, and she sent them a bit of cash. It took two months to make the arrangements. Leila's father refused to go, and the rest of the family argued with him for days and days. He insisted that if he left, someone would occupy their house. If they left the house and the farmland unoccupied, it wouldn't be theirs for much longer. He would rather die on his land than live without his home. They countered by saying that this was no longer a question of saving their lives. It was now a question of saving their family's honor. If he stayed, he would stay alone because all the young men would be conscripted to fight and all the women would be shamed. He insisted that he intended to stay, even if everyone else left.

Then a bomb destroyed the front half of their house. It was about 5 in the morning, and the family was fast asleep in beds and mattresses scattered around the house. The bomb hit the front of the building and destroyed half of their living room and half of their kitchen. The debris came within inches of Mama's head, and fragments hit Baba in the arm. He bled out for several minutes, but they managed to tie the top of his arm so it would stop bleeding. After that, he could no longer lift his right arm. And he no longer had a house worth protecting, so he agreed to go.

The family piled into the back two rooms for their last few days in Syria.

When the day of their departure finally came, they left early in the morning, well before the sun awoke. Mama, Baba, Leila's three younger sisters, three sisters-in-law, and five grandchildren. Leila's brothers' wives had not kissed their mothers one last time nor hugged their sisters because it was too dangerous to tell people of their plans. The children didn't have a chance to choose their favorite toy to pack, nor did they play one last game with their neighbor friends. With no warning, they were pulled out from under their covers, the young ones bundled up in the arms of adults and the older ones dragged sleeping into the hallway. The women had prepared a bag of sandwiches so they wouldn't have to stop to eat breakfast.

No beds were made, but everything else was left tidy.

Down the stairs and onto the street the women carried three enormous woven laundry bags filled with changes of clothes, towels, and sheets, along with a few other sundry bits and bobs. With no able-bodied man among them, the women dragged the bundles silently to the edge of the village where a flatbed Suzuki truck was waiting. The men in the truck, smugglers whom Mama had somehow discovered and contracted though no one could quite figure out how, silently lifted the bags into the truck but did not offer to help bring things from the house. The women's purses were bulging with every remaining item of jewelry they owned. Everyone silently piled into the back, and Rana handed out some scruffy blankets, some of which they lay on the bed of the truck and others that they wrapped around themselves to keep warm. It was a very chilly night in late November.

The smugglers did not turn on the truck engine. Instead, one man steered while the other two stood behind the truck and pushed it down a dirt road heading up into the hills to the East.

Jordan was south.

"Why are we going east?" asked Nuha.

Her two sisters-in-law looked at Mama expectantly.

Mama shushed her and looked ahead.

An hour later, they finally turned a bend in the road. Everyone looked back, silently, as their home village faded out of sight.

Once they were in the hills, away from any settlement, the driver turned on the truck engine. The sound blasted the night silence and awoke the children who had drifted to sleep in each other's arms.

"What now?" asked one of the younger boys.

His mother wrapped her arm around him and drew him in under her shoulder. "We wait."

Everyone rode along in silence for several minutes, until they came to a checkpoint. As they approached the ragtag collection of soldiers, one of the men in front poked his head out of the passenger window and turned back. "Just stay sitting there. Don't say anything, and try not to look."

"*Yallah*," said Mama, and everyone else kept their mouths shut.

They all listened to the exchange between the driver and the soldier.

"Who are you?" asked a soldier.

"*Ya Kheie*, it's me," answered the driver.

The family heard the sound of slapping hands as the men greeted each other. Then an exchange of carefree how-is-your-mother and how-is-your-brother and how-is-life comments.

"How's the road up ahead?" asked the driver. No one in the family ever learned his name nor the names of either of his companions.

"Well, wait a second. Who do you have with you?"

"These? These are just some friends."

"Are they with us?" asked the soldier.

"Of course! What do you think, I'd take just anyone?"

The soldier then shouted in the general direction of Leila's father, "*Ya Hajj!*"

The driver interjected, "He's an old man, don't bother him."

"I'm just greeting him," responded the soldier.

Baba poked his head up out from where he sat buried under the blanket. Covered up the way the were, they weren't trying to hide, but it was easy to imagine how the soldier might have thought they were.

The soldier walked back and looked at Baba. He stared at the old man, who blinked back at him.

Then he walked back to the driver and said, "Go on. It's calm tonight."

They exchanged half a dozen warm farewells and wishes for each other to enjoy peace and safety, and then the truck drove off again.

At the next checkpoint, only half an hour later, a similar exchange took place, but this time, the soldier directed them off the road and into the fields, recommending they again turn the engine off. The two passengers up front got out and pushed, this time through bumpy terrain that until recently had been a cabbage and cucumber farm.

Seeing them struggling to push, the younger women hopped off and walked alongside the truck. Even so, the men were barely able to get the truck to move, so two of the half-dozen FSA fighters at the checkpoint left their positions to cross into the field and help.

Though Jordan had previously been about a 45-minute drive from their house, by the time the sun came up in the morning, Leila's family were a mere three villages away from their own. The Suzuki pulled up to a small country house.

"We'll rest here today and continue in the morning," said the man who seemed to be in charge as he hopped out of the passenger seat.

The group quietly climbed down and walked into the little house, where they found a big bottle of water for drinking, bread, and a stock of labne, olives, cheese, olive oil and za'atar. As good a meal as they had enjoyed in months.

The two sisters-in-law set out the meal in the middle of the mat while the others settled on mattresses that lined the room. Their smugglers joined the family for the meal, and as soon as they were done politely stuffing their faces, everyone drifted off to sleep.

Except for Nuha, who was feeling as awake as she had felt in a long time. She had not rested well since the incident in the shop, and the face of that young FSA fighter kept appearing in her conscience. She was struggling with hatred, guilt and a nagging shameless curiosity about what might have happened next.

She wandered out of the little house, which was really just one spacious room surrounded by concrete blocks and covered by a tin roof. The sun was blinding, and it took a few moments for her eyes to adjust. The rains had recently begun to fall again, and the surrounding land was beginning to show little signs of green. Little pink, yellow and white wildflowers were scattered across the landscape. There was not a soul in sight, and Nuha couldn't hear anything at all except for the buzzing of a bee near the roof of the house. No human voices, no donkeys braying, no cars or motors of any sort, not even any birds chirping. She wondered if they could just stay here, rather than venture into a new strange country.

She walked around the house and down the little slope into a tiny ravine. It was dry, but she could see that the ground was soft and imagined water would be trickling through the gully any day now. She poked the flowers on its sides with her toes and the blossoms flittered. She leaned down to pick a few, and wandered along the riverbed for a couple of minutes, holding the flowers up to her nose.

Where was that soldier now? What had happened to him? Probably nothing. How old was he, anyway? Had he finished his education? Maybe under other circumstances, he would have been a good respectable local boy with a promising future. In a different Syria, instead of forcing her out of town he might have been a suitor. He was quite attractive, and she knew that he was a distant relative by marriage. Beyond the hatred and greed in his eyes, she believed she had seen some hint of kindness and desire, not the perverted desire that he chose to manifest, but an innocent desire, a yearning to do the right thing.

Then her thoughts brought her to her schoolbooks. She had brought three books and two notebooks with her. Though the University of Damascus felt like a universe away now, a dream that had slipped irrevocably out of her hands and into an abyss, those books gave her solace. Only one semester away from graduating. A mere semester had remained, but now it was as if she'd never studied at all. Those books were the one thing that proved otherwise. Her books tied her to a larger world, a world where she could talk to boys and be smart and make a difference.

While her Baba was mourning loss of house and land, and her Mama was mourning the loss of her sons' careers, and her sisters-in-law were mourning the loss of the family life they had been building, and her nieces and nephews and younger sisters would soon – once they understood what was happening – be mourning the loss of their friends and games, Nuha was oddly mourning the loss of the little shop. At the shop, she had done something. She had given out food and clothes to the hungry and destitute. She had helped people in need to access the help they needed. She had helped create a space for religious learning and prayer. She had smiled and said kind words to people whose own smiles had faded. It was a small project, but it was a source of hope for a village under siege. Those two men – and her uncle – had taken that away from her and she could never forgive them for that.

Now, she was on the road to becoming a refugee. As soon as she crossed the border, that was what she would be. A refugee had nothing to give to anyone else and had to ask others for everything. She was going to be someone else's charity case. She was smart enough to know that the world saw her as an uneducated village girl, just the kind of neglected soul who couldn't help but to become a war refugee. She would no longer encourage others in their day of pain; now she would become an excuse for others to say they were encouraging a poor young lady in her day of pain. To preserve her honor, she was turning in her dignity.

She turned and began to head back up the little hill to the house where everyone was sleeping, but just then she heard the first shot. Not even a second later, she saw a splash in the sand just up ahead. She turned around and saw nothing, but she did catch a glistening flash of light. She had lived in a war zone long enough to recognize the barrel of a gun, maybe one or two hundred meters away. Another shot. She sprinted up the hill and into the house, casting all decorum aside and shaking the man sleeping nearest the door. "Brother! Brother! They're shooting outside!" she shouted.

Within seconds, the three smugglers were awake and pulling guns from holsters that they had thus far concealed from their clients. The rest of Nuha's family were groggily sitting up.

More shots rang out as the men tiptoed out the front door, one headed to the left and the other two to the right.

What seemed like an eternity was spent huddled together as a family, listening to the shots grow louder. It sounded like various types of artillery were being used. At some point, they heard an engine roar. The Suzuki drove away, leaving dust flaring up in its wake.

"What do we do now?" asked Baba, rather harshly.

Mama didn't answer.

"Where did they go, Mama?" the youngest child asked. Her mother hushed her and didn't answer.

There wasn't much to say. A fight was raging outside the house, and they were stuck inside. They had fled the war in their village to get caught in the war on a plot of countryside several miles away. They had paid a sum of money known only to Mama, to men who had just abandoned them.

The battle continued, but nothing hit their house, and no soldiers came barreling down their door. There was more shouting, and there were more shots, but over time, they drifted away, until Nuha could barely hear anything anymore. The silence restored, Nuha and her sisters-in-law tiptoed up to the front door and peered out. Nothing. No soldiers. No FSA militias. No tanks or guns. No car. No smugglers. No laundry sacks full of their only remaining belongings. To return home now was unthinkable – it would be obvious they tried to leave, and their tenuous position in the community would all but crumble. The only way to go from here was forward, and so they packed up all the food in the house to take with them, then tried to get some more rest until night fell. As the sun was setting, they opened the front door again and slowly stepped out. Nuha took charge, leading the group in the opposite direction than the one from which they had come. Judging from where the sun was resting in the sky, it seemed that this was Southeast. The known border crossing was Southwest, but any variation on South would get them to Jordan eventually. And so they started walking.

Fifteen minutes later, they heard a car engine in the distance and Nuha pointed to the extremely scanty brush on the side of the road. They tried to hide, but with little success.

As it turned out, their conspicuousness was, for once, a good thing. The engine belonged to the Suzuki, which held their three smugglers. They got out and apologized, explaining that the battle had nothing to do with them, but they didn't want any of the fighters to know that the house was occupied, and a car out front was a clear giveaway, so they had left for the sake of the family's safety.

Nuha, for one, was skeptical of that explanation, but at least, they had returned.

They piled into the back of the Suzuki and headed off again, Nuha's two sisters-in-law rummaging through the three big plastic bags to ensure that nothing was missing. All appeared to be well, and yet they still praised God for the wisdom to keep their most valuable items on their persons.

All along the harrowing journey to Jordan, they found the FSA fighters whom they encountered to be kind, gracious and hospitable, nothing like their own extended relatives in their home village, who had taken advantage of them in so many different ways.

Along the way, they did pass two inevitable government checkpoints. But Mama whispered to the family that she had already included money for a bribe in her payment, and all went smoothly.

Just as the first rays of sun were beginning to fall on their second day, they pulled up to a fence in the desert. A military tower stood in the distance, and a voice spoke through a blowhorn. "Stop there!"

The Suzuki stopped. The three men in front shouted for them to get out as quickly as possible, and helped them unload their bags. Then they jumped into the cab again and, this time drove off for good.

Seconds later a Jordanian soldier appeared and pointed a gun at them. The family let out a collective sigh. It never ends.

Using the butt of his rifle, he pointed for them to walk over to the tower and made them sit at its base. They obeyed, but he still kept his gun trained on them as he radioed someone.

Half an hour later, a truck appeared and they were loaded into it. The truck picked up three other families along the border, then took them all to Za'atari Refugee Camp.

In Za'atari, they encountered everything that Nuha had feared, but it was even worse. They were taken straight to a registration center where they ate one semi-decent cooked meal. Then they received food ration cards, one mattress and blanket per person, a bucket and some other basic hygiene items, and assistance putting up a tent.

After that, it was up to them to figure out how to arrange themselves in the tiny space and to think up strategies for warding off the dusty wind that never abated and shielding themselves from the relentless sun. There were latrines and shower stalls a hundred or so meters away, but they looked unsafe for the women and were rather filthy. Water was collected from communal taps, not too far away but even so, a gruesome trek in the grueling desert heat.

They were so exhausted that they spent most of the first day sleeping, but after that, they slowly began to learn their new surroundings. No one whose name or family was familiar lived anywhere near them, so even though they were surrounded by fellow Syrians – many from Dera'a region just like them – they were strangers in a foreign land.

No one questioned their loyalty to the cause. They were surrounded by fiercely anti-regime families, who whispered curses against Bashar al-Assad and proudly waved the flag of the

Free Syrian Army. It quickly became clear that they were not yet freed from their secrets. They couldn't admit that Leila's brothers had opted to defect instead of kill, that a family member lived in Kuwait, or that two of the women had been shamed by FSA fighters. The children were sat down for a careful talking-to and a stern warning not to open their mouths about these things, ever.

Meanwhile, they began to hear the stories of the other families whose tents lined their little sandy walkway. Their stories were even more agonizing. Hardly anyone they met had not lost at least one close family member, and most everyone also had, at least, someone who had spent significant time in jail. The stories from jail were the most horrific. Men were put into cells so crowded that no one could even sit down, much less lie down. They slept with their heads on each other's shoulders, urinating and defecating where they stood. The torture was legendary, and few prison survivors came out with full use of their limbs or without an assortment of scars. Noise and lights were a given, at all times.

Almost every single family had been separated, like Leila's own family was scattered across Syria and its bordering countries.

As Mama and Nuha finished telling Leila all these things over bottomless cups of tea, Mama would point to a Caravan nearby and tell of what that family had suffered, or to another Caravan and complain about how that woman may have lost her son to the regime but that didn't excuse her for the scathing remarks she dropped on the neighbors.

Leila, wrapping herself around her mother's arm, asked what life was like in Za'atari.

"It's awful. You can see the conditions," began Nuha. "We're in the desert, far from everything. For six months now, I've seen nothing but the desert and the Caravanat. It's better now than before, though. Now we, at least, do have this Caravan to live in. The tent was awful. We were never clean, never. Critters came into the tent at night, and there was nothing we could do about it.

"But praise God, we're making a life here. The children all go to school. They only missed one year in the end. I volunteer at the local youth center, where I teach French and math to teenage girls. Many of them dropped out of school even before the crisis. Most of the other families here are so backward. There aren't even many people who can read at all. And most of the others didn't bother to finish their school." Nuha sighed. "They're not like us."

"And you?" asked Leila. "Is there any chance you will finish university?"

"It's difficult." Nuha looked up and gazed into the distance.

"I heard that Jordan University is allowing some Syrians to finish there. Is it true?"

"I heard that too, but couldn't find any information about it."

"Maybe we can investigate together. I'll ask in Amman."

"So you're really leaving us again so soon?" asked Mama.

Leila hugged her arm more tightly. "That's the plan. The car is waiting."

"Tell him to go. Stay here."

"I don't know if the camp would let me."

"This is a big camp; no one knows anything!" added Nuha. "The things people get away with here..."

"Like what?" asked Leila.

"People leave all the time. Do you know, down the road there, is a 19-year-old boy who has three Caravanat just for him? He has arranged them in a triangle, so there's a little courtyard in the middle."

"Just for him?"

"Yes. His whole family was here, but they got themselves released from the camp. I think they're even living in Qatar now and working there or something. He didn't want to go and said there wasn't anything for him to do out there. So they left their camp ID cards with him, and he collects rations for 20 people and has three Caravanat just for himself."

"That's crazy! Why doesn't he leave if his family is all gone?"

"I don't know. Maybe he's just lazy. Here all he does is hang out and make friends and eat his food rations. He's a 19-year-old boy who doesn't care that the food is crap."

"What else?" asked Leila.

"Well," Nuha rolled her eyes. "You saw the new little market on your way in, right?"

Leila nodded.

"Almost everything they sell in those little shops is from Syria. It's not even Jordanian merchants who smuggle it in. There are people who live in the camp but go to Syria every week and bring back produce. Even with the war and the way prices have soared, fruits, vegetables, simple things like these, are all much cheaper there. The shops take Syrian lira, too: no Jordanian money in this camp."

"Are you saying that they live in a refugee camp and are refugees, but that they go home every week?"

Nuha nodded.

Leila shook her head. "And what about you? Do you think of going home?"

"Never." Mama gritted her teeth.

"What about leaving the camp? If it's that easy, why don't you leave?"

"We don't know how," Mama said, shrugging.

"Ok, then, let me go back to Amman and study the issue."

"Stay with us," said Mama.

"Yes, you only just got here!" exclaimed Nuha.

A little bit more arm-pulling and expressions of love later, Leila agreed to spend the night. She went out and brought in her bags of gifts, then sent the driver away, saying she would call him tomorrow to set a time for him to fetch her and the boys.

Meanwhile, the boys were playing ball with some of the other children in an empty patch of sand behind the Caravan. They seemed to be as happy here as they'd been in their airconditioned flat full of brand-name toys back in Kuwait.

Second Trimester

Chapter Eight

A month later, Leila was still at Za'atari. She couldn't seem to pull herself away. She found joy in helping Mama with the cooking and in struggling alongside her sisters and sisters-in-law to keep the dust out of their little space. The desert was as brutal as everyone said it was, and she felt her skin tightening a bit more with each day that passed. She wasn't getting enough water, and her bowels were all plugged up. The boys seemed to be happy, but their faces were several shades darker from spending so much time in the sun, their hair was a little bit sun-bleached, and overall they looked much more like village farm boys who had never been to school, than like sons of a doctor living in Kuwait City.

The camp was not a very safe place, and no one ventured far from home alone. Leila went with Rana to collect the family's monthly food rations one day, experiencing the arduous wait in a stuffy tent and witnessing a fight at the distribution point. On an outing to the vegetable market with Nuha, she saw a political rally crying for the downfall of the regime, then witnessed Jordanian police break it up as quickly as it started. She accompanied her younger sisters to the youth center a few times and was everyone's sweetheart as the young girls asked her questions about English language, about traveling, about life in Kuwait, about anything that might pull their hearts and minds away from camp life. She joined the weekly attempt at washing their clothes, moaning in frustration as her nails broke in the brutal bucket-and-soap routine she'd not followed since her student days. Then wanting to cry when she hung the clothes to dry and watched them collect dust as quickly as they released moisture.

But she loved every minute sitting with her family, listening to their stories and telling them her own. It warmed her heart to see her boys play with their cousins, accept kisses from their aunts, and cuddle up next to their grandparents.

Slowly, as the days wore on, the weight of what her family had told her began to grow. She had known the general outline, but the details were new. She'd known that her brothers were in Lebanon, that her nephew had briefly joined the FSA, about the good work being done at the store, that there was tension in the village, and that her mother had asked her for money to help pay the smugglers. But she had not known the nuances or little stories that filled out the tale. She tried to imagine herself trying to advise her brothers what to do when facing the pressure of the militia. She tried to put herself in Nuha's shoes as she faced down a rabid FSA boy. She tried to imagine waking up in the middle of the night to see the front half of the living room gone, dust floating in its place. She tried to imagine picking up her two boys in the middle of the night and leaving everything behind, aware that she would never see her home again.

She couldn't.

She couldn't even begin to process what her family had experienced and survived. She couldn't understand how they were still able to laugh or smile. Instead, a seed of guilt began to grow, fueled by ideas about what she could have, should have done. She should have brought them to Kuwait from the very beginning. She should have been with them at home. She should have sent more money. She should have joined the FSA herself. She should have, she should have, she should have.

Hassoun called every day, promptly at 7 pm. He was not thrilled that Leila had stayed in the camp, and it had fallen on him to inform his cousin that their houseguests would reappear only at some moment unknown and unexpected to all.

He was a patient man and was careful not to pressure her. But he did ask her how much longer she was staying. He also asked her how her family was doing, asked her to tell him about the camp and asked her how the boys were faring with the dust and the sun. In every question, Leila heard judgment. She heard him telling her that he didn't want her to stay any longer, that her family could get on without her, that the camp was no place for her to keep his children.

Most phone conversations ended with Leila shouting at him that he didn't understand and hanging up.

The next day, though, promptly at 7 pm, he would call again.

His dependability, faithfulness, and tenderness was wrong, just wrong. She didn't deserve it. So she began to tell herself that he wasn't actually that good, that it was all a cover for the anger that he harbored towards her and her family.

When she spoke with her husband, she kept the conversations short. Then she went and worked as hard as she could to help her family with their daily chores. Meanwhile, her sisters looked out for her boys, whom Leila had all but forgotten.

A month had now gone by without news. A whole month. In fact, a month and a few days. A friend of a friend of a cousin said he'd learned that Samir was still in the holding area by the border crossing, but no one could know for sure. Why Samir? Why now?

Roxy stayed with Maha during the first two days, helping with the cooking and the cleaning and creating endless distractions for her friend. They went for walks on the seafront, did some shopping in the big mall, and started half a dozen little home projects. "For Samir," Roxy would say. "He'll like this."

Maha followed along, doing whatever Roxy said, gladly letting her friend do all the talking. If Roxy said to rearrange the knick knacks on the shelf, she did. If Roxy got up on a chair at one end of the curtain rod and told Maha to grab the other end of the rod, she did. And then when they were done, she either went straight back to the sofa or wandered into the kitchen to make some tea. Or she ran to the bathroom to be sick, yet again.

A woman whose husband has been arrested, even more so when his crime was helping people somehow or another, is likely to lose some weight. Maha could hardly keep a bite of food down, between her despair and her changing bowels. She lost 5 kilos in her first trimester, and the doctor was worried.

After a few days, even if not yet fully herself, Maha understood that Roxy needed to return to her family. Her children needed their mother. So she tried to tell her friend that she would be ok, but Roxy's response was to take Maha back to Aley with her. Maha protested that she wanted to be home in case Samir arrived, but Roxy assured her that he would call first anyway.

Once in Aley, Maha felt like a lump on a log. There was nothing for her to do except take up space in an already very cramped flat. Roxy's children were happy and playful and served as a distraction at times. Until they reminded Maha of her future.

Even so, she kept coming back. Every couple of days or so she would go back to the Beirut flat she and Samir shared, then when she could bear the solitude no more - usually after a day or two - she headed back up the mountain. She drifted through a month like this, not truly anywhere and doing little regardless of what house she found herself in on any given day.

Over time, the grip on her stomach let up. It also helped that the nausea was passing. Slowly, anxiety was replaced by dullness. At first, Maha had been keeping her makeup fresh and dressing carefully each morning, ready for her husband's arrival at any moment. With time, she cared less and less, and by the third week, she had stopped changing out of her pajamas or leaving the house, except to come or go from Aley. The Beirut flat was a mess, and Maha wasn't much help to Roxy or her mother-in-law either.

One afternoon, Maha was at Roxy's house when Samir's brother called from Damascus. He had called once every few days since Samir had disappeared, and this conversation went much as it had every other time.

"Hi, sister. How are you?"

"How are you?"

They both asked but neither had an answer, and neither expected an answer.

After a second, Maha asked, "What's the news?"

"Still none. But I spoke with my cousin who talked to his friend and it sounds like he's still there at the border. There is talk of a transport soon."

"Transport to where?" asked Maha, her voice raised.

"I don't know. Sednaya, maybe?" suggested her brother-in-law.

"That place is horrid!"

"Which isn't?" He was careful not to say the words "jail" or "prison", but the Sednaya prison – just a mile down the road from Maha's now-demolished childhood home – was one of the larger and more infamous, known for holding hundreds of political prisoners, often for decades on end.

"Don't say that."

"Maybe that's not where."

"Can you imagine..." Maha pondered aloud. "He could be just down the street from my own family? As bad as it is to know he is where he is, it would be torture for him to go to my hometown but see it through bars."

"We're not giving up yet. We have a plan to try something."

"What?"

"I know someone who has a contact–" he cut himself off at this point. This was not a conversation to be shared with the phone waves. "Just trust me, we're not giving up."

"Thank you, and let's keep trying. What can I do?"

"Pray, just pray."

For some reason, on this particular day, Maha's temples began to burn when he said this. "Pray" was not the answer she wanted. She blurted, "I can do more. I need to do more."

"Don't you worry yourself," repeated her brother-in-law. "Your husband will not be forgotten."

"Thank you," she said as quickly as possible. She wasn't feeling very thankful.

"Rest, ok?"

Rest. All she did was rest. "Let's talk soon then. *Yallah* bye."

"Bye."

When Maha hung up the phone, little electric currents were pinging all over her body. Men! They thought women were useless and had nothing to offer. It was her husband, the father of her baby, in that holding cell. And he was being held for a cause that she had fought for alongside Samir. She had never been a wallflower housewife before, and it was unthinkable that she might start now.

She went to the little bag she had brought up with her and pulled out her makeup and street clothes. She asked Roxy's mother-in-law if she could take a bath. An hour later, Maha was clean, tidy, and looking as good as she had the day she was wed. Even better, her body allowed her to forget she was pregnant. Her energy was high, and her nausea was low.

Roxy was putting the finishing touches on lunch in the kitchen when Maha walked in.

"I'm leaving," she announced.

Roxy looked up from squeezing a lemon into the salad. "Leaving where? Why?"

"I'm going to go help Samir."

Now Roxy put the lemon down and turned to her friend. "How are you going to do that?"

"I'm going to the border," announced Maha. "I'll appeal to their compassion, offer myself in his place, start a protest at the border, I don't know, but I'll get their attention, and I'll get him out."

"Are you insane?" asked Roxy.

"Maybe. But he's my husband, and I'm tired of being the patient war widow waiting at home."

"I understand, but--"

"But nothing, that's what I'm going to do."

Roxy opened her mouth and started to say something, then shut it again. She turned back to the salad, saying, "Well, you can't travel on an empty stomach. Let's eat now."

Maha had an appetite for the first time all week, she realized at that moment, and her mouth began to water. They sat down to lunch, Maha, Roxy, Roxy's mother-in-law and her two children.

At first, they talked of the sundry everyday things of life as they ate. Then after a few minutes, Roxy abruptly jumped into her arguments. She reminded Maha that she had to think not just of herself but of the child she carried. She pointed out the utter futility of walking into a Syrian police station and asking that someone be released. It always was a crapshoot, but in the current days, it was a non-option, insanely dangerous. She suggested that Maha, at least, find someone to go with her and even offered herself – but not today.

Maha just let her talk. From the moment she had hung up the phone, her mind was made up.

"You are probably right, Roxy," she said. "Probably everything you just said is wise and practical. But I'm still going. I have to. For my own sake, for the sake of the honor of my child, for Samir's sake. He needs to know he's not forgotten. I need to know that I didn't give up. That's just the way it is. I don't want you to come with me. It's dangerous, and your children are exactly the age where they need you the most. I'll be ok, you'll see."

They kept arguing, but Roxy seemed to realize that there wasn't much point. Though she kept talking, instead of saying, "you shouldn't" she said, "you will." For example, Roxy may have said, "You shouldn't have to deal with the abuse of police officers and possible torture." But instead, she said, "You will probably be abused by police officers and tortured." As if that helped.

Finally, Roxy succeeded in obtaining a small concession from Maha: she would wait until morning rather than traveling over the mountains now since the sun was about to set.

Chapter Nine

The next morning, early, with two cheese sandwiches, a bottle of water and a change of clothes tucked in a plastic bag in her purse, Maha left Roxy's flat and walked straight to the Damascus Road where she flagged a minibus to Chtaura, the Lebanese outpost where she could catch a ride to the border.

She sat quietly by the window and watched as the houses and vegetation thinned with each switchback on the way up the crevices of Mt. Lebanon. Billboards for Coca-Cola and Lebanese television shows peppered exits for summer mountain resorts. At the very top of the highest mountain, they went through a checkpoint. The soldier waved them through with nary a glance into the bus. Two smaller checkpoints and a steep downhill drive later, they were in Chtaura, one of the biggest towns in the Bekaa Valley. The ubiquitous golden arches of McDonalds signaled their entrance into the commercial hub.

The minibus continued to Zahle but half the passengers, Maha amongst them, disembarked in Chtaura. The others, all men, scattered and disappeared into the milling and bustling of the town center.

Maha went straight to the taxi garage, a parking lot full of yellow cars with Syrian plates tucked behind a grungy restaurant.

She walked up to a man who was leaning against his car. Before the problems started, she could have barely stepped one foot off the minibus before half a dozen taxi drivers would pounce. From all sides, she'd hear "Sham, Sham, Come here, sister!" Inevitably, some ambitious character would grab her bag and tote it to his vehicle, and she would be stuck accepting his services. Occasionally, a fight would break out, if the winning driver had only just arrived while another had been waiting hours for passengers. In those cases, Maha would just wait until someone not too young and not too old, but a tad better-dressed than the others, came up and told her which car to take. It mattered little to her since there was not a soul in Chtaura who didn't know the price of a seat in a taxi to Damascus, 200 Syrian lira per seat, 1000 for the entire vehicle and immediate departure. Otherwise, the car didn't move until all spots were claimed.

All in all, before the problems, it had always been a very passive process for Maha, her job being simply not to look foolish and gullible, and to make sure that the taxi drivers realized that she knew what she was doing. She did this trek often enough that some of them had come to recognize her, which helped.

But now, it was Maha who walked up to the driver and initiated the conversation. It fell to her to figure out which car was next in line for departure.

This was also the first time she was only traveling to the border. Entering Syria would not be an option for her today.

"Are you available to travel, uncle?" she said to the graying thick-waisted man with a two-day growth on his face, dressed in khaki jeans and a dark-brown button-up shirt.

"To Sham?" he asked, still leaning against the car with his arms crossed.

"Just to Jdeideh, actually," she said.

"Same price as Sham. I can't pick up passengers in Jdeideh to come back."

"Shared taxi?"

He looked around and extended his arms to the quiet, mostly empty lot, waving them around a bit. "If you want. We might leave tomorrow, though." He lifted an eyebrow for good measure.

"Is there another car?" Maha asked. "A car leaving sooner?"

Again he waved his arms around and turned his head, saying, "That's hard." Maha wondered if he would tell her if there were.

But she wanted to be a confident bargainer. "Where are the other cars?"

"There aren't many people going to Sham these days, sister. Most of the cars go straight back to pick up more passengers coming this way."

"What about you?"

He shrugged.

"So, how much for the car, to Jdeideh?"

"To Sham, you mean."

"*Ya'ani.*"

"Five hundred a seat."

"Five hundred?" exclaimed Maha, sounding as indignant as possible and gearing up for a bargaining session.

"That's what it costs now. When is the last time you went back?"

"Last month," she fictionalized. Her last trip had been closer to three months ago. "It wasn't like this."

He shrugged. "That's the price."

"Well, if you don't usually get any passengers at all entering Syria, then shouldn't you take me for free?" She didn't imagine such logic would do any good, but it made sense to her.

He shrugged yet again and re-crossed his arms.

"*Taieb*, how much for the whole car?" asked Maha.

"Four seats in my car, so 2000."

Clearly there was no point wasting any more time on this conversation. This looked to be her only option. So now Maha shrugged and walked over to the back passenger-side door.

"ID card, please," said the driver.

"We still need this?" asked Maha.

"Syria's at war. That doesn't mean the whole world has collapsed."

Maha reluctantly pulled out her Syrian ID card and handed it to the driver who walked away into the building to register the trip with the local authorities. Registering felt like a very bad idea, even though as far as she knew she was welcome in Lebanon. Plus, everyone figured the Lebanese and Syrian governments still talked. She could imagine that conversation.

Lebanese police officer: "We had one person leave Chtaura for Sham today. A Syrian, Christian."

Syrian counterpart: "What was her name?"

Lebanese police officer, glancing at the otherwise-blank logbook: "Maha Yousef, father Younis, mother, Marie Sausan."

Syrian counterpart, glancing at his log: "That's the wife of Samir Aflaq, currently detained at Jdeideh border."

Lebanese: "She must be insane."

Syrian: "Insane indeed. We'll keep an eye out for her."

But there was no way to go, but forward and so Maha waited what felt like an entire hour but was actually just five minutes, for her driver to return and plunk into his seat. He passed the ID card back to Maha, put the car into gear and drove off.

As they headed down the flat stretch of highway towards the border, the driver asked, "Bread? Medicines?" These were the most common products people generally purchased on the Lebanese side of the border to take to Syria.

Maha shook her head no.

They continued on in silence a few minutes and then Maha had a thought. "Since I've rented the whole car, can you wait for me a bit in Jdeideh? I will probably be coming back to Chtaura pretty quickly."

"What are you doing in Jdeideh."

"*Malish*. It doesn't matter."

He glanced back in the rear-view mirror, and Maha saw his eyes narrowing.

So Maha added, "It's nothing too much. I'm just visiting my husband."

"Visiting your husband?"

"Long story. But don't worry, it's nothing wrong." Maybe it was, Maha didn't know, but she'd best be positive. She would walk into the immigration hall, find the little office of the officer on duty, explain that she was there to get her husband, then ten minutes later she and Samir would walk out together and head straight for Lebanon. She would never let her husband go home again, as long as chaos and suspicion reigned in their country.

It was as simple as that.

A few minutes later, they pulled up to the Lebanese side of the border. The driver offered to take Maha's papers in for her. She thanked him, handed him her ID card once again, and leaned back in her seat.

The nausea was beginning to creep back. She grabbed the bottle of water that Roxy had given her and took a sip, then slouched as far as she could in her seat, with her head tilted back, and took a few deep breaths.

She tried to squelch the desire to vomit by planning what she would say upon arrival at the Jdeideh crossing. But as the scenarios worked themselves out in her mind, the insanity and likely futility of what she was setting out to do became increasingly obvious. Her determination and excitement about actually doing something, rather than just sitting around waiting, began to fade, quickly being replaced by pregnancy feelings.

Wasn't her condition supposed to be a physical thing? Why did she feel nauseous when she was discouraged? And how did she then manage to forget the symptoms for several hours?

Maha sighed loudly and accepted the inevitable: she hopped out of the car and ran behind a little mobile phone hut to vomit.

Then she wandered slowly back to the car and lay down in the back seat, lifting her head just far enough to take another sip of water.

Would a sickly pregnant lady garner more sympathy from the officers, or would it be a turn-off, she wondered?

It was fifteen minutes before the driver reappeared and drove up to the checkpoint, where the soldier looked at Maha's ID card and little receipt, then glanced into the car to verify it was the same person.

She was sure her face was deathly pale as she struggled to stay seated, but neither her driver nor the soldier commented, and they were soon speeding across the 8-kilometer mountainous passage through no man's land.

Halfway to Syria, Maha asked the driver to pull over. As soon as the car was stopped, she ran out to the side of the road to be sick.

The driver then asked if she was ok, and she pretended she was. It garnered enough sympathy, though, for the driver to offer to wait with her in Jdeideh – as long as it didn't take too long, he said.

A few short minutes later, and they were there. The driver pulled up to the entrance of the immigration hall for arrivals, which looked more quiet than Maha had seen it in a long time. She asked him to stay there, took one more sip of water followed by a deep breath of air, patted her hair down and gave it a little combing with her fingers, then stepped out of the car. She told herself to not be sick again.

She set off to the immigration hall on the other side of the facility, the hall for exiting Syria. The driver called out that she was going into the wrong building, but she turned back, smiled, and said, "I know where I'm going. Thank you!"

Then she set her eyes on the big white construction, completely unchanged from days of peace when thousands passed through this border every day, on business and family visits, without a care in the world. The only difference was that everything now looked eerily quiet.

She walked in and, as she had envisaged, found the little office for the officer in charge.

A graying man with three stars on his shoulder was sitting at a desk, smoking a cigarette, and chatting with a much younger soldier who stood by handing him documents to sign.

"Excuse me?" began Maha.

At first, neither man looked her way.

"Excuse me?" she tried, a bit louder.

Then the officer looked up. He raised his eyebrows, inviting her to talk without stooping so low as to ask her a question.

"Are you the officer in charge here?"

He nodded and may or may not have grunted quietly.

"I want to talk about someone who is being held here."

The officer raised his eyebrows again.

Maha wasn't sure what to say next. As she had played it out in her mind, the officer had actually engaged in the conversation. After a horribly awkward delay, she repeated, "I want to talk about someone who is being held here." Then, stammering, she continued, "My...my...erm...my husband is...is...well, I understand that he has been detained here at the border."

The officer waved his adjunct away, and the younger man quickly exited the room with the pile of signed papers, barely glancing in Maha's direction.

Now that she had started, she went on, "It was the 17th of April. He was traveling to Beirut. I really don't understand why he would be stopped, but they say he's being held here."

The officer waved his arm limply to a chair, and Maha sat. Then he said, "I don't know anything about that."

But, Maha reasoned, if he didn't know anything he wouldn't send the soldier away or ask her to sit. So she sat down, perched stiffly on the edge of the enormous brown leather armchair.

Eventually, he did answer. "We don't take civilian petitions in this office."

"I'm not here for a civilian petition," Maha said. She had no clue whatsoever what a civilian petition might be.

"Oh? Why are you here?"

"He's my husband, and I want him to know that he's going to be a father." This was not part of her rehearsed strategy, but Maha muttered a prayer of thanks under her breath to God for giving her the idea. After all, how could an honorable man – which the officer would surely want to appear to be – deny a request to inform a man that his wife was expecting?

The officer lay his pen on the big gilded blotter that covered half of his monstrous carved wooden desk. He leaned toward Maha and asked, "Where have you come from?"

"Beirut." She looked him straight in the eyes.

"You came from Beirut to ask me to tell your husband that you are pregnant?"

"No."

"So why did you just tell me that?"

"I want to tell him myself. Surely you would not deny a woman's right to visit her husband with such wonderful news?"

"Surely I might," He said, but his lips were curved ever so slightly up. This man just may be won over.

Maha didn't reply, but kept staring him down.

He stared back for a bit, then looked down to his pen a moment. He reached for the ancient green phone on his desk and dialed – yes, dialed a big round phone dial that was very possibly inherited from the Soviet Union – two numbers. A moment later, he told someone to come to his office.

When he put the phone back in its cradle, he asked Maha if she wanted tea or coffee. She politely refused, but the officer went ahead and called for someone named Mustafa, who must have been right outside the office, to bring two coffees. Mustafa immediately entered and asked Maha if she wanted hers black, sweet or medium. She asked if they had *zuhorat* instead, and so one black coffee and one flower tea were summoned. As they waited for their drinks and for whomever the officer had summoned to appear, the man went back to signing papers and Maha twiddled her thumbs.

The drinks arrived at the same time as a smart-looking young officer entered the room. The officer-in-charge had him sit in front of Maha. While Maha slowly stirred some sugar into her tea – she did not usually drink her tea with sugar but felt she could use the extra energy right now – the officer asked her for her husband's name.

"Samir Aflaq."

The older man turned to his junior: "Is there someone hosted here named Samir Aflaq?" he asked. Maha couldn't help but roll her eyes at his use of the word "hosted" as she copiously averted her gaze.

The younger man pulled out a notebook from his breast pocket and consulted a moment. Did he really keep a record of all prisoners in that notebook? That seemed absurd, and Maha assumed it was just for show. She wasn't very impressed.

"Samir Aflaq, 17 April."

"That's him!" exclaimed Maha. He was close by, maybe in this very building. "Please, can I see him?"

The junior looked to the senior, whose hands were outstretched, with each finger touching its counterpart on the other hand. "She wants to tell him that she's carrying his baby," he explained. "If it's ok with you, it's ok with me."

The junior shrugged and stood up, gesturing for Maha to come with him. She had not actually drunk any of her flower tea yet.

"Don't forget to check her papers first," said the senior.

Maha's heart froze. Surely they wouldn't arrest her, too? Not a pregnant woman who lived in Lebanon?

Her hands trembling, she reached into the purse that she had slung diagonally across her shoulder and midriff, resting on her lower belly, right in front of where this strange child was growing. She pulled out her Syrian ID card along with her Lebanese residence permit, hoping that that would help allay any temptation the military might have to see her as a threat.

She handed them, barely managing to conceal the shaking in her fingers, to the younger officer, who returned her Lebanese card to her then walked away. She looked back to the officer in charge.

"Go with him!" he barked.

"Thank you, sir, for your assistance," she said, resting her right arm on her chest in a gesture of deference.

He nodded shortly and called out for Mustafa again.

Maha followed this young officer, whose name she did not know, whose rank she was unable to determine, and whose role she could only suspect. He was clean-shaven, with green eyes peering out from a smooth tan face, well-built and athletic but not chunky. Muscles rippled under his sleeves. He walked tall and assured, but not cocky. The stories about men such as this, about the brutalities they conducted on a daily basis, things like the murder of civilians and torture of detainees, belied such a clean-cut, fit man. He looked like the boy next door, one of Samir's mates, and he acted polite and gracious. Maha struggled to imagine what he did behind closed doors, or even out in the open in rebel areas. She shivered, and her stomach began to churn again.

She determined to think of something more mundane. There was nothing mundane about this building. Almost everyone she could see wore a Syrian military uniform of one kind or another. Very few people were leaving Syria this way. The United Nations released monthly figures about refugees crossing from Syria into Lebanon, estimates that ran into the tens of thousands each month. But very few of them journeyed through this, the largest official crossing between the two countries. The Syrian government didn't want to let them out, thereby admitting a problem, and the Lebanese government only let in people who could present a legitimate reason to visit – a justification for a temporary visit, that is. A family celebration, or an onward ticket from Beirut airport, perhaps, though in fact many would stay in Lebanon. Instead, countless Syrians traveled across the steep desert mountains that roamed across the border between the two countries, a no-man's land that had always been the terrain of trafficking and contraband. Now, instead, of trading in goods, it traded in humans.

So Maha found no happy families or cute children or unusual outfits on which to set her attention. What she did find were little bits of this and that which managed to decorate the massive, dank room. The beige-colored walls may be covered with cracking paint; the marble counters faded with years of sun and usage, the windows dirty and smudged, but at one end of the long row of interview counters, there was a lone fake daisy sitting in a pink porcelain vase. On one windowsill by the entrance sat three dirty coffee cups all painted with bright floral patterns. Under a bench in the corner, a cat stared at her.

She took in these things as she waited in the plastic chair as per the officer's instructions. He went up to the immigration counter and handed over her ID card. While the man behind the counter entered her details into a computer, the officer made a call on his mobile. He exchanged a few words into the mouthpiece, then hung up and chatted briefly with his counterpart on the other side of the counter. Then he took her ID back and walked over to were Maha sat waiting.

"I'm sorry. It won't be possible to see your husband."

The words landed on her like a lump of clay thrown right at her chest.

She began to pant, and all of a sudden, she needed desperately to vomit.

"Please, sir, just a second," she panted, and ran out of the building.

Barely in time to find a patch of dirt behind a bush, she emptied what little remained in her stomach. She grabbed the smaller bottle of water from her purse and took a quick swig, swishing the water around in her mouth as she walked weakly back into the immigration hall.

The young officer was already chatting with someone else as he headed towards a side door.

"Please, sir! Don't leave!" she shouted.

Every head in the room turned to look at her.

Maha put a hand up and turned her head down, "Excuse me," she whispered in no particular direction.

The officer turned to look at her, questioning with his eyes.

"Please forgive me. I get sick sometimes, now, with the pregnancy."

He kept his gaze on her, waiting.

"I want to know why you said I can't see my husband. I came all the way from Beirut."

"It was a long journey to make for something you couldn't have expected to happen," he pointed out.

"But I was led to believe..." No one had told her anything, but God would forgive the white lie. This was a negotiation.

"Whoever you talked to was misinformed."

"But why?"

"It is simply not possible," he stated.

"But the officer in charge—"

"He said he would allow it, but the details of your case do not permit it."

"What details?" she asked.

"You need to trust me."

"Trust you? But all you've done is deny me the right to see my husband, the father of my child!"

"Sister," he said, narrowing his eyes. "Come, let's talk in here," and he gestured for her to follow him into a side office. He closed the door.

Maha's stomach began to tighten again, and she took some deep breaths. Fortunately, the nausea did not take over, and she was able to look at the officer again. She wasn't sure if she should be scared or hopeful. Was he going to help her, or take advantage of her? He looked nice, but it was often the nice-looking ones who did the worst things. She had heard stories, many stories, even had friends, who had been horribly treated in such situations.

She dared herself to stare at him defiantly. "My husband is a good man," she muttered. "His arrest was a mistake, I'm sure of it."

The officer sat down and gestured for her to sit down. Reluctantly, she did so.

But she kept talking, blabbering on about why she wanted her husband released, promising to take him straight to Lebanon and keep him away from Syria for as long as they wanted, about Samir's loyalty to the regime and his good work on behalf of Syrian civilians. Not everything she said was true, but much of it was.

When she finished, the officer let out a little chuckle. "You do love your husband," he observed.

"Of course, I do."

"God bless you, sister." He leaned forward, his eyes turned down. "I am very sorry I cannot let you see your husband, but I strongly advise you to return to Beirut right now."

"Why?" she almost shouted. "I have no intention of leaving here before I see Samir, much less without him accompanying me."

"You must," he said. Then, before Maha could launch into another tirade, he said, "Listen, sister. It is not up to me to have an opinion about these things, but if you stay here any longer, you too could be arrested. If you must know, the officer told you that you could see your husband just to get you out of his office. No one simply visits a prisoner here. I did look into your husband's case, and there is no way you would be permitted to visit him. Even more, your own name is on a list. I had taken your ID card back before anyone else noticed; fortunately, it was my friend who ran the number. I don't know what you did or what your husband did, but for the sake of your unborn baby, I am giving you this chance to return to Beirut. I will give you the benefit of the doubt that this was a mistake. But you must go now."

It was clear from his words, the look in his eyes, and the tone of his voice, that there was no real option. Maha had to accept that, not only was she not going to see Samir, but she too had better stay away from Syria if she didn't want her baby born in jail.

Tears began to well in her eyes, but she pushed those down. It was the nausea that she couldn't stop, and she excused herself again, running out to dry heave into a bush. Then, without turning back to say goodbye to the officer, she ran to her taxi and negotiated a fare back to Chtaura.

The dull feeling in her stomach gained weight, becoming unbearable as Maha made the journey back to Beirut. By the time she stepped into her all-but-abandoned flat two hours later, her disappointment had transformed into rage. She slammed her keys on the table and walked to the back veranda, grabbing a pack of cigarettes out of the bottom kitchen drawer on the way. A smoke couldn't be any worse for the baby than her electric nerves. Or a dead daddy.

Just as she was holding a match up to the tip of the cigarette, she noticed a yellow lump at the bottom of the birdcage. She blew out the match, let the cigarette fall from her mouth to the floor, and stepped closer to investigate. Figures. Bird was dead.

Chapter Ten

Meanwhile, Leila was raging a growing battle.
Hassoun wanted her to leave the camp.
She was ready to leave the camp.
Her hosts back in Amman were calling her, asking her what to do with the luggage she had left at their house.
But she could not bear the thought of leaving her family. Again, as it were.
Her family could not feed three more mouths on their food rations. Sure, there was food for sale in the camp, but pitching in for fresh fruit and vegetables wasn't really enough to keep Leila and the boys from adding to an already heavy burden.
Then, one day, the boys were playing ball in the clearing behind their Caravan with their cousins when some bigger boys came out and started teasing them. By the time the adults noticed, Hammoudi had a black eye and Saleh was prostrate on the ground wailing.
This little incident finally pulled Leila out of her funk.
She was the wife of a doctor with a good career. Her family was one of the most honorable in their village back home, her father a man of respect, and before the problems her brothers had been people to whom others came for help or advice. Her sister was one miserable semester away from a university degree. They did not belong in a refugee camp. Refugee camps were for people like those boys who bullied her sons – ignorant, violent, uneducated, dirty folk. If they stayed, it was only a question of time before she, or her sisters, or her sisters-in-law, were put into a vulnerable situation, and Lord knows Nuha and Rana had already been through enough, already been punished plenty for their attempts to do the right thing.
No, they absolutely did not belong in a refugee camp, living alongside fighters and their families, swindlers and perverts.
If Leila couldn't help her family get out, then she was not worthy to call herself their daughter.
So one evening, she called the taxi driver and told him to come get her the next morning, then she called Hassoun's cousin

and informed him, without any consultation or asking, that she would be back at his house the coming afternoon.

"I'm going to get you out of here, Mama. Be ready," she said, as she explained her plans to leave the next morning to her family. "I'm not leaving you, not at all."

"But daughter, you have your life, her mother replied."

"I'm staying in Jordan until I get you out. I'm going to find someone to spring you from the camp."

"Are you sure that's a good idea?"

"Do you want your girls to live under threat and your grandchildren to be bullied? Don't you want to start your life again?"

"There is no life for us outside of Syria, my girl." Mama shook her head.

Leila wrapped her arms around her mother's plump and slumped shoulders.

"How will we eat? Where will we live?" asked Nuha. "Will the children go to school?"

"Anything is better than this, isn't it?" interjected Rana. "Maybe my husband will be able to come join us if we're out of the camp."

"See?" said Leila. "Once you're out, you can start to make plans again. *Khalas* – no more waiting. Who knows how much longer this evil will continue, and only God knows what has happened to your house and land. Don't worry, I'm going to figure something out for you."

Mama looked at Nuha who looked at Rana who looked at her two sons who looked at their silent grandfather sitting in the corner. The other women in the room all looked at Leila.

"It's decided," Leila declared. "I can't bear seeing you like this and I won't go back to Kuwait. It has to be." She felt the selfishness in her words even as she uttered them, but held steady.

Nuha stood to fill the teapot with water, and they spent the rest of the evening talking about what city in Jordan they might like to live in.

The next morning, Leila flashed her passport with her Kuwaiti residence permit at the mildly stunned Jordanian guards, piled her boys into the taxi, and drove away from the camp without even bothering to look back at the sea of white Caravanat and tents. She pulled a tissue from her purse, dipped it in her water bottle, and attempted to wipe the sand from hers and her sons' faces. Only a little bit of the brownness budged: most of the coloration was good old-fashioned suntan. Hassoun would be furious to see his sons looking like peasant boys.

Upon arrival in Amman, Leila lost no time. Hassoun's cousin could not stand up to her determination. She insisted he vouch for her family, or help her find someone who would. She promised money, enough money that eventually he agreed to do it himself.

The next morning, she got the boys dressed, ate a quick bite offered by her hosts' Sri Lankan maid, then hailed a taxi. After a little informal surveying of taxi drivers and her host family, she decided to head for Jabal Hussein where she hit the pavement in search of a little flat to rent. Though she'd heard the Jordanian housing market was beyond tapped-out by refugee families not unlike her own family, within a few hours she'd found the perfect spot, in exchange for an exorbitant price.

Leila had the best husband in the world. After viewing the flat and expressing her interest to the estate agent, she found a little café where the boys could sit and play a game on the tablet while she called Hassoun. He didn't hesitate, and it was as if they'd never argued at all. He agreed to dip into their savings to pay off his cousin as well as give a six-month deposit for the flat. The rent for two rooms, tiny kitchen and even tinier bathroom, complete with cracked tiles on the floor and flaking paint on the walls, was almost as much as what they paid to rent their three-bed, three-bath marbled Kuwait home, even though Jabal Hussein was a poor neighborhood and the flat didn't have an ounce of marble. What it did have was cockroaches and a fair bit of grime that her sisters would need to scrub away.

The boys were tucked away and breathing their soft snores. Leila had bid goodnight to her hosts and was seated in the dark on her mattress, listening to the whir of the air-conditioner and the sweet sound of little boys sleeping. She knew she should get some rest herself, but instead she sat, back leaning against the wall and legs bent. She gave her knees the embrace she would give her husband if he were by her side today. Sitting there, curled into a ball, she struggled to sort through the dozens of thoughts that were all crowding into her consciousness.

She felt guilt and gratitude, anxiety and anticipation, regret and relief, fear and frustration, hate and hope.

She thought of her mother and how grateful she was to get to spend time with her. Mama had aged decades in the last couple of years, and now held more responsibility for the family's welfare than she ever had before. It was just wrong to reach the life phase where a woman should sit back in the home she built over the course of a lifetime, and enjoy the respect and care of younger more sprightly offspring, but instead, watch it all disappear. Most of her earthly possessions were lost, and the house over which she had ruled since before Leila was born was a heap of rubble. Her family was scattered, and the only way to ensure the survival of those still nearby was to keep on trying.

She thought of her sister whose life ended right about at the moment it was due to begin. During her time in Za'atari, Leila had started to avoid Nuha because the sensation of guilt was too overwhelming. Now, back in a posh Amman flat, she again felt her breath catch in her throat as she remembered her last visit to Nuha's dorm room. She'd been so proud of her sister following in her footsteps, but in many ways far out-performing Leila. If anyone deserved a university degree and a job in the city, the chance to map out her own future, it was Nuha. Yet Leila was the one with a diploma and work experience and stamps in her passport. Considering her current circumstances, Nuha might actually be better off if she just got married and started making babies.

Her thoughts moved on to her husband. She knew that she should be grateful for a man who loved her so much and who cared for her so sincerely. And she was, truly, grateful even if she struggled to feel it. What she felt was humiliation and resentment. His family had not had to flee their home; instead, they had voluntarily set up life in another country and were doing quite well for themselves. Hassoun's own life had continued relatively unscathed by the war. The only thing that changed for him was that, with each passing day, Leila grew more indebted to him. Even so, he never seemed to do anything that actually merited her wrath, and so she was stuck feeling like she owed him. But as kind as he was in the practical ways, he wasn't here with her right now, when she felt like she most needed him. Leila longed to feel his firm arms holding her and affirming that everything could indeed be ok. But then again, she knew that the first thing she would do when she next saw him would be to spew out a long list of grievances.

She looked at her two sons, the most important little human beings in her life, and wished they weren't. She wished they had never been born into this world, a world that she had now discovered to be full of such filth. She felt exhausted, knowing she could never leave them to their own devices yet wishing she could devote her full energy to helping her mother and her sisters and her nieces and nephews and other members of her extended family that did nothing to deserve the poverty and uncertainty that now defined their existence. Her sons were well-fed and wore clothes that fit. They didn't mind playing in the sand with illiterate refugee kids, and they had actually found desert life to be an adventure. But Leila knew better and would do everything in her power to protect them from any harm. And she wished she didn't have to do that.

Leila was too tired, too overwhelmed, too sad to cry. She just sat staring blankly at Hammoudi, Saleh and the wall, her brain racing from doubt to question to idea to worry. She was not remotely sleepy, though eventually she did lay down on the mattress, still curled up in a ball and still hugging her legs. Eventually, she closed her eyes.

Just as she was beginning to think sleep might actually come to provide some reprieve, Leila felt her mobile phone vibrate under her. She pulled it out from where it had fallen under the covers and saw that it was Maha, calling over Viber.

She pushed the green button and whispered, "Hi beautiful. How's your health?"

"Why are you whispering?" Maha got right into it.

"The boys are sleeping. I'm in Amman."

"Should I call back later?"

"No, no. It's good to hear your voice," Leila conceded this as much to herself as to her friend.

"So, how are you? How is your family? Tell me about Za'atari."

"It has been a long time, hasn't it?"

"Too long. You can't imagine the month I have had."

"Me too," Leila sighed.

"So?" nudged Maha. "Tell me."

"I wouldn't even know where to start..." Leila left the thought hanging as she tried to compose a few short sentences in her head that might summarize the camp, her family's story and her own journey into their new world. Maha patiently waited, so she tried, "The camp is awful, worse than the stories. So tomorrow I'm going to pick them up. I got a Jordanian to vouch for them, bring them to Amman. They can't live like that. It's awful." She stopped there.

After a pause, Maha asked, "Did you stay at the camp at all?"

"Yes, for a long time actually. Pretty much from when we last spoke, until a couple of days ago."

"So you really got deep in there." Too far.

"You sound chipper," Leila observed, changing the subject.

Silence on the crackly wavelengths was followed by, "Thanks for saying so. I'm trying."

"How are you feeling? Has the nausea passed yet?"

"Mostly. I went to the border last week."

"You what?"

"I went..." Maha couldn't finish the sentence. Leila heard soft sobbing filtering through.

And then Leila started crying. Something about hearing her friend's voice, the shared burden of knowing that Leila's family had been reduced to brown lumps sucking up oxygen while Maha's husband was in effing jail because he found out he was going to be a father. Both needed a good cry and needed to share the cry with someone whose heart was also broken.

So through the cell waves that floated between Jordan and Lebanon and rippled over their own beloved Syria, the salt of two friends mixed. Leila, the Sunni whose family, had stood against the resistance, one of the only Sunni families to do so. Maha the

Christian whose husband was arrested for supporting the resistance even though he didn't care about politics and Christians were supposed to be with the regime. Two women who didn't care very much about who was in power but who would lay down their lives for their families.

Leila was vaguely aware of all the ironies surrounding this moment. The irony that the true Syria had now moved outside of its borders, and the beloved Bilad al-Sham, the historic land of Syria, was now occupied by some genre of evil that no true Syrian could understand. The irony that she had never suffered so much yet was sitting in an air-conditioned room in the flat of a well-to-do Amman family. The fact Maha was supposed to be that girl for whom everything always came easy, but it didn't anymore. The irony that her husband had just given up no small portion of their life savings so she could keep her loved ones alive for a few more months.

She was vaguely aware of all these ironies and more, but her brain couldn't hold them. Nor could her soul. A few minutes of tears were a gift. They were an outlet to drain a tiny bit of the emotion that was accumulating within her, ballooning and threatening to explode. She felt the pressure on her heart lighten ever so slightly.

Eventually, the call dropped. Neither friend tried to call back; that would be for another day.

Chapter Eleven

The next morning Leila awoke with the phone still clutched tightly in her hands. The pillowcase was lightly streaked from the saltwater that had continued to pour out well into the night. She was shivering, but she felt ready to face the day, better-rested than she had felt for quite a while.

She lifted her head a few inches and tilted it so she could see the boys. They were sitting together on the same mattress, little feet dangling off the end as they leaned their heads against the wall. They were doing something together on the tablet. They looked serene, content.

"Good morning," she tried to sound cheery as she called out to them.

"Good morning, Mama," Hammoudi said without even looking up.

Saleh, her baby, got up and came over to the bed. He took Leila's neck in his tiny arms and planted a kiss on her cheek. Then he ran back to his brother's side.

Today was the day. It was a big day. It was the day her family returned to the world of the living. Leila had heard enough tales of woe from refugees living in Jordan's cities to know this would not solve their problems, but it was a start. Right? Or was she just ruining her husband in order to move them from one woe to another?

Ah, but she had to. The camp was no place for them. What options existed? Could she get them to Kuwait? What would they do there? Could they apply for asylum in Europe? Them and two million other Syrians...their request was not likely to be approved. Would some of them find jobs in Jordan? Perhaps a handsome, wealthy Jordanian man who believed in education would fall in love with Nuha and give her her life back? It was possible, but now her beautiful, intelligent little sister was "one of those poor Syrian refugees" in the eyes of most Jordanians. Her whole family was a charity case.

The simple truth was that there was no life for them that wasn't in Syria. Their life was their home, their village, their work and studies and friends, their extended family. There was no fresh start imaginable without those things. If she truly wanted to help her family, she would get them home.

But, of course, return likely meant death.

Jordan was a lifeless existence, but Syria was simply death.

Was it a waiting game? Or was this the functional equivalent of seeing a loved one in a coma after the doctors had determined that wakefulness would never return? Was Leila seeking a comfortable bed and respirator for her family so that she wouldn't have to pull the figurative plug?

Probably.

So she sat up because they would not breathe their last breath on her watch.

They would survive, even if their lives were over.

And she would help them do it. Because it was, simply, not fair that her life could continue, that she had a home and a husband waiting, or that her sons could soon be back in a top-ranked Kuwaiti school. It was unfair that she could easily pick up some translation work when she was ready to resume her career. Her life was unchanged, but the woman whose birth canal had guided her into life, and the women, men, girls and boys whose blood she shared, had no life left at all.

Leila was simply helping them to continue not living in a slightly less shameful venue. That was the long and the short of it, she pondered as she folded the last few items of clothing, laid them in the last suitcase, and zipped it up. It went without saying that she would now stay with her family rather than rely on the hospitality of Hassoun's cousin.

"*Yallah*, Hammoudi. Finish that level and come have breakfast. Come here, Saleh!"

She took the tiny hand of her youngest in her own and walked out into the corridor. Breakfast was laid out on the big oak table as it had been every morning this week. Hammoudi followed a minute later. Their hosts were not there.

Leila silently rolled little sandwiches for her boys, yogurt with apricot jam and a bit of za'atar sprinkled on top. Then as they chomped away, she dipped little pieces of bread into each of the smattering of small plates.

The three were silent. She glanced from one boy to the other and occasionally set her bread down to pat the head of one or the other. She drew strength from their purity. They didn't understand much of what was going on and saw life as an adventure. She remembered when she was like that. She hoped they would never lose that quality. For now, she found that they had hope enough for themselves and a bit extra to share with her.

As they were sipping down their sweet black tea, Madame Muna appeared. She was wearing a glorious red silk housecoat.

"Good morning, Auntie," Leila smiled at her.

"Good morning." Muna sat down at in an empty seat and ripped off a little piece of bread for herself.

When Leila saw this, she wondered if it was ok that she and the boys had started to eat. "You haven't had breakfast yet? Can I serve you some tea?"

"No, no. I've already eaten. Hours ago. Just snacking."

As Muna made herself a tiny roll-up of cheese and za'atar, Leila sipped her tea. The boys sat politely, holding their glasses carefully in both hands. Saleh's head was barely high enough to peer over the table. Hammoudi was only a little taller.

Eventually, Leila found the words. "May God bless you and your husband, your entire household, for the goodness you have done to us. May God give you good health and peace and comfort."

Madame Muna nodded slightly in response. Leila knew her hostess felt strongly that more important than gratitude, hard cash was due her in exchange for the assistance she was providing. She would receive it, and everyone would get what they wanted. But it was a bit painful to feel such an untenable divide. She was sure she had never been so unwanted in her life.

After a bit more silence, the hostess found her own words. "I pray safety and wellness for your family. I hope that they find their new home satisfactory, and I hope that they can return home soon. We all pray for peace in Syria."

"Mama, should I also pray for peace in Syria?" Leila looked at her eldest to see two large round eyes peering at her curiously.

"Yes, Hammoudi. We should all pray for peace in Syria."

"I haven't done that before. Will God be mad at me?"

"No, Mama," Leila replied affectionately, calling her son by her own title. "We should pray for peace because Syria needs peace. But God will not judge you for what you pray. He only asks that you live a life of devotion and obedience."

"Why does Syria need peace?"

Leila let out a heavy sigh. She knew the question was valid, but she had worked hard to protect her sons from the realities of war. They could never understand what she herself was still incapable of understanding. She had tried to shelter them because she had no answers.

In a rare moment of compassion, Madame Muna offered an answer. "Son, there are many people in your country that are making bad decisions. But there are also many good people from your country – like you and your parents. We pray for peace because it's important to make good decisions and to listen to good people."

"If we listen to good people, will that bring peace?"

"Usually, it will, yes."

"Oh."

Leila looked up and exchanged a grateful knowing look with her hostess.

But it wasn't over. After Hammoudi had gulped down a bit more of his tea and placed his glass carefully back on the table, he asked, "Is Grandma a good person?"

Leila reached across the table and took her son's hand in her own. "She is one of the most good people in the world."

"Am I a good person?"

"You're young, but so far, yes, you are growing into a good person. It is important to be a good person. And to make good decisions."

Hammoudi nodded, and that was that.

While Leila reflected on whether she had said the right thing to her impressionable young son, saying a prayer under her breath that he would resist any temptation to join a militia or engage in any form of violence when he grew older, Madame Muna was addressing her.

When she realized that she'd missed something, Leila apologized and asked Muna to repeat what she'd said.

"I was asking you whether you have everything you need for the flat, or if anything is still missing."

"Oh! Yes, well, we have the basics, but the kitchen doesn't have much. And also we're going to have to go out and get some cleaning supplies – my sisters won't accept living in a dirty house, and I know they are going to get straight to work as soon as they arrive!"

"Well, if you go ask the maid, she can show you our storage room. It's full of things we don't need. Feel free to take whatever you want."

"That is so kind of you! Thank you."

"It's nothing. It will help us clear out some space, too, eh?" Madame Muna said and laughed. Then she continued, "Anyway, my husband will be here in half an hour to go to the Camp with you. Everything is ready."

"God give you health, auntie." Leila got up from the table and took the boys back into the room. They settled back into their game on the tablet while Leila went to find the storage room. It was chock full of practical items. Most of them were old and worn thin, but she was beginning to realize that a Jordanian's rubbish was a Syrian refugee's treasure in this day and age. Leila, the charity case, filled up two large shopping bags with kitchen and cleaning supplies to take to her family. Everything was ready.

That evening, Leila sat on the little balcony of her family's new flat. She had found a rickety little blue plastic three-legged stool on which she could enjoy the great outdoors and a bit of solace. A tattered beige-colored canvas drape with red vertical stripes surrounded the balcony, allowing her and other covered women a bit of privacy, but blocking the fresh breeze that could have provided some reprieve from the sweltering air inside the flat. A dozen people can fill a small space with a lot of heat in a very short time, so the balcony was still fresher than indoors.

The boys were downstairs playing with their cousins. She marveled at the resilience of children, who barely seemed aware of what was happening around them.

The day had been chaotic but had gone much more smoothly than she could have hoped. The vouch-and-release procedure at Za'atari had been spectacularly easy. No wonder so many Syrians had gotten themselves released. A bit of money exchange and a Jordanian willing to take the time to drop by the camp was all it took. Leila could hardly believe how hard it had been to convince Hassoun's cousin to do this: as far as she could tell they had not even written down his name.

It had taken three taxis to transport the entire family back to Amman. Children piled on laps and luggage in the back and by people's feet. The resourceful women of the family had gathered all their food, mostly rations distributed to them by the World Food Program, into little bags and were leaving with a month's supply of grains and lentils. A van would have been easier, but taxis were what Leila could find.

She wondered what would happen to her family's Caravanat, to their mattresses and blankets, and to the other items that they had returned to the camp management upon departure. She imagined a new family would be using them shortly. If her own family weren't so obsessed with cleanliness, she'd feel guilty.

Arriving in Amman, the taxis had all been a bit lost. Leila knew where the flat was, but the driver didn't believe that a Syrian woman could know her way around better than him, and he ignored her instructions. The other two taxis followed them around a few circles, but everyone eventually pulled up under the flat.

All the bags and children were unloaded and toted up the stairs to the second floor. Leila used most of the rest of her cash to pay the driver.

Rana and Nuha had left immediately to register at the nearby office for refugees. They were gone all afternoon, but they came back with an appointment for the entire family to register. Then they would begin receiving food vouchers for exchange at a nearby supermarket, as well as possibly a bit of cash assistance to help pay the rent. Leila hoped so. She was tired of asking her husband for favors.

The kids had started tumbling on the rug, and her father had turned on the television. Leila and her mother made tea, drank it, then set about cleaning and arranging the kitchen.

The flat was filthy, even dirtier than Leila remembered from her visit with the estate agent. She and the other women did enough cleaning to breathe in that first afternoon, but several more days of work lay ahead for all of them before they would consider the flat livable.

When they began to prepare dinner, the stove's gas tank quickly ran out. It had apparently been on its last leg. So Leila sent her nephew, the one who was still not speaking, down to the shop at the end of the block, and he returned gesturing that it could be changed out that very afternoon. An hour later, they were able to start cooking. This was the first time her mother had been in an actual kitchen in more than six months.

Tidying, settling, arranging, and orienting were the activities that made the day pass by quickly. The girls kept marveling at their newfound privacy. Leila might have liked a breeze, but her sisters and sisters-in-law were glad to, for once, be able to let their hair out of their scarves and robes, and sit comfortably somewhere that wasn't coated in a layer of dust. For almost a year they'd not had a room of their own with a door that closed.

They were inside now, five of them all sitting together on one mattress, chatting and giggling. They had just finished taking turns doing evening prayers, and now they were looking at photos of something on a mobile phone, acting like they hadn't a care in the world, like they hadn't fled bullets and threats and assault and abuse and hunger and desolation to get where they were now. They had each other, and family plus a clean bed and a room with walls was enough.

How was it that they were her family, her flesh, and blood, but she didn't feel welcome in that bed? She still went through the motions of praying with them when it was time to pray, and there was a pleasant familiarity surrounding their mealtime routines and decisions about how to organize the flat, but Leila felt like they allowed her to join in, not that they wanted her participation in family life. How was it that, after all, Leila had done for them, rescuing them from the camp and spending so much on their behalf, that they cuddled up together and none of the girls so much as cast an eye at her as she walked through the room to the balcony? How was it that she had felt more at home amidst her loved ones in that accursed camp than she did now in this Amman flat that she and her husband had rented?

She missed Hassoun right now, knowing that he, at least, would prefer to sit with her. She also craved her own bed, the sofa that she had custom-ordered from a designer furniture shop, and the shiny countertops in her kitchen, which were kept clean by a conscientious lady from the Philippines who came two days a week. She was of half a mind to grab her little boys from their football game with the neighbor kids on the street below – how was it that children made new friends so easily? She wanted to grab them and their suitcases, which were still unopened after leaving the house this morning and hail a cab to the airport. It couldn't be that many hours until the next flight to Kuwait.

She wanted to get out. She was done. Her family was safe now so maybe it really was time to move on. God knew she didn't see how sticking around any longer would do any good.

But, the moment she got into her head to lift herself from that wobbling blue plastic stool and head off, an invisible force pulled her back down. She felt she couldn't move at all, and she knew that she wasn't going anywhere. She was not going back to her shiny flat and her sparkly life and leaving her family in a country where they weren't welcome, in a flat that would take weeks for an industrious crew of women to clean, in a neighborhood where rubbish accumulated in every nook and cranny, in a building with unreliable electricity and even less reliable water. And most importantly, in an existence where their identity was that of refugees. If her family were refugees, she too was a refugee.

As all these thoughts swirled around in her head, Leila's hands and knees grew shaky. A horrid migraine began to creep up her spine and into the top-right of her head. She leaned forward, resting her head on her knees, to stave off a wave of nausea.

She hated when this happened, and it was happening more often. She'd done a bit of web surfing and discovered that these were common symptoms of anxiety attacks. Other possible symptoms that she'd not yet had included: sweating and chills, choking, chest pain, numbness in her limbs, a dry mouth, and ringing in her ears.

Also, on the list was a feeling of dread or a fear of dying, but since the war had started in Syria that had been a constant.

Even if she didn't have all the symptoms on the list, Leila was pretty sure that this was, indeed, an anxiety attack, because the nausea, trembling and headache came so suddenly and the Internet said that anxiety attacks were sudden and lasted 5 to 20 minutes. Like tonight: one moment she was enjoying the fresh evening breeze while thinking about her family, and the next moment she could barely breathe, overwhelmed by pain and dizziness. In half an hour she would probably enjoy the night air again.

The Internet also said that the best treatment was to address the lies that were building up in her heart, which were the cause of the attacks. This particular piece of the Internet had clearly not been written by a Syrian, as there could be no lies in her spirit that were any worse than reality. Medication was also an option, but medication was for people much worse off than her: old people, sick people, disabled people, people who had to go to doctors. Or perhaps for people who had cash to spare after taking on the livelihoods of a dozen relatives.

There was nothing to do but wait it out. She leaned over, head between her legs, and closed her eyes.

As she sat there, doubled over in pain, working hard not to vomit and hugging herself to control the shakes, the thoughts continued to build up, swishing around like a whirlpool filling from a big pump below, waves crashing into each other somewhere in the innards of her soul. On top of everything else, she now felt angry at her family for ignoring her. Yes, they needed her. But she needed them too!

In short, life was so unfair.

Eventually, Leila sat up again and breathed deep. She still felt a little queasy, but she pulled out her phone and opened Viber. Almost by rote, without thinking, she dialed not her husband but her best friend.

"*Aloh*?" Maha replied.

"*Habiby*!" Leila's voice was too excited. She felt some force inside her reaching through the telephone waves, grasping at her friend as if Maha were the last rung on a ladder. If she let go, she might fall into an abyss.

"It's good to hear from you!" Maha exclaimed. "I didn't expect you to be able to talk so soon. Oh, wait, did something go wrong today? Were you able to get your family?"

"Yes, they're here. We're all in their new flat now."

"Congratulations! You must be thrilled!"

"I must..." Leila couldn't muster up any joy to accompany this statement.

"Uh oh. What's the matter? What happened? Is everyone ok?"

"Everyone's fine." She gulped down the catch in her throat.

"Tell me, sweetie."

"I don't know what's the matter. I think the world is just going up in flames, isn't it?"

"It sure is. I know my world is."

"Tell me, do you have any news from the border?"

"No, no. But I'm ok. It sounds like you're not."

"It's just that..." Leila struggled to find the words. "How can I be so close to the people I love most in the world, but feel so alone? Mama is resting, the girls are chatting with each other, the kids are playing in the alley, and I'm here all by myself on the balcony. They don't want me, and honestly, I'd much rather sit here and talk with you than be with them."

"That's normal," replied Maha. "I actually feel like we might have had some similar conversations when we were students.

"Yes, but we were young. I know I was a little bit rebellious. You maybe weren't, but you know I was."

"Maybe, but that doesn't change the truth."

"I think this is different. I think – I know, this is terrible, shame on me – I think I don't want to be here because I don't want to be a refugee like them. I don't want to be homeless."

"Who does?"

"Well, but shouldn't being near family matter more than a piece of land?"

"Maybe it should, but what should be isn't the same as what is," observed Maha.

"Keep talking."

"I don't know how to explain it, but think about Palestine. Think about all those people who lost their homes more than fifty years ago and have never been able to return and who have never been able to build new homes. Millions of people who are, essentially, homeless. Yes, they have a roof over their heads and walls to shelter the wind. In some cases very luxurious roofs and walls and nice furniture and great kitchen appliances and even their own washing machine and all. But all they ever talk about is going back home."

"Do you think that is what will become of us?"

"I don't know. We might become like the Palestinians. Or we might go home soon. Everything could go back to normal or maybe nothing ever will. We might be allowed to buy and build new homes here in Lebanon or over there in Jordan. Probably not. But I don't know. What I do know is that we can learn from history. If you have a home, even if it's temporary, enjoy it. Gain strength from it. Grow your family in it. Take advantage of every moment, because we never know when we will lose it. It's a sad lesson, but it is what it is, right?"

"It is what it is," Leila agreed, but she didn't actually agree. It felt wrong to her. She didn't want to accept this. She wanted to lose this icky feeling and feel right again. "Remember when we were all so innocent?"

Maha just sighed over the phone.

A few moments of pause later, it was only politeness that brought Leila to speak again. "Now, how are you? How is Samir? How's the baby?"

"There's no word. I have no idea. None at all."

"God is generous."

"Yes, I suppose. God is generous."

"I will continue to pray for his safe return."

"Thank you, dear." Maha sighed again. "And you, and your family. And your people who are stuck in the war."

"God bless you. And your family as well."

"And you, don't go and do anything stupid, right?" warned Maha.

Stupid? "What do you mean?"

"Oh, I don't know. You just sound a bit, not like yourself. Don't make any poor decisions."

"I don't know what you mean. Do you think I made the wrong decision bringing my family out of the camp or renting this flat or something?"

"No. I think you're amazing. I don't know. Just, just...well, be careful. I love you."

"I love you, too," replied Leila and then she quickly hung up.

And right as she started to stand up, a realization flashed. Her boys were content as could be with their cousins, her family was as safe as she could hope, her sisters had each other, and her husband would probably be better off without the burdens she was currently bringing. It occurred to her that it all might be a bit better if she weren't alive.

Chapter Twelve

Maha hung up the phone, set it back on the little nightstand and rolled over. She'd been in bed since the sun had gone down at six pm, but Leila hadn't woken her up. It had been weeks since she'd last slept a proper night's sleep. At some point in the wee hours of the morning, she would doze off for a bit, long enough to be able to make it through another day. But the need for sleep wasn't why Maha had crashed with the sun. She was just weary and preferred the solace of a soft mattress in a dark room over silly attempts at pretending she had any interest in the life Beirut currently afforded her. No husband, few relatives, no work, a baby that she couldn't even begin to plan for. A church, yes, but Maha didn't feel very comfortable with Samir's parishioners. The dark room and soft mattress were highly preferable.

So Leila's call was a respite of sorts. Maha had always taken comfort from trying to comfort others. Leila's husband was free, and her father was alive. An outsider looking on might assume that Maha had every reason to envy her friend and would in some respects be right. But in other respects, Maha had a new life growing inside her, which deep down gave her some tiny seed of hope, though she wasn't yet ready to admit it, and she had a good network of friends lobbying on Samir's behalf. In contrast, Leila and her husband were alone in caring for their loved ones.

Maha didn't like to criticize anything about religion – especially since the war started; she was determined that Syria's heritage of inter-faith coexistence be preserved, prized and held out like a diamond. "See?" she wanted to tell the media outlets and European governments and everyone who dared talk about Syria, who didn't know Syria. "We have something you can only dream of having. In Syria Christians, Muslims, Druze, and Alawites all get along. There's no tension. My best friends are Sunni and Druze. We love each other, and there is a bond deeper than the bond of sisters among us. Who else in the world can brag of this? Not you. Take that!" So, far be it from her to criticize people of other religions.

But, at this particular moment in time, she was actually very glad to be a Christian and not a Muslim. Leila's brothers were almost forced into the FSA because a good Sunni boy from their village was expected to join the fight. Loyalty was assumed, even demanded. But when the family lost everything because of the fighting, no one from the Sunni community stepped up to help. Leila's family didn't get any compensation or a safe place to stay. Instead, they spent their own life savings to get across the border, where they were herded like cattle into a refugee camp paid for by all the other governments of the world. The FSA could only go on existing because of the generosity of the outsiders caring for the needs of the fighters' families and neighbors who were living as refugees in neighboring countries. Some of those charitable outsiders were Muslims, but more of them were Christians. There was little rallying in support of one another, it seemed, and Maha saw proof of this in how it had fallen to Leila and Hassoun to help her family. They had no one else to go to.

Maha, on the other hand, had a dozen numbers on speed dial to call that night when she had begun to worry about Samir. There was a whole network of people in Damascus advocating on his behalf. She hadn't attended any meetings while Samir was in Syria, but she knew that a whole church full of people was just waiting for a hint as to how they could be of assistance.

Maha was even more touched by their kindness considering that Samir was arrested by the regime, and most of their Christian friends were loyal to a fault. But the fact that he was a member of the "family of Christ" was enough for them, maybe, even more, important than his supposed politics.

Because of that, though Leila's family may today be safer than Maha's, Maha worried for her friend. She would like to be of comfort to Leila just now; her friend did not sound right. Maha couldn't put her finger on it, but she was worried. She wasn't being flippant in asking Leila not to do anything stupid. Something stupid was in the air. But what, she didn't know.

Maha buried her face in her pillow. The pillowcase smelled like stale sweat. Her head had spent a lot of time on this pillow in the last few weeks and hadn't been washed for even longer. She couldn't be bothered: by now she was used to it. It was almost a friendly, familiar smell, so she buried her face in further, shut her eyes, curled her legs under her and pretended to sleep.

The sun was shining through a crack in the curtains when Maha awoke on the first day of July. As had become her norm in the months since Samir disappeared, it was more than fifteen hours after she'd gone to bed the night before but only a few short hours after she'd fallen asleep. By now, her nausea had passed, and she knew her energy should have returned, but her sleep routine had not improved at all. She rolled over groggily and pulled her arm up to shield her eyes from the rays of light.

She reached over to the nightstand for her. 9:30 am. Still early. She was starting to roll back into a ball to try to sleep a bit longer when she heard the pounding at the door. What a racket.

As she slowly sat up and began to clear the cobwebs from her head, shaking it ever so slightly as she blinked, the knocking came again. Louder and faster. It might have been the knocking that had awoken her. If they had been knocking a while with no reply, why didn't they just leave? She pondered ignoring them, but since she'd been in bed way too long anyway, she stood up and stumbled through the living room to the door.

"*Yallah*. I'm coming. Just a minute!"

That stopped the knocking, praise God. She couldn't hear any voices outside; hopefully, that didn't mean they had left. If they walked away right as she finally got to the door, she swore under her breath, she would go to the balcony and tell them off in front of the whole neighborhood. All that knocking, and only 9:30 in the morning?

Maha prepared a scowl – not a difficult feat with her groggy head and bleary eyes – as she unbolted the door. She opened it a couple of inches and tilted her head so she could see through the crack.

Then she blinked both eyes shut hard. She opened them; then she blinked again. Then her jaw dropped open. She just stood there for a few moments and stared, speechless.

"Can I come in?" Samir asked.

One more blink of the eyes and Maha believed it. Her husband was standing on their doorstep, in the exact same spot where she had bid him farewell more than two full months ago. He was alive and in one piece. He was back.

Finally, she yanked the door open wide and allowed Samir's arms to sweep around her. She fell into his embrace, which he freely gave. Maha clung back, timidly at first, but then a bit more tightly as she relaxed in the familiar big strong arms that she had missed so much in the past weeks.

"God, I missed you," he whispered into her greasy, stinky hair.

Maha just purred in response.

After a few moments, Samir let go and reached back to shut the door and led Maha to the sofa. They sat side-by-side, legs touching legs, Samir's arm still around Maha's shoulders.

"What happened? How did you get out?" Maha asked.

Samir laughed as if he hadn't a care in the world as if he hadn't spent the last two months in a prison cell enduring all the horrid things Syrian prison cells were famed for inflicting on their occupants. He just threw his head back and let out a "ha ha ha ha". Not loudly or boisterously, but freely and with a smile. "The short answer is, I don't know. The long answer is, there's a lot to tell but how about some coffee first?"

Maha jumped up. "Have you had breakfast yet?"

"No. Oh!" Samir jumped up, too. "Not only that, but the taxi driver is waiting downstairs. I forgot about him the moment I saw your lovely face." He stood up and gave her shoulder a squeeze. "I need to pay him." He walked to their secret stash of cash in an envelope that they tucked under some trinkets in an intricate Damascene carved box. He navigated the flat with ease as if he was just returning from a routine business trip. Maha had used a bit of their cash for this and that during the month, but the envelope was right there where he left it, and it still held a hefty pile of US 20-dollar bills. He pulled one out and said, "Just a minute," as he strode back out the door.

Maha followed him to the door and stood in the doorway listening to his footsteps descending the stairs. Once he reached the entryway, she ran out to the balcony to watch him pay the taxi driver. She followed his every step, his every twitch of the fingers, his every word, observing him carefully as he leaned into the driver's window and exchanged pleasantries then shook the driver's hand. He looked so...so...normal. Wasn't someone just out of jail meant to look different, something other than human?

Maha continued to watch Samir as he walked back into the foyer, then she ran back to the door and listened to his footsteps growing louder. Eventually, his thick brown hair emerged from around the bend in the stairwell, and he was there again. He grinned. She grinned back.

Maha held the door open for her husband, then gently closed it, bolting it twice as if that could keep them safe for eternity.

"So... breakfast?"

Samir sat on the sofa, leaning back with his arms and his legs spread wide, a picture of relaxation and yet of territoriality. He was claiming his home for himself again. It had never stopped being his. Except for a few more dust bunnies in the corner and a little less evidence of cigarette ashes in the little metal tray on the coffee table, everything was identical. Even the book Maha had been reading when Samir left remained untouched on the TV stand.

After a minute gazing around, taking it all in, he said, "Sure. I'm ravenous, actually."

"Great. I'll make us an omelet."

Maha started to walk back to the kitchen but then stopped. She didn't want to leave Samir's line of sight. What if some mysterious force grabbed him and whisked him out of the front door again? What if she came out of the kitchen and he was gone? What if he'd not really returned and this man in her living room was nothing but a mirage, or worse, a ghost?

"I've missed you so much," she began.

Samir looked behind him to where Maha stood frozen. He had been gazing out the window, towards the balcony. "Me too, darling."

"Why don't you come sit on the back veranda while I cook? We can catch up."

Samir stood immediately and followed her to the little wicker chairs under the now-empty birdcage. He sat again, this time crossing one leg over the other as he positioned himself to watch her puttering in the kitchen.

While the coffee boiled, Maha scurried around getting the eggs and some veggies ready for an omelet. She was out of bread. Again. But for this occasion, she would break out that frozen pack she kept in the freezer. There was no way she would consider sending her just-released husband out for bread.

"Hey, what happened to Bird?" Samir called into the kitchen.

"He died," Maha replied flatly.

Samir didn't respond and for almost fifteen minutes neither said a word. Samir mostly gazed at the sky and occasionally threw glances at his wife. Maha did a bit of this and that and occasionally threw glances at her husband.

It was as if he'd never left. And it was as if he were a complete stranger.

The coffee done, Maha carried it and two little cups over to the little plastic table. As they waited for the grounds to settle, and for the eggs to cook in the other room, she sat down by his side. "I kept everything the same. Well almost everything," she observed, thinking of their dearly departed Bird and the curtains Roxy had insisted on hemming.

Samir just gazed at her and smiled. He reached forward and cupped her face in his hand, stroking her cheek gently with his thumb.

They just sat like that for a few minutes until the coffee was ready. Then Maha pulled away and poured a cup for Samir. He didn't comment on the fact she – coffee addict that she was – abstained. He took a sip, and she quickly went to check the eggs. The initial joy and relief of seeing her husband, alive and free, was slowly being replaced by a discomfort she couldn't quite define. It didn't feel right, not like it always had been.

She let him sip his coffee while she heated the flatbreads directly on the burner, keeping the fire at its minimum so as to bring life to the bread without burning it.

Still without speaking, Maha brought out the bread and the omelet still in its pan, laying them on the little table. Then she sat down across from her husband, ripped a piece of bread and gave him half. Simultaneously, they broke off little bits of bread and used them to grab up bits of the omelet, Samir from his end of the pan and Maha from her end. Little by little they ate away at the omelet until their bread scoops met in the middle.

Once Samir had taken a few bites and given the obligatory compliments for her great cooking that was as good as he'd remembered it, Maha asked again. "How did you get out?"

"Honestly," he said, "I don't know."

"What do you mean? They just came in and opened your cell door and told you that you were free?"

"Something like that," he replied. "But it's never just that, is it? There's always a reason."

"There is? Nothing about this war seems to have a reason."

"The stories I heard while I was in there... each person had a story. The reasons often seemed silly, but there was a reason given for everything."

"So you think that they solved your case? Realized that your arrest was a mistake?"

"It wasn't a mistake," Samir said. He just dropped those words like it was no big deal, like it was obvious that he'd had it coming.

"It wasn't?" Maha's voice raised.

Samir then chuckled. He actually chuckled.

"Why are you laughing? You think this was a joke? You were in jail. Well, I've been here, worried sick, unable to sleep, making a million phone calls...and you think it's funny?" By the end of this rant, she was almost screaming, and she felt her face flush red and prickly.

That tugged the grin off of his face. Samir scooched his chair over to bring him closer to Maha and lay his hand on top of hers. "It's in the past now, anyway."

"You're sure?" She glared at him.

"Yes. I can't go back to Syria, though." Two pats on the hand. Then, cheerily, he added, "I'll be safe now! There's nothing for you to worry about anymore."

"What aren't you telling me?" One eyebrow lifted.

Another pat on the hand. "It's in the past now," he repeated.

"Samir, you and I were never that couple. We're supposed to be the ones who actually talk, who, you know, share life with each other. I'm not just your toy, and you're not just my protector. That's not changing, definitely not now after what happened."

"Sweetie, you know I love you. But you have no idea what happened. Let's just leave it at that, alright?" His hand was now gone and his arms crossed.

Maha watched as her husband pulled himself away from her. She saw him receding not just physically but in some other way as well. She had this sickening feeling that she'd had her husband back for fifteen minutes, but that was all she would get. Had jail followed him back to Beirut? What was controlling his mind right now? Because the Samir she knew didn't keep secrets or tell her to stop asking stupid questions.

To hide the tear that was creeping into her eye, Maha stood up and grabbed the empty coffeepot. "More coffee?" she managed to choke out.

All smiles again; Samir accepted, and then himself stood and walked into the living room.

In the kitchen, Maha struggled to get her feelings under control. It was weird that they hadn't talked about the baby yet. But as her eyes welled up and her nose twitched, she feared she'd be unable to get a full sentence out before she'd break down in sobs. As the water heated for the second pot, she scrubbed not just the pan in which she'd made the eggs but a dozen other dishes that had piled up in the sink. The water on full blast, the sponge full of soap, she quickly sudsed up all the dishes and then rinsed them all, splashing water halfway across the kitchen floor. The rapid movement of her arms pulled her attention away from the hurt and confusion that had sprouted so quickly and helped her regain her composure. By the time the water had boiled, she was able to spoon the grounds into the pot and stir with a bit more calm, and by the time the coffee had boiled over its customary three times, she was able to walk into the front room with a hint of a smile on her face.

As she lay the coffeepot and the cups on the table, Maha said, "I still can't believe you're back."

Samir was staring out the front window, to a point beyond the veranda. Maha sat down beside him, but he just kept staring.

"Samir?"

He turned his head slightly and raised his eyes; a gesture Maha had always found heart-melting. But then he turned away again and resumed his blank stare.

"Samir, I..." she started. Maha needed to acknowledge the third member of their family in this reunion moment but had no idea how to bring up her pregnancy. The last time she had talked to Samir, he had sounded so excited to learn that he was going to be a father, but now it was like that conversation had never happened. Except, of course, it was that news that put him in the taxi to the border where he was arrested. If there were no baby, perhaps none of this would ever have happened, or at least, that was what Maha had been telling herself for the past two months. Now Samir had dropped a hint that his arrest was not a mistake, after all, words that echoed what the police officer had told her in the dank immigration hall on that day she had trekked up the mountain. But none of this erased the fact that she was now in her second trimester, the baby had a heartbeat, and her body was beginning to change shape.

So, as Samir continued to stare out the window, Maha formed the words, "I had a doctor's appointment last week. She said everything was fine. Isn't that great?"

He shrugged.

She reached out and took his hand, sitting limply on his knee, in hers. She tried again, "The baby? The doctor said that I am now at 17 weeks – almost halfway – and the baby is as big as an avocado!"

"That's good," he replied. "I'm glad to hear it." But he didn't sound very glad.

Maha prayed a prayer under her breath. She let go of his arm and poured out a little cup of coffee then pulled up close to Samir, finding a way to inch herself under his embrace, uninvited though she may feel. Then she took his hand and lay it on her belly. "So, meet your child."

No reaction. None whatsoever. No joy, no tenderness, no shock, not even anger. He just kept staring. Then he took his hand away to pick up his coffee cup and leaned further back, slightly away from Maha, who was still curled up next to him.

"What happened? You were so excited. Did you forget that we're going to have a baby? We're going to be a family!" She forced more cheer into this final statement than she herself felt.

Samir then stood up, walked into the bedroom, and shut the door.

Maha didn't try to contain her tears any longer.

Chapter Thirteen

That evening, Leila was back on her little blue veranda footstool, which had come to be seen by everyone in the household as her special spot. The day had been devoted to more cleaning, more cooking, more paperwork, more television, and more moments in which she felt completely expendable.

She was staring at the rails on the veranda, imagining whether she could fly off of them into an alternate universe like in a fantasy novel, where she could be a heroine, where people would need her and where she would share wonderful adventures with a group of fellow super-heroes of some variety. She pictured unicorns, flying white horses, fairy godmothers and the odd dragon.

She also pictured what might happen if she attempted to fly off the veranda and failed. Splat.

So she tried to think of something else. Anything else.

It was on this mental treadmill that she remembered her old friend Nisreen, the Mockingbird. With her mind on other things, it had been a few weeks since she had checked the blog. What did Nisreen have to say these days? What was going on in her precious Sham?

Leila picked up her phone and opened the browser. She typed "Moc" and the auto-complete recognized the entry. One click more and The Mockingbird was loading. Leila felt a rare bite of anticipation and adjusted herself on the stool as she prepared to read.

Friends with Death

Death no longer teases. Who no longer knows death? Who fears it? Who worries that its talons may creep in and overpower them? No one I know. We used to. We used to believe that keeping the heart beating and the lungs breathing were the most important things for a person. Now, really? What are the odds that hearts won't stop beating? What are the odds that lungs might actually maintain their capacity of taking in a new pulse of air every few seconds? That is the true miracle. Life is a miracle.

Death is just something that happens. Me, I'm one of the lucky ones. I've lost two cousins, one aunt, and one uncle to death in this war. That's all. My brother is still alive, if on the other side of the world. My parents still breathe, although they do little more than that these days. I'm one of the lucky ones.

Most of my friends have been lost not to death, but to migration. I don't know many people in this, the city of my birth, childhood and coming-of-age, anymore. They've all left. A few have died. But only a few.

Two years ago, losing a few of my friends to death would have been the ultimate tragedy. Not one, not two, but three of my close acquaintances? All killed within a year of each other? How can anyone survive such loss? You might have prayed for me, prayed for my soul, that I might maintain my belief in God amidst my grief.

But now, it's different. It's a handful of friends, plus a handful of distant relatives, plus God-only-knows-how-many old acquaintances from school, from the market, from walking down the street a thousand times. Do I no longer see them because they've left the country? Or do I no longer see them because they've been claimed by death? Or, possibly even worse, do I no longer see them because they have been captured – by anyone and for any reason?

No wonder we've given up on God. Me, I won't say that God doesn't exist. He probably does. And I won't say that God is sadistic and evil. He's probably good. But I rather leave it at that. Because to try to wrap my brain around a God who exists and is good, who is watching all this horror run rampant, who is seeing these little human beings whom he created, dropping like flies...that's not anything I can understand. And why would I want to have anything to do with such a God anyway? Life is too complicated as it is without bringing God into the equation.

No, instead, I think we should walk down the streets of Damascus and ask anyone whose paths we cross: Who have you lost? Then when they tell us – and everyone will have an answer – give them a hug. It's a small gesture, but when the big things have gone to shit, there's something to be said for the small things.

Then there was another post.

Life goes on

A friend was down to visit from Homs today. We all know what is going on in Homs. But in case you've been under a rock for the past few months, here's a summary: FSA took over the old city, regime laid siege, people starving because of the siege, lots of houses and buildings destroyed as often as not with families inside them. Fighting fighting fighting, regime slowly gaining ground, no one in Homs likes the regime anymore. Perhaps the only ones who did were the Christians, and they've all fled. I don't know if that's true, but it's what the media tells us. And what YouTube confirms. But that's all selective information. People who want to say something say it. There must be a lot of normal people in Homs who just want to go about their own business, right? Plus, as far as I could tell all these months, the fighting was almost entirely in the old city.

So I was looking forward to seeing my friend. She works at the university there. Yes, you read that right. She works – present tense – at the University in Homs. The university is still open. There are still students and teachers and classes and exams and everything. Life goes on.

That in and of itself was a reality-check. It turns out that Homs has not all gone up in flames.

But then again.

She had too many stories to tell.

One day she was walking to work from her family's house, about a ten-minute walk, when she all of a sudden found herself in the crossfires of two snipers. She ducked under a wall by an abandoned house and waited it out. For a couple of hours. She just sat there, slouched as low as she could, waiting until the cracking of the sniper shots went silent. Then she waited a bit longer, until the rifles had stayed silent for about fifteen minutes. She figured they might have stopped because they ran out of ammunition, and she had no idea who or where, exactly, these snipers were. She did catch a glimpse of them, and one of them was a woman. Neither looked very much like an official regime soldier. Were they two rebel groups in a dispute? Two families in a dispute?

With laughter, she told me of the first time she heard gunfire as she walked to work. She painted a humorous picture of herself, walking with her sister who is in her final year of engineering, jumping out of their skin then scrambling to find somewhere to hide. At first, they hid under a jasmine bush but quickly realized that those flimsy little leaves and even flimsier white flowers wouldn't protect them from anything. Screeching out loud and fidgeting didn't help their cause. So then they scrambled right out into open space, making themselves targets, as she realized afterward, and finally just ran away. Thank God they were kept safe. But my friend told me of the panic she felt at that moment, how fear had overcome her. Unlike this more recent sniper fight, which has now become just a routine delay to her daily commute. Now gunfire on her way to work isn't anything out of the ordinary, she said. She just keeps walking if she can, or settles herself behind a wall if she can't. Just another day in the life of a working woman in Homs these days.

Another time, her family was sitting down to dinner. Yes, her family still lives together, in their house, and shares family dinner. Life goes on. But then again, not exactly. There was a knock on the door right as they were dishing out, and my friend's mother went to answer. It was a family of refugees from the Old City. They had managed to escape the siege during a lull in the fighting that afternoon. It was a man and his wife and their seven-year-old son and their four-year-old daughter and a little baby. The baby was so young, my friend said. The baby had probably been born in their besieged home, without the benefit of any sort of medical care, which might explain why the little one was pale and colicky; it was the sickly baby that finally persuaded them to risk the wrath of all factions to flee. They needed to get medical care for the baby and food for the other kids, but they didn't know anyone outside their neighborhood, they said. This was a very traditional family. The father protective, the mother submissive, the children scared of everything. They had an ancestral village in the mountains to the north, but it was cut off.

So my friend's mother fed them all, and then my friend's father hailed and paid a taxi to take them to the nearest working hospital. My friend said that she and her sister went to visit them the next day and found that the family had indeed checked the baby in, but then they had all left in the middle of the night after just one round of medication. They most likely fled to Lebanon, but do they not know that it's almost impossible to access medical care in Lebanon if you're a refugee? They would have been better off in Homs.

And that's saying something.

My friend went on, story after story after story, for a couple of hours as we drank cup after cup of tea and chomped on hundreds upon hundreds of sunflower seeds. It seems every day is an adventure for her, but on the other hand, every day she wakes up and gets ready and goes to work as a secretary who responds to students' routine queries. Then at the end of each day, she goes home and eats and watches TV and does her nails. There is much that is extraordinary about her very ordinary life.

What I loved most about her visit was how much we laughed. Each story she told, she told it as a joke. I pictured her there slouching behind that wall playing Tetris on her phone while she waited for two snipers who had been armed and trained to fight a war of ideas, to finish shooting out a family feud. I pictured two giggling sisters jumping from bush to bush, holding up jasmine leaves as an attempt at camouflage, as they tried to dodge bullets. I tried to picture a family so jittery that the kids barely touched their dinner, their mother unable to so much as say a single word, fleeing a regime-operated hospital in the middle of the night. Those aren't funny stories, but we laughed. Because when you live in hell, laughter is the most logical response.

Leila was crying and laughing by the time she got to the end of the second blog post. She scrolled down and saw that she had already read the next one. There were only two new posts since she'd last checked two weeks ago.

Only two posts?

She went back to look at the date on each post and saw that nothing had been posted for more than a week. Remembering Nisreen's pattern of three posts a week, maybe only two on a slow week but never less than that, Leila's jaw slowly dropped. She knew what it meant if it had now been more than a week.

Nisreen had been taken.

There was no point trying to sleep or join in the family routines, Leila quickly realized. And jumping from that balcony window would have to wait, she thought wryly.

What had happened to her old friend Nisreen?

This was an omen. Nisreen was Leila's personal symbol of the good that might potentially come of the devastation sweeping over their country. Spirit, heart, and courage. Commitment to the truth. Protests for justice, not for politics. Over time, Leila had also observed an increasing attention to humanity on The Mockingbird. Stories of people, real people. Syria was about people, and Nisreen had always been one to tell it like it is. Leila had found so much hope in seeing that spunk devoted more and more to loving friends and strangers, individuals and families. Girls, boys, women, and men.

If Nisreen had been taken, there was no good left in this revolution. She had been that little flickering candle in a very large, very dark room. Had she been snuffed out? Had she met death? Or was she merely waiting it out in a torture chamber somewhere? Leila found herself praying under her breath for death. It was the greater mercy.

What could Leila do? How could she help? How in the world could she find out what had happened to Nisreen?

She opened WhatsApp and began typing: Our friend Nisreen has disappeared. Do you know anything? How can we find out what happened to her?

She sent that message to Maha, Hassoun (although Nisreen was Leila's ex-boyfriend's sister and Hassoun had most certainly never met her) and Roxy.

Then she stood up and began pacing the balcony. What else could she do? She wracked her mind for other possible mutual friends, but none came to mind. She wondered if there was some kind of online service for helping trace the disappeared. If anyone would know about that, it was Maha, but she daren't send Maha any more than one message, figuring Maha had her own disappeared husband to worry about.

After a few minutes, Leila found herself scrolling through Nisreen's blog posts again, re-reading every word going back several months. She read carefully, searching. Searching for what, she didn't know, but she felt like if she read, she might find direction.

At some point, Leila stopped reading and looked blankly out at the dingy curtain surrounding the balcony. She noticed a little rip part way up which had grown into a bit of a hole. Through it, she could barely make out the lights in a flat across the alley. That flicker of light kept her gaze for a while as she pondered what she had just read.

Nisreen had no fear, never had. Her writing expressed as much courage and strength as her tirades in the coffee shop had done back in the days when they had called themselves study-buddies. Leila had often attempted to shush her friend, looking around to check no one was eavesdropping. Nisreen's words could easily anger the ruling leadership of Syria. But though she was critical, Nisreen didn't have a beef with them, per se. She was a soldier for Truth, not for Revolution. Her words had the potential to bite as sharply against the rebels – any and all factions of them – as they did against the regime.

In short, she probably made everyone angry, and could have been taken by anyone.

How long had she been gone? Leila had been so absorbed in her own family's drama that she'd not been checking the blog, but the last post was almost two weeks ago. Probably Nisreen had been gone for more than a week already.

Was anyone else looking for her? Why had no proclamations of loyalty been posted on her blog? Or had they? Leila scrolled back up to the top post and clicked on 'comments'. Sure enough, there were a couple: "Mockingbird, where are you?" and "No posts lately. I wonder why. I'll say a prayer."

So she wasn't the only one who had noticed. But, still, no one seemed to have rallied the troops on her behalf.

Of course, Leila acknowledged to herself, if she wanted to track down Nisreen, put her heart at ease that her old friend and longtime heroine was well, she should contact the person closest to Nisreen that she knew. That was Nisreen's brother, Ahmed, Leila's old boyfriend, the only man she had ever cared for other than her husband, and a man who had most unkindly broken her heart. Leila had preserved her dignity by managing to never speak to him again. When he showed his true colors, Leila had turned around, walked away, nursed her wounds for several months, then met the actual man of her dreams. And she had never spoken with Ahmed since, never so much as acknowledged his existence. Through the grapevine, and through late-night hormone-induced websurfing, she knew where he lived and which was his profile on Facebook. He'd be easy enough to contact, but for the past six years, they had happily pretended each other had never existed.

No, she would not be contacting Ahmed.

She had met Nisreen and Ahmed's mother, but the thought of speaking with that witch was even worse than the thought of contacting her ex.

And Leila had completely lost touch with the few of Nisreen's university friends whom she may have met, crossed paths with on campus or been introduced to because they happened to be in the same coffee shop at the same time.

Nisreen's blog was full of stories about encounters with people. She had many, many friends and many more acquaintances. But she never named them. And Leila had the impression Nisreen existed mostly on her own and lived on her own, with friends passing through but not participating in her life – an odd choice considering that her parents' home was in the same city. It spoke to some kind of a falling-out or suggested her parents had fled. No young woman in Syria lives by herself, much less if she has relatives within driving distance. So a massive number of acquaintances, a large number of friends, but possibly no one close enough to have been there when she was taken. And possibly no one close enough to be running around police stations trying to find her.

That is, assuming she was alive. Leila's breath stopped for a moment as she considered the possibility that it might not be rescuing that Nisreen needed, but burial rites.

Just then, her WhatsApp dinged. Hassoun, God bless him, had replied: Nisreen...is that your friend the blogger? Are they looking for her? What do you know?

Did this man ever have an unkind thought? Did he ever, ever allow himself not to care or to grow bitter? He was some kind of a god, Leila thought ruefully. She was always asking him for things, and he was always delivering.

She replied: I know nothing. Just that she disappeared from her blog. A few other readers have noticed, that's all I know.

A minute later, his reply: What's the name of the blog? I can text some mates and ask them.

Leila: The Mockingbird. Love you, *habiby*.

Hassoun: I love you, too. And miss you too much.

Leila longed to hop a plane and be near this wonderful man who said he missed her. But she couldn't bear the thought. She already felt like a burden, like a dirty smudge on his charmed life. She had dragged him so low. He would lord it over her, make sure she never forgot what a disaster she was, find little irritating ways to remind her on a daily basis how much she owed him. And she would nigh kill herself trying to make it up to him. It wasn't fair. Leila would end up the worst-off of everyone. Her family may not be in a great position, but they would be alive and together. Her husband would be just fine. Her kids would never notice anything ever happened. And Leila would spend the rest of her life picking up the pieces.

She was just beginning to think she should feel jealous of Nisreen when a little voice spoke from the doorway at her back. "Mama?"

Leila turned and saw little Saleh, the cutest little three-year-old she had ever laid eyes on, staring at her. "Come here, Mama," she said and reached out her arms to him.

He willed himself to be pulled into his mother's embrace. Leila held on tight to her little boy, her arms wrapped around his back and his face snuggled in her bosom. It was just a year since she had weaned him, and she missed the time they had spent daily in a similar embrace. She missed her little baby. A tear snuck into her eye, but she willed it back.

Too soon, way too soon, he pulled himself away from her. Leaning against his mother's leg, Saleh fiddled with a tiny rip in her pajamas, which he stared at intently for a moment before asking, "What is rape?"

Leila's hand lost its grip on Saleh's shoulder and fell limp to her side. Then she choked out, "What is what?"

"Rape."

"Oh, Saleh, *habiby*, where did you hear that word?"

"Just now, downstairs, we were all playing. And cousin Mohammed said we were going to play a game called Shooting And Raping. He said it was a game he had learned in the camp, and it was lots of fun."

Leila just stared at her little three-year-old for a minute. She withheld the urge to march downstairs and grab her eight-year-old nephew by the ear, drag himself upstairs and give him the whipping of a lifetime.

But first, she asked Saleh, "Did you play the game? What did you do?"

"Well..." Saleh muttered. "He had me and Hammoudi and Tamer – that's the boy from next door – pretend to be the women, and then he and the other bigger boys started shooting fake guns made out of sticks at each other. Then Mohammed said, 'I win! Now I get to rape the girls!' I don't know why he won. Then he made the three of us lie down on the ground, and he sat on top of us and started bouncing. It hurt a little bit."

Halfway through her little boy's account, Leila started to shush him but then stopped, willing herself to hear more. "What next?"

"We asked him to stop, but he didn't stop for a while, but then the other boys got bored and decided to play football. So Mohammed gave up and joined them. Hammoudi is downstairs playing football with them, but I didn't want to play anymore."

"Saleh, darling, thank you for coming up to visit with me. I love you so very, very much." And she gave him another big, strong hug, the strongest she could, hoping he would forget his initial question.

It worked. A minute later, he found Leila's phone in her pocket and opened the games app, like only a 3-year old born in the new millennium could.

Leila gently stood up and placed her little boy, now engrossed in a game of Bejeweled, on her little blue stool and patted his head before she left him safe on the veranda, where he would be exposed to nothing but silly phone apps, wishing he would stay there for the next twenty years.

She walked inside, where the sisters were all watching the latest Turkish soap opera. She planted herself in the doorway, hands on her hips.

"Rana?" she said, tentatively at first.

Her sister-in-law acknowledged her with a quick glance that lasted all of half a second. Then her eyes were back on the shiny blond man on the TV screen.

"Rana!" Leila tried again, this time, more insistently, and a fair bit more loudly. "We need to talk. Now."

"*Yallah.* Just a minute," she replied.

"No. Now." Leila's authority was finally coming to her, she who by virtue of her husband's generosity was now the head of this household.

Rana untangled herself from Leila's youngest sister and pulled herself off the sofa. Leila marched through the living room and into the kitchen, Rana following.

Once Leila felt confident they were out of earshot, she said as quietly yet as boldly as she could, "What is the matter with your son?"

Rana shrugged. "What do you mean?"

"Mohammed. Your. Eight. Year. Old. Son. How long has he been sick and twisted?"

"I have no idea what you are talking about," Rana replied, disinterested. She made a move in the direction of her Turkish heartthrob.

"You should spend less time watching teenage soap operas dreaming about men who aren't your husband, and pay more attention to your children," Leila hissed.

"Who are you to talk? When is the last time you had a proper conversation with your kids?"

"Just two minutes ago," Leila replied smugly. Before that? It had probably been way too long. She would be spending more time with her boys after this, though. "And the story Saleh, Three. Year. Old. Saleh told. I could barely believe my own ears!"

"Ok, I'm listening." Rana shrugged again. Shrugged.

"Your son just pretended to rape my boys!"

"He what?"

"You heard me."

"Sure, I heard you. But this is not something you joke around about."

"I'm not joking."

"Well, then did you ask Saleh? Why would he make up a story like that?"

"Saleh?" Leila let out a chuckle. "He's too young to know. He came in because he wanted me to explain what it meant. Can you imagine, having to explain to a child what rape is?"

"Yes, I can!" Rana replied indignantly, her voice now raising to a point where the girls in the other room might hear. "Do you have any idea the things our children have seen? Have experienced? No, you were living your happy, sheltered life there in the Gulf, completely oblivious to the horrors that took over our country. My own son came to me asking these same questions because he saw it, with his own two eyes."

"Well, he has no right making my sons experience the same things. And do you know how twisted it is that he would subject my boys to that? That he would make them pretend to be girls? That he would think of something so disturbing, as a reward for winning? A reward! And, for that matter, that winning would mean shooting everyone else to oblivion?" Leila was horrified by the image even as she said the words. Then she added, "You deal with your own, and keep them away from mine." Then she started to walk out.

Rana held her arm and kept her from moving. "I'd say the same to you. Don't you make false accusations against my son. You know nothing. You should look at your own first." Then she walked out first, leaving Leila behind.

Leila fell back against the sink. Her legs felt weak. She had no idea what Rana's last words meant, but one thing was now clear: it had been silly to suppose her boys might yet come out of this ordeal untouched, unaffected or unaware.

Chapter Fourteen

Maha was alone on the sofa, crying out the few final tears that her body could generate after ten hours straight. Samir was still in the bedroom. She'd heard not a sound since he'd locked himself in there that morning. For the past ten hours, she had huddled on the sofa, tears slowly welling and dripping as the same triad of thoughts repeated themselves in her mind: considering that this emotional exile might actually be worse than a husband in prison, wondering if this new reality meant her child would be raised unloved, and plain old simple hurt. What was he thinking in there?

It had not occurred to Maha to inform anyone that Samir had come home. This was in part because she did not really feel sure that he had in fact come home. It was also in part because she was not thinking of anyone besides her own little family: Samir and the baby growing in her womb. No one else existed to her today. The people we love the most can hurt us the most.

A ding on her phone interrupted her self-pity session. It was a WhatsApp message from Leila. At first, Maha thought of ignoring it but brought herself to do the second slightly useful thing of the day, after making breakfast. She clicked on the little icon and read the message.

"Our friend Nisreen has disappeared. Do you know anything? How can we find out what happened to her?"

Maha dropped the phone to the sofa. It thudded on the firm cushion as her arms, and her shoulders fell limp. Her eyelids began to close but ended up just staring blankly at the empty coffee cups in front of her. Her brain and every bone in her body was overcome by weariness. Just on the very day that she got her husband back from captivity, in body, at least, another person in her network of friends was taken. It would never end.

She couldn't bring herself to reply. After a few minutes, she picked up her phone and read the message again. Clear as day, it said that Nisreen was gone.

Her back limp, Maha lay down and curled herself into a little ball, both hands tucked under her head. She willed herself to cry a bit more. What other reaction would make sense? Not that anything made sense.

Eventually, she drifted off to sleep.

The next morning, a hand rubbing her shoulder woke Maha from a black and mercifully dreamless sleep. She slowly opened her eyes and looked up at her husband, sitting by her head, giving her the most gentle of massages.

She sat up slowly, and he quickly pulled her into an embrace. Maha curled into the spot under Samir's arms that had long been hers.

"The size of an avocado?" he asked.

Maha felt a tear welling already. So she didn't say anything.

"I am still having trouble believing it's true, even more so after all this time without any news. But you know, 70 days in prison was a fair price to pay for such a treat." He lifted his head back and laughed.

"Fair price?"

"Well, in that place, I needed some reason to feel like my imprisonment was justified. At first, it was the baby. Then I began to wonder if I'd dreamed up our last phone conversation. I didn't know what was real and what was my imagination, and I was looking for something to be angry at. So I told myself to stop thinking about, or hoping for, a baby. It was too hard to believe anything good could be happening because, inside there, everything just felt so pointless. I mean, I know why they did it, but that doesn't make it justified, right?"

"Samir, dear, I really don't understand how you could have done anything worthy of imprisonment."

"It's a complicated world out there, you know," he replied.

"Of course, I know," Maha responded, now stiffening and sitting up straight. "You think I haven't spent two months asking all the questions you've been asking? And on top of that, I've been trying to grasp the thought that I could be bringing an orphan into this world."

"Honey, I do know that this affects you as well. Though perhaps I didn't realize just how much. Mostly I was just grateful that you are strong and an incredibly capable woman because I needed to trust you were safe."

Maha let out a grunt.

"So I don't know how many times I wished I had just stayed in Damascus that day," he continued. "But it wouldn't have made a difference: when your name is on a list your name is on a list. Of course, a baby is worth it and much more, but you know, nothing feels worth it when you're in there. So you can't imagine how hard it was to keep believing."

"Trust me, it's real. All the vomit I've deposited in the toilet this month is evidence enough."

He chuckled. "Well, thank God for vomit then. But I don't even know this little guy--"

"Or girl."

"Oh, it could be a girl!" Samir exclaimed and now turned to face Maha, putting his two hands on her belly, staring at the spot where the child must be growing inside. "Well, even more for a girl, I'd do anything to keep her safe."

Maha sighed. "I don't feel anything yet. Other than nausea, though that phase is mostly over now. Thank God!"

"I look forward to watching him, or her, or it or whatever, grow. We'll watch together."

"So..." she hesitated. "What did happen? Why were you arrested?"

"*Malish*. It's not important."

"Yes, it is!" She grabbed his upper arms and leaned forward, bringing her face close to his.

"You are my husband, and I need to know. What could have possibly happened that justified such, such, such...that."

"I promise you, you don't want to know."

"I do. I've spent these months, which felt like a lifetime, fretting, worrying, crying, making phone calls, trying to lobby people at the border--"

"You went to the border?"

"Of course, I went to the border. My husband was taken at the border!"

"You shouldn't have done that," Samir said in a dark voice.

"My ass."

Without replying, he stood up and walked into the bathroom. Maha watched him walk away. Then she stood up and went into the kitchen. A bright ray of morning sun was coming through the window, shining right on the stove. As she waited for the coffee to boil, she stared at the bright spot on the stovetop.

The coffee was almost done when she heard Samir come back out. He appeared in the doorway, arm on the doorframe, face poking into the kitchen. Tentatively, he said, "I'm sorry."

"No, no," replied Maha. "I'm sorry. You're the one who was in God-knows-what-awful a place."

"I worry about you, that's all. This whole time, knowing you were carrying our baby, I worried about you."

"Thank you, dear. But do you think I don't worry about you, too? I do. I love you, and I'm not a helpless child. I did everything I could to get you out, and now it sounds like you kept secrets from me, so I didn't do a very good job of helping. I just wish you didn't feel like you had to protect me from everything."

"It's what a good husband does," he observed.

"We're not that kind of couple. We never were," she countered.

"I can't talk about it, though."

"But why not? What if you get arrested again? What if something else happens, something we can't even imagine?"

"I'll stay here. We are safe from now on, I promise. But I can't tell you. It involves other people, and I promised them, too. Plus, it's over."

"Is anything over? This war just gets more and more crazy."

"That's for sure," Samir chuckled wryly. "Too crazy. But it's no good. From now on, I'll tell you anything else that comes up, or, at least, I'll tell you as much as I can. I won't keep secrets. But this one, I can't tell you. I'm sorry."

Maha gazed at him. She was angry and nervous and so very, very relieved that he was alive and safe. And she wanted to know, needed to know, anything that might help her feel like she had even the tiniest bit of control over the situation.

But he was adamant, and she knew enough to know that secrets were a highly valued currency of the revolution. She admitted to herself that she wasn't actually all that surprised to learn that Samir was wrapped up in something political. Disappointed, yes. Frustrated that she'd been kept out of the loop, even more. But this just made her a normal wife in a war that made no sense. The last 70 days had awakened her to the reality that she didn't have the perfect marriage, the idealized connection with her spouse that other women dreamed of and that she had always smugly assumed she did have. She still hoped she could salvage a good marriage, but she was beginning to realize that this reality was all she could hope for.

And she still loved him. Looking at her husband, her heart overflowed with gratitude that he was back, sympathy because she knew that whatever he did was with good intentions, and he didn't deserve to pay the consequences, and just a little flutter in her belly at the sight of his hazel eyes and thick eyelashes. At this moment, he didn't need her protests or pleas or judgment. She actually had no idea how pained he might be, what he had endured during the past month. Just an uncomfortable cell and uncertainty? Or solitary confinement, or overcrowdedness, or torture? And what had he seen? These were the questions she should be asking.

"Alright. I'll trust you. I won't ask you again. But, you need to know how much I care, how I will do everything to protect you. So I hope that, whatever you were involved in, it's really is over. I may be just a woman, maybe you think it's your job to protect me, but we are partners and nothing you say will convince me not to be your partner or to try to defend you, too. So...what do you want to talk about?" She grabbed a fresh coffee cup from the dish drainer and picked up the rakwa and led him out to the veranda, then went back for a cup of water for herself. They both sat.

"It's awful. Syria is really and truly lost," he started.

Maha nodded. Even from her comfortable flat in Beirut, she had already lost so very much.

"They treated me better than most. I don't know why, honestly. Someone else in the prison told me it was because I'm a Christian, but who knows, really? They mostly left me alone. They brought me in for questioning once a day, but they didn't do anything. Just set me in a chair, asked me questions that I – honestly - couldn't answer, then sent me back to the cell. But I saw things. Oh, Maha, all the stories, they're true. And more."

She poured his coffee and encouraged him to keep talking. And he did. For three hours, until the sun was high in the sky, he talked. Maha listened, absorbing as much as she could of the stories, of the horrors that were happening to her people. Syria's prisons had always been infamous, and probably all these horrors had been going on all along, but somehow it seemed worse now. Much worse. Worse because it had reached her own most beloved. Worse because if it had reached him, and had reached Leila's old friend Nisreen, it had reached too far. Way too far.

When he finally finished, Maha asked Samir if he wanted her to make brunch. He said he'd rather go out and celebrate. It was a momentous day, he said, and he wanted to see the sea, breathe fresh air or, at least, air as fresh as Beirut might be able to offer.

But instead of getting ready, Maha found herself preparing more coffee. Then, offhandedly, she commented, "Do you remember Leila had a friend at university called Nisreen? Nisreen was actually the sister of that guy she was seeing."

"Yes, sure, I remember," he nodded. "Why?"

"Well, apparently she went and became some big-name blogger. Tales of justice from Damascus or something like that."

"Yeah? Do you remember the name of the blog?"

"Just a sec," Maha said. She stirred the coffee grounds into the pot then went to get her phone. She scrolled through her messages until she found it: "The Mockingbird. Do you know it?"

Samir, who had gradually been relaxing through the telling of his stories in the comforts of his own home, was suddenly tense again, frowning and leaning forward. "I do. Let me guess. She's gone."

Chapter Fifteen

Leila was in the kitchen helping her sisters finish preparing the big meal of the day when she heard a ding on her phone. She put down the knife and a half-chopped cucumber, wiped her hands on her *galabiya*, then went to pick it up.

It was a WhatsApp from Maha. Took her long enough! Usually, her friend was responsive and helpful, but last night Leila had hardly slept, fretting about Nisreen, and Maha hadn't so much as bothered to reply with a word of sympathy. Leila opened the message.

It said: Samir is back. Samir is back! Can you believe it, he's back! He just walked up to our door yesterday!

Leila didn't know whether to smile or frown. Smile for Maha's joy, or frown because she didn't find this news as exciting as she knew she should.

But another message came through just as Leila was putting the phone back down, unsure of how to reply.

Maha: He knows about Nisreen. When can you Viber?

Leila felt a chill go up her back and her hands trembling as she composed a reply: One hour?

Maha: Ok. I'll look for you in an hour.

Leila went back to the kitchen and got the cucumbers chopped as quickly as she could. Then she stood around the kitchen asking if they could finish cooking any faster, and once the food was ready she rushed to lay out the meal on newspapers on the floor of the larger of the flat's two rooms. She rushed to eat and feed her boys, then rushed into the back room, letting her younger sisters deal with the cleanup.

She opened her Viber app, looked for Maha's name and tapped on it.

Maha picked up quickly enough. "He's back, Leila, he's back!"

"*Mabrouk*," she replied, with less enthusiasm than she should, but as much as she could muster.

"At first, he didn't seem to even want to be home. He was awful. He even got mad when I mentioned the baby. But he came around, and we had a long, long conversation this morning. He said he won't go back to Sham – of course - and that he'll focus on me and the baby now."

"That's great."

"But of course, we're all still very worried."

"Of course."

"Anyway... there's so much to tell. So much."

"Yes."

"When did you find out about Nisreen? How did you find out about her?"

"Just last night. With everything going on with my family, I hadn't checked in a few weeks. But last night I went to read her blog and saw that it has gone silent."

"So, Samir knows about her. She was arrested, Leila."

Leila didn't reply.

Maha added, "I'm sorry. I'm so sorry."

Then Leila said, "I figured as much. But how did Samir know?"

"He... well..." Maha's voice caught. "He's keeping secrets from me."

"Like what? What do you mean?"

"He told me that he knows why it happened."

"It? Like, the–"

"Yes!" Maha cut Leila off in a hurry.

Leila caught on quickly. Another thing not to be said over the phone lines. "I see." Then again, "I see."

"It's like there's a whole side to him that I never knew," Maha's voice choked up a bit more.

"I guess it wouldn't be easy getting him back after...after...after... well, he must be like a new person in some ways."

"New? Or ruined."

Leila chuckled. "Well, what have you done with him so far?"

"Mostly just talk and wait while he slept. He slept for like 24 hours yesterday. And he's sleeping now. We did go to the Port for lunch, though."

"Nice."

"I guess. Like I said, he's keeping secrets. I never thought my husband would keep secrets from me."

"Well," commented Leila. "They always say that every couple has a few secrets. Hassoun doesn't know everything about me."

"Does he know about Nisreen?" Maha asked.

"Yes, and he said he'd help find her. But he doesn't know how I know her."

"I guess he wouldn't, would he?"

"No. Some things we really don't know about each other. I bet that's why Samir isn't telling you, because he knows that you don't actually want to know."

"Perhaps."

"Darling! You sound so sad. Be happy; your husband is back!"

Maha didn't respond. After a moment, instead, she changed the subject. "So, about your friend."

"Yes," Leila sighed. Maha's marital woes had actually felt like a welcome distraction. Easier to use platitudes to comfort one friend who is a little sad than to wonder about the eternal fate of the friend who, she now knew for certain, was rotting away in a Syrian prison cell somewhere.

"So now you know what happened to her. Samir knows where she is, and apparently knows who to talk to about it. But he wouldn't tell me, and plus, he doesn't seem to think there's much to do."

"There must be something!"

"Pressure, he said. It's all about pressure," Maha commented.

"What kind of pressure?"

"Public, visible stuff."

"So like media and protests?" asked Leila. She was not sure what else she should ask or say over the airwaves.

"Um... I'll text you," Maha said abruptly. "I've got to go. Love you, bye!"

Leila stood holding her phone in her hand. The Viber connection had held remarkably well. Why did Maha cut the conversation short? Had Leila said something wrong? Too much?

Regardless, she was so grateful for her friend and for her friend's connections, even if they came at the cost of Maha's husband's sojourn through the Syrian prison system. Perhaps.

Maybe that wasn't how he found out. The way Maha talked, Samir could be involved in anything.

But still, they were her friends, and she was glad for friends like them. Now, instead of Kuwait, she wanted her next airplane to be headed for Beirut. Oh, how she longed to sit in Maha's living room just as she had so many times back during their student days. How she longed for a sip of Maha's bitter black coffee, and a conversation in which they could say anything, freely, share each other's hearts, and do so without wondering who else was joining in and without fear of the connection dropping.

To Leila's relief, a message did come from Maha on WhatsApp: They're saying this is the safest way now.

Leila understood this to mean that WhatsApp texts were the most difficult to bug, or track, or intercept, or whatever word secret police gurus used to describe their technical strategies for stealing other people's conversations. No one really knew what was safest, but they tried to follow general wisdom as best they could.

She replied: Ok, thanks.

Maha: So, use your contacts outside. Your husband's co-workers, people you've met from elsewhere.

Leila knew that 'elsewhere' meant Europe or the United States. She didn't like that they mattered more, but they did.

Maha continued: Tell them her name, her full name. Tell them about her blog. Give them a photo. Use Facebook, Twitter, whatever you can, and tell them to use whatever they can.

Leila: Ok. Will you do the same?

Maha: I don't know. I never really met her. She doesn't have other friends?

Leila: Good point. I don't know.

Leila: But I'm worried about her!

Maha: Do you have a photo of her?

Leila: I might have an old one from university days, I can ask Hassoun to look through my albums.

Maha: Don't worry. I think I can get a copy, I'll send it to you.

Leila: How?

Maha: I just can.

How in the world did Maha have a copy of Nisreen's photo? Leila imagined this must be another piece of Samir's secret life.

Leila: Ok.

Leila: Thank you.

Maha: Love you. Peace to your family.

Leila: Peace to you too.

Left alone to her thoughts, Leila found she had few. It felt like a weight of sandbags surrounding her from all sides. She could barely breathe, felt no desire to cry or laugh or even pray. She just wanted this all to be over and her simple life to come back. She lay on the pile of mattresses in the corner of the room, mattresses that would be strewn around the flat when it came time to sleep at night.

The next thing she remembered was hearing the new message sound, accompanied by a vibrate, on her phone. Sure enough, it was a photo of Nisreen. And Leila had slept for two hours.

Chapter Sixteen

The next morning, Samir got up early and prepared to head to church. Maha begged him not to go, to rest up a bit more, to just enjoy being home, and to remember he had promised to put her and the baby first. But he insisted that this was his job, and his calling, and he needed to check in at work and report to them on, well, something. So Maha asked to go with him, but he insisted she stay at home, rest, and care for the baby's health. This was fine, as Maha did not actually want to go to church herself. She just wished Samir wasn't going either.

But she gave up insisting, knowing that her concern could be mistaken for suspicion about the world of his secrets that he'd asked her to ignore. There was no point causing undue tension. He wasn't going to tell her. She loved him too much to argue with him or to lose him over it. Plus, it was very unlikely that whatever he was wrapped up in, which she suspected had something to do with politics and revolutionary activity, had anything to do with his job at the church. So she let him go back to work, just another normal day.

As soon as he was out the door, she dialed Roxy.

"*Aloh*, who is it?" Roxy answered with a question.

"It's me," Maha replied.

"Of course, it is, darling. How are you doing?"

"What are you doing today?"

"I'm just home with Mom and the kids. We're stuffing *koussa* with rice and chickpeas."

"Do you want a visitor?"

"Sure! *Ahlan wa Sahlan*! You're very welcome!"

"I'll be there in an hour or two."

Before setting out, Maha made herself a cup of flower tea, then decided it was high time she wash her hair. She also quickly washed the dishes and threw out the cigarette ashes and did a quick once-over on the flat so that Samir wouldn't come home to the mess he'd left behind. After throwing on a loose-fitting white summer dress, applying a bit of eyeliner and choosing some big earrings, Maha almost felt like a normal woman for the first time in months. She had a home, she had a husband, her husband was employed, and she had a friend to visit.

Traffic was at its Beirut best, so it took more than an hour to get to Aley. By the time the bus was done winding up the mountain, Maha was thoroughly nauseous. She disembarked a kilometer before Roxy's house, was sick on the cliff overlooking the mountain, then let the fresh mountain air clear her head and freshen her belly.

When Roxy opened the door, Maha couldn't wait any longer. "He's home! Roxy, he's back!"

Roxy's enthusiasm did not disappoint. She let out a scream surely heard throughout the town, then embraced Maha tight. Then she started jumping, pulling Maha with her. Maha hugged her friend back and jumped along.

She felt happy. For once in she-had-no-idea-how-long, Maha felt a pure and simple happiness overcome her. It filled her from her hair to her toes.

Roxy pulled her into the house and kept jumping, now laughing uncontrollably. Maha watched her for a few seconds, but the laughter was contagious. She quickly slipped out of her shoes and fell to the sofa, leaning her head back and bellowing out unrestrained laughs. Soon Roxy's kids were skipping around the salon laughing as well. They had no idea why they were dancing, but such glee couldn't help but spread.

Fifteen minutes later, giggles, chuckles, and snorts all spent, Roxy fell to the sofa alongside Maha and leaned up against her back, long red hair fanned out creating a halo over her head. She took Maha's arm in a tight embrace.

"Tell me," Roxy commanded.

So Maha did. She told of how Samir appeared on the doorstep two mornings past, but had little to say of where he came from and how he'd managed to return. She told of his horrid rejection on that first day, and of the better conversations that ensued. She said that he was mysterious but then said she didn't want to talk about that. Then she told Roxy that he had already gone back to work today, leaving her alone, but that he promised to stay away from the border.

Roxy listened without a word, other than groans and gasps at just the right moments to show she was paying close attention, and sympathizing.

When Maha was done, her friend stood up and said, "I am so glad that he's back. So glad that you have your husband again."

"I'm sorry," said Maha, suddenly aware that she was one of the very few Syrian women in Lebanon whose husband was near and healthy and working. "Have you heard from your husband?"

"*Malish*. It's no big deal," Roxy replied, waving a hand in dismissal. "Let's make some deceitful *koussa*," the name given to vegetarian stuffed courgettes. *Koussa* for squash, deceitful for tasting good but not actually delivering any meat. The cheap version.

For the next hour or so, Roxy, her mother and Maha sat on little stools in the kitchen, gutting little green squash and chatting about banalities. Then Roxy mixed up the stuffing of rice, herbs, tomato paste and chickpeas, and passed it to Maha who deftly filled every nook and cranny of each piece with the mixture. They would swell as they cooked, but not burst.

Once the food was on the stove, Roxy got to tidying the kitchen, leaving Maha to sit back on her stool, back up against the kitchen wall.

"How's Leila?" asked Roxy.

"Oh, Leila," Maha sighed. "She's alright, I guess. It's not easy in Jordan. I talked with her yesterday. Do you remember that girl Nisreen, her boyfriend Ahmed's little sister?"

"I remember how much Leila loved her, almost as much as the brother."

"Yes. Well, she's been taken now. Literally we learn that Samir is free, and then that Leila's friend is in jail."

"Oh, no! God have mercy."

Maha just nodded.

After a moment, Roxy glanced over from the sink where she was washing dishes, and asked, "So, do you know what happened to her? Where she is? Anything?"

"Well," considered Maha. "I know Leila reads her blog and apparently it has gotten a fair bit of attention lately. I don't imagine any well-known Syrian blogger these days has much reason for optimism if they've been marked by the regime. Samir knows what happened to her, at least, he acted like he knows, but he wouldn't tell me much."

"What do you mean?"

"Samir knows she was arrested. He said that he has friends who were talking about her before and that he's sure they know where she is. That's all he'd tell me."

"So what can we do?" Roxy asked.

"I don't know," Maha replied.

"Well, ask Samir."

"You know how mad he was when I told him I'd gone to the border?"

"That was really a stupid thing to do, sweetie."

"Wouldn't you have done the same?"

"For my husband?"

"Of course."

"Well, look at me. I'm here in Lebanon while he's alone back in Sweida, so I don't know what that says," Roxy groaned.

"It means you care about your kids, right?"

"I suppose. Or that my husband is a stubborn donkey." Roxy burst out in happy chuckles.

Maha laughed along.

"Well, he is, you know," she said. "I talked to him this morning, and he said that the fighting is now within earshot of our house. A stray bullet came through our living room window this morning. Wait a second, I'll show you. He sent me a video of it."

Roxy wiped her hands on a tea towel and picked up her phone. A moment later, she thrust it out towards Maha, who stared at the ten-second clip, showing a bullet hole in the window then spanning across the room to show where the bullet had lodged in the wall.

"Roxy!" Maha exclaimed. "He could have died! That's awful!"

Roxy let out a grunt and half-smiled. Then she shrugged her shoulders.

"What is he doing to stay safe?" Maha pressed.

"He said he'll sleep on a mattress on the floor in the basement, and he has moved the television down there. That's a bit better. But he still putters around in the kitchen and tends his olive and apricot trees. I know him. Like I said, stubborn donkey."

"I'm so sorry. You must be so worried."

"Of course, I'm worried. But I'm staying here for now. Sure I miss him, sure I'm terrified something will happen to him. But let him be, I say."

"Seriously?"

Roxy shrugged again.

Maha stared at her a moment more before it dawned on her that this was Roxy's defense mechanism. She'd seen the same thing back when Roxy had divorced her first husband. She'd cooked up a storm, kept their little dorm room as clean as could be, and planned dance parties. The tears lasted less than a day; after that, it was all fun and games. She had showed a tiny bit of her heart to Leila; Maha knew, but no one else saw anything but cheer and playfulness.

So Maha let her keep her pride. "You're a stronger woman than me. If something happened again to Samir tomorrow – God forbid – I'd be right there at the border again. Or I'd just collapse into a broken lump of misery."

"You can't, you know," Roxy observed. "It's not just about you anymore."

Maha knew Roxy was right, and so she just really, really hoped nothing would happen to Samir.

"But our husbands are in God's hands," Roxy continued. "Let's talk about Nisreen. We should do something."

"Like what?"

"I don't know. Start a Facebook campaign? Raise money to bribe someone? I don't know."

"Facebook is exactly what Samir suggested. Leila wants to do something, but I'm not sure. I mean, Nisreen has a family and surely she has better friends than us. Maybe someone else is already doing something."

"She's Leila's friend, isn't she? Us Medina girls have to stay together."

"She's not Medina. She's from Damascus."

"Close enough. If Leila cares, I care."

"Speaking of us Medina girls, have you found out anything more about Huda?" Maha changed the subject.

"Nothing. Still no response to my friend request."

These days in Syria, a non-response could be horrible news, or it could just be bad news. Huda could be dead. Or she could be stuck somewhere that the phone lines were down or without electricity to charge her phone. Or she could have traveled, become a refugee somewhere. Or she could have just not accepted the friend request.

"Matte?" Roxy asked.

What Maha really wanted was a strong cup of black tea, but matte would do. She nodded.

As the water boiled and Roxy laid out the herbal leaves into three small glasses and rinsed out the metal straw, still by the sink from the previous usage a few hours earlier, she turned the conversation back to Nisreen. "I'm just saying. Ask Samir and ask Leila. Let's track her down, find enough information to do something. We're not just going to sit by and watch this happen."

"I don't know if he'll help," Maha said, thinking of their argument just the day before. "But I'll ask."

On the bus back down the mountain from Aley to Beirut, the temperature rising with each inch closer to sea level, Maha found herself wondering why Roxy had grasped so strongly onto the idea of helping Nisreen. Of course, Roxy knew about Leila's relationship with the chic Damascene girl who, though a few years younger than Leila, had been a mentor to her. As much as Leila had been Roxy's confidante, Roxy had been Leila's. Everyone within a fifty-meter radius knew of Leila's crush on Nisreen's brother Ahmed, saw him steal her heart then act so aloof, and sympathized when she finally realized she'd been dreaming up a life with a man who had never thought of her as more than some college-time diversion. But it was to Roxy that Leila had asked her questions, and on Roxy's shoulder that Leila had wept.

So Roxy knew more about Nisreen, perhaps, than most of Leila's friends did, but as far as Maha knew not even Roxy had ever actually met her.

Why would Roxy want to rally behind this city girl, but so willingly leave her husband to the elements of war in Syria? If Roxy was capable of such activism, why had she done so little to support Maha in Samir's absence, beyond providing that reliable shoulder upon which to spill tears?

Was it a bond of sisterhood? Or was it something about what Nisreen stood for?

Regardless, Maha found herself oddly encouraged. After all, Samir was now safely back and, of course, Samir's brother and a few other friends had worked hard for his freedom: though Samir had made his release sound random, Maha knew it wasn't.

Who did Nisreen have? Roxy, Leila, Maha, even Huda, were from villages speckled around Syria. They had few influential connections – Maha more than the others since she was part of a church network with friends around the world and also since she had relatives in Damascus. And Leila had her own assortment of international friends. Maha imagined that Nisreen must have plenty of her own connections because she was a city girl. But maybe not.

Maha pulled out her phone and wrote a message on WhatsApp to Leila: *Habibty*, any news about your friend? Remind me of the link to her blog?

Though the morning sickness phase should already have ended and, indeed, Maha felt much better, it still hit her now and again. Today, the roads were too curvy and Maha's stomach too unstable for reading a phone screen on the bus. She dropped her hand holding the phone to her lap and looked up, then she dropped her head against the window and stared out at the cars whizzing past on their way up the mountain. Everything was so fast on this road! This road that connected her two homes, her Beirut flat and her family's house in Sednaya. Except, of course, the house in Syria was gone, and her ability to cross the border that lay behind her had been revoked. This was no longer the road from home. Now it was just a dangerous highway.

Very few cars with Syrian tags passed her way, but there were a few. Longingly, she tried to catch a glimpse of each passenger in those cars as they headed to a land so precious to her, but which might as well be a million miles away.

A light vibration in her phone jerked her attention back down. She risked the nausea to read Leila's reply, which included a link to the blog.

Maha clicked on the link and put the phone back in her lap as the website loaded. She would have to read it later, once she was back on her own two feet or once the bus stopped swerving back and forth from one switchback to another on its way into the heart of Beirut.

When she finally did make it back onto flat land, Maha decided to walk a ways rather than catch a taxi straight home. She opened The Mockingbird and read as she walked.

Chapter Seventeen

It was a balmy morning in late July, hot even as the day began. This had been a brutal summer already, and August promised to be worse. The breeze from the sea kept the air bearable, but even so, Huda felt sweat gathering under her blouse as she walked the twenty minutes into Latakia City center. It was still early, and the streets were just beginning to wake up. She passed a handful of housewives washing their front courtyards, a street sweeper, and several shops in which the owners were just lifting the heavy, noisy metal gates.

As was her tradition, she popped into the bakery halfway to work and purchased a small chocolate croissant. She nibbled at it as she kept walking. Mid-way through Ramadan, many people were fasting, but the bakeries in Latakia stayed open, and the city's residents could decide whether or not to fast. Huda had never seen the point of fasting, and she had no idea why an Alawite girl like her should be expected to do so. It was not enough that someone had once told her that Alawites were a type of Muslim.

Huda was one of the first people to arrive at her little law firm. She always had been a morning person, and she treasured the half hour or so during which she could make her tea and tidy her desk in peace.

Hot mug in hand, she booted up her computer and moved a few contract files from the top of her desk to their proper homes in her filing cabinet, then she arranged her purse neatly into the top drawer of the desk. As soon as she could, she opened up her browser and typed in www.facebook.com. She logged in and clicked on the icon for friend requests. It was still there.

One night a few months ago, Huda had seen a notification of a new request. It was from someone named 'Roxy', whose profile picture was of two little kids on either side of an enormous daisy. Huda had clicked on the name and found that the security settings wouldn't allow her to see any more of this "Roxy" profile, so she had gone to sleep and thought nothing more of it.

But come morning, she'd awoken with a start. Roxy was, of course, the name of an old friend of hers, and who was to say that this wasn't that Roxy. Roxy was quite an unusual name, after all.

The possibility of reconnecting with an old friend from university had intrigued Huda, and she had found herself pondering this friend request – indeed, one of few – often in the past few months.

Today, once again, Huda clicked on Roxy's name, and once again she saw a blank wall. She clicked on 'about' and found little more. This Roxy did, however, declare herself to be from Al-Sweida, the very city from which her old friend Roxy had come. Then she clicked on the profile photo and the two little children all of a sudden were much larger. And incredibly cute, dressed up in matching outfits. The image of children made Huda wonder, though, because the Roxy she knew had never seemed to be the procreating sort. She clicked on the image and this Roxy's previous profile photo appeared. It was of the same children when one of them was little more than an infant, laughing together. Next photo was of just one baby. Then the next was of an array of stars in technicolor The final photo, however, held the confirmation: it was a glamour shot of a woman with long black curls falling down her back into the scooped curves of a red evening gown, face turned back but just slightly tilted toward the camera and lips formed into a deliberate pout. One glance at that woman and Huda knew that her old friend Roxy had somehow found her on Facebook.

Intriguing.

Huda sat back into her chair and pondered for at least the thirtieth time whether she should accept the friend request.

There were few signs that life in Latakia had changed since war had come to Syria. Her job had remained the same. She was still little more than a glorified paper pusher, though fully qualified as a lawyer, at a male-dominated law firm whose clients were mostly shipping companies. Business had slowed considerably since much of Syria's maritime activity had ceased, so Huda was just grateful she still had a job. If the firm began to struggle, the women would expect to be fired first.

Her family still had a little home in the village where life went on much as it always had. Fruit trees, a cow to milk, an annual cycle of picking and pickling and preserving, and a houseful of three generations. They still had their little home in the city where Huda and one of her sisters spent most of their time, along with their mother from time to time.

She still walked to work each day around 8 am, and she was still usually the first one there and one of the most productive and, therefore, one of the first to leave each day. She still bought her croissant on the way in and groceries for dinner on her way home. She still made the exact same salary as she had for the past five years.

She was still single and still spent most of her free time either reading or watching television with her sister.

But some things had changed. Prices had risen considerably, so her family was beginning to struggle to make ends meet. Her sister and her brothers also continued to make the same amount of money, though their monthly expenses were easily five times what they had been three years ago.

Also, Latakia had become rather overcrowded. Dozens of beggars flocked to cars stopped at traffic lights where, previously, an odd tissue vendor may have tried halfheartedly to sell his wares to the drivers of stopped cars. Dozens queued each day outside the community association and the charitable office of the mosque that she passed on her way to work. On her street, about half the homes were now rented to people from other regions of Syria, and multiple families crowded into each small flat. Garbage production had increased, traffic had grown unbearable, and it was not unusual to see men sleeping in the parks.

And while Huda had never been one to describe Syria as a country where freedom reigns, she had never bemoaned the general restrictions imposed by the local authorities. She had grown up with the idea that any neighbor may report on any untoward activity and had just always been careful to avoid being untoward. But this too had changed. Now, she felt like her every move could be monitored, and that someone was just waiting for an excuse to make her family's life a tad more difficult. One wrong move at work, or one accidental rebuff to the wrong person, and Huda might soon learn that her oldest nephew had been demoted at work or that her cousin had failed an exam at the university.

Access to Facebook was one of the more positive changes that had come to Latakia since the problems began. Before, she had had a Facebook account, but finding the VPN to log on clandestinely had been so complicated that she hadn't bothered to use it. One of the first initiatives of the government after the protests began had been to legalize Facebook. So now, Huda, like almost every other Syrian who had enough education to be able to read, was an avid Facebook user. But she wasn't naïve. She knew that Facebook access had been less to appease the protestors than it had been to introduce a new mechanism for monitoring the country's citizens.

Friending the wrong person on Facebook was one of those little things that could have consequences. But on the other hand, a reunion with an old college friend would be a big event in her routine of a life.

As she mused these things and again pondered what to do, people began to drift slowly into the office. Chatter in the little kitchen area began to pick up, and one by one, the dozen or so other people who worked in her little law firm sat down and booted up their respective computers.

Huda shut her browser, opened her email and got to work.

Chapter Eighteen

"Well? How did it go?"

Maha lay her bag on the coffee table and fell onto the sofa next to Samir, who was typing away on his laptop. He put the computer off to the side and pulled her into an embrace, a pleasure that was once again beginning to feel familiar to her.

"Fine," she sighed. "She said everything looks normal."

"That's good, right?"

"I guess."

"Why do you not sound convinced?"

Maha pulled herself to a sitting position and pulled her legs up onto the sofa. She sighed again. "She did the scan."

"Really?" Samir's muscles tightened in anticipation. "Did you get a copy? Can I see my child?"

"Here." Maha pulled a rumpled black-and-white photo out of her pocket and handed it to him.

"Seriously?" Samir said, exasperated.

"It's just a fuzzy blur, nothing special."

"Let me take a look at this." And he began to study the image, which would be blurry even if the sheet of paper it was printed on were not so wrinkled. "Oh! I think I see the head, there! And is that a leg?" He held it close to his face and retrieved his left hand from Maha's shoulder to point at parts of the image as he investigated. Maha sat and watched, saying nothing.

"Did you find out the gender?" he asked.

"No. The doctor didn't say, and I didn't ask."

Samir kept gazing at the image. Finally, he declared, "I think he looks wonderful. It makes me even more in awe of the beautiful creation God created."

"You're kidding, right?" Maha let out a scoff.

"Kidding? No. It really is spectacular."

"I hope I come to see it that way soon."

Samir didn't reply, just sat there studying the photo.

After a few minutes, Maha continued. "Seeing that scan made it so real. Too real. The nurse showed me the heartbeat. This thing inside of me has a heartbeat. But I can't stop thinking about my mother, still holding on to the tatters of her life that remain, of Leila's family, barely scraping by in some Jordanian slum, of Nisreen, the poor girl. Why create new life when we can barely hold on to the lives that we have?"

Samir turned on the sofa, so he was facing Maha and lay his hands on her bent knees. "You know, I have stopped asking the question 'why.' This world makes so little sense that I need to just hold on to the truth that I have. I know that I love you, and you are here with me, and we are going to have a baby. And I know that only God could create something as magical as this tiny person who is taking shape inside of you."

Maha gently pulled herself away and stood up. "Coffee?"

"Always," replied Samir.

She went into the kitchen to boil the water, wiping her eyes with the heel of her hand as she walked. She wasn't sure whether the tears were more the fault of hormones or of the nightmare that life had become.

That night, over dinner, Maha broached the subject that had been nagging her, and which Leila had texted her about half a dozen times over the course of the last few weeks.

"I've been thinking about Leila's friend Nisreen. I think we should start a campaign for her. I told Leila what you said about drawing international attention to her situation, and she wants to do it, but we don't know enough."

"What do you mean, you don't know enough?" Samir asked.

"Well, Leila wasn't able to track down her family yet. Except for her brother who lives in Canada. She was embarrassed to write him, so I did. He said that he doesn't know anything. He wouldn't give Leila his parents' contact information, just told her that they wouldn't be able to help anyway. There's some weird history there."

"What kind of history?"

"I don't know. And Leila and Nisreen's brother have a really awkward relationship so it's not like we can push it."

Samir nodded as he took another bite of his okra stew.

Maha continued. "So either her family is being very unhelpful, or they are completely lost themselves. Ahmed sounded grateful enough for our offer to help, though. I have no idea why he doesn't fly back to Syria to help his sister... maybe he is wanted too?"

"Seems unlikely. Didn't you say he has lived in Canada for several years now?"

"Yup. Odd, huh?"

"Well, he must have his reasons."

"He must. Or he's just a moron. Either way, Leila says she wants to do this, but she doesn't have any contact with Nisreen's family and doesn't know any of her friends. We have searched the Internet, and it doesn't seem like anyone has mentioned this except for a handful of people who commented directly on her blog, which is odd if you think about it since The Mockingbird was so popular."

"It does seem odd."

"So, what do you think we should do?"

"Just start, I guess."

"Start what?"

"Have you tried just posting a photo of Nisreen and a link to her blog on your Facebook page? Label it 'Missing now for X number of weeks' or something like that. Then ask people to share it. Go from there."

For the rest of the meal and as Maha washed the dishes, they talked about activism and what it meant to raise public awareness, to garner the attention of random people, then of the governments of the world. They began to dream big. Why stop at Nisreen? What about the thousands of other people unjustly imprisoned, or the countless other atrocities happening every day? Also, everyone knew that it wasn't just the Syrian government's fault. Why stop at pressure on Syria? How about some advocacy for Russia to stop supporting the regime's abuse of power? How about stopping the flow of arms from the Gulf and the U.S. that went to violent militias?

Now that the door was closed to helping people meet their most urgent immediate needs, Samir and Maha began to consider whether they might help to change the entire system that had created those needs in the first place. As they talked, Maha felt a growing sense of excitement, something she had not felt in a long time.

The next morning, Samir headed off to church to meet with the head pastor, as he did most mornings. The pastor had asked him to take on more responsibility now that he was going to be in Lebanon for the foreseeable future. The church had received a large grant to help Syrian refugees living near their facility in one of Beirut's poorest neighborhoods. They had opened a little school and were distributing food, mattresses and blankets. Every month, the church put aside a small amount of the grant to cover overhead expenses, and this was beginning to add up. Plans were in motion to build a larger space for worship and to do some much-needed repairs on the rest of the building, and Samir was asked to manage that process. He would also be preaching every Sunday next month while the head pastor traveled to America to raise funds in churches there.

His life went on almost as if two months' imprisonment had not separated his past life from his new. His role was changed, but the meaning of his life was not. He was still a pastor, he was still involved in the ministry of the church, and he still kept busy.

Maha, on the other hand, had no idea how to start arranging her life now that half her family was dead and the other half inaccessible, now that she could no longer find meaning in helping people who had lost more than she had, and now that she was meant to be slowing down and focusing on preparing her home to receive a new family member. She had not really done anything at all during Samir's absence, but now that she wasn't worried about that ordeal anymore, she found that she was fairly bored.

So no sooner had Samir walked to the end of the street and hailed his cab, than Maha got to work.

First, she did as Samir had said. She uploaded her photo of Nisreen, the one that Samir had obtained from the source he would not acknowledge, and captioned it with a link to The Mockingbird and an appeal in English to share. She shared it to Leila's and Roxy's pages, then re-posted it in Arabic and re-shared. Then she started tagging her friends. Every last one of her friends got tagged. Then she sent personal notes to the dozen or so friends she had who lived in Europe or America, asking them to share.

Share, share, share. Was sharing all it took to make some noise? She would soon find out.

A minute later, her Viber began to ring. She picked up her phone and was greeted by Leila's icon. All of a sudden, she remembered that this week was *Eid*, the holiday to mark the end of Ramadan and she had not sent her friend holiday greetings.

So Maha pressed the green button and immediately gave the traditional holiday greeting: "*Kul al-am wa anti bikheir.* Happy Holiday, dear friend!"

Leila replied the standard response: "*Wa anti bikheir.*"

"Have you had a good holiday?" Maha asked.

"It's nothing special. The boys miss their father. The whole family misses having enough money to cook the way we used to. We miss my brothers. It's not like anyone has a job anyway, so no one got vacation days. My Mama is trying to make it special. I think she has become too religious since all this began. But poor Mama, none of the rest of us are very excited."

"Well, God watch over you anyway and bless you."

"I'm just glad Ramadan is over. It was just exhausting this month. Too hot to be fasting all day. And no big parties in the evenings like we have in Kuwait to break up the monotony. Hassoun was going to come out, but he was on call. He'll come in a few weeks."

In response, Maha just sighed.

Leila continued, "Look at me, rambling! That's not why I called. I just saw your Facebook. Thanks for doing that."

Maha perked up again, replying, "Dear, we are only just getting started. We have plans, I mean, plans." She could hardly contain herself.

"Tell me."

"Last night I had a long chat with Samir. There is so much we can do, and what we don't know how to do, we'll find someone who can help us. We live in the age of the popular citizen, so what are we standing around doing nothing for? Maybe we can even end the war."

"What in the world are you talking about?"

"We'll start with your friend, of course. We'll start mobilizing for her release. But once she's free, we can push push push."

"I am so confused."

Maha started laughing. "Me too. I have absolutely no clue what I'm doing. But I'm going to do it. And you're going to do it with me."

"Do what?"

"Campaign. First for the freedom of a leading Syrian blogger, a voice for truth and justice. Then for the freedom of all political prisoners. Then for outside governments to stop making things worse by weaponizing our country."

"That sounds like a little bit more than something just you and I can do," mused Leila.

"And Roxy. I'm sure Roxy will be on board."

"Three of us? Change the world?"

"Exactly. Why not?"

Maha could sense Leila rolling her eyes on the other side of the line.

But she kept going. "Samir and I were talking last night, and here's the thing. To get Nisreen released, we are going to need to get the attention of some people in very high places. We are going to have to go seriously global. And we need to fight for your friend, right?"

"Definitely. I've already shared--"

Maha cut Leila off. "So once we've made the connections and got the attention of the people who will pressure the – them – to set her free, then we'll use those connections to start fighting for other things." She could really not contain the excitement in her voice.

Leila broke in, though. "Maha, stop. Just stop there. Can we just focus on Nisreen for now? I've got my family to worry about, and there's too much going on to start changing the entire world right now. But for Nisreen, I'll do anything. So can you just tell me what to do about that?"

"Alright. But mark my words. We will do so much, so soon. This is the first time I've felt excited in months, at least, maybe years. Since the war started, maybe."

"Good, I'm glad. Keep me posted. What should I do about Nisreen?"

"Share. Share share share, on Facebook, and do you have Twitter?"

"No."

"That's ok. Facebook then. Join pages and groups and share there too. Then email your friends. Email everyone that you know and ask them to share. Focus on your Western friends, the Americans, the Brits, and Europeans."

"What do I write them?"

"Not much. Just say that she has been arrested and she wrote the blog and she's a good person and ask them to share share share."

"All this sharing is really going to do something?"

"It's a start, anyway."

Leila hung up her Viber and stared at her phone. Maha was unnaturally excited, to say the least. How could one person be so excited about sharing things on Facebook?

But if sharing was what would get Nisreen out, then share she would. She tagged and shared and messaged everyone she knew. She even texted a few of her friends who had previously lived in Kuwait but had now returned to their home countries with the link to The Mockingbird and the request for sharing.

Half an hour later, she could think of no more sharing to do. She wondered if Maha had come up with more to do than just this, but all that enthusiasm was not something Leila wanted to face again so soon.

She got up from her little blue stoop and walked to the railing. The big curtain surrounding the veranda was flapping in the breeze, and she held it out with her arm so she could peer down to the street.

She knew it was time to get out of here. The boys looked happy enough in their football game on the street, but after Saleh's story, she worried about them every moment that they were not within earshot, and every day somehow felt heavier than the day before. The excitement of the big move was fading, the flat was mostly clean and reasonably livable, the UN registration had come through and food vouchers scheduled. School registration was going to happen in a few hours.

Leila still hadn't decided if she should register Hammoudi and Saleh for school in Jordan. Hassoun wanted his family to be together again back in Kuwait, she knew. But somehow, Leila couldn't quite fathom the idea of leaving. It just seemed like an utterly idealistic and unrealistic proposition.

Last night, when Hassoun had called, he had spoken with each of his sons for a few minutes. Leila could tell, as she watched one side of the conversation, that the boys missed their daddy but didn't want to leave their cousins.

Hassoun was coming for his holiday in a few weeks. They would talk about it then.

Huda decided it was time to stop resisting, even though the more she thought about it, the more she was convinced that it would be a bad idea to accept Roxy's friend request. Some people were just looking for a way to get her, and Huda didn't know enough about Roxy's life to be sure if it was safe. It was really just too risky.

In fact, just a couple of days ago at lunch, Marwan, who sat at the desk across from her, had told a story of someone who was arrested for something equally innocuous. His friend had retweeted a cute video of someone's baby doing something adorable. The retweet may not have been a problem, but the commentary of "Check out the cutest baby in the world, son of one of my favorite people," was.

Now Marwan was one of those figures who liked to make an impression. He was tall and loud and often walked into the office either with a crude joke on the tip of his tongue or with a big box of chocolates or dates to share. So he might have been exaggerating. But what he said was that that the father of the cute baby turned out to be a well-known member of the Syrian National Council based in Turkey. The tragedy, according to Marwan, was that his friend, the one who retweeted the post, had never met this guy and had no idea who he was.

So Huda asked Marwan why this guy had said that the man was one of his favorite people in the world? He deserved to be arrested for his stupidity because no idiot living in Latakia tweets his admiration for a rebel.

No, Marwan insisted. The man had two Twitter accounts, one for his politics and one for his family. Marwan's friend didn't know anything about the man, just that his tweets were hilarious.

The story sounded like gossip, a rumor conjured up and passed from lunch table to coffee shop to family dinners, throughout regime strongholds. Some secret police member had probably told a less shocking version of the story and hoped that guys like Marwan would make it sound worse than it was. The thought of getting arrested for complimenting someone on Twitter who posted cute baby photos was a bit too much. Sure, mistaken identity and all that, but the prisons were full as it was and the secret police had no time to be tracking down people for such ridiculous offenses.

But the story had its effect. It freaked Huda out.

She shouldn't accept a friend request from an unknown element. Roxy was an old friend, but too much water had flowed under the proverbial bridge during the past decade. Huda had successfully kept her head down and weathered this war, working diligently and keeping up with her family responsibilities and doing nothing to stand out or excel or draw attention. Mediocrity had become her greatest weapon, because if anyone took interest and started trying to push her buttons, she wouldn't be able to resist the temptation.

The fact is, she hated her president, and she hated the system that kept him in his seat of power. She felt personally wronged by the system because the system didn't protect her rights as a woman. From the first day she began her university studies, she had felt pressure to do exactly what she was doing now: excel at mundanity. When she was younger, she'd had dreams. Big dreams. But the Syria she lived in had solidly squashed those dreams. When her professors had noted her ambitious spirit, rather than encourage her, they'd made her life hell and then punished her with marks well below her performance. When it came time to apply for jobs, she had refused to use family networks – of which she had few anyway –

and so had been lucky to find employment at all. Work-related decisions were constantly made over *arguile* between brothers-in-law and male cousins and their mates from schooldays. Since she didn't smoke and wasn't related to her colleagues and wasn't part of any boy's club, she had quickly learned that decisions were going to be made about her or around her or ignoring her, and never with her best interests at heart. Realizing she would not be finding affirmation at work, she had begun to volunteer at the local woman's union, but after a couple of years, she'd quit. It was impossible to get anything done. The authorities approved charity bazaars, Ramadan *iftars*, and crochet clubs, but nothing more substantial. Huda thought a union was supposed to challenge society, but apparently not.

Now, five years into her current job, she had not had a single promotion, nor any opportunity to pursue promotion. No one asked her opinion about anything, even though she had the highest closure record in the office and at least once a month seemed to save her boss from some ridiculous mistake.

In the privacy of her own bedroom, she could fume or even scream her head off. At all other times, she could fume all she wanted as long as it was only in her head. These days, the greatest investment of her intelligence was in maintaining two simultaneous conversations: a politically correct interaction with other people and a much more interesting discussion with herself. Making sure no one ever knew what she was actually thinking required a fair bit of mental investment. One little slip and it might all come out.

Of course, a Facebook friend request had nothing to do with her political views, one way or the other, but nowadays everything was connected, especially when it came to politics. Everything had something to do with her political views.

If she was honest with herself, Huda had to admit that seeing that image of her old friend may have opened a tiny crack in the dam of emotions that she had worked so hard to wall in.

It brought back a flood of memories. She had kept in touch with her university friends for a while, but they had slowly lost touch, speaking a little bit less often with each year that passed. Since the war began, she'd had no contact with her old best friend, Leila, nor with any of the other friends in Leila's band of sisters. There was no good explanation why, though Huda wondered if they wanted nothing to do with an Alawite. After all, few people did nowadays. Then again, maybe Huda had preempted their rejection by withdrawing herself; she didn't want to put them at risk. Maybe they had all become too busy, dealing with the everyday business of survival. It was also possible that they had all left Syria, and maybe even left the region. For all she knew, by now Roxy could have attempted crossing into Europe by boat and sunk. God knew it happened to enough other Syrians these days. There were a hundred and one ways in which they might have died, and if, for no other reason, Huda was glad for the friend request because now she knew that, at least as of a few months ago, Roxy was alive.

Since receiving the request, Huda's thoughts had often drifted not only to Roxy, but to Leila, Maha, and the many other girls who had lived on their floor of the University of Damascus dorms. The memories of those days were like a morsel of Swiss chocolate. Delicious and worth savoring, but certainly not sufficient. She wanted more than a morsel.

As Huda pondered why these happy memories frustrated her so, she began to realize that she was lonely. She was most spectacularly lonely. She had no friends, no kindred spirits at work, not even any nieces or nephews close enough to shower with love. She had one sister living with her, but she and her sister did not understand each other at all. They spent time together almost every day, shared meals and occasional outings around Latakia, but they never talked. They were a relationship of convenience, nothing more.

No, Huda had no one. It was just her and the running diatribe in her head. If she allowed herself to imagine seeing those girls again, just one hour catching up with them, the longing would grow and grow until it overcame her whole being.

So, two months after the request came, she gave up and threw caution to the wind. She clicked "accept".

Chapter Nineteen

"Do you want the good news or the bad news first?" Roxy said as she finished planting a kiss on each of Maha's cheeks and walked over to the sofa.

Maha followed her. "Hi, Roxy, How are you? Welcome."

Roxy set her feet on the coffee table and pulled her phone out of her purse. "How's the baby?"

"I did a scan yesterday. The doctor said everything looks good."

"Thank God for that," Roxy sighed. "So? Which news do you want?"

Maha stuttered a bit. Not entirely sure she still believed in good news, she truly dreaded bad news. "I don't know. I guess good news first," she replied, considering the possibility that the bad news would be so bad she would no longer be able to tolerate good news.

"Great," said Roxy. "Come here."

Maha moved over to where Roxy was pointing at her phone.

"Look who accepted my friend request and who is still alive and everything!" She held her phone so Maha could see.

"Huda..." Maha breathed.

"It's her!" smiled Roxy. "We chatted for a while last night. She's completely fine. Still living in Latakia, still working as a lawyer. She never got married. But she's well. She said that life is calm and safe where she is and that her family is well."

"Let me see." Maha took the phone from Roxy's hand and began to scroll through Huda's profile. It might as well have been the profile of a stranger, because nothing looked familiar and, other than the outdated profile image they had recognized a few months ago, there were no actual photos of her. There were some pictures of assorted nieces and nephews and one family photo in which Huda may have been third from the right, but it was too blurry to tell. Most of the posts were bland motivational sayings, like 'Eighty percent of success is showing up' or 'Beauty is not in the face; beauty is a light in the heart.' There were also some cute photos and videos of cats and dogs and babies doing heartwarming things. It was thoroughly impersonal.

"Are there no photos of her?" Maha asked.

"None that I could find," replied Roxy. "But let me see, maybe she's online, and we can chat."

She wasn't, but Roxy sent her a message asking if she could talk and giving Maha's Skype.

Maha turned to Roxy, then, and said, "I guess it's time for the bad news. Or do you want some tea first?"

"Nah, might as well get it out of the way." Roxy sat up and turned to face Maha.

"What is it?" Maha asked, feeling her friend's entire mood transform.

"Our house was bombed this morning."

"Bombed?" Maha asked dumbly.

"Yup."

"How bad?"

"I don't know. I haven't been able to talk to my husband yet."

"But do you know if he's ok? Is he..."

"He's in the hospital. That's all I know."

"Who did you talk to?"

"My mother. My parents heard there was bombing in our area so made some calls. They heard about it, and I guess they are the ones who got an ambulance to go out there."

"That's amazing, that an ambulance could get to the village."

"Things are different in Sweida. Everyone is determined to try as best they can to act like nothing has changed. So the hospitals stay open, and there are still ambulances."

"But they were willing to go out to a village that had just been bombed?" Maha asked.

"I don't know; that's what my mother said."

"I'm glad they could go. At least, he's still alive."

Roxy sniffled ever so slightly and put a finger up to her eye; Maha turned away out of respect until her friend could regain her composure. It didn't take more than a few seconds before Roxy continued. "My father was going to the hospital to be with him. As you know, almost everyone in our village left. It hasn't been safe for a while. His family is all gone. My parents live in Sweida city that has stayed mostly calm. At least, they can be with him."

Maha lay a hand awkwardly on Roxy's arm. "We will pray for him," she said softly, all she could think of to say.

"Thanks," Roxy forced out, laughing but clearly not amused.

So Maha stood to go to the kitchen, asking, "Flower tea, black tea or coffee?"

"Whatever you're drinking."

"I can't have caffeine, remember? Don't worry, it's easy to make two. I have teabags."

"Flower tea is really fine."

Maha left Roxy in the living room and went to the kitchen. She found an open package of biscuits bordering on stale and decided her friend wouldn't mind. She placed those, along with some apricots she had picked up at the market the day before, on a tray. When the water boiled, she dropped the dried flower mixture into the pot, put it and two little cups on the tray along with a little bowl of sugar, and walked back to where Roxy was texting.

"Any news?" Maha asked even though she had been gone all of five minutes.

"There is," Roxy uttered slowly.

"Oh no," groaned Maha. "What?"

"My father just got to the hospital and spoke to the doctor, then he called my mom. She says that my husband is alive and stable. He's awake even."

"That sounds hopeful!"

"But he's been paralyzed. The doctors don't think he will be able to walk anymore."

"Oh, darling! No!" Maha let her jaw drop and sat dumbly staring at her friend, wanting to comfort her, but unsure of where to begin.

"Our house is ruined, too. The bombing even got most of our olive trees."

"I remember you telling me about those olive trees. Your husband loved them. He must be devastated."

"He must be. I need to talk to him," said Roxy. "Do you mind if I try to call?"

"Of course not."

So Roxy stood up and went out to the veranda. She paced back and forth holding the phone up to her ear. Maha could see her fiddling with the phone then put it back up to her ear again, then again. After a few tries, she walked back in. "I can't get through."

"Maybe he had to leave his phone behind. Did you try your dad?"

"Yes. His phone is off too."

"Try again later," suggested Maha. There was always some reason the phone lines were touch and go when calling Syria.

"Right," replied Roxy, who sat down and happily helped herself to some tea.

Maha had been looking forward to Roxy's visit this afternoon because she wanted to start planning their advocacy campaign. But her friend was clearly not going to be interested now. So as they sipped their tea, they chatted about other things.

Not much time had passed when Maha's computer, which sat abandoned in the hallway, dinged. It was the ding of a Skype contact request.

Maha looked at the computer, then at Roxy. Roxy looked back at Maha, then at the computer then at Maha again.

"Go check!" Roxy instructed.

So Maha stood up and walked over to the computer, which sat on the floor next to a power outlet. She unplugged it and carried it over to the sofa as she tapped on the mousepad to bring the screen back to life.

She sat next to Roxy and placed the computer on her lap at an angle so both women could see the screen. They sat studying the screen as if they were waiting for their final scores to be released from their university entrance exam.

When finally they were able to view Skype, Roxy let out a little yelp. "Call her! Call her!" she screeched like a little girl.

So Maha accepted the contact request and clicked the green button.

Predictably, after a few rings, someone answered, but the voice on the other end was completely unintelligible.

"*Aloh*? *Aloh*?" Roxy said, and repeated it every few seconds.

Maha randomly scrolled the mouse around the screen, as if that might somehow reveal or, better, resolve a connectivity problem.

After a minute or so, the call dropped.

"What do we do?" asked Roxy.

Maha replied with a thoughtful sigh. "We could–" she began.

But Skype was already ringing again. Maha quickly clicked the green button.

"*Aloh*?" came a woman's voice, loud and clear, through the airwaves.

Roxy stuck her head in front of the computer screen and nearly shouted, "Huda? Is that you?"

"Roxy? Is that you?"

"It is!" Roxy was almost shaking as she started speaking quickly. "I'm here with Maha in her house. This is Maha's computer. We're in Beirut. I can't believe it's really you! Say hi, Maha."

So Maha did. "It is so wonderful to hear your voice, darling. We have been wondering about you so much."

"I was shocked when I got Roxy's friend request. It has been so long. Another life."

"Another life, indeed," mused Maha.

"So tell us everything," Roxy then said. "Where are you? What are you doing? Are you married? Children?"

Huda laughed. "I had forgotten how much energy a person could have. I missed you Roxy, more than I knew."

"And us you. You have no idea how much we have been talking about you and wondering where you are and what you're doing and everything. So talk!"

"Well," began Huda. "Where do I start? There's not really anything to tell, actually."

"Are you married?" Maha suggested.

"No, nothing like that. I'm married to work, I guess. Still living with my sister."

"Why not?" asked Roxy. "What kind of idiot men have not yet stolen your heart? Or is there someone? Are you dating, engaged?"

"Sorry, girls. There's no news at all from me on that front. Nothing interesting to tell. I'm still single and have always been single. There are no interesting men here, and even if there were, I don't know... it has just never happened and probably never will."

"Don't say that," protested Maha. "You never know."

"True, but you do. You know what I mean? So, what else?"

"Just tell us everything," suggested Roxy. Start with five years ago and tell us everything that has happened.

"You are so sweet. But really there's nothing to tell. I graduated, and then I moved home, and I got an internship in my city."

Roxy and Maha looked at each other. Both had noticed that Huda had not used any names yet.

"The internship went fine. Nothing really interesting, I guess. Men were pigs just like always. But I survived, and they offered me a job. So now I'm a lawyer doing tax stuff. I work all day, then I come home and watch TV with my sister, and that's my life. My family is all fine. Most of them are still in the village, it's just my sister and me in the city, but I see them most weekends. It's a good life."

Then Roxy ventured, "Are you safe?"

After a heavy pause, Huda said, slowly, "Perfectly. Here life is fine, and we're all well."

"We worry about you," commented Maha. "We already did when we didn't know where you are. But now we will still, maybe even more."

"Don't. I'm fine, really," Huda said in a flat voice. Then, "But tell me about you. I mean, you know, what you can."

Maha whispered in Roxy's ear to be careful. Roxy nodded and rolled her eyes.

Maha then said, "You go first, Roxy."

So Roxy told Huda that she was married, happily so, and had been for almost five years already, which meant she had married shortly after they had all last seen each other. She had two kids, and she lived with her mother in law about an hour away. Then she stopped.

When it was Maha's turn, all she offered was that she married the man whom Huda had met, if she remembered, when they were students. She had just started seeing Samir when Huda moved back home. They had moved to Beirut for him to continue his studies and then stayed. Then she told Huda that she was expecting her first child, and received the compulsory enthusiastic congratulations.

Then they told Huda the unlikely story of their reunion at the shop downstairs. "It was all because of a haircut!" Roxy exclaimed. "People tell me not to waste my time or money, but look what I got because I did. I have my friends again. I have missed you all so much."

Then Huda asked, "And what about Leila?"

"Leila..." began Maha, unsure of what to say. Roxy looked at her, waiting for Maha to explain, so she began to pick her words. "She's fine. She is still living in the Gulf. You knew her husband, right?"

"I never met him," replied Huda. "But I did know she got married to someone from near her village, and that he's a doctor."

"None of us have met him, I guess," said Maha. "But he sounds like a really kind man and a perfect match for her. So he has worked for years as a doctor in the Gulf, and that's where they live. They have two children. I talk to her often, and she recently traveled to spend some time with her family, I guess."

"Please give her my love," Huda said.

"Of course. She'll be so jealous that we spoke with you. Do you want her number?"

"Not now. But maybe that would be nice later."

There was little more to say, it seemed, so after a fair degree of pleasantries and kind words, they hung up.

Maha turned to Roxy. "She's alive! And she's well! And she sounds miserable."

"Yeah... it was wonderful to talk to her again. But wow, that was awkward."

"Can you even imagine what life is like where she is? She's in Latakia, right?"

"That's what I understood," agreed Roxy.

"I was nervous to say anything at all!"

"She was, too, I think."

"But still, thanks for getting in touch with her. It is good just to know she's alive. It's too bad she sounded so lonely."

"So very lonely. Poor girl. I wish she could come visit."

Huda closed the Skype on her phone and put it down on the bed where she sat. She was struggling to keep the tears in. But she was alone in the room, and her sister was out running errands, so she lay back on her pillow and allowed a few stray drops to roll down her cheeks.

She should be happy for being reunited with her old friends; it was wonderful to hear their voices. So why did it hurt so bad? Why did it feel like, quite literally, her heart was breaking? No, not breaking, being squeezed tight, leaving no space for it to beat.

Why was it so hard for her to breathe?

Why did she want to scream at the top of her lungs, and why did only a few tears come down?

People she cared about were well. They were alive, and they were safe. They were married with families, with a future and dreams. Huda did feel happy for them, she really did.

No, she told herself, she was not jealous. That wasn't it. That wasn't the reason a reunion with her friends felt like such a let-down. It had to be something else.

If the flat weren't so small and the walls so thin, she would have screamed. And thrown something at the wall. In the films, people punched their pillows, but Huda couldn't bring herself to try that. She just felt the frustration mounting.

Why?

Why had Huda never fallen in love or been wooed by a man? A few had tried, but halfheartedly at best, and she'd done nothing to encourage them.

Why did she not progress in her career? Why did she stay in a job where she got no credit for her work and allow herself to be pushed around?

Why did she still live with her sister in Latakia, a city where every day she had to lie?

Maha and Roxy, and even Leila, by all accounts, were living the dream. But they had made their dream. They had moved to a new country; they had married the men of their choosing. They were caring for their loved ones.

And there was more. Huda could hear it in their voices. She knew they had chosen their words carefully for her sake, and perhaps for the sake of their own families back in Syria. But their voices were filled with passion and purpose. They cared about more than just husbands and babies and the safety of their parents. If nothing else, they apparently were looking out for each other.

Huda felt so lonely at that moment. She had moved home to Latakia after university in part to help support her family, but circumstances had changed. She did still set aside a bit of her monthly salary for her mother, but it was a gesture of respect, not a response to need. Her father had passed away two years ago, and her mother had moved in with her brother and his family. They were renting out the other village home to refugees from other parts of Syria, and rent income was fairly good these days.

She didn't have to stay, but she did.

If she was jealous of her old friends, it was not because of what they had that she didn't have. It was because they knew something she didn't. They knew how to live. They knew how to reach out and love and take initiative.

Ten years ago, a bright and cheery school student, Huda would have scoffed if anyone had told her that she would go to university and graduate, but then, of all her friends turn out to be the least ambitious of them all.

But here she was. Now she did punch the pillow. It was too soft, so she tried the mattress. She punched it with her right arm, then her left, then her right a few more times. It helped a little.

What the heck had happened to her? How had she let life run away with her?

Syria was at war. Everything was on pause. This was no time to be planning for the future. These were the excuses and truisms that floated around Latakia's smoke-filled coffeeshops and *arguile*-scented courtyards these days.

All of Alawite Syria, all of Regime-loyal Syria, was lying in the shadows, nursing their wounds and waiting, hoping that things would Just Go Back To How They Were Before.

The choice to wait and hope and hide was, of course, because they were scared that they might lose – though no one would ever admit it. And because they could not imagine a future that was better than the past.

What was Huda's excuse? She wasn't under the illusion that no future could be better than the past. Or at least, she hoped as much, because the past pretty soundly sucked. And the only reason she was a bit concerned the regime might lose was because the victors would not likely have mercy on a girl raised a stone's throw away from Bashar al-Assad. But still, she did not imagine their justice would be any worse than her own community's mercy.

Huda's thoughts continued down this path until she could think of absolutely no justification for the life she was living.

She needed to leave Latakia. Maybe leave Syria. Or stay and become an informant for the revolution. Or join the fighting. Or stand up to her boss and create some shockwaves. Or something.

Her friends had moved on. She had stood still. Well, no longer.

But a tiny voice of reason told her to sleep on it before she did anything radical. And, well, she was quite tired. She went into the bathroom and brushed her teeth and washed her face and readied her bag for work the next morning and did all the other steps in her daily nighttime routine. Then she turned off the light and crawled into bed.

As was often true on a weeknight, Huda was fast asleep by the time her sister got home.

During the next month, the campaign came along nicely. Leila had made a few contacts with American and British doctors who promised to call their embassies in Kuwait and their elected representatives back home.

Nisreen's photo and name and blog address had been shared to more than 10,000 people and counting. They'd created a Facebook page for people to like, called 'Free the Mockingbird' and Twitter hashtag #FreeMockingbird was gaining some traction.

Maha was getting ready to schedule some meetings. She had friends who knew people at the French, Italian, Spanish and Venezuelan embassies and had also met someone who had a friend who worked for a major UK-based advocacy human rights organization. She found fulfillment in chasing these people down, knocking on their doors, usually by phone or email but in person when necessary, and presenting a simple, clear request to them.

She found that activism came naturally to her.

Unfortunately, though, she was on her own from here on out. Roxy had just phoned to say she was going home.

"Maha, *habiby*, I need to go care for my husband. He is paralyzed now, and he isn't well enough to travel. He needs me. And my parents tell me that Sweida city is safe, anyway. He sent us away for our safety, but it's time to go back."

"I understand," said Maha, reluctantly, feeling the dread overtake her as she imagined the rest of her pregnancy without a friend by her side.

"I'm sorry I can't help with your campaign. I will pray for Leila's friend's safe release."

"Thank you." What else could she say?

"Take good care of yourself. Eat well, and sleep enough. Don't overstretch yourself. Tell Samir that I said to take good care of you."

"I will, dear. I'm going to miss you."

"Me too. So much."

"What about your kids and your mother-in-law? Will they stay here or go back with you?"

"We are all returning. My mother-in-law wants to be near her son, and there's no life for the kids here. Sahar is due to start school next year. It was probably not going to happen in Lebanon, but the schools in Sweida are still open. Syria is her best chance now."

"Take good care of them. Give each a big kiss from me."

"I will."

"I love you, Roxy."

"I love you, Maha."

After hanging up, Maha had a sense that this was an ending. Would Roxy and her little family survive? When the dust settled on this conflict, would they still be allowed to be on the same side of whatever new borders may be drawn? She feared that this little rekindling of their friendship was like a blossom of a flower in an Indian summer: a beautiful explosion of color before death set in to stay.

Third Trimester

Chapter Twenty

Leila was beginning to wonder if there was a point to any of it now. Maha had ambitiously taken over the free Nisreen project, leaving Leila with little to do but sit and fret. Maha kept talking about calling contacts at embassies and humanitarian offices and human rights agencies. But those words hardly made sense to Leila: she wouldn't even know where to start. She didn't have any international friends in Jordan, and her international friends in Kuwait were all doctors. The very thought of trying to find a friend who knew someone who knew someone who was somehow connected to people of power baffled her. The thought of actually using that friendship to get a meeting of some sort, somewhere, saying something...it left her brain in a tizzy and made her want to boil a pot of tea. Or even better, take a nap.

Hassoun was coming tomorrow, and she knew she should be getting ready. She should do her hair and go shopping to buy his favorite foods to bring to his cousin's house, where they would stay with their boys during his visit. It was a bit unthinkable to imagine that Hassoun would stay with Leila's family in their substandard flat in an area little better than a slum. Not when he had relatives in the swanky neighborhood just down the street.

She knew she should be excited, and doing those little things and saying those intriguing things that would build up her husband's sons' sense of anticipation. Things like "I wonder what Baba will bring us from Kuwait!" Or "Won't it be great to take your father to that ice cream place that we discovered last week?"

Instead, she let the boys keep playing on their gameboys - the cousins had just started school this week, but Leila was waiting for Hassoun to arrive to decide whether Hammoudi and

Saleh would return to school in Kuwait or whether they should join their cousins in a Jordanian school, stubbornly insisting to herself that she'd have no trouble finding an available space for them to start a few weeks late in Jordan's already overcrowded schools.

Leila curled up on a mattress in the back room of the flat and took a nap. A four-hour nap.

She had been sleeping a lot lately. With half a dozen aunts and cousins and grandma sharing the parenting load, Leila had fallen into the teenager's trap. She was hooked on the soap operas that started at 10 pm and continued until the wee hours of the morning. Then, most nights, she watched a cheesy romantic comedy before finally drifting off to sleep shortly before the sun would make its appearance. She'd emerge at noon and eat the food given to her by her mother, then lounge around again until sleep took over her afternoon. When evening came, she checked Facebook, re-shared the Nisreen story, maybe texted Maha or some of her old friends in Kuwait, and similarly whiled away the time until the soap operas came on again. The boys got a few hugs in here or there but were mostly left to the natural waves of family life. After the incident with Muhammad a few months ago, Leila had intended to be more careful and set more clear boundaries, but somehow it seemed that life took over.

With this routine, the thought of engaging an activism campaign was utterly unthinkable. Even the thought of helping her sister-in-law make dinner was hard to imagine.

When Leila woke up from her nap, filled with strange dreams involving photos of bloggers on Facebook and lots of desert sand and vague memories of the village home, it was all she could do to get herself dressed in outdoor clothes.

But Hassoun was coming tomorrow, and she needed to get her act together.

When was the last time she had set foot outside the flat?

She couldn't remember, but it must have been a while because her tailored overcoat was near the bottom of a suitcase, too rumpled to wear without ironing. So she hung it up and grabbed her sister's clothes instead of going to the effort of finding something suitable to wear among her own things.

Pulling a scarf sloppily over her head, she walked out to the veranda and lifted the curtain so she could peer down at the street. "Hammoudi!" she shouted. "Hammoudi, *ya Mama*!"

Her oldest looked up from where he was sitting on a concrete stump sharing a bag of chips with a neighbor boy. Chips? Who let him eat those?

"Hammoudi, bring your brother and get ready to go out. We need to prepare for your father's arrival tomorrow."

Slowly, with the reluctance of a pre-adolescent kid, though he was barely even school age at this point, Hammoudi stood up and said, "*Yallah*," which Leila understood to mean that he was on his way.

She walked back in and looked at her suitcases piled up in a corner. She should go through and find nice clothes for the boys to wear tomorrow. She should go through and figure out what it would take to look nice herself, as a good wife would, when her husband arrived tomorrow.

That was going to be a lot of work; food shopping would be easier.

So, wearing whatever they were wearing - which was much dirtier than Leila had ever allowed them to dress before - the boys followed their mother out the door and to the store.

When they got home, Leila sent them off to the shower while she began the onerous task of getting herself organized.

Hassoun's flight was due to land at 12 noon, which meant he wouldn't be at his cousin's house until 1 pm at the earliest, though possibly a fair bit later. But if he arrived before Leila, she could not bear to imagine the humiliation she would feel.

So she managed to pull herself out of bed by 10. She had planned on going down to the hairdressers, but now she really wasn't into that idea. Breakfast seemed like a much more urgent necessity now. Hassoun wouldn't mind - surely the important thing was that he see her, not her hair. Or so she rationalized.

She did manage to get her own clothes looking reasonably neat and tidy, and Nuha helped her brush out her hair, then tie it up in a decently attractive do. Then she got the boys into clothes that befitted sons of a Kuwait doctor rather than refugee boys from a village. They enjoyed breakfast with the family, possibly the last depending on what was to be decided in the coming days.

By noon, Leila and the boys were in a taxi headed to the cousin's house.

Madame Muna met them warmly, like a long-lost relative should. The snobbery of past conversations was gone, and entering the spacious flat with Italian furniture that was kept clean by a Sri Lankan maid, was like returning to Kuwait. Leila felt like she'd walked through a magical door, from the world of refugees to the world of the living, and well-to-do living at that. It was hard to believe that the taxi ride took less than 10 minutes. And now Leila wished she had not only done her hair but had her clothes dry cleaned. Or even better, bought a new outfit. As clean and tidy as her sisters kept their little flat, dirt off the street had a way of wafting in. And even more than dirt, the smells! Anything that had spent months in that flat did not belong in this shiny domain.

But Leila would have to make do. She told herself to remember who she was, who she had been a few short months ago. She reminded herself of her past job accomplishments and who her friends were in Kuwait. She knew how to operate in this world; she just had to switch modes. Like switching from Arabic to English, she had to switch from refugee to professional.

Muna ushered Leila and the boys into the salon and called for tea for herself and Leila, and juice for the boys. A few minutes later, the Sri Lankan woman brought the drinks along with biscuits. The boys gulped their juice down and asked if they could go to the playroom that had been their bedroom on the previous visit and would be so again tonight. Madame Muna nodded graciously, and the boys ran off.

The maid in the kitchen was cooking up something that smelled wonderful. When Muna noticed Leila's eyes and nose gravitating to the source of the smell, she announced that they were making mansaf, the Jordanian national dish. The most appropriate fare for receiving a beloved relative back from the Gulf, Leila had only tried mansaf once before, at a birthday party hosted by one of Hassoun's Jordanian colleagues. It was an extravagant expression of bounty with roots in the nomadic

Bedouin tribes of the Arabic desert. Mounds of lamb piled on rice over a bed of traditional flatbread, covered with a sauce made from camel's yogurt, it was served on massive round trays. Traditionally, friends and family would all sit around the tray and reach in to grab bites with their fingers. Communal eating at its best. And the lamb, which had been boiled in the yogurt, was as tender as could be. Leila's mouth began to water. Meat was a luxury her family could rarely afford anymore.

Leila and Muna made polite conversation, avoiding the topic of Leila's family. Instead, Muna told Leila about her recent shopping trip to Europe and about the newest hip cafés in Amman. Leila shared about some of the interesting shops and restaurants that she had discovered in Kuwait. They compared the products readily available in Jordan's supermarkets with those in Kuwait.

It was just after 1 pm when Leila's phone dinged a text message. It was from Hassoun: Landed and through security. Just waiting for my bags and then I will be on my way. I can't wait to see you!

She zapped off a reply: *Alhamdulillah a-Salameh*! Praise God you arrived safely! We are waiting.

As Leila was typing, Muna took her leave with the pretense of preparing more tea. Leila could hardly imagine what she and her hostess could possibly come up with to discuss for another full hour of waiting; she hoped the next pot of tea would take a long time to brew.

Alone on her oversized earth-toned armchair in the front salon, Leila felt her hands tremble just a bit. It had now been nearly two months since she had last seen her husband, and for most of that time, she had been living an existence that he could not possibly imagine. He was the world's most loving and faithful man, but she still couldn't contain a pang of fright. What if he didn't think she was beautiful anymore, or had he already begun to allow his eye to wander due to loneliness? What if he arrived irritable and rough?

There was no point pondering these things, and there was no mattress here in this luxurious house decorated for image rather than for comfort, where she could curl up and fall asleep, as had become her habit of late.

She opened her phone and scrolled through her recent WhatsApp chats.

The first name was that of Maha. Preoccupied and exhausted, Leila had completely forgotten that a message from her friend in Lebanon had come through late the previous evening. She clicked on the message to open it.

Maha: Hi, my beautiful! How are you? When does your husband arrive? Roxy is back home safely. She called yesterday. I'm going to miss her so so much.

This was news to Leila. Now that she read the message, she vaguely remembered her last Viber with Roxy a few weeks before. It had been a very short conversation, but it seemed that Roxy may have been talking about plans to leave Lebanon. Leila had made nothing of it, assuming it was just Roxy sharing a new idea. Or perhaps she had dismissed it the way she dismissed the majority of things that other people told her these days. Her own life was too weighty to start taking on the burdens of others. And either way, Leila had probably not taken any talk of moving to Syria very seriously. Who in their right mind was moving to Syria these days? But Roxy had never been one to do things because they were associated with people in their right minds.

Poor Maha. Leila still spoke regularly with her. Maha had become the sister that Leila's own sisters could never be. She was that person who was just always going to be there, and who was her equal. But, of course, Leila and Maha never saw each other. They hadn't seen each other's eyes or shared an embrace for five years, at least. Furthermore, Maha's own cousins were still in Syria and only rarely made it to Lebanon for a visit, and now Maha could not go back to visit them. Life in Lebanon was lonely for Maha, as life in Jordan was lonely for Leila. Leila had been so jealous that Roxy had re-entered Maha's life during these past few months. But with Roxy leaving, Maha would have to get used to being alone again, and Leila did not envy the way her friend must be feeling right now.

And Leila had ignored her message last night. So she quickly sent off a reply now.

Leila: Hassoun just landed in Jordan, and will be here soon. I'm at his cousin's house.

Leila: Roxy is moving back? I didn't think that she was seriously considering it. Why????????

It didn't take more than a few seconds for Maha to reply: Did she tell you about her husband?

Leila: No. Well, she mentioned something a bit. But tell me.

Maha: You know about the attack?

Leila: What attack?

Maha: Ohhhhhhhhhhhh. His house was bombed last month. He was injured.

Leila: What????????? I can't believe I missed this!

Maha: You have had a lot going on, haven't you?

Leila didn't reply. She had had much less going on than she had allowed others to think. Much sleep and little thinking had been involved. She was a terrible friend.

Maha kept going: Anyway, the house is pretty much destroyed.

Maha: The village isn't safe anymore, I guess, so I'm not sure they have seen the damage yet.

Maha: They're going to live with Roxy's family in Sweida City.

Leila: Why doesn't he come to Lebanon?

Maha: That's the other thing. He was injured. He's paralyzed now.

Leila: NOOOOOOOOOO! That's terrible! Poor Roxy.

Maha: It can't be easy. But you know her, she is talking like it doesn't matter. Going to care for him is her next big adventure.

Leila: And she's taking the kids back?

Maha: Yes. There's no life for them in Lebanon. They hated it here. Their flat was tiny, and they were having trouble finding a school with space for her daughter.

Maha: Plus, Sweida is safe. Or that's what they say.

Maha: And if her husband can't work anymore, I don't know what they would do for money. They'll live with her parents in Sweida, at least for now.

Leila: You're going to miss her, aren't you?

Maha: So much. You have no idea.

Maha: She was so good to have around, especially when Samir...you know.

Maha: And she was giving me pregnancy tips. She was being my mother.

Leila: And how is your mother?

Maha: I don't think she is very well. We aren't talking much. She has hardly even congratulated me on the baby - she's the only one who hasn't, it seems, and that's fine. I'm still learning to be excited. But I don't think she is in a place to think about things like being happy. Plus, I hear she is hardly leaving the house in Damascus, wearing black, acting like a typical widow in mourning. I wish she would come here.

Leila: You do?

Maha: Of course!

Leila: But you never seemed to get along with her.

Maha: I guess. But she's my mother, right?

Leila: True.

Maha: But back to Roxy, yes I will miss her so much. You should call her or message her or something. It's going to be hard.

Leila: I can't even imagine.

Leila: Makes me feel sad. Here I am waiting for my husband to arrive for a visit, just because. And her husband is now...wow.

Maha: We will have to keep in touch. She will need friends even when we are far away.

Just then, Madame Muna walked in with a fresh pot of tea, sage tea this time. As she was pouring out, there was a ring on the doorbell.

Leila typed in: I need to go. Everyone's arriving now.

Maha: Enjoy Hassoun's visit.

Maha: When you have some time let's talk about Nisreen and the project.

Maha: I actually have a lot of news.

Maha: I miss you.

Maha: xoxo

Leila couldn't reply because the ring at the door was Hassoun.

She heard his voice the moment the maid opened the front door, so she stood up to greet him, but the boys beat her to it.

"Baba! Baba!" screamed two little voices as they ran through the flat, all manners forgotten.

When Leila arrived in the entry hallway, she saw both boys clinging to their father's shoulders, Hassoun holding one boy in each of his arms, with a big smile on his face. Leila was relieved to realize that she had not had to work hard to prep her sons. But saddened to realize just how much they had missed their Baba, and yet she had not noticed, thinking they were perfectly happy playing in the grimy alleyway with their cousins.

Then Hassoun turned and caught Leila's eyes. To her shock, she saw a tear begin to gather in the corner of her husband's eye.

Something broke in her heart at that moment. Later she would ponder whether it was the feeling that, for the first time since she'd left the flat in Kuwait she could let down her guard, or whether it was just an overflow of love for her husband, or whether it was because she was so touched by his tenderness. But at this moment, it was as if a dam broke in her soul and her own tears poured over. She ran to her three men and joined the group hug. After a few precious moments, Hassoun let the boys down and pulled Leila into a deep embrace all her own.

Leila led Hassoun, with both boys in his arms, into the salon where she had just been sitting and where Madame Muna now waited. She stood and shook Hassoun's hand, commenting that her husband was on his way home from work and would be there shortly.

The boys soon went back to their toys, but for the grown-ups, an uncomfortable couple hours of pleasantries followed. They spoke of anything that no one in the room cared about: the weather, foods, tourism in the Gulf states, horse breeding, and embroidery. Yes, even embroidery came up when Leila complimented a piece of artwork in the room after an awkward lull. Tea helped grease the conversation, then when Hassoun's cousin arrived home, mansaf helped a great deal. Fruits and nuts and more tea were then consumed as quickly as possible without anyone admitting to the fact they would all rather be doing something else.

Hassoun's cousin stood after finishing his apple, saying he had to get back to the office to finish out business for the day. After he left, Madame Muna kindly told the young couple that she was going to run some errands herself and allow them time to catch up.

Leila felt her muscles begin to relax the moment she walked out. Finally, it was just her and Hassoun.

Finally, they could talk.

Hassoun now turned to Leila. "Wow, you are a wonder to behold. I may have forgotten just how beautiful you are."

Leila, to her shock, felt herself blushing. She looked down to her hands and pulled slightly away from her husband's arms, which were seeking to pull her in.

He kept trying. "You have no idea how I've missed you. I mean, I knew I would, but it has hurt so bad how much I have missed you."

"I've missed you, too," she murmured, still unable to bring her eyes to meet his. Then, before he could romanticize the moment any further, she began, "We have so much to discuss. I don't even know where to start. Maybe, how about if you tell me your news first. How is the hospital? How is Kuwait?"

"Certainly not the same without you."

"You've missed the boys, haven't you?"

"The boys, and you, my dear."

Leila chuckled. "I've missed you too. But tell me, how is the hospital?"

Slowly, Leila began to get a fact-based conversation moving. She could tell her husband was needing affection right now, but with the emotions of their initial reunion now past, she couldn't find it in herself to offer it, nor to receive it.

So they spoke about the recent managerial shifts at the hospital, an unending saga to which there was always an update, about which of their foreign friends were still in Kuwait and which of them were returning to their home countries, and new arrivals who had taken their place. Hassoun informed Leila of a new construction project near their building and shared about how he had trouble sleeping during the day when he worked night shifts because of the noise.

Once there seemed to be nothing left to share about their life in Kuwait or about Hassoun's job, he finally asked Leila about her family.

From their many brief phone conversations, he knew the outline of events well, but now Leila began to draw a more complete picture for him. She told him about her brothers who had still not been able to be reunited with their wives and children, about how her mother seemed to be fading with age and worry, about how their Syrian accent had become a way of ensuring a cold reception at just about any shop or government office. She then told him about the incident with her nephew and his lurid game, and how she wanted to have compassion for what her brothers' children had experienced, yet feared for the well-being of her own children.

Hassoun mostly just let her talk, asking few questions. Mostly just hmm'ing or ok'ing.

But as the stories grew more tense, Leila noticed he too became more tense. As she finished the story of the kids' game of war-and-rape, he stood up and began pacing the room.

"Why didn't you tell me this before?" he asked.

"A story like that doesn't get told over the phone, does it?" Leila pointed out.

He considered this a second, then said, "You should have come back. I can't believe you spent one more day in that house after that."

"After all, they are my family," she observed.

"They're your family, yes, but Hammoudi and Saleh are my sons."

"They are my sons, too."

"I thought they were. But what kind of a mother...no don't answer that. Just..." His voice trailed off, and he kept pacing.

Leila sat on the sofa and looked up at her husband. Somehow, this didn't seem like a good moment to introduce the question of whether she would stay in Jordan or whether to register the boys for a local school. For several moments, she watched Hassoun work his irritation out of his system while she pondered what to do next. She needed to find some way for him to understand the pull that drew her here and the need she felt for her young little family to be integrated with her extended family.

So she reminded him of their plans. "They are expecting us this evening. My mother is so excited to see you."

"Let's do it tomorrow. Tonight let's just enjoy each other, ok?"

"But Hassoun, they have been looking forward to this for so long! They want to express their gratitude to you. Plus, they're family."

"They are your family not mine. I want to spend time with my family who I haven't seen for months."

Leila could tell from his tone of voice that his mind was made up. But still, she wanted to find a way to convince him. She felt like she needed him, but she needed them as well and feared she would crack into pieces if she couldn't have both. Surely he must understand this, she thought, but could think of no words to persuade him.

So she tried imploring, "Please? We have tomorrow together just us. It will mean so much to them. And to me."

Hassoun, who was still standing, came near to Leila but didn't reach out to touch her. He just towered over her. "Leila. This doesn't make any sense to me at all. Haven't you missed me? Haven't you missed being us: you, me and the boys?"

"Of course, I have, dear."

"So it's decided. Tonight we are going out to explore Amman together. We can visit your family tomorrow."

But it wasn't tomorrow, nor the day after. A full week passed during which Leila forced herself to be the faithful and cheerful wife and mother. They went to a local fun fair, they visited shopping malls, and they did a day trip north to the famous ruins of the ancient city of Jerash. They ate at some of the same chain restaurants imported from America that they had occasionally frequented in Kuwait, like Burger King and Chili's. They enjoyed the hospitality of Hassoun's cousin and visited some of Hassoun's other extended relatives in town.

But they did not venture any closer to Jabal Hussein than the major roundabout that separated that poverty-stricken haven for migrant Jordanians and refugees, from the posh West Amman where they were staying.

Every morning and every evening, Leila called Nuha with apologies. Nuha transmitted back their mother's disappointment. But Hassoun was Leila's husband, not to mention their benefactor. There was nothing to be done.

Leila began to despair that her husband would never see her family, that she would never even find a way to suggest he allow her to stay in Jordan and register the boys in local school, and that he might even insist that she withdraw the support that paid the rent for their overpriced little two-room flat.

Sure enough, at the end of a week, Hassoun went out early in the morning when Leila was still in bed. When he returned, shortly before noon, he announced that he had changed all of their tickets to return to Kuwait next week, just in time for the boys to catch their first day of school there.

Chapter Twenty-one

Without any explanation or forewarning, Huda dropped a letter of resignation on her supervisor's desk on her way out the door Thursday afternoon, knowing he wouldn't see it until Sunday, after the weekend.

By Sunday, she hoped to be far from Latakia. She had a feeling she would not be coming back for a very long time, if at all.

From work, she went straight to the little bus depot where she caught a minibus up to her family's village. She often went home on Thursday evenings and spent Fridays with her family, but this would be her farewell, even if her family was not aware of it.

The journey took forty-five minutes, most of which was spent winding up small country roads into the hills. The city quickly thinned out, and the lush greenery of the Nusayriyah Mountains took over the landscape. Orchards and farmland alternated with the occasional village. Huda's was just one of many villages in the foothills, little more than a row of houses, each with its own courtyard and grapevines. To her, of course, it was completely distinct from any other village. She had made this trip every week for many years now, and the other villages had each come to distinguish themselves in her psyche as well. One village she remembered because of the house with a statue of a dog in the front courtyard; another because an antique pink-colored pickup truck was parked right after the last house; and yet another for its half dozen or so mansions surely built by absentee owners making their fortune in Europe or the Gulf.

But as Huda's village came into view at the end of series of switchbacks, it was like she was seeing, yet again, a very familiar face. It was not entirely unlike the feeling she had when she got off the bus and saw her mother greeting her. Huda recognized the contours and the colors of each house, the details of the walls and fences that surrounded each property. She had been inside each of these homes at some time or another; most were the residences of distant relatives or old friends from her school days. Little had changed over the decades: occasionally the owner of a house audaciously painted the façade a different color, perhaps mint green instead of gray or white instead of pale yellow. Every so often a new floor would be added onto a house, usually an indicator that the owner's son was ready to get married. But such changes were rare and few, and the entire village contained no more than a couple dozen family homes, and for Huda, there was a story behind each one. Each turn of the head brought back a new memory.

Just before her house, Huda called out "*Aindak, ya 'ami.*" As she said it, the thought came to her that in Turkey, they would likely have a different way of stopping buses. Huda had even read of countries where buses only stopped at pre-set points on their route; she wondered if Turkey was one of those countries. By Saturday evening, she would know.

But this was the time to embrace the present reality one last time, not think about tomorrow. The bus stopped right in front of her house – indeed, Huda had recognized the driver and was not surprised to see that the driver knew where to stop – and Huda's mother came out the front door. "*Ahlan*! Welcome, daughter!" She held out her arms to receive her daughter's embrace. Huda held her mother for a few seconds longer than usual, then forced herself to release because she would not be able to explain herself if she was caught behaving oddly.

Her mother led her into the house where Huda could smell food in the final stages of cooking. Within fifteen minutes, she was seated on the floor with her older brother, sister-in-law, mother and two nephews, around plates piled with stuffed cabbage and courgette, salad, olives, yogurt, and bread.

As they filled their plates, Huda's brother asked, "How is Latakia? We hear there are more migrants arriving."

Huda nodded. "You can definitely feel it. The streets look the same, but everything just feels more crowded. I don't know where they will all stay. They were setting up tents in the park for a while, but those have been taken down."

"Well, I suppose if you don't set limits, then people will just push, push, push."

"It depends, doesn't it? Where have those families gone instead?"

"You're the one who lives there," observed her brother with a half-full mouth. "Where do you think they are?"

"I honestly don't know. Like I said, you can tell there are more people in the city – longer queues at the stores, crowded buses, more people walking. But I have no idea where they are living. I just hope they are warm and able to feed themselves."

"Feed themselves?"

"Yes," nodded Huda as she scooped some yogurt onto her plate. "These migrants are fleeing here with nothing but the clothes on their backs. Most of them aren't educated and don't have any skills but farming, or herding sheep, or maybe physical labor. There are no jobs for them in Latakia - unemployment was high even before this all started."

"Why are they coming, is what I want to know. Shouldn't they be defending their country and their homes?"

"Would you stay here if this house were being bombed?" retorted Huda.

"Of course," he shot back. "It's my village, and it's my country. I can't just give it to the rebels. Just think what they would do to this place. What they would do to us Alawites."

"It's easy for you to say," she replied, before stuffing a cabbage roll into her mouth, hoping this signified the end of the conversation, during which none of the other women and none of the children had said a word. Every Thursday it was like this, and Huda had told herself this morning, as she had packed her tiny overnight bag, that this week would be different. She would not let her brother draw her into a political argument, and she would not compromise her own views. But here she was, fearing that, if she couldn't be honest with her family, she couldn't be honest with anyone, yet still frightened to think they might discover just how much she hated being an Alawite.

The meal continued in peace. After a few moments of silence, Huda's sister-in-law asked about more mundane news of Latakia, like which fruits were available in the market and how busy work was. Each of these topics could also be easily drawn into a political debate; little about Syrian life had been untouched by conflict. But Huda's sister-in-law, unlike her husband, didn't care for politics, so accepted Huda's simple answers for what they were.

The rest of the evening continued in the typical weekend routine. Huda's sister arrived from the city a few hours later.

From there on out, the entire household occupied itself with sitting, television, chomping of nuts and sunflower seeds, a bit of music played by her 12-year-old nephew who was already reaching an advanced level on the 'aoud, and only a little conversation. Huda sat close by her mother throughout the evening, alternately leaning her head on her meaty shoulders and jumping up to bring tea whenever the cups were running low. As, one by one, people turned in for the night, Huda stayed up enjoying the fresh air, the sound of crickets and the stars.

Friday dawned sunny and fresh. Huda was the first one up though she had been last to bed and then had slept nearly seven hours. She decided to go for a walk around the village. As she let herself out the gate, she tried to make as little noise as possible, happy to let the family doze so she could enjoy a few minutes alone.

She walked uphill, taking in the familiar array of flowers, bushes, trees, iron fence work, mosaicked pathways, stone walls, and other bits of beauty, both manmade and God made. The air was cool, but it felt good to walk briskly to brave off the chill. Huda found her mind surprisingly empty. She was content simply to take in the village for what it was, nothing more and nothing less, searing its beauty and calm into her memory. Though the entire world seemed to view this little pocket of Syria as a politically-charged zone, for Huda, home was home, an a-political place.

The day continued in a similar vein as the previous night. Little was said and little was thought, but much was eaten and many small gestures of affection given and received.

As was their weekly tradition, Huda said her goodbyes after dinner, at the hour when everyone else was laying down for the siesta. Her sister would return to the city early next morning, by which time Huda expected to have disappeared.

She planned on leaving no note and no evidence of her plans. She would pack a small bag, something easy to carry, containing little more than a couple of days' worth of clothing along with the paltry supply of cash that she had been able to withdraw from the bank without suspicion. Over the past month, she had managed to purchase a humble stock of jewelry, as well, with her meager savings. No one knew she owned any valuables, so they would not be missed.

Through a dummy Facebook account, she had befriended some NGO workers living in Antakya, right across the Turkish border. From Latakia, Antakya was a mere 100km away, if traveling directly were an option. But of course, it was not. Traveling there would require a detour through one of the strongholds of the Free Syrian Army, the vanguards of anti-Alawite sentiment. Huda's name did not immediately identify her as an Alawite, and she had learned a pretty good imitation of a Damascus accent when studying in the country's capital, so she had told her new anti-regime friends that she was a Damascus native who had been working in Latakia since before the crisis began, and she was ready to jump ship. Her entire family had been cut off from her, so she asked them for help. In response, they had offered to escort her to Turkey if she could make her way to Idleb. Once in Turkey, another contact she'd made on Facebook had offered her a place to stay in his house in Gaziantep, the new honorary Syrian capital of Southern Turkey.

Traveling from Latakia to Idleb would be no small endeavor, but again, Huda's new friends had given her some tips, mostly tips they had picked up from refugees arriving at Turkey's border. It would be harrowing, but she needed to be in Idleb by early afternoon on Saturday for her new friends to collect her and journey to the Turkish border before the curfew imposed by their employer, an international NGO with strict security protocols.

So when Huda arrived home, just as the sun was setting behind the mountains from which she had just come, and indeed to which she would have to return tomorrow - though of course taking a route that would divert her from passing her family's home - there was little for her to do. She packed her little bag, made herself some sandwiches, and tried to rest until dawn, when she would head out into the unknown. Tomorrow she would finally begin to learn how to be loyal to her convictions and how to live for something bigger than her own survival. She was fully aware that her own survival was far from guaranteed, and by this time tomorrow she might have been captured or dead. But she hoped that, instead, she would be seeing a new country for the first time in her life.

Again, she surprised herself in that, when her head hit the pillow, she drifted off almost immediately. She would have imagined that running away from home, quitting her job and her family, and making friends with revolutionaries would guarantee a sleepless night on the eve of this new adventure. But instead, this surprise at her drowsiness was the last thought she registered before the alarm awoke her at 5:00 Saturday morning.

After a busy afternoon phoning embassies and doing a quick Skype interview with a London-based human rights organization, Maha opened her Facebook, just to see what was what. There was only one new notification, and it was of a friend request. Curious, she immediately clicked on the little red icon, and when she saw who it was, let out a gasp. It was from one "Huda Houria", which she immediately understood to be not a real name, but rather "Huda Freedom." She clicked on the name and a smiling image of her old neighbor from her dorm days at the University of Damascus stared back at her.

She scrolled down the page and saw a newsfeed very different from the one Roxy had shown her just last month. This one was full of revolutionary slogans and pictures of 'martyrs' fighting for the liberation of Syria. It also had a fair bit of communist and atheist rhetoric peppered throughout. Gone were the cute cats and bunnies and babies. This was clearly the same Huda, but some Mr. Hyde iteration to the Dr. Jekyll Roxy had friended previously.

Maha was trying hard not to take sides in the conflict. She had not friended the cute little bunny Huda because she didn't want to bring risk to her old friend by inviting her to associate with the wife of a recently released political prisoner. And now, it was she who was unsure whether she should accept the request from this new Che Guevara version of Huda. Maha was trying to build a reputation for herself as an activist for justice, not an activist for the Syrian Nationalist Party - though of course few people imagined a Syrian activist with friends in the West could be anything else.

But Maha reasoned that some of her other Facebook friends posted the occasional anti-regime cartoon or revolutionary slogan, and she could always unfriend Huda later if need be. This wouldn't threaten Maha's life, just perhaps her reputation.

She clicked "accept" and was glad she did, because now the Newsfeed repopulated with the private posts, and the top post said, "Safe in Turkey. Here to stand in solidarity with all Syrians fighting for freedom."

Huda was in Turkey.

Maha's first impulse was to pick up her WhatsApp. She wrote the same message to both Roxy and Leila: Got friend request from Huda. She's in Turkey. What about you?

Then Maha messaged Huda: Thanks for the add, old friend. I miss you! You're in Turkey? We should chat sometime. Call me on Viber?

Then she typed in her Viber phone number.

Just a minute later, Roxy replied: Yes. Me too! Good for her. I hope she can be happy now.

Something about this left Maha feeling a bit uncomfortable, though, so she replied: You think so? Did you read her feed?

Roxy: Reading it now.

Maha: What do you think?

Roxy: Thinking I should not accept her friend request. Roles reversed now.

Maha: Good point. I accepted.

Roxy: Yes, you should. You can. Tell her I send my love?

Maha: Of course.

Maha: But do you really think this is good?

Maha: I mean, this is so different from the Huda we spoke with before.

Roxy: Now I guess we know why she was so sad.

Maha: Good point.

Maha: But Turkey. Can you believe it? That's a big move.

Then, apparently Roxy's Internet died, as so often happened in Syria these days, especially towns easily forgotten by all sides in the conflict like Sweida. Maha's last message stayed with just one check, indicating Roxy hadn't received it, and her profile showed her offline.

So Maha went back to reading through Huda's profile and noting the groups that she had joined. It looked like Huda had been busily networking with the dreamers living in Southern Turkey, the artists and intellectuals who continued to hold out hope that a better Syria was just around the corner. Maha was glad that they existed, and in fact, she had many friends of a similar ilk in Lebanon. She also knew that most of her contacts at the Western embassies and NGOs saw her as a Syrian secularist dreamer as well, and perhaps in some ways she was. Her pastor husband could hardly be mistaken with those chain-smoking arak-drinking creators of gruesome or soft porn films, but Maha herself had tended to avoid church since the day of Samir's arrest. Samir had graciously not insisted, perhaps thinking it was healthier for the baby if Maha stayed home and rested on Sunday mornings though for Maha it had nothing to do with her pregnancy and everything to do with her suspicions that her country needed a medicine much stronger than religion.

Huda had become one of those idealist revolutionaries. Interesting.

As Maha mulled over these things, her Viber began to ring. It was an unknown number, but with at Turkish country code. Her heart skipped a beat.

"Huda?"

"Maha, dear! How are you?"

"How are you? You're in Turkey?"

"Yes. I just arrived two days ago, Saturday night."

"Wow." Maha found she had no words. So she repeated, "Wow."

"Wow is right. But I have you to thank, you and Roxy. I want you to know that."

Maha felt her grip loosen on the phone when she heard those words. "What?"

"Thank you. I wouldn't be here if it weren't for you."

"How so?" Maha began to wonder if she hadn't already become a little more political than she meant to.

"Well, when we spoke, I was so inspired. You and Roxy - and Leila from what you said - you're doing important, meaningful things. You have taken big steps because of what you believe is right. I never did that before."

"No?" Maha felt like some more detailed response was needed, but couldn't think of the words.

"Ever since university, every decision I ever made was for survival. Keep my job, make my home livable, keep the peace with my family. But I hated that. I never wanted any of that, and when the conflict started, honestly, I was on the wrong side, in the wrong city. I should have joined the resistance from the beginning, but I never even thought of it. I just got mad at what we were doing, and the fact that I was a part of it simply because of my family's religion and my hometown. It never occurred to me that I had a choice until I spoke with you."

"But none of us left our families. Or, did your family come with you? Are they alright?"

"Sadly, no." But Huda didn't sound very sad. "They would never understand. I had to leave them behind."

"That must have been hard," Maha sympathized.

"Not really. I mean, it was kind of hard to leave, and I know I'm going to miss them – especially my mother – so much. But you can't believe how thrilled I am. I honestly feel like I've been let out of jail, or like a bird released from a cage. It's an amazing feeling."

Now it occurred to Maha that to ask Huda to reveal more might attract the attention of the mysterious listeners who seem to pick up randomly on any type of electronic communication. So she made her excuses. "Darling, it is so good to hear your voice. I'm so glad you're safe. I have to run out now, but maybe we can talk later. Enjoy Turkey!"

"Thank you! I just wanted to thank you. Thank you so much."

Rather than acknowledge the thanks, Maha simply said, "Take care of yourself. Bye!" Then she quickly hung up.

As she sat on the sofa, rubbing her belly as had become her new habit since the baby had begun to flutter around in there, Maha concluded that her panic may have been unwarranted. But Maha was still glad the conversation was over. She had felt sorry for the Huda of last month, but she wasn't sure what to think about the Huda of this month. She was glad her friend was happy, finally, but it was hard to imagine that this was a good kind of happy.

Chapter Twenty-two

Bags were packed, and Jordanian shopping rounds were complete. When Leila had left her mother's side two weeks ago, she had not known it might be permanent, and she now determined that it couldn't be. She pulled Hassoun into the hallway and said, "We have to see my family before I go. I have been supportive of you all week, but this is ridiculous. They are family. We'll go right now."

To her relief, the determination in her voice seemed to resonate, and he didn't protest.

No one spoke during the brief taxi ride to Jabal Hussein. The boys had been excited when Leila told them they were going back to see "*Teta*," "*Khale* Nuha" and the others. But they had quickly caught on to the somber mood of their parents so contented themselves with peering out the windows.

When they pulled up into the little alleyway which had been home to Leila and the boys for all those weeks, she felt her heart quickening. She still couldn't quite explain why, but she very much wanted to stay. This was her last ditch effort to find a way. Hassoun paid and they all piled out.

"*Ahlein! Ahlein! Ahlein!*"

Four sets of eyes peered up to see Rana sticking her head through the curtain encircling the balcony, waving down at them. A couple of small boys were peering over her shoulder.

"Good morning!" Leila shouted.

Rana replied with all the pleasantries that could be mustered up for an occasion like this, then beckoned them up.

When they had mounted the two flights of stairs, the door was open and all the women were standing in the hallway, still in their pajamas but heads covered, waiting to welcome their guests. Leila was greeted with many kisses by all, and the boys, too, were smothered with kisses. Hassoun received many head-nods and hands on hearts. They all hovered around him, asking if he had made a safe trip from Kuwait, about work and whether he wasn't pleased to see how they had fattened Leila up, though they hadn't really succeeded in doing so. In the family room, Leila's father awaited, sitting on a mattress in the corner of the room. Hassoun went up to him and shook his hand, then sat down by his side.

No sooner had formalities been completed than the boys ran off to play with their cousins in the back room.

Leila followed Nuha and Rana into the kitchen, where Mama was already boiling water for tea.

"What happened?" asked Nuha.

"Can you blame him?" Leila shrugged.

"But he has been so good to us. He was so supportive."

"I don't think he plans on stopping that. He just has different ideas about the boys and me."

"So..." Nuha faltered. "Does that mean you are definitely leaving?"

Leila found herself wringing her hands. "We have a flight at two in the morning."

Her mother kept working on the tea without so much as a glance Leila's way. Rana said, "*Inshallah bitruhi bi-salama*. Go in peace."

Leila automatically replied as per custom, "*Allah yesalamek*." But then she continued, "Between you and me, I don't want to go. I am still looking for a way."

"We don't want you to go either. We already miss you so much," Nuha sighed. Leila could imagine how Nuha, of all members of the family, would feel isolated without her older sister, the only other university-educated member of the family, around. She and Leila had been brainstorming ways that Nuha could apply for scholarships to complete her education in Jordan, or find some online program. Who would care about helping Nuha resume her studies after Leila was gone?

But before Leila could think of a reply, her mother said, "He is right. What kind of a life is this?"

"But Mama, I don't want to leave you! You are my home."

"We live in strange times, dear. Nothing is as it should be. You have a husband, a visa, a house. Don't waste your blessings."

Leila saw the logic in these words. This was what had made it so difficult for her to challenge Hassoun's plans: her only counter-argument was that she belonged with her family. But, of course, Hassoun was also now meant to be her family.

"Love him, Leila," her mother continued. "He is a good man and he cares for you."

Leila felt tears welling up in her eyes. She didn't want to hear this. "What about registering the boys for school here? There are good schools in Jordan."

Rana then commented, "Listen to yourself. You know you are always welcome here, but don't waste your blessings. Which of us wouldn't send our kids to a private school in Kuwait if we could? Which of us wanted to be here?"

"But you are, and your children are from my blood," protested Leila.

"We would love for you to stay," Nuha then said. "But we can't ask it of you."

The tea was ready and biscuits laid out on a tray. Leila knew that her family needed Hassoun's money more than they needed his wife. As long as she could guarantee that the stream of financial support would continue, there was not much left to say. She was sure this was what every woman in the house was thinking, though none would stoop so low as to actually verbalize it. She felt dirty, like getting on that plane tonight, resuming married life with Hassoun tomorrow, submitting... like all of this had been diminished to nothing more than glorified prostitution.

Mama carried the tea out, followed by Nuha with the tray of biscuits. Leila followed them, and Rana hovered in the hallway. They served Hassoun with as much honor as their simple circumstances would allow them, giving him the only unchipped glass, piling biscuits on a plate in front of him, keeping watch to ensure his cup never ran low.

The conversation was stilted. They discussed mundanities of life in Jordan, complaining about the treatment of refugees by the international aid agencies as well as by their Jordanian hosts, but avoiding specific examples. They spoke of Hassoun's family, whom Leila's parents had known as casual acquaintances back in Syria. His family had all left the moment the first rumblings began, and had done quite well for themselves running a busy Syrian restaurant in Istanbul. They exchanged news of other mutual friends from Dera'a'. Throughout the visit, Leila saw his eyes taking it all in, the mold stains on the ceiling, the flimsy mattresses, the lone light bulb that hung precariously from the walls. She imagined he was horrified at how little his contribution had secured, and breathed a silent prayer that he would not see this as reason to walk away from his commitment. On a purely financial calculation, Za'atari was a much better deal. It was an all-expenses covered lifestyle and the facilities were not much worse than this. But there was no dignity there and even less humanity. Her family needed at least that.

The visit ended quickly. Her mother begged, implored and pleaded with Hassoun that he stay for dinner. She promised to make his favorite food and insisted that he needed to allow her to care for him, even if only for a single meal. She asked him if he had other pressing engagements, and when he deferred the question, she declared it was settled and stood up to start preparing the meal. But, to Leila's horror, Hassoun stood too and announced that it was time to go. He would not allow her family this one little honor; instead, he called for the boys to say their goodbyes.

Hassoun bade farewell to each member of the family, then walked out to the landing, leaving Leila behind to give her mother and her sisters and her sisters-in-law each one last hug. The farewells were simple but prolonged: tight hugs, a few tears threatened but secured, and many kisses. Then it was up to her to pull the boys away from their cousins, which was no easy task. By the time she got downstairs, Hassoun was waiting with a taxi ready to go.

They spent the rest of the day lounging around the house, doing nothing planned or interesting as they whiled away the hours until their car arrived to take them to the airport. Amman airport seemed to be the busiest in the middle of the night, and a 2 am flight time would be a nightmare for the mother of two small children. Leila tried to convince the boys to take a nap, but they were not interested. So she let them watch television, hoping that at least their bodies would be rested. Hassoun did doze off a couple of times throughout the afternoon. He knew that he needed to rest since their flight would land in Kuwait around breakfast time and he would head straight to the hospital.

Hassoun's cousin was, as usual, at work. Madame Muna was also staying out of their way, out visiting or running errands or something.

So Leila took the afternoon to catch up with her social media. She chatted a bit with Maha on WhatsApp, as well as with a few other friends, though she found she had little to say. She didn't want to talk about her own life or how she was abandoning her family or how little she wanted to return to Kuwait or how she was mad at Hassoun for making what she felt was a difficult decision with so little hesitation. She didn't want to talk about these things, but they were what filled her entire consciousness. On these brief chats she didn't ask anyone about their family or their news, nor was she particularly forthcoming herself. She deliberately evaded any mention of Nisreen when chatting with Maha.

She also scrolled through her Facebook feed and clicked on the various links that presented themselves. She watched the ubiquitous videos of cute babies and cats, took a couple of quizzes that told her what her heart color was (green) and where her true home was located (Paris), and read about the advancement of Islamic groups in Syria. Of particular concern was a feature article about European teenage girls traveling to Iraq to marry fighters in the name of Islam. Disgusting.

At some point in the afternoon, Leila received a new friend request. She immediately clicked on it and was a bit shocked to see that the request was from someone named "Huda Houria" and was accompanied by a photo of her closest friend from university days, Huda, the would-be powerful lawyer. Leila recognized her eyes, but her head was wrapped in a green, white and red headband, with three stars on the white stripe. This was how members of the resistance dressed, but Leila thought Maha had recently told her that Huda was still living in Latakia. People in Latakia were not dressing for the resistance.

Leila was excited to be in touch with her old friend and curious where she was. She wondered, briefly, if Huda might actually be in Jordan. There were only six hours remaining before they left for the airport, but Amman was a small city.

So she clicked 'accept' then began scrolling through the Facebook feed of one of the most politically active lividly anti-regime profiles she had ever seen.

Leila knew Huda's story well, that is, her story up through university days. Theirs had been a close and precious friendship, but not the type of friendship that lasted a physical separation. When they had graduated, Leila had walked Huda to the bus stop and helped her load her bags onto a minibus headed to the station on the north side of Damascus, to return to Latakia in the north of Syria. Then, a day later, Leila had herself traveled to the station on the south side of Damascus, where she had taken a bus back to Dera'a in the south. Many promises of meeting half-way and calling each other weekly notwithstanding, that had marked the end of their friendship. The minimal contact they had had since then was superficial and brief.

But in university, Leila and Huda had been the best of friends. Their hearts had connected from their very first conversation. They shared a passion for learning and a sense of frustration that those nearest and dearest to them did not feel the same way. They had been able to talk about anything and, indeed, had. At least Leila had. In their final year at University of Damascus, Leila had learned that Huda had been sexually abused by one of her professors. Leila had not imagined that Huda's depression was caused by anything other than academic stress, and if she was honest with herself, she admitted that she had not wanted to understand. The abuse Huda had suffered had been absolutely unforgivable, and it had tragically transformed her friend from an ambitious woman motivated by hope and expectation of a better life, into an unhappy hard worker who found it difficult to open up to her friends and impossible to confide in her family.

Leila was not surprised that Huda's bitterness had continued to grow over the years. She was, however, surprised that Huda would risk her family's wellbeing by visibly protesting against the regime. She and Huda had shared their desire to break out of the mold, but only if they could do so without disappointing their families.

Now, Leila reflected, the tables had turned on her own life. Breaking out of the mold would mean choosing one part of her family over another, a choice she felt unable to make. Two years ago she had been the exotic daughter making it big in Kuwait, with international friends and – heaven forbid – working after having children, even if it was just light translation work at home. Now she was having trouble even looking at her husband, much less sitting by his side and joining in his attempts at conversing about life back in Kuwait, because she felt she belonged on a dingy mattress in an even dingier neighborhood being a dutiful daughter.

Just as Leila was reflecting on these things and beginning to concentrate her efforts on keeping the tears out of her eyes, a message dinged on Facebook.

It was from Huda: Thanks for the add! And so quickly. How are you? I've missed you so so so much!

Without thinking, Leila replied: Me too. How are you?

A moment went by before the little "Huda is writing..." icon appeared in the messenger box, then another long moment before the reply came: I'm well. I am in Turkey. Came last week.

Leila, again, somewhat by rote and without much reflection, wrote: Why?

More delay, then: It's time to do something I believe in. I'm joining the struggle.

Leila: You mean...

Huda: Yeah.

It was like they were back at university. Leila knew exactly what Huda meant, and Huda knew exactly what Leila was asking. Huda was preparing to return to Syria to fight.

It was Leila's turn to pause before writing: Go with God.

What else could she write? What else could be said? Security concerns aside, if Huda was in the same room with her and they had all day, Leila might try to talk her out of a suicide mission, but this was not a conversation to be had over Facebook Messenger.

Mercifully, Huda quickly replied: How are you? How is your family?

Leila: They are well. I have two sons now.

Huda: *Masha'allah*. I am looking at photos on your profile now. They are beautiful. May God give them many years.

Leila: God keep you.

Leila: What about you, are you married?
Huda: No. It's just me.
Leila: Why?
Huda: Honestly, for a long time I wondered too. But no one really interested me, I guess. Now, I think it was so I would be free to do what I believe I should do.
Leila: It's your right.

A moment went by, and then Leila asked: What city are you in? How long have you been there?

But Huda didn't reply. Not in the next minute, nor after five minutes, not even after half an hour during which Leila's eyes shifted back and forth between the images flashing on the TV and her phone. She wasn't sure if she had said something wrong, or if Huda's Internet had just gone off.

These days, Maha was Leila's only true friend of confidence, and Maha also knew Huda. Leila thought about calling Maha to ask if she too had heard from Huda and what she thought. But the very idea left Leila feeling a bit weary, so she joined the boys on the sofa and watched cartoons with them until their hosts came home with rotisserie chicken for dinner.

In Turkey, Huda's heart was racing. She had grown so accustomed to suppressing her thoughts, feelings, urges, interests, desires, ideas and anything else internal that could be suppressed, that she found she no longer knew how to talk. When Leila asked her what city she was in, was it out of suspicion, or was it simple curiosity, or was it nothing more than politeness? Would Huda get in trouble for reaching out to her old friends and failing to hide her new adventures? She had no idea. Until last week, she would always and inevitably choose the most cautious route, and the most cautious route was usually the right one. But she was no longer planning on doing anything cautious; in fact, she was working her way up to the boldest of moves. Did this mean it was time for her to speak openly with her friends as well?

"Chai?"

Huda looked up and saw her host, a very handsome young man named Adnan from one of Damascus's oldest and most established families. Adnan made no secret of his refusal to believe in God, his suspicion of all governments of the world, and his love of Che Guevara. He had been in Turkey for about a year; before that, he had been working for the Syrian Arab Red Crescent society in Damascus, but organizing freedom protests in his spare time. Eventually, his employer, a humanitarian division of the Syrian regime, had caught on to Adnan's extracurricular activities and fired him. The threats to his family had started after no more than a couple of hours, so Adnan had caught a shared taxi to Lebanon that night and flown to Gaziantep in Turkey a week later. His family was still in Damascus, and he had no contact with them, allowing them – and hence the regime – to think he was dead. Mutual friends occasionally sent him news of their welfare, so he knew they were still alive and still living their Damascene life.

Huda had befriended him through a Facebook group called Syria Justice, and he had offered for her to stay with him when she arrived in Turkey. She had no idea how he supported himself, but he seemed to have at least five jobs. He worked for the Syrian National Council, frequenting Gaziantep's coffeehouses looking for small Syrian associations with whom the Council could partner. He recruited fighters for the Free Syrian Army. He coordinated collection of food and clothing packages to be delivered through an informal humanitarian corridor he had helped establish between Gaziantep and Aleppo. He played the kanoon in a band and taught music to refugee children. And he ran a hostel. He had rented a large old run-down house on the outskirts of Gaziantep and welcomed orphaned revolutionaries like Huda to live with him. He didn't charge rent and, as far as she could tell, none of the other jobs were lucrative either.

"Thank you. Some tea would be lovely," Huda replied, blushing.

Adnan was everything she aspired to be: passionate, convicted, friendly and energetic. He was also very, very good looking.

He disappeared back into the kitchen and re-emerged with a rusty old copper pot in one hand, a box of Lipton tea bags tucked under his arm, and two mugs in the other hand, a little bag of sugar and a spoon tucked into one of the mugs. He crossed the little courtyard to the old sofa where Huda was sitting and sat down beside her, placing the supplies on a little stool.

"Where is everyone else?" Huda asked.

"They're all out," he replied. "I think there's a theater presentation down in the town square tonight."

"That's right. They invited me, but I completely forgot."

"You only arrived a few days ago. It's good for you to rest," Adnan put a hand on Huda's shoulder and gave it a gentle tap. Then he put a tea bag in each mug and poured hot water out of the pot. "Sugar?"

"No thanks."

As Adnan dipped two spoonsful of sugar into his own mug and stirred, wrung out his teabag with the spoon, then did the same with Huda's teabag, she couldn't help but gaze at his hands. They were soft but muscular as the hands of a kanoon player must be. She liked the way they went about doing what, in Huda's experience pre-Turkey, was generally a woman's job.

He handed her mug to her, and she thanked him, then asked, "And you? Why didn't you go to the theater?"

"No reason, I guess. I just preferred to stay home."

Huda didn't answer, just sipped her tea while she tried to keep her eyes averted from his wavy hair, goatee, and intelligent-looking glasses.

"So, Huda," Adnan said after a few moments during which he had leaned back on the sofa and tucked his legs up under him. "What do you think of Turkey?"

"I just arrived," she giggled. "It's too early for me to have an opinion. What do you think?"

"It's no Syria," he sighed, completely serious.

"No, it's not Syria," she agreed. "Do you miss it?"

"In a month, you won't ask me that anymore because you'll miss it too. I couldn't miss it more. My body is here, but my heart will always be in Syria."

"It's odd, isn't it, to come to another country because we love our own?"

Adnan took a slow sip of tea, then leaned forward to put his mug on the stool. Huda couldn't help but comment to herself that his arms, too, were quite strong. Then he leaned back again and said, "Nothing in this war makes sense. Nothing at all."

"Well, it's an honor to be here," Huda said brightly. "So far, I'm much happier here than I ever was there."

He turned his eyes to her questioning.

Huda gasped ever so slightly. "I'm sorry. I didn't mean... I mean... I really love Syria. I want to go back, too, just like you. But I'm glad to be here instead of living the lie that I was there."

"Tell me," he said, turning now to face her, cross-legged. He leaned forward and gently removed the mug from her hands and put it next to his own. Then he took both her hands into his and began to rub them softly. "What are you running from? What is your dream?"

Huda's blood all rushed right into her head. She couldn't remember the last time she had felt such thrill or warmth in her hands or, for that matter, at all. It was all she could do to keep his gaze and more than she could do to frame her words. She knew she should not tell a near-stranger where she came from or that she was Alawite or just about anything else about herself. But it was her heart that began speaking, not her head, as the words came tumbling out.

She told Adnan everything. Where her village was, what her family stood for, what she had studied at university, how she had realized in her twentieth year that there was no justice for a woman like her in their country, her disappointments ever since. She spared few details and kept talking about her desire to do something meaningful and her dreams for seeing human rights and opportunities for women and justice for all.

As she spoke, Adnan continued to hold her hands and listen intently, barely blinking as he gazed into her eyes and nodded his head at all the right moments.

When Huda began to narrate what her professor had done to her in her second year of university, he registered shock and shifted his body to pull her into a full body embrace. He leaned back and pulled her back into his arms.

Beyond the obligatory handshakes at work and cheek-pecks from her brothers, Huda had not been touched by a man since the day her professor had molested her. She didn't know what she was saying, and she had even less idea what she was doing.

Eventually, she ran out of words. She had no idea how long she had been talking, but she wished she could keep going. Her heart was racing, and she felt tingly all over. She did not want this moment to end but had no idea what one did next.

But Adnan did. He shifted his position and tactfully guided her body so that she rolled over to face him. His face was mere centimeters from hers, and he just smiled at her. After a long moment, he said, "Welcome. It's time for you to start living." Then he put his arm around her head and drew her lips to his.

The shock of that gesture brought Huda back to reality for a very brief moment. It was wet and sloppy and confusing. She had met this man all of three days ago and was a guest in his house.

But that moment of sagacity quickly passed, and she began instead to tremble with excitement. His arms were strong but caring, and her entire mouth tingled as he kissed her. He seemed to realize very quickly that she was inexperienced because he took her hand in his and guided it around his neck and paused to give her instructions as to how to kiss him back. Then he began to caress other parts of her body and pull her arms to himself, showing her where to touch him.

Completely caught up in the moment, feeling her body come alive in a way it never had before, barely able to believe that this man, an icon representing everything she ever wanted, had chosen to spend the evening with her, Huda was stunned and immediately heartbroken when he suddenly pulled away, sat up and began gathering the mugs and teapot.

She sat up and stared at him for a brief moment, her eyes barely able to focus, when she finally heard the voices at the door and realized that their five housemates had just returned home.

A minute later, Adnan was back in the kitchen, heating coal on the stove to prepare an *arguile* while he made a pot of flower tea, and Huda was sharing the sofa with three others, two sisters from Aleppo and a boy barely out of his teens from a small town in Syria's eastern desert whose entire family had been killed the year before. Two other guys, slightly older in their early thirties, had pulled up little stools. They were telling her about the play, written by a young man who had completed his studies at the University of Damascus College of Arts in the same year as the revolution started. He had come to Turkey that same year and immediately begun writing sketches about the regime, putting together a troupe, and performing on the streets of Turkey's major cities, making sure that each performance was filmed and uploaded to YouTube. They included caricatures of Bashar al-Assad, of his wife and his advisors, and of major Islamic figures. The housemates told her in intricate detail about the playwright and the play, interrupting each other to make sure they got every detail right. From the kitchen, occasionally Adnan shouted out questions or made comments. Eventually, he rejoined them and they kept talking about artistic movements that had popped up across the Syrian diaspora in the past two years. He was attentive to her needs, making sure her glass was always full and inviting her to join the conversation. A few times, Huda caught him looking her way, caressing her with his eyes, it seemed.

Huda tried hard but struggled to keep her eyes off of him. She was silent, not participating in the conversation any more than necessary. She was in awe of this man who had welcomed her into her house, how he was able to maintain so many projects in the air, and how he could show her so much personal care and attention yet still be such a gracious host to a group of disparate rebels.

As she half listened to, and half participated in, the conversation, a bit of logic reestablished itself and Huda felt a wave of relief come over her as she realized how quickly and suddenly she had surrendered any and all control over herself. She did not know Adnan and she had enough experience of men to know that once they got what they wanted from a girl, they often walked away. As much as she felt every vein of her body craving his touch again, she told herself that this was not the reason she had come. She had a higher calling.

This resolve was difficult to keep, though, even more so when, many hours later, after the conversation had exhausted itself and everyone had drifted off to his or her little corner to sleep, Adnan knocked on her door. She opened the door to his dark hair and smiling eyes and tender facial hair and strong arms that held up a bottle of wine and two glasses. How could she resist? But she found it in herself to do so, claiming she had already fallen asleep and could they continue tomorrow.

But tomorrow came, and it seemed a single night's sleep was all it took for Adnan to lose interest. In the morning he barely spoke with her over breakfast and then he left the house, leaving Huda to fare for herself. All of her housemates were working, in fact. Each one had an interesting project to work on, whether for an NGO or in journalism or community mobilization amongst the refugee population. Huda knew what she wanted her project to be, but had only briefly mentioned it to Adnan, who said he would help. That was before she came to Turkey, and was largely the reason she came to stay with him. But since she had arrived, the topic had not come up, and she had no idea how to broach the subject.

So she decided to cook. Her journey through contested Syrian territory had left her with a ravenous appetite which she had not yet come close to satisfying in the Turkish restaurants and snack shops to which her hosts had introduced her. At this particular moment in time, she was craving about three things at once: tabouli salad, kibbeh meatballs boiled in yogurt, and cheese saj sandwiches made on a traditional round flatbread grill. Not having access to a traditional round grill, she decided to get to work on preparing the other two.

A rummage around the kitchen revealed that Huda would need to do some shopping first. The cabinets were full of half-used bags of coffee grounds, tobacco for *arguile*, ashtrays, a random assortment of sugar bowls, and a few different types of tea. But it didn't appear that this kitchen was used for cooking very often, if at all. There were only two pots and half a dozen mismatched bowls, and a variety of cracked mugs and teapots and saucers. There was the bare minimum in utensils, with which she would make do.

As she let herself out of the heavy iron door to find a supermarket, Huda decided she was too hungry to cook. She walked down to the end of the street where a doner kebab - the Turkish version of shawarma, shaved grilled meat - shop was already serving sandwiches. She ordered one with ayran, the yogurt drink which Adnan had told her all Turks ate with their doner, and sat on a stool watching people walk back and forth on the street. She was enjoying this Turkish food, and so far she hadn't eaten anything that she didn't like. But she wouldn't admit that to her housemates, who had little good to say about Turkey and in particular liked to complain about its food. But this doner was so good that, using hand gestures, she went ahead and requested a second before she had even finished the first.

The sandwiches were not small, but Huda was still not full after eating two. She decided that it was enough to tide her over, though, and she headed out down the street in search of a grocery store, which she was relieved to find on the very same street, just one block down.

She walked up and down the aisle, taking it all in. Though she had grown up no more than an hour's drive, possibly even walking distance, from Turkey, she had never been. She knew enough English and French to feel comfortable with the alphabet, so she sounded out the words written on the packets of food that caught her eye. Most things she recognized, but there were quite a few odd items on the shelves as well, things she couldn't even begin to identify. Some of them looked quite intriguing, though, and Huda selected a few to try: something she assumed was a packet of olives though she couldn't be sure from the wrapping, a flavor of tea that seemed to be some kind of a green leaf, a hard cheese, and a few other bits of this and that. Everything looked appetizing, and she wasn't sure whether it was because - two shawarma sandwiches notwithstanding - she was still hungry, or whether it really was good food. She couldn't wait to find out.

Huda wandered toward the check-out queue and was waiting behind two other customers when she realized she had forgotten to buy the groceries for which she had come. Exciting as these new foods were, she was looking forward to satisfying her cravings for some good food from home. She was also excited to serve home-cooked Syrian food to her housemates. Especially Adnan. She loved the idea of preparing a meal for her host.

So she returned into the store and filled a cart with an assortment of vegetables, meat, yogurt, bread and other sundry items. For good measure, she also selected some fruits, some more familiar-looking cheeses and olives, and a few other staples to stock the kitchen. She had no idea how long her stay in Turkey would last, but she didn't mind playing housewife to her activist companions. She didn't mind at all.

Back at home, she decided to clean the kitchen before cooking. It needed a good clean. Huda hummed to herself as she worked, imagining how pleased Adnan would be when he arrived home to a house that was more of a home and less of a crash pad.

Still hungry, she took out the Turkish foods from the shopping bag and decided to try them out. Everything was delicious, except for the tea, which tasted like it was made for detox and not for daily consumption.

Then Huda began to cook. She had chosen some complicated dishes, which she had not actually cooked for a few years. It took her a while to remember what she was doing, and the quality of the knives and spoons did not help. She worked diligently for most of the afternoon.

The rice was boiling on the stove when the sisters from Aleppo came in.

"*Ahlan!*" Huda called from the kitchen. "How was your day?"

"Fine," replied the older of the two. "But I'm exhausted. I'm going to take a nap."

"Me too," said her sister.

They wandered into the room they were sharing.

Huda wasn't phased, though. They would eat after their nap. The kibbeh was smelling fantastic, after all.

Half an hour later, one of the older men arrived. He noticed the food immediately.

"Hi, Huda!" he said as he poked his head into the kitchen. "What smells so good?"

"Kibbe labaniyeh," she replied cheerfully.

"I love kibbe labaniyeh! It was always my favorite treat when my mom made it."

"Well, I'm not your mom, but I hope you enjoy this, at least, a little bit," she replied. "I made tons."

"Oh no," he groaned. "I already made plans to go out this evening for dinner. I can't cancel."

Huda swallowed her disappointment, by telling herself that this was just one of her housemates. The others would eat, and of course, she was mainly interested in feeding just one particular housemate. She replied, "Well, maybe just taste a little bit. Eat twice!" Then she giggled.

So he did. He told her it was fantastic, but he ate in such a rush, she couldn't be sure.

Eventually, Huda did sit down to share dinner with the sisters and the young boy from the East. At that point, it was 8 pm, and the other older man and Adnan had not yet returned home.

Everyone enjoyed the food, though, and there was still some left when they were done, which Huda left on the stovetop for whoever might want it later.

The girls invited Huda to go with them to a friend's house, but she demurred, claiming she was tired after a long day, but really because she wanted to be home when Adnan arrived.

Again alone in the house, Huda washed the dishes, then spent some time on Facebook, looking for more old friends to contact. She looked through Maha's and Leila's photos and commented on many of them. She particularly enjoyed seeing Leila's sons and how they were growing. They were adorable, and Huda wanted to reach through her little phone screen and eat them up.

Eventually, she grew too sleepy to keep waiting. Even if he arrived home now, she would be terrible company. So Huda turned in for the night. She thought she heard all of her housemates returning together at some point in the early hours of the morning, but she wasn't sure.

The next few days went by in a similar manner. Her housemates all seemed to be friends with each other and have plenty of friends of their own. They all had jobs and places to be. Huda continued to play housemom, but she didn't see housedad again until the weekend. The next time the girls invited her out with them, she did accept, and on that visit, she met the playwrite they had all been raving about before, so she was glad she went. Her appetite continued unabated, and she continued experimenting and exploring new Turkish foods. Every day she cooked some more Syrian food, as well. But she was struggling to keep her excitement up.

She wanted to do something. Something meaningful and significant. Or, at least, she wanted to be with someone meaningful and significant. Before she had come to Syria, she had met a lot of different activists on Facebook, some who had helped get her across the border, and others who had offered to help her find work in Turkey. But she had accepted Adnan's invitation because he was the only one who also seemed to be able to help her begin to do something more bold than just aid work. Then, the moment she had laid eyes on him, she stopped wanting to consider pursuing any of those other friendships. She didn't move to Turkey to fall in love, but it was as if all her senses were on overload: her appetite for food, for sleep, for keeping busy around the house, for doing something meaningful, and for a beautiful man.

But if she didn't see Adnan, the romance that had just begun to blossom couldn't go anywhere. It had clearly already cooled though she kept reminding herself that he was very busy with his five jobs and couldn't keep up with everything at once. Maybe he was just waiting for a few free minutes.

But if she didn't see Adnan, how was she going to figure out how to join the FSA? This was what she had decided she wanted. Talking to her housemates, and to the few other Syrians in Turkey to whom they had introduced her, Huda was learning that there were many effective means of making a difference. In fact, most of them were pacifists and worked hard to stay away from the fighting. So she didn't mention her plans to them, and actually began to question her own intentions. Perhaps community mobilization, helping to network local civil society organizations inside Syria, was a better plan. Or perhaps she should do what she had discovered Maha was doing, according to her Facebook feed, and get involved in engaging Western governments to help the Cause. Huda had no interest at all in doing humanitarian work because it looked a bit too much like a band-aid. She didn't want to save lives; she wanted to create a reality in which lives were not at risk to start with. But even after she heard all these stories and saw the wider reality and was convinced that these other moves were important for building the

Syria she dreamed of, Huda's hatred was not satisfied. Before she could think of helping to build something new, she had to destroy the old.

As Huda heard the stories shared by the members of her small network of Syrian friends, her anger burned deeper. In Latakia, she had been sheltered. She had been bitter because of the limits she had faced in her own life, but she had not realized that so many people had suffered so much more than she had. She heard stories of men who disappeared for as many as twenty years because they so happened to make the wrong friend or say the wrong word on the phone, of women who were raped in prison after being arrested for allegedly trying drugs one time, of the constant harassment faced by the family of the young man who had started the whole thing by spraypainting anti-regime slogans on his school wall.

So Huda still wanted to join the army that had been established to bring down the regime. The real FSA, not those local factions just trying to make money off of rich Saudis, and certainly not those bands of brothers who talked about making Syria into an Islamist society. She wanted the Free Syria Army, the one that really understood the importance of freedom.

Her fury was growing quickly, and this was only her first week in Turkey.

She wanted to see Adnan and get some time to talk with him, but she wasn't sure whether it was because she wanted to talk to him and spend time with him, or because he was the only path she knew of into the army.

Chapter Twenty-three

Today was a big day. Maha had a meeting with a representative of the United Nations Commission on Human Rights who was visiting from Geneva. This person had all the contacts she could hope for to pressure the Syrian government to release Nisreen.

Nisreen had now been disappeared for fifteen weeks. During the past two months during which Maha had been fighting for her release, Nisreen's story had been shared 100,000 times on Facebook and nearly that many times on Twitter. Articles had been published in the New York Times, the Guardian, Huffington Post, and the Atlantic, as well as a broad assortment of other lesser-known news outlets. Maha had also conducted brief radio interviews with BBC Lebanon, Le Monde, and two local German channels. Word was getting out, and the Mockingbird might be added to the list of issues to be discussed at the next Geneva conference, bringing together representatives of the Syrian regime and its supporters, the Syrian National Council and its supporters, and a few other Syrian factions which no one in the international community wanted to take seriously, mainly because they were advocating for extremist Islam in Syria.

Maha's hope was that the Mockingbird would not be on the conference agenda because Nisreen would be released in private negotiations prior to the event starting.

She had learned a lot in the past weeks about advocacy and lobbying and political demands. She still had a lot to learn but felt like she was making progress.

Today's meeting was to ask the special rapporteur for Syria to lobby on their behalf to get Nisreen out before the conference. Maha felt she had a real chance of succeeding.

She asked Samir if she could purchase a new outfit for the occasion, and he graciously agreed to let her buy a maternity business suit, something she would use no more than a few times in the coming months – she was now in her third trimester. The suit was a work of art: navy blue satin, with folds in all the right places that didn't hide the fact she was expecting, important to Maha as she had found that most people in these human rights circles were disarmed by a 'family woman', but which still looked professional and serious.

In her lobbying and networking, Maha had begun to collect a list of other people wrongly imprisoned. It had started when a friend on Facebook had re-posted the Mockingbird announcement with a photo of Nisreen then private-messaged Maha, asking for advice. This friend's cousin had been arrested in the first month of the protests because he had been on the street in Dera'a during the initial clashes. They knew where he was being held, and the family visited him every month, but they had no idea how to get him exonerated. There was no evidence that he was participating in the protests at all, much less engaging in violence or making trouble of any kind. But he had never come before a judge; he just sat in jail.

Maha had replied, sharing the same tips that she was following, but it felt to her that such words were not enough. She was fortunate to have friends living in many countries, and from many countries. She was based in Beirut with time to spare. Plus, she was having great luck making contacts and couldn't be sure her friend would have the same luck.

So Maha had asked her Facebook friend - no more than a distant acquaintance from her university days - for the name of the cousin in jail and a photo, the date of arrest, which jail he was in, and any other details she could provide. Then she had begun to look for opportunities to introduce his name when meeting with other activists. She also posted his photo to the Save the Mockingbird Facebook page.

Next, a gentleman had come up to Samir after church one Sunday and told the story of his wife's nephew, a student in Aleppo who had been stopped at a checkpoint attempting to deliver food into a neighborhood that was under siege. Samir had been struck by the story because it was not unlike his own. Over dinner that evening, Samir had shared the story with his wife, hoping for some sympathy, and wanting to pray with her for this man and his relative. Maha had responded more pragmatically, though, suggesting that they mount a campaign on his behalf. Samir had taken the suggestion back to his congregant who had discussed it with his wife who had decided it was better not to publicize his story for the safety of their family still living in

Aleppo. But they said that if Maha could keep her ears open and let them know if there was any news, they would be grateful. So his name was added to Maha's list.

As Maha heard stories, she added them to her list, which now contained almost three dozen names and was growing by the day. She had already experienced some success, too. A couple of weeks ago, she had been invited to a meeting at the office of the United Nations mission in Lebanon. The meeting was for planning the agenda of the Geneva conference, and a friend from a UK-based advocacy organization had invited her to come along. At the meeting was a Syriac Orthodox priest from Aleppo, who had good relations with the government but who also traveled regularly to Lebanon to meet with other organizations. He had news of the young man from Aleppo, who had been arrested delivering food. Maha had spoken with him afterward and one thing led to another until the priest successfully negotiated his release just a few days back. Maha had been there when the man arrived at his aunt's house in Beirut and had not even tried to keep back the tears. She hoped to see Nisreen soon at a similar reunion. And she hoped that the handful of other cases that were currently being negotiated would also lead to happy endings.

Maha knew that bad news would come soon enough. Not everyone would be released, and some might suffer a great deal before meeting an untimely death. But she chose not to dwell on that possibility. She had endured her own days of unbearable torture when her own husband was being held. Dealing with the unknown was a terrible fate, and Maha wanted to do whatever she could to bring truth to light. That was her focus. That, and those precious moments of reunion.

She had started recruiting a team to work with her. With Roxy gone, Maha tried to use social media to keep in touch with her friends and get their moral support. But back in Syria, Roxy was unable to engage at all, and it seemed that Leila was not herself anymore. Maha had not heard from Leila at all in the week since she had returned to Kuwait. She was worried about her friend and decided it would be best not to bother her with these things anymore, even if Nisreen was Leila's friend and not her own.

So Maha turned to her other acquaintances in Beirut, people she didn't actually particularly like, but who lived in the neighborhood and who had a habit of stopping by from time to time to drink coffee or watch television. A young couple from Syria, who had come to Lebanon together ostensibly because they were known amongst their friends for their somewhat leftist ideologies, but probably mainly because they wanted to live together and their Damascene families would never allow it, had jumped into the project with gusto. They were both working for international NGOs and were able to help Maha network for lobbying purposes; but, even more, important, they still had friends in Syria. They knew people in every major city, and many of their friends were active members of the resistance themselves. They also had a few friends still working for the regime who might be induced to help. As names were added to Maha's list, this industrious young couple took it upon themselves to find out where they were being held, whether charges were being filed, and what the odds were that negotiation could take place.

Just yesterday, Maha had received an email from a large international advocacy organization suggesting that she apply for a small grant to begin a research project analyzing the use of arrest and detention by all factions in the conflict. She herself did not particularly enjoy writing, but just downstairs lived a British Arabic student who might be looking for work. They could make a great team, and Maha was enjoying daydreaming about the possibilities that name recognition from a published report with her name on it, and perhaps a little logo she had been fiddling with would bring.

She would have to start working on that grant application tonight, but first she had her biggest meeting yet, due to start in one hour.

She was dressed and ready to go so she took a minute to look over her notes one more time. In her folder, she had ten copies of a one-page brief including the photo of Nisreen with some text about the Mockingbird blog. She also had a sheet of talking points she had compiled for herself. After a few stilted interviews, she had quickly caught on to the importance of being prepared for what she wanted to say. Last week, she had been meeting with an independent negotiator who was liaising with the

British government and the Syrian regime on some other issues, hoping to get her agenda inserted into the negotiator's discussions, and had almost been railroaded. The negotiator tried to turn the conversation against her and focus on some stupid debate about the destruction of a church near her hometown. If it weren't for her talking points, Maha might have lost control of that conversation, but she felt proud of how she had steered the large and loud Italian gentleman back to the human lives she sought to represent. Also, Maha had a few other sheets of information she might need, and her list of souls tucked in the back for quick reference.

She came out into the living room where Samir was seated at the table preparing his Sunday sermon.

He looked up and whistled when he saw her in her suit. Then he asked, "Who are you meeting today again?"

"The member of the UN Human Rights Commission from Geneva, remember?"

"That's right. No wonder you look so amazing. Come here," he said as he stood up.

Maha walked into his arms.

Samir embraced her shoulders with one arm and lay his free hand on her tummy. "He is looking good! What a gorgeous belly."

Maha shrugged the comment off with a giggle. With each centimeter she grew, she was one day closer to the inevitable slow-down that the baby would bring to her life. While her affection for the little one was certainly growing, the now near-constant flutters and kicks helping her to bond with little human being, she was still not as excited as Samir.

"Come, sit down," Samir then said, walking with her to the sofa. "You have a few minutes, right?"

"Just a few minutes."

"Let's pray."

Maha smiled and took his hands in hers. She bowed her head as he bowed his.

"Lord, we thank you for the doors you have opened for my dear wife and for the way you are using her so powerfully to enact good in the lives of others. I am proud of her, and I know you are too. She is your loyal servant. Please, oh Lord, go with this your servant today. Walk with her. Send your spirit into that room with her. Anoint her mouth. And give the others the ability and desire to hear what she has to say. I pray, Lord, that you would work a miracle in the lives of each and every individual on her list and in their families. In particular, Lord, I pray that we will see her friend Nisreen soon. Lord Jesus Christ, we ask this in your name. Amen."

Maha looked up tears in her eyes. She was no loyal servant of Jesus. She was doing this for Nisreen and for Leila, not for God. Sometimes she thought she wasn't even doing it for Leila, but rather for herself. She was enjoying this season of her life more than she had enjoyed anything in a long time and found advocacy ever so much more interesting than preparing a baby room.

But she was grateful for her husband's faith. She reached over her belly to hug his neck.

A moment later, Samir was ushering her out the door, one final peck on the cheek. Maha trundled down the stairs and hailed a taxi.

The meeting went well, or, at least, she thought it did. Maha was still gaining a sense of gauging when encouragement was real and when it was forced. But she felt a growing hope that Nisreen would be arriving before the baby came.

On the ride home, Maha wrote Leila a quick WhatsApp, saying, "We're making progress with your friend! I think she might be released soon."

Not too surprisingly, no response came.

Then Maha thought of Huda. She had not heard from Huda directly since that odd Facebook chat a couple of weeks before, but she was following her old friend's Facebook feed.

Huda seemed to be enjoying Turkey and had posted at least a dozen photos of Turkish foods in the past week. She was as political as ever, posting articles and blogs about the situation in Syria, photos of children attacked by the regime, and calls for people to take up arms. It seemed, also, that Huda may have met a man. There were a few photos of her with new friends, and one particular face seemed to be predominant, in photos of just her and him.

Maha wondered what kind of network Huda was developing in Gaziantep and whether she might be able to help with the new research project and with identifying what had happened to some of the people on her list whom her Beirut team had not yet been able to track down.

So she opened her Facebook Messenger and wrote: *Ahlan* Huda! How are you and how is Turkey? Do you remember Leila's friend Nisreen, sister of that guy she used to go with? We are working to get her freed. It looks like she will be out soon, Praise God!

Maha hesitated before writing more and then pressed send. She would wait to see how Huda responded before introducing more of the idea.

It was only a minute before her friend wrote back: Nisreen? Really? I'm so sorry. What can I do?

Ah, this was what Maha had hoped for. She continued typing: I think Nisreen is going to be ok. It has been two months, but we are making progress. Did you know my husband was also taken for two months? I am so glad to have him back with me.

Huda: Maha, I'm so sorry. I have been hearing lots of stories since I've been here. I had no idea it was so bad. I was so sheltered.

Maha: Be grateful for what you had. We all want it.

Huda: Don't say that. It was its own form of torture. And even worse for me to be remembering those days, now that I see what is happening in the rest of our precious country. I need to go back to help.

Maha: Well, as it turns out, I could use some help with something if you're interested.

Huda: Sure! Absolutely. Tell me.

Maha: Let's Skype sometime? How is your day tomorrow?

Huda: Ugh. So far, every day is free. I hope that will change. But now I'm just playing housewife.

Maha: Oh, so you have met someone! I wondered from the photos.

Huda: Maha...you have no idea.

Maha: Tell me! Us married women need to live a little through others.

Huda: I've only been here two weeks. But he's amazing. I am so in love. He is passionate; he's so good at getting things done and engaging people. And he's so caring...

Maha: So?

Huda: I don't know. One minute he is all over me. Then he disappears. There have been days when I thought he was completely in love with me, and then three days passed without even seeing him. And we're living in the same house!

Maha: You mean....

Huda: No, no. Nothing like that. Well... not exactly.

Maha: ??

Huda: It's not just the two of us in the house. There are seven of us total. All Syrian.

Maha: I see. But you and he have something special.

Huda: I think we do. We've... you know... a few times. Maha, did you know that I've never really dated in my life? It was my first kiss last week!

Maha hesitated before responding. She could easily imagine how naïve Huda might be, and while this disappearing three days thing could mean anything, Maha knew too many men for whom it meant three other women. She hoped Huda hadn't done anything she would regret. As she thought this and pondered what to write that would be encouraging yet sufficiently warn her friend, Huda started typing again.

Huda: He's so wonderful. He does humanitarian work but also advocacy. And he's a musician. He has lived here for a few years: he was one of the first Syrians to come here. I wish you could meet him.

So Maha replied: Be careful, dear. Don't go too fast. How long have you known him?

Huda: Two weeks.

Maha: Yes, be very careful. Go slow. If he's worth it, he'll wait for you. Let him chase you a bit.

Huda: But he's so busy. He does so many things that I don't know if he has time to chase me. I'm just cleaning his house.

Maha: Then it sounds like it's time for you to get something else to do. Let's Skype tomorrow.

Huda: Alright. Thanks, dear!

Maha's taxi was pulling up to her house, and Samir would be waiting for a report on her meeting; then it would be time to prepare dinner.

Maha: I have to go now. Is eleven tomorrow morning good?

Huda: Sure.

Maha: Kisses.

Huda: Kisses.

Huda already knew that she was in trouble. She had never been in love before but was beginning to understand how it could be described as torment. She waited for him every day, looked out for him when she was on the street, figured out what foods he liked and made them, and even cried a few times when he didn't come home in the evening. She had begun to make a few friends but found it very hard to engage in conversation with them and even harder to go out with them when she just wanted to be at home with Adnan.

So far, she had actually not seen him outside the house, ever. It had just never worked out that way. She was also frustrated because when they were together, she found herself talking a lot – it felt like he knew just about everything about herself – but he offered little by way of his own reflections.

The long intimate conversations and the kissing and the making out had continued on and off, and Huda was finding it increasingly difficult to figure out what was reasonable and where to draw the line. She wasn't even sure she wanted there to be a line. But Maha's warning echoed in her own head. She didn't like the idea, but she had to take it slow. She didn't know him well enough. But surely such a kind man must be everything she could hope for.

Indeed, Maha's warning was something that her heart had been shouting already. No man was perfect, and Huda really should figure out what his imperfections were before giving her heart over to him completely.

But more importantly, she didn't come to Turkey to fall in love. She came to Turkey with a task and a goal.

She had not yet had an opportunity to discuss her future with him. After two weeks into her time in Turkey, she had not changed her mind. She still wanted to join the fight. She would hear what Maha had to say tomorrow, and if it would keep her busy for a while, she would do it. But her heart was with a newly-formed regiment of female fighters.

Chapter Twenty-four

"*Sabah al-Kheir*!" Maha chirped over the surprisingly clear Skype line.

"*Sabah al-Ward*," replied Huda.

"So... Turkey? Tell me everything!" Maha started.

"Everything?"

"Yes. A few months ago, we skyped with you, and you were working as a lawyer near your family in Latakia. You sounded stable and committed to what you were doing. We thought you sounded kind of sad, but still...how did you land in Turkey?"

"Like I said the other day, it all started when you called last month."

"Go on," Maha prodded.

Huda hesitated a bit. She started saying something a couple of times but stopped herself before even a full word could come out of her mouth. Then, finally, she said, "You know what? I'm here now. I'm not sure I want to go back to all that. I am glad to be here now."

"You are? For sure?"

"Yes. Absolutely. Even more now that I'm learning the entirety of the story about the war. In Latakia, I was somehow complicit with the abuses of the regime. Either I fight against it, or I support it."

"You really think that?" Maha asked.

"For sure. We made money, my firm, you know? We worked in import and export of materials, and that included things being brought in for the war. I didn't know many details, but I'm sure my firm was profiting from the import of explosives, the fact that more food needed to be imported than before, and even from bringing in construction materials for humanitarian agencies. Not that they ever gave me a raise, but I kept my job when our country reached 60% unemployment. And I know my bosses profited nicely."

"That doesn't make you complicit, though."

"Sure it does. At the time, I was just kind of miserable. I wanted some appreciation for my contribution at work. I was very good at my job, and always covering for my colleagues' mistakes. I was bitter against a system that held me back. But now that I'm meeting people from all the other parts of Turkey..." Her voice drifted off.

"What do you mean?"

"You must hear them in Lebanon, too, right? The abuses, the torture, the unfair arrests, the aimless bombings?"

"Sure," agreed Maha. "But it seems to me that everyone is guilty. I won't name names, but I couldn't support a side if I wanted to. I'd rather fight for people than fight for a side."

"You can't mean that. I heard what happened to your family."

Maha gasped slightly.

Realizing Maha might be suspicious of how she learned about the bombing that had destroyed her childhood home, her brother, and her father, Huda added, "I mean, I figured it out from your Facebook page."

"I see," sighed Maha. Then she added, "But you don't know who did it."

"I don't?"

"You can't. Because we don't know."

"What do you mean? Of course, it was--"

Maha cut her off. "Watch what you're saying, dear."

"Sorry," conceded Huda. "But still... how can you not know?"

"We don't. I know who you think. But my family thinks it was someone else, so I'm not going to even pretend I know."

"But the others, they're not..." Huda was choosing her words, or lack of words, carefully now.

"Everyone is, my dear. That's what you hear here in Lebanon. Everyone has something to ask forgiveness for. At least, everyone who is involved."

"Some fall-out of conflict is to be expected, I suppose," acknowledged Huda.

"So, is it worth it?" Maha asked.

"Of course," Huda stated immediately. "That's why I know I'm in the right place. I don't plan on staying long, though."

"Oh no?" Maha asked.

"I'm going home. I mean, not home to Latakia. Home in the broader sense. I'm going to get involved."

"Girl, be careful! By now, everyone has figured out what happened to you. Your face is all over Facebook and Twitter and stuff. You've gathered a bit of attention."

"Why? Just because I'm finally being myself?"

"I think you are doing a little bit more than just being yourself," Maha observed. Then she ventured, "And this man, the one you are seeing, or maybe seeing? What does he say about all this?"

"That's why I came to live with him. He's going to help me. At least..."

"What is it, dear?"

"Well, I've been here two weeks, and he seems to be avoiding the subject. He keeps asking me about myself, my life, my history, my interests, my dreams. He's eating my food. I'm sleeping in his home. But I came to live with him because he said he could put me in touch with the right people to send me back, although since I came, he hasn't mentioned it. At all. I tried talking about it last night, but he just shushed me and told me I was cute."

"Maybe he does like you. Maybe he wants to keep you around," Maha encouraged.

"Maybe..." Huda replied dreamily.

"Or maybe he isn't who you think he is."

"What do you mean?"

"Do you think maybe he's trying to check you out, make sure you're legit? And are you sure who he is loyal to?"

"Don't even!" Huda exclaimed.

"Darling, I'm glad you're finding yourself, and I'm glad you're discovering a more interesting life. But these are dangerous times. Yes, take risks, but don't take too many. Be smart."

Huda kept silent. What could she say in response? Yes, Mama? Maha was being a bit bossy.

Then Maha mercifully changed the subject. "The reason I called you was that I'm doing a project. It sounds like everything you want to do. Except for the taking-sides thing. But to be fair, this is mostly going to support the people you want to support."

This got Huda's attention. "Tell me."

"So, like I said, we're making real progress with getting Leila's friend released. Did I send you her blog?"

"No."

"It's called The Mockingbird. Google it; it's easy to find. She didn't take sides, just tried to point out the need for justice in various situations. Though it's easy to see how they got upset with what she was writing."

"I'll look it up."

"The point is, we are arguing that she was taken under illegitimate pretenses. She didn't do anything worthy of arrest. But the project is growing. Now that we are gaining traction with her story, new stories are coming up."

"Who is 'we'?"

"Just me and a couple of friends. Leila and Roxy were involved at first, but they have had family stuff come up, so had to stop. But a few other friends here in Beirut are working with me."

"Don't worry. I don't have any family stuff. At all!" Huda forced a laugh.

Maha laughed, too. Then she announced, "Actually, I do. I'm due in a couple of months."

"*Mabrouk!*"

"Thanks. But I'm going to keep working on this as much as I can. I really believe in it." Maha took a deep breath. "We now have almost forty names, all of the people who, according to what we have been told, were taken, but without a legitimate reason. We want to find the truth about all of them and, if the story is true, lobby to get them out."

"That's great!" Huda said. "Just yesterday someone was telling me about his old school friend who was taken, and they didn't know why or where or anything. Those devils!"

"So, if I sent you a few names, do you think you could do some research for me? Talk to your friends, get their contacts in-country in the different cities of the north, find out what really happened?"

"People here talk so much, I kind of think that if anyone knew, they'd tell," Huda observed.

"That may be," said Maha. "So sometimes maybe your friends even know. But more often, I'm thinking it would be their friends inside who can help us."

"True."

"So, are you interested?"

"Ummm," Huda hesitated. "Is this a job?"

"No. We don't have any money," Maha pointed out. "But we might soon. If you're interested. For a bigger research project."

"Sure. If I'm still in Turkey, that is."

"So, let's start with these names and see what you can find out."

"Sounds good. I've been spending too much time sitting around the house anyway."

The conversation ended rather abruptly after that. They said their quick goodbyes, and then Huda quickly shut the computer because she heard someone coming in at the door.

As she had hoped, it was Adnan. Huda could tell even before he walked into the room because he was whistling. She loved that he whistled.

Huda adjusted her position on the sofa and put his computer, the one she had been using for Skype, on the floor.

When he walked in she said, "Welcome home! How was your morning?"

He dropped to the sofa by her side, snug against her body. Huda shifted her weight to lean against him.

Adnan pulled out his phone and tapped on a few apps absentmindedly. Then he said, "Honestly, hard. It's one of those days when I don't know why I keep trying."

"I'm sorry to hear that. What happened?" Huda peered up at him.

Still staring at his phone, Adnan didn't answer for a minute or two. So Huda peered down to see what he was looking at on the phone. Photos.

"Who are they?" she asked.

He didn't answer immediately, instead kept scrolling. Eventually, he said, "My family."

Huda brightened. "Let me see!"

He turned the phone toward her, and she reached out to scroll through the photos at her own pace. A traditionally-clad woman with wrinkled skin embraced a much younger version of Adnan. "My grandmother," he said. "My mother's mother."

"She looks sweet," Huda commented.

"Very much so. She taught me a lot."

She scrolled again and saw a couple of teenage boys. "Your brothers?"

"Yes."

"They're still there?"

"For now. My brother will be 18 soon, though, so we need to get him out before he's drafted."

"You'll bring him here?"

"Probably."

Huda kept scrolling through photos of his mother, his father, and a few uncles and aunts. These photos revealed more of him than he'd allowed her to see thus far, and she felt this was a special moment. She had understood he was from an established Damascene family, and now she saw that he came from wealth, too. They were a secularized family. His grandmother was clearly conservative, but his mother was clad in Western dress. His brothers were dressed exactly like the rich kids in the Damascus cafés that Huda remembered from her student days.

As she kept scrolling, Adnan leaned forward and pulled the already-full ashtray to him, took out a cigarette, then offered Huda one. As he lit hers, he said, "The worst thing about all this is the separation, isn't it?"

Huda handed the phone back to Adnan and concentrated for a moment on getting the smoke going. She had never smoked before coming to Turkey, other than an occasional *arguile*. She had considered it a disgusting habit and had preferred to live a healthy life. But in the first couple of days with her new friends, she saw how integral a part of life cigarettes were going to be here, so had decided to learn. She still found it disgusting, but she was learning to enjoy the sensation of heat flowing down her throat and of blowing smoke out into the air. It felt symbolic of the way in which all her senses were coming alive these days.

They sat in silence for a bit, each in their own thoughts. Once Huda had found the relaxation in the puffs of smoke, she reached forward to tap the ashy tip into the tray. Then she garnered up the courage given by his tiny window of vulnerability, and their shared camaraderie smoking side-by-side, to broach the subject. She decided to start by asking, "Why don't you fight?"

"Me?"

"Yes. You told me that you help recruit fighters and get them trained. Why not go yourself?"

He stared at her blankly.

So Huda continued, "I mean, I do think it's a bit surprising that you told me that, since everyone else around here seems so opposed to violence. But I agree with you. I don't think this conflict will resolve itself peacefully the way they all want."

"How so?" he then asked.

"You know. The regime needs to be destroyed, right?"

He still didn't say anything. Instead, he took another long drag on his cigarette. Huda did the same.

Finally, Adnan spoke. "I've been trying to figure you out, you know? This Alawite girl who told me that she's Alawite – which, honestly, you probably shouldn't have done – who comes here looking to martyr herself or something. It doesn't make any sense."

"It doesn't?" Huda asked this with disappointment, realizing that he'd once again evaded revealing any of his own thoughts. Some family photos were as far as he would go. But at least, they were finally talking about her plans.

"You had a good life," he continued. "It's not like the rest of us. We all had to leave. I'd do anything to be near my family again, but you ran away from your family. Look around. Everyone here lost a job or had to drop out of university, was arrested or had a family member in jail and tortured, and lost a home. Everyone. My situation is probably the best. I was just threatened. But you came because you wanted to."

"Am I not allowed to believe in something?"

"*Taieb*. What do you believe in?"

"Freedom, for one. And equal opportunity. A fair chance for everyone. Respect for women and for minorities. It doesn't have to have happened to me. I know it has happened to others, and I believe it shouldn't."

"You really want to risk your life for it? More specifically, you are ready to die for some ideals?"

Now Huda smushed out her cigarette and leaned back into Adnan's arms, taking his hand in hers. "Adnan, the life I was living before I came here was death. I have lived more in the past few weeks than I did in the past five years. We are the living dead, those of us pretending that nothing has changed. Syria came to life, and it has taken me two years to realize that. I'd rather die on a battlefield than walk around living no better than a zombie."

He patted her hand and turned to look into her eyes. Then he gave her a quick yet deep kiss on the lips before saying, "That was poetry."

She smiled and absorbed the warmth of his gaze.

"I still think it's a bit naïve," he continued. "Surely when you hear the stories of how much our friends have all suffered it makes you wonder if it's worth it."

Huda nodded, then said, "Yes it does. But that's why the cause needs willing volunteers like me so that fewer innocents are forced to pay the price."

Adnan pulled away and stood up. He looked around the room. "Where's my computer?"

Huda reached down to where she had laid it and handed it to him.

He sat down again and opened the laptop. While he waited for it to come out of sleep, he said, "I'll write now to my contact who knows the commander of the female regiment. We'll find a way to get you back in soon."

"Thank you!" Huda exclaimed, then reached over to give him a big hug and a peck on the cheek.

Chapter Twenty-five

Back in Beirut, Maha hung up from the Skype call seriously worried for her old university neighbor. She had never known Huda very well, but she knew that Huda had had a reputation for being a hard worker, the early to bed and early to rise type, studious, neat and tidy with everything in its place. She had been friendly but always a bit formal. The only friend who she had felt truly comfortable with was Leila. Maha had become briefly close with Huda, right at the time that Huda had an emotional breakdown. Later, Maha learned that it was because her professor had taken advantage of her. No woman would respond well to that, but Maha had been particularly concerned that Huda had no one to turn to and had shied away from friendship or comfort.

After the incident, Maha had tried to keep an eye out for her neighbor and had never felt that Huda was truly happy, though depression had not overtaken her either. Huda had finished out her university years as well as could be hoped given the circumstances.

But one thing Huda had never been was reckless. Maha found this transformation a bit disturbing, in part because it was out of character, but even more because she had a feeling Huda had no idea what she was actually doing. It was clear that a raging swathe of emotions was eking it out in her heart, and Maha could only hope that the more mature, wiser emotions might prevail.

So Maha hoped that having something productive and positive to do would help. Perhaps this project was exactly what Huda needed. To that end, still seated in front of her computer, Maha composed an email to Huda with the names of five people who had disappeared in the northwestern parts of Syria, along with the known details, which were few. These were people whose stories Maha's team in Beirut had not been successful in discovering. Then Maha gave Huda a list of seven questions to answer about each.

Maha uploaded the email to a secure server, as one of Samir's friends had taught her to do, and emailed the access details to Huda, Facebooking her the password separately.

That done, she took a moment to browse through her messages on Facebook. There were a few new ones that day.

Most were regular updates and hello's from friends, but one message caught her eye. It was from the old university friend whose cousin had been taken in the early days of the conflict. She clicked on it and read the words she had hoped never to see, the words she had dreaded when her own husband was in jail. "Thank you for trying, dear. My cousin's body was delivered to his parents this morning. Please keep us in your prayers."

The emotion overcame Maha like a wave, a tsunami set to knock down anything in its path. She couldn't breathe, and she felt a deadening weight on her back. For good effect, the baby kicked hard at the same moment. Maha stood up and staggered over to the sofa, where she collapsed in pain, gasping for breath.

She tried to imagine what that poor boy's parents were feeling right now, what his friends and his family might be feeling. And she couldn't help but imagine what it would mean if it happened to others on her list, or even if it had happened to her. It came so close to happening to her.

For several minutes she lay on the sofa, cringing in pain and dread. The physical pain was easier to react to than the emotional pain of the thought of what that moment must have meant to this family. She spent so much energy trying to create the other kind of moment, the moment of joy, that she didn't want to even imagine the moment that this young man's parents had just experienced.

In the minutes that followed, a bit of rage began to grow in her heart. Rage against people who could do such a thing, who could make a family suffer so, who didn't have the least bit of respect for human life.

This anger was what got her back off the sofa. Maha walked over to the computer and called up his file, with the photos and anecdotes that his family had sent her to help garner human interest in his story.

She began to draft a little obituary for him that she wanted to send via the various outlets of social media in his honor, but also by means of very subtly pointing the finger at his grim reapers.

Half an hour later, she had a few paragraphs written and two photographs selected. One was the photo that her friend had begun spreading around Facebook, and the other one was of him playing with a football. That one was so endearing and so human; Maha was sure it would capture the pain she felt at a life ended too early, for no good reason.

She sent it off to her friend to ask permission to share it then went to prepare some tea.

By the time Maha arrived back at her computer, her friend had already replied giving her the go-ahead, so she had begun her next campaign. She posted the photos, and the brief text in both Arabic and English, to her Facebook profile and tagged several dozen of her friends asking them to share it. Then she shared it to the Mockingbird page, the group she had started called "Let's Get our Loved Ones Out", and a few other Syria advocacy groups that she had joined. Then she got started on Twitter and created a hashtag for him: #RIPMahmoud. She broke the message up into small pieces, then tagged various people in her posts and asked them to retweet. Within minutes, as she was just starting to post it to some of the blog forums she followed, the messages of support began to come in.

The trickle of comments of support, shares, retweets and queries about how the family could be helped grew into a flood of social media activity greater than anything she had ever been involved in before.

For the rest of that afternoon and into the evening, Maha just sat at her computer and watched the comments and the story of young Mahmoud go viral.

That evening, Maha's team came over for some of her famous strong coffee and some television. And to catch up on the project. They filled the room with cigarette fumes, giving Maha an opportunity to build her fortitude of character as she longingly inhaled a bit of secondary smoke. She updated them on her conversation with Huda and asked them if they had seen the online excitement about Mahmoud.

They had seen it, of course, and had themselves contributed by commenting and sharing on their networks. By this point, adding up the various posts and shares, they estimated that as many as 50,000 people had already read about what happened to Mahmoud, and as many as 3,000 had written messages of support and sympathy. A large number of those were asking what they could do to help.

The three of them brainstormed a bit, then decided to start a fundraiser for his family on YouCaring. It took no more than an hour to set it up, even though they toiled over the exact wording of the appeal and fiddled to get the photo just right. They decided not to tell his family; instead, they would surprise them with whatever funds came in.

Once the YouCaring crowdfunding page went live, they posted and tweeted a dozen or so links to the page, and then they went home to go to sleep. By the time the sun awoke the next morning, $10,000 had already been contributed.

"What are they going to do with $10,000?" Samir asked when Maha showed him the fruits of her labor during the past 24 hours.

"I don't know. Maybe escape Syria? They can't want to stay after all this has happened."

"No, I don't suppose they do. So how are you going to get it to them?"

"I don't know that either," Maha giggled. "Right now it's all dropping into my PayPal account. *Habiby*, we're rich!"

Samir laughed with her for a moment, then stopped himself. "We need to be careful. We can't mess around with other people's money. You need to figure out what to do with this, and give it away fast."

"I know. And I will – but let me just take a few hours and enjoy the success."

"Success?" Samir lifted an eye.

That immediately squashed Maha's lighthearted sense of satisfaction. "Oh. I didn't mean. I didn't think... No, of course, this boy's death is not a success."

"It definitely is not," Samir said, then smiled broadly. "But I do think it's commendable that you are bringing something good out of a terrible situation."

"I suppose it will be small comfort to the people who loved him," Maha groaned.

"Do you know what I think?" Samir asked.
"What?"

"I think that they are not going to be as pleased with the money as they are going to be pleased that his story is being shared. That people all around the world have seen his photo and joined them in mourning for him."

Maha flipped over to his Facebook page, which someone had created in his honor in the middle of the night. Indeed, the messages of support were touching and may be some slight comfort to his family.

"Can I make a suggestion?" Samir then asked tentatively. Though they had conceived of it together, once the project started Maha had avoided involving him, partially because she wanted it to be her own, and also because she knew he was busy. There was also a part of her which wasn't sure it would be good for their marriage. Samir had always been a religious man, but he now spiritualized things even more. With everything he had suffered, he was finding his comfort in faith. Maha had also always been a faithful Christian, though perhaps never quite as fervently as her pastor husband. But she had gone the other way: struggling to imagine how God could allow these things to happen, she chose not to think about God at all. Many of her Syrian friends in Lebanon, most of whom were either involved in humanitarian or advocacy work of some sort or were artists, had rejected God entirely. Maha had never had so many atheist friends as she did now. She herself didn't go that far. She just chose not to think about God.

Working together with her husband on a cause would force them to talk about their religious differences, and neither she nor he wanted that. She didn't want it because she didn't want to think about it. But she also knew that it would destroy Samir if he had to add his wife's disbelief to the demons that he had been battling since he returned from Syria.

But one little suggestion? Why not. "Tell me."

"Change the description on the YouCaring site. You know we will meet more families who have suffered the same tragedy. Or if they haven't they will. You've touched the hearts of people all around the world, people who want to give to help Syrians. Give this first 10,000 to Mahmoud's family. Then, starting now, take donations for all families who have lost loved ones in the war. It can be some kind of a fund that gives grants to families in need. If you have made $10,000 in one night, you're just getting started. But you need to change the description of the site. As long as people will think they are giving for Mahmoud, we will need to give it to him."

Maha looked at her husband in wonder. He was a genius.

Chapter Twenty-six

Already back in Kuwait for three weeks, Leila had not yet once left the house. She just couldn't find the will. It was as if she had used every last little ounce of human energy remaining during the days that Hassoun had spent with them in Amman. She had been tired before, spending long mostly-unproductive days in her mother's little flat, but the level of exhaustion that had overtaken her, the moment she set foot back in her own beautiful Kuwait home, was of an entirely different order.

She stayed in bed, with the blinds down in the room, only rising to use the toilet. Hassoun had taken over the kitchen, something she had never imagined she would see him do. But someone had to care for the family and Leila just didn't have it in her.

Every day he brought her breakfast in bed. She usually picked at it, but sometimes it felt like even sitting up to sip the tea demanded more energy than she could devote.

She heard noises around the house that suggested the boys were somehow making it to school every morning and getting home every afternoon. Though the room was dark and Leila was always somehow half-asleep, she got the impression that there was another woman in the house, at least, a few hours a day. She suspected that Hassoun had asked Mila, their Filipina housekeeper, to take on more hours to help with the cleaning and to look after the boys when he was at work. She thought that made sense. Then she fell asleep.

In the evenings, Hassoun again brought her food, which she sometimes picked at and sometimes didn't.

After their first night back, when Leila ignored her husband climbing into bed next to her, she never noticed him coming to bed. She figured he was sleeping on the sofa, maybe watching television or something. It didn't occur to her that her unbathed body was emitting an aroma that kept him away, or that her room had not been aired out at all for weeks. If anything, she was relieved. She was too tired to talk, much less make love to her husband.

Two weeks to the day after their arrival, Leila woke up. She sat up sometime mid-morning and looked around the dark room, then got up and peeked into the corridor. The house was empty.

So she wandered into the living room and saw everything just exactly the way it had always been: a little play area set up for the boys, sofas arranged in a U formation, every woman's dream kitchen off to the side, clean and tidy as it ever was. She was now sure that a maid was looking after their house.

Leila wandered into the kitchen and put some water on to boil. She wasn't yet hungry, but some tea would do her good.

When the tea was ready, Leila wandered into the living room, fell on the black leather sofa and threw her feet onto the little coffee table. She pulled the remote control out from between two cushions and turned on the television.

She didn't watch, though. Instead, she began to think.

She hadn't done much thinking lately, and when the thoughts began they were like an avalanche.

There was little logic to her thinking. Instead, she felt like she was dreaming the past five months of her life, the events, and emotions since the day she had the idea of visiting her family.

She fingered the soft leather of the sofa, then thought about the sandy mattresses that had served as her family's living space in Za'atari. This stood in stark contrast with the equally dingy but considerably cleaner mattresses that kitted out their flat in Jabal Hussein. But neither held a candle to this sofa, much less to the four-post bed and thick mattress she had slept in for the past few weeks. Her family's living room was morphed into a bedroom each night, half a dozen souls or more piled onto mattresses. The children had to share mattresses. There were not enough mattresses to go around, but there would not be enough space on the floor even if there were. Her boys, in this spacious flat, had bunkbeds. Bunkbeds! What a luxury, she thought now. She had never considered them to be anything other than a practical choice.

How was it, though, that Hammoudi and Saleh didn't seem to care about sharing mattresses? For that matter, neither had Leila. She had had a mattress to herself but had needed to step over an entire collection of sisters and sisters-in-law just to get to the bathroom in the middle of the night. But she had been happy because she had been with them. Her boys had been happy because they got to cuddle up with their cousins.

Who cared about bunkbeds? They just kept everyone isolated away from each other.

This flat would fit everyone. Sure, she didn't have that many beds or that many mattresses, not now anyway. Hassoun liked the look of a sparse flat and Leila had never had reason to disagree; after all, they lived too far away from family to have guests on any regular basis. On the rare occasions that company did come to stay, the spare room was more than enough. A spare room. What a laughable luxury. Surely there was no justice in a world where her family had long given up any dream of privacy, yet Leila and her husband could enjoy privacy every night if they so chose.

Not that they did. Leila was relieved, really, that Hassoun was keeping his distance. As time had passed by, she had grown less and less encouraged by his touches. By the time they had boarded the plane to Kuwait, not only was she disinterested, but she found herself shrinking away from his arms. Arriving home, she was if anything disgusted. The thought of sharing a bed with Hassoun again gave her the heebie-jeebies.

She didn't know why, exactly. They'd fought before. She was still mad at him for pulling them back to Kuwait, but she also knew that it was his right. What she felt now was something different. She didn't know what and wasn't sure she wanted to know. She just didn't want to have to touch him.

Lost in this sea of thoughts and emotions, Leila sat on the sofa staring blankly at the television for several hours. When she finally drew her eyes to the clock, she saw that the boys would be returning from school shortly. Completely unaware of what routine had been developed since their return from Jordan, Leila knew that they had a routine and could hardly bear the thought of putting on a smile to greet her sons, much less kissing her husband.

She stood up and walked into her room, closing the door behind her.

Standing in the dark, stuffy room, Leila leaned back against the shut door. She was panting ever so slightly. Her head had started throbbing just in the few short moments it had taken to walk back to the room.

She let her legs give way and slid to the floor. Several deep breaths later, she closed her eyes and leaned her head back in relief.

Her limbs felt like jelly and little by little she slumped further back until she was laying on the floor.

Sure enough, she soon heard a key turning in the vast expanse of the flat on the other side of that bedroom door, and then the bubble of tiny happy voices. She thought she could make out Mila's voice as well.

Every afternoon, Hammoudi and Saleh had come in to give her a kiss on the cheek. Their endless happiness and flexibility after they, too, had now seen and lived through a refugee ordeal, baffled Leila. She shuddered as she remembered her littlest asking her about rape. But he seemed to have forgotten that disgusting game already; she hoped to God that he would never remember. A few times the boys had tried to clamber up into bed with her and cuddle, but Leila had curled into a ball and ignored them in her zombie-like state. But they still came to give her a peck on the cheek.

This afternoon, Leila had the presence of mind to reach up to the door and turn the lock. Then she lay her head on her arms and closed her eyes.

It was a pounding sound that pulled her back to wakefulness some time later. The banging on the door was making her headache worse, and Leila found she couldn't ignore it. So she stood up, opened the lock and walked back to bed. Hassoun came in and followed her, perching himself on the edge of the bed, inches away from where Leila was already snuggling herself up under the duvet. He sat down beside her. Leila felt the soft pressure of his hand on her back.

"Leila," he began in his interminably patient voice. "My life, I don't know what is going on with you. We are all waiting for you to get better or to wake up or whatever, but the boys miss their mother. And I really, really miss my wife. I've called a doctor, and he'll be here in half an hour. We need to get this room ready to receive him."

"No!" Leila exclaimed. "No doctor."

"It has been three weeks already," Hassoun pointed out. "You're sick, and you're not getting better on your own. We should have called a doctor right at the beginning. That was my mistake. I'm so used to you taking care of these details..." his voice trailed off.

"I'm fine, really. Just tired," Leila lied. She knew she was not just tired; she was terrified. Terrified of facing the world out there. Terrified of Hassoun's hand that still lay somewhere on her upper back.

"Darling, it's too late, anyway. He's already on his way. If you're really just tired, then it will be good to confirm it."

"Please," she begged. "Please don't. Call him and cancel. I can't face a doctor right now." To her chagrin, she felt her nose twitch and tears begin to gather behind her eyes. She buried her face a little further below the duvet.

But Hassoun wasn't swayed, and Leila didn't have the energy to continue resisting. She hid under the covers while he opened the curtains and threw the windows wide open. Then he called out "Mila!" and Leila heard steps approaching in the hallway. Leila attempted a frail smile and a nod by way of greeting the housekeeper who had been her regular companion around the house for the past few years but who now felt like a complete stranger. Then she closed her eyes. Hassoun instructed Mila to mop the room and change the bedding. He picked Leila up and carried her into the bathroom. Slightly shocked by so much bright light and fresh air and the smell of cleaning supplies and being gathered into her husband's arms and deposited on the covered toilet seat, Leila sat obediently while Hassoun gently lifted her pajamas off of her, washed her face and arms with a cloth, then dressed her in a clean *galabeya*, a housecoat that could double both as new pajamas and as appropriate garb for receiving a guest.

When he arrived, the doctor took her temperature and her blood pressure and her pulse. He asked some questions, most of which Hassoun answered while Leila lay back on the fresh, clean pillows Mila had fluffed for her. Then he diagnosed her with hypertension, a catch-all diagnosis that Leila had at various times heard pronounced over her mother, her aunt, and a few cousins.

He prescribed more bed rest, a specific diet, and a few pills that Hassoun could easily procure at the pharmacy downstairs.

More awake than she had been in weeks, Leila found she no longer wanted to sleep. The excitement over the doctor's arrival and diagnosing, along with the cleaning and partial bathing, had actually woken her up.

The fear was still there, though. She avoided eye contact with Hassoun when he returned with the medications and a tall glass of water. She grunted when he asked if she was ready to see the boys. Instead, she stood up and, hoping to make her meaning clear, yanked the curtains shut then marched back to bed.

Hassoun made one more attempt at a peck on her cheek, but when she turned her face away, he simply walked out of the room. Before he left, though, he said, "Take the time you need. Your family is waiting for you. But from now on, this door stays open. A locksmith is coming tonight to remove the latch. You have no idea how frightened we were when we couldn't get into the room this afternoon. Please don't ever do that again." Leila thought she heard his voice catching as he said these words and she felt a brief pang of sympathy for someone other than herself.

But it didn't last. Alone in the mostly-dark room with light and the sound of the television and the whispers of Hassoun and the Filipino maid all filtering in through the open door, Leila sat on the edge of the bed and fumed, feeling a prisoner in her own home. She couldn't leave her room because there were people out there. She couldn't leave the flat because that was simply too frightening. She couldn't sleep anymore, either.

She stood up and wandered over to where her suitcase lay half unpacked, her purse to the side. She rummaged around until she found her phone, the battery of which had long desisted, and her charger. She plugged it into the wall socket by her bed and settled herself back against the pillows while it turned on. A flood of messages greeted her within the course of a minute. There were WhatsApp messages from her sisters, her sister-in-law Rana, Maha, and a couple of her friends in Kuwait who no doubt were wondering why she had come back but not called. Missed-calls on Viber from her sisters and Maha as well. Facebook messages from Maha, her sister Nuha, Huda and half a dozen friends with whom she kept occasional contact. There were also emails from assorted friends and acquaintances, mostly people in Kuwait with whom she had done fundraising before leaving for Jordan.

Scrolling through the messages, she realized that she had never told her family that she was home safely. They must have called Hassoun by now, and he must have given them some story. They were probably worried about her, but surely they knew she was alive and safe. A few other friends might have no idea, though. In particular, Leila was concerned that Maha may be worrying about her safety. Maha had experienced dead silence from loved ones before and had learned to expect a tragedy. So she typed a brief message on WhatsApp, just informing her friend that she was back in Kuwait.

Leila was intrigued by the messages from Huda. There was one every few days. The first were just friendly hello's. Then they referred to how much she absolutely loved Turkey. The last couple of messages were more cryptic, mentioning plans but not giving details. The final message, two days ago, simply said, "Well, I'm off. Wish me luck and I'll see you when this mess is over!"

So Huda had gone to war.

Leila knew she should call her mother, but that was another thought that she couldn't bear. One more day wouldn't hurt, she reasoned.

The noises of life continued in the hallway. Leila heard rummaging in the kitchen and felt the scent of food wafting down toward the room. She didn't like the smell, she thought, as she began scrolling through her Facebook feed; in fact, she was still not hungry at all. After a while, Hassoun appeared in the doorway, carrying a tray of food. He put it on the bed by her side. Standing over her, he informed her that after eating something, she should take one of each of the three types of pills. Then he walked out again.

Leila did pick at the food and took in a few tiny bites.

Curious, she picked up the boxes of pills that had been laid out on the nightstand. Reading the boxes, she saw that one was, indeed, a medication for hypertension. The other two, however, looked like they had nothing at all to do with blood pressure. She pulled out the informational leaflet and discovered that one was recommended for anxiety and the other for depression.

This did not surprise her. She felt anxious and depressed, after all. But she didn't like a doctor saying so. He may not have said so in so many words, but Hassoun had seen the medications, surely read their descriptions just as she now was. So now she was his mentally unstable wife.

This thought did not help her mood, but at this particular moment, Leila felt more anxious than depressed, and she felt twitchy all over. She stood up and paced the room by the curtains that shielded her from the world beyond.

As she walked out her frustration, deciding whether or not to admit to the doctor's diagnosis by taking the pills, she heard the door shut. Mila must have left. The water in the boys' bathroom was running, and she soon heard happy splashing sounds. All of a sudden, longing gripped Leila's entire being, and she wanted nothing more than to be wrapped in the embrace of those four little arms. She began wandering to the open door, but the bright light in the hallway stopped her. She wanted her little boys but not enough to push against the fear. So she walked back to the bed and perched on its edge, hands in her lap.

Hassoun found her sitting this way, staring at her palms when he returned some time later. A few minutes or a few hours later, Leila wasn't sure. The flat was now silent, so she imagined the boys were tucked into bed.

"The locksmith just called. He's on his way," Hassoun announced.

Then he picked up the medications and furrowed his eyebrows. "You haven't taken them yet! Leila!" His voice rose in a desperate tone. "We need you back."

Leila just sat there. So Hassoun popped out three pills himself, one from each box, and sat down between Leila and the nightstand. He turned and held her mouth open with one hand, dropping a pill onto her tongue with the other hand, then holding the glass of water up to her mouth until she had no choice but to swallow. He repeated this twice, then stood up, took the tray of half-eaten food from where it sat on the bed, and walked out.

The locksmith came and went, and Leila kept sitting there. She was beginning to feel the effects of the medicine. It was dulling her senses, and as terrible as the fear was, the awareness that it was being suppressed chemically scared her even more. But there was nothing to do, she thought, so she turned on the television and leaned back in the bed. She flipped through the channels until she found news of Syria. For several hours, she stared at images of fallen buildings, houses riddled with gaping holes, kitchens and bathrooms hanging precariously from these holes, men groaning in pain as they were carted away on stretchers, children screaming, hospital beds covered in blood, youth throwing Molotov cocktails on the streets, and women marching smartly with revolvers in their arms. She looked closely to see if Huda might be among them, but she wasn't.

Many hours later, Leila stood to go to the bathroom. As she walked back to bed, the sight of those ghastly medicine boxes caught her eye. Afterward, she couldn't tell exactly what overtook her mind, but she felt a moment of lucid determination. She decided to take every single last pill from all three boxes, at once.

Hassoun had an early shift at the hospital the next day, so he came in at 5 am to check on Leila. He found her asleep on the bed, looking more peaceful than he had seen her in a very long time. He leaned over her and gave her a soft kiss on the cheek, breathing a prayer under his breath that she would return to him soon.

He turned to go to the closet to select his clothing for the day. As he did so, he saw the empty packets of medication tossed on the nightstand. He picked up one little metallic tray and confirmed that it was empty. Then the next, then the next. His heartbeat quickened as he leaned down under the bed to look for the dropped pills. They weren't there. He pulled open a drawer and lifted the edge of the duvet. They were nowhere to be seen, which meant one of two things. Either she had destroyed them, or she had consumed them.

Oh to God that she had destroyed them. He shook her shoulder. No response. He shook it again, and again no response. He began shouting her name, "Leila! Leila!" All his medical training left him at that moment as he desperately grabbed her head and held it to his, shouting her name again and again.

Two bleary-eyed boys appeared at the doorway seconds later, and it was the sight of them that jerked him into action.

Hassoun once again swooped Leila into his arms and beckoned the boys to join him. He told Hammoudi to grab his wallet from the counter and to lock the door as he flew down the stairs and into the street. He ran to the car and lay Leila on the back seat. The boys piled into the passenger seat behind him, and with no thought to seatbelts or any other such formalities, he sped into the rising sun.

In the Emergency Room, Hassoun was told by an American doctor who was a friend of the family that Leila's situation was precarious. She was not too far gone, though, and they were pumping her stomach. Any further delay and it may have been too late.

Hammoudi and Saleh, meanwhile, sat side-by-side in two chairs in the waiting room, still in their pajamas, legs flapping back and forth beneath them. Hammoudi's right hand gripped Saleh's left as they stared at the door through which their parents had disappeared.

Chapter Twenty-seven

Huda was somewhere east of Aleppo. She wasn't exactly sure where, but it was some village that had been among the first areas liberated almost two years earlier and now came under the command of a local general who seemed to be more accurately described as a spoiled son of a local landowner. He respected the women, though, allowing them to bunk in some of the abandoned houses and making sure that none of the locals took advantage of them.

She had joined a regimen of female soldiers a few days ago and was currently being trained, which meant that a very gruff middle-aged woman who had lost her husband and all her sons in the Battle of Homs was teaching her how to shoot different types of guns and advising her about survival techniques. Huda was expected to pick the rest of her military knowledge up through the learning-by-doing technique, and she was anxious to get out on the field and start learning by doing.

In the three days she had been here, Huda had already mastered a pistol and an AK47. She was proving herself to have a good eye and was now practicing with a sniper's rifle.

The regimen had no more than two dozen women, and they were divided between three houses. Their captain lived in the flat above the one Huda shared with six other women. The gruff widow slept in the living room by herself. She snored and was known to wake up in the middle of the night screaming from nightmares, so the others generally left her alone at night. Huda had been assigned a room with two other women about her age. Both were from Homs - in fact, everyone Huda had met so far was either from this village near Aleppo or from Homs. One of her roommates had been working as a secretary in the National Bank and had lost her job the moment it became known that her brothers were joining the resistance, but this was after the siege of Bab al-Amr in central Homs had begun, so she stuck on the pro-regime side of the barricades. Returning home was too dangerous, so she had set off north, where her brothers had introduced her to the captain. She had been a soldier in the Free Syrian Army for six months now.

The other roommate told one of the most tragic stories Huda had heard since the day she left Latakia. She was from a well-to-do family from one of the most established Sunni Muslim families in Homs. They were generally apolitical but were particularly intentional about not speaking against the regime. A year after the protests began, in early 2012, an old classmate from her school days, the son of a family with whom her father had good business relations, had returned from Norway, where he was living and working. His visit was to be for two weeks only, but the moment she had set eyes on him, she was drawn to him. And he to her. He extended his stay into a month of whirlwind courtship, and they planned a rushed wedding, after which he would return to Norway and apply for her visa to join him. The wedding was a large family affair, a rare moment of festivities in a city which was increasingly tense, a frontline of the "problems" which were quickly growing into an all-out revolution or, perhaps more accurately, civil war. But for one night, the elite of Homs celebrated this union of two families joined together by money and love, a party uniquely devoid of political overtones. The next day, the young couple planned on traveling to Lebanon for a few days' honeymoon. After that, the groom would fly back to Norway from Beirut, and the bride would return to Damascus, which remained relatively calm, to wait for her visa. The party danced on into the early hours of the morning, and the happy couple finally retired to their bridal suite an hour or so before the sun was due to rise. Dawn, however, brought an aerial attack on the rebel faction based in a nearby neighborhood The regime bombers missed their aim, though, and a loud blast flung them out of each other's arms. When the bride, Huda's new roommate, returned to consciousness a few minutes later, she found the room half-destroyed and her new husband's body on the floor in front of her, arm blown off and guts flowing onto the bright yellow Persian rug.

 Needless to say, from that time on the erstwhile bride took a side in the war. Her loyalties were fiercely anti-regime, but her family, though sympathetic to what she had suffered, feared any loss to their own holdings, business or social status. They tried to assuage her and encourage her to forgive the regime for what was clearly an honest, if costly, mistake. But a few weeks later, she ran away and joined the FSA, determined to bring justice, nay revenge, upon the heads of those who had stolen her beloved from her, so carelessly.

For her part, Huda had a story as well. She had made it up because Adnan had warned her to never, ever, let on to her identity. So she made herself a lawyer from Dera'a, like her old friend Leila. She said her family had all been killed in a random bombing one day when she was out shopping for food. To answer any other questions, she just imagined how Leila would answer.

Tonight, the regiment was out scouting the frontline with the Islamic Front, which had advanced several miles closer to them in the past week. Huda was not yet declared field-ready, so had been left at home to practice her aim and to study up on some strategic warfare texts that were being passed around. She did not like being home alone. It was scary being a single woman in this little village on the outskirts of Aleppo. This was a very conservative village, and in her three days back in Syria Huda had quickly discovered that the FSA's style of governing was a little bit more like anarchy, or chaos than anything that might be described as 'governance.'

Not only that, but she was beginning to feel antsy. She had come to fight, not to study!

But Adnan had warned her of all this, so she knew she had to take it all in stride.

Adnan...at least once an hour in the past three days, she had posed to herself the question of whether she had done the right thing or not. Should she have stayed for him? Clearly, there was something there; Huda was absolutely convinced that she was something special to him, not like the other girls that she eventually came to accept he was also seeing. He spent more time with her than with them, and he had finally begun to open up to her. Should she have changed her plans to stay with him? She knew, in her heart, that he was a great man or, at least, a man destined for greatness. She could make a difference simply by helping him. But every time she posed that question to herself, she put it quickly back to rest. She would not have forgiven herself if she had not followed through on her plans, or what she described to herself as a 'calling' from some unknown deity - for Huda had happily joined the ranks of her atheist housemates.

But as soon as that question was put to rest, she then wondered if she had done the right thing on her last night in Gaziantep, when all was settled and she knew she may never see him or Turkey or anyone who wasn't involved in the war again. Huda refused to allow herself the luxury of hoping to survive. In the month that she spent in Turkey, she had experienced an awakening of her senses such as she had never felt before, and that last night, every last one of her nerves had been completely tingling. She had felt it in her toes and her fingers, in her throat and in her eyes. She had enjoyed shots of arak while laughing and crying and dancing, all at the same time. She had tried her first - and possibly last - puff of marijuana and wondered at the hazy cloud that drifted through her head. As the night had gone on, one by one the guests had gone home and Huda had continued dancing. No one but Adnan knew that she was leaving the next day. The other housemates had no idea of her plans. So they had rolled their eyes at her excess and they, too, had one by one turned in. Adnan himself had eventually tired and tried to leave her still floating around the courtyard area of the house. But she had not let him. Instead, she had followed him into his room and removed her clothes and begged him to take her, not let her go into war a virgin. He had hesitated for only a very brief moment, probably wondering if she was in the right state of mind to make a decision like this. And, indeed, Huda's senses, already buzzing from one end to another, felt things they never had before that night. And may never feel again.

    Had she done the right thing? She little cared for her purity or her reputation. That seemed a laughable thought to her as she sat in a dingy bedroom, all the doors and windows locked, under strict instructions not to let anyone in who didn't know the secret knock and, for heaven's sake, not to sit anywhere near a window at any time because you never knew where stray bullets might fly. The sound of shots were now steady in the background, at all hours of the day. Turkey was a world away. She had to dull her senses now. There were plenty of cigarettes to go around, but no alcohol and certainly no men. At least, no men who could hold a candle to Adnan. She wasn't sure if she had done the right thing, though, because leaving in the morning had been difficult. More difficult than she could even begin to imagine it would be, and she knew that she was now forever tied to this man who, granted, had had many women before her and was surely with another woman now. But that didn't change the fact that he was still somehow in her, and so she was struggling to focus now. Not only had she not heard from him since she crossed back into Syria, but there was no safe communication mechanism and so she probably never would. His silence felt like torture, so did this mean that she had made herself a worse soldier? Because, in her consciousness, her head was entirely still burrowed into his neck, her arms still in his embrace, her legs still intertwined with his.

She didn't know the answer, so at every hour that she asked herself this question, she again reminded herself to keep her mind on the task at hand.

If only the task at hand were more interesting than some boring text of guerrilla warfare strategies.

Chapter Twenty-eight

Leila was released after nearly two full weeks in the hospital, during which the doctors had not allowed her any access to phone, Internet, television, or media of any sort, and visits from Hassoun and the boys were limited to one hour each afternoon. She was given medication that kept her asleep most of the rest of the time. In her brief moments of wakefulness, the irony of being forced to sleep was not lost on her, and she asked the nurse - who was assigned to her bedside at all hours when Leila was not sedated - to please let her just get on with her life.

When Leila woke up for the first time, two days after swallowing a lethal dose of pills, the doctor had to tell her what had happened - what she had done to herself. She was beyond horrified. She felt some relief that her insane attempt at self-intoxication had failed, but mostly disgust at herself for losing control not just on that last day but for the weeks since returning from Jordan, remorse at what she had put her dear boys through and, more than anything, guilt that she made herself so reliant on her husband's care and, furthermore, for embarrassing him at his place of work, among his colleagues at the hospital.

She immediately resolved to pull herself together and be the daughter, wife, mother, and friend that her loved ones deserved.

But the hospital staff were not convinced. And when Hassoun came for his hour-long visits each afternoon, she could tell he was not convinced either and that he wanted her under supervision in the hospital. He wanted to be sure she was better though of course there was no way of being sure.

During Leila's few hours of wakefulness each day, she couldn't repress a feeling of self-hatred. Before, she had felt self-pity and frustration with an unjust world. Now, she knew she could blame no one but herself. So, when on the thirteenth day after Leila awoke from the after-effects of the overdose to which she had subjected her body, she was told she would be discharged that day, she began to prepare herself meticulously. She showered, asked the nurse to help her get some perfume and makeup and applied those with great care, dressed herself in the outfit Hassoun had brought for her, and was perched on the edge of her bed, hands daintily in her lap and a demure smile plastered on her face, when Hassoun walked in, Saleh and Hammoudi trailing behind him.

It would be different this time, she told herself as she stood to give each a solid kiss on the cheek. She took Hassoun's hand in her own and allowed him to lead her down the hall to fill out the discharge paperwork.

When they arrived home, it was dinnertime. Hassoun had arranged for the delivery of a nice meal of American-style burgers, the boys' favorite.

Drawing from her newfound mental resolve, Leila asked the boys about school and their friends and the games they were now playing. She forced herself to glance at Hassoun every few minutes and throw him a smile. Once they were both done eating, she even took his hand and held it gently while they waited for the smaller mouths to catch up. This took a fair bit of mental wherewithal, as she still felt repulsed by his touch. But she forced herself to do it and was feeling quite pleased with herself by the end of the meal.

She offered to bathe the boys and put them to bed while Hassoun rested. Hassoun thanked her but decided they would do it together. She felt his mistrust when he positioned himself between her and the tap when he walked behind her to tidy everything in the boys' room, and when he re-tucked the boys under their covers to make sure they weren't too tight.

Leila gritted her teeth and kept smiling throughout the bedtime routine. Finally, she kissed each boy on the forehead and walked out, turning the light off behind her. Hassoun followed.

The next moment was the most difficult of all. Leila had allowed the boys a longer bath and had read them an extra story, not out of a desire to spend more time with her sons, but rather out of dread for what might happen once she was alone with her husband.

Now, the boys' door pulled shut, they stood facing each other in the hallway. Leila tentatively looked up and saw him staring at her, oddly. She said nothing, as did he.

Eventually, he sighed and walked away. A moment later, from where she still stood in the corridor, she heard him turn on the television.

If she was going to resume her role as mother of the family, Leila knew she had to ask a few questions. She needed to know what she was and was not allowed to do according to doctors' order, she needed to know Hassoun's work schedule, needed to know what arrangements had been made with this Filipina girl, needed to agree on the use of their bedroom. But Hassoun was mad at her, and rightly so. She just couldn't bring herself to begin that conversation.

So she turned around and walked back into her bedroom, whose door could still not be closed. The room had been fully cleaned and tidied during her internment. She opened the closets and saw that her clothing had been rearranged. In the bathroom, all scissors and tweezers and anything else that might cut was gone, as well as, of course, any medications. Hassoun had told her that he would be bringing her pills according to the schedule prescribed. Everything else was locked up in a cabinet in the kitchen to which he held the only key. Leila didn't like being treated like a child, and almost retorted that she was better now and could take care of herself, but caught herself. She knew she would have to prove herself.

Nothing was where she had left it, but rather than ask Hassoun for help, Leila rummaged around the newly-organized bedroom until she gained a sense of what was where. She found her phone in a drawer by the bed and picked it up, holding it to her chest in a tiny hug. To her surprise, tears came to her eyes with this little find.

She attempted to power on the little device, her link to the world outside this posh marble flat which now felt more like a prison than a haven. Finding that the battery was dead, she looked through a few more drawers and shelves until she found the charger. Déjà vu.

Leila sat on the bed and was about to lean back into the pillows when she remembered what she had done last time she had settled into that position. With that memory came an urge to curl up again, to withdraw from reality and shut her eyes on life.

Gasping at the shock of such a strong sentiment, she stood up quickly.

Looking around the room for another place to sit, she finally settled on the floor next to a wall socket under the window.

Again, there was a barrage of messages.

Leila was relieved to find that Hassoun had informed her family that she was unwell. He had not, of course, told them the nature of her illness, so she had voice messages from everyone in that precious little dingy Jabal Hussein hovel wishing her well and a quick recovery. Leila opened her Viber and was about to dial Nuha when she felt tears catching in her eyes. So instead, she recorded them a quick message instead. "Sister, I'm home. I got home last night. So glad Hassoun told you so you wouldn't worry. So don't worry. I'm fine. But I'm still supposed to rest so can't talk now..." Her voice began to catch, so she stopped talking and quickly sent the message.

Maha, though, had no idea, and there were a couple dozen frantic WhatsApp messages from her:

Maha: Leila, how are you?

Maha: Dear, things here are going well.

Maha: We have started a fund for families of victims. I'm not sure if you've seen the page. It's amazing. Take a look at the Facebook page, but also the link to the fund. It's really something incredible.

Then, the next day: Leila, where are you? Are you ok? Have you heard from Huda since she left last week?

Then, the day after: I'm getting worried. Send me a message, dear! There's so much to talk about!

After that, Maha had apparently given up as several days went by with no messages from Beirut. But last night, Leila had received a few more messages.

Maha: Incredible news. You HAVE to call!

Maha: Please tell me you're ok.

Maha: Dear, we need to talk!!!!!!!!!!!!!!!

When Leila opened her Facebook, she saw that Maha had copied the same message this morning into Facebook messenger.

So Leila typed into WhatsApp: I'm here. Sorry for my silence. Long story. What's up?

Almost immediately, Maha replied: Girl! Don't do that to me! I was so worried!

Leila: What's going on?

Maha: Can you Skype?

Leila: Can you believe that I still have not turned on my computer since I've been back in Kuwait? I'm not even sure where it is.

Maha: Viber?

Leila: Sure.

She again opened her Viber, but first popped into the bathroom to check her reflection in the mirror and splash water on her face. Then she told herself to hold it together and went back to where her phone sat plugged into the wall. No sooner had she logged into Viber than the call came through.

"Leila! Where have you been?"

Leila hesitated, then said, "Actually, I was sick. I was in the hospital. I just got back."

"Darling!" Maha exclaimed. "Why didn't you tell me? I had no idea what had happened to you. I was worried sick. If I'd known..."

"What does it matter?" Leila asked, a bit bitterly.

"We're friends! At least, I could have prayed or something."

"Sorry," Leila offered flatly. "Anyway, I didn't even have my phone with me there."

"What happened?" Maha asked.

"*Malish*. No big deal," Leila replied. And, before Maha could insist, she asked, "What's going on with you? Your message made it sound like you had big news? Was the baby born?"

"Not yet. But soon. It's due in a month already, can you believe it?"

"Wow, that went by fast."

"Indeed. I'm not ready. At all."

"Why not? What do you need?"

Maha laughed. "Honestly, if it weren't for Samir's relatives here in Beirut, I'd need everything. But his cousins planned a little party and invited women from the church. Between them all, I have a ton of diapers, some clothes, lots of random cleaning things and oils that I'll need to learn how to use, and an assortment of adorable outfits. Oh, and like five blankets. They're so cute and small."

Now Leila let out a soft chuckle. "You sound like you've become more excited about motherhood."

But instead of enjoying the joke, Maha replied, "But I'm not, not at all. I mean, I guess I've gotten used to the idea, and everyone tells me that when I see the little one I'll fall in love. But other things just feel so much more important to me right now."

"How so?" Leila asked. A year ago, she could not have possibly imagined anything more exciting than becoming a mother. But during these months that had passed, her own precious darlings had faded in importance in her everyday life as the trauma of reality had grown and grown. This was not really a great world into which to be introducing new life, after all.

"Oh, you know, the usual."

Leila hesitated, unsure of how to reply.

Maha quickly filled the silence, though, announcing, "But I have great news. Not great. Amazing. Incredible. Enormous!" Her voice was trembling with excitement.

Leila, doubtful of her friend's enthusiasm, simply replied, "What?"

"Guess."

"Oh, I couldn't possibly begin," Leila replied.

"My goodness. This is too big to just say. You're really not going to believe it."

Leila was not impressed by this little game. "Just say it," she said wearily.

"Ok." Leila could hear Maha taking a big gulp of breath. "She's being released."

Leila was, at first, confused. Who was 'she'? And released from where? She tried to think through different members of Maha's family that Leila knew or had heard about. As far as she knew, Maha's family was all alive and well - except, of course, for her father and brother. Samir was already free, and of course, he was a 'he'. Then Leila's thoughts went to Huda. Was Huda needing releasing? Leila had missed a lot, then, in the weeks that had passed.

"Did you hear me?" Maha asked. "Isn't that amazing? She's being released. Day after tomorrow. She needs to leave Syria, of course, so we're expecting her in Lebanon on Wednesday."

Then, Leila said, "Maha, I have no idea what you're talking about."

"Nisreen!" Maha practically shouted. "How could you have forgotten about your friend?"

Then a wave of fresh emotion came over Leila. More than emotion, it was a form of conviction, a rebooting of her entire system. She knew in that minute that the depression was behind her, but that she would never again be the wife Hassoun wanted nor the mother her sons had grown accustomed to. But maybe she would be something better. She was suddenly confident that her family was going to be alright, and that it was no longer her job to care for them, at least not for now. For now, she was once again that twenty-two-year-old perched on the roof of her old residential building at the University of Damascus, wind blowing in her face, the world before her just waiting to be conquered.

Nisreen was being released. Leila had played a small part in it, and Maha, who had clearly done all the hard work, was a genius.

Leila dropped the phone to the floor and stood up and started dancing around the room, head tilted back and laughter bubbling over.

"Woohoo!" she screamed at the top of her lungs.

Hassoun appeared at the door, out of breath and deep worry on his face.

Leila ran up to him and planted a big kiss on his mouth. "Nisreen is being released!" she grinned, arms around his neck.

He seemed confused and did not share her enthusiasm for the news, but seemed to appreciate the kiss well enough, taking her into his arms and kissing her back with a fervor and desire that betrayed the months of growing frustration on his part.

As he hungered for her, Leila found her desire begin to well up within her, and she started pulling him to the bed while she pulled his shirt open.

Hours later, laying naked under the covers, Hassoun fingered Leila's hair tenderly in the same way he had once done, in the early days of their marriage.

She stared back at him and caressed his whiskery cheek with the back of her finger.

"It's different now," she ventured.

"It doesn't matter," he replied.

"Yes, it does."

Hassoun pulled his hand away and sat up. "What do you mean?"

"I'm going to Beirut to see the girls. I want to be there to receive Nisreen."

"But you only just got back," he pointed out.

Leila sat up and faced him, cross-legged. "I know. But there's work to be done."

Her heart tugged at the disappointment that passed over his face, the raw emotion in the eyes of a man who had been required to hold it together for the sake of his family for too long, who just wanted his wife back.

So Leila tried to explain. "I do love you. Really, I do. And I won't stay away forever. And this time, it will be different, I promise. I know what I want and need. And so do you. Someday, I think, you will see this as good too. But this is who I am. I'm not just about you and the boys. I'm not even just about you and the boys and my family. They're going to be alright. I understand that now. But you and me? We're Syria. Those two little boys sleeping in the other room, they're the future of Syria. You have your work to do here. And I need to go do my work for Syria."

"What is your work?" he asked.

"Maha has started a fund to help families who have lost loved ones in the war. No doubt Nisreen is going to have a large platform for her writing after all the publicity she has received. She is the voice for the Syria that we all dream of building. Huda has gone to fight for what she believes."

"And you?" he asked again.

"I belong by their side. Before all this started, remember I was helping raise funds for relief aid? I was thinking I might start an aid division to go with Maha's fund."

"You can't do that from here?"

"Probably. But not now. For now, I need to be there."

"Leila, I have missed you so much," he protested. "I need you. The boys need you."

"You will have each other."

His eyes raised in surprise.

"I know you have done well with them this month," Leila explained. "Honestly, I think you can care for them better than I can right now. They need more daddy time anyway, after our months in Jordan."

He stared at her for a moment, then took her hand and gave it a soft kiss. "Come back soon."

Leila repositioned herself so that her head was resting on his shoulder, and wrapped her two emaciated arms around his one strong arm. Then she said the words that she knew he had been craving for too long. "I love you, Hassoun. Really, I do."

"I love you, too."

It wasn't that Leila was all of a sudden all better. Not even remotely. The feelings of remorse, guilt, hatred, and hopelessness were all still there. She was still angry at the universe for putting her family where they were, and for making her choose among her loved ones. She still felt frustrated about her marriage and disgusted when she thought of the world into which her two boys had been born. She still hated herself for her weaknesses as well as for her privilege.

These feelings were all still there, and not a few times in the two days since she had been released from the hospital did she again contemplate ending it all. When on the highway in a taxi, she caught herself daydreaming about jumping out; when getting something in the kitchen, the sight of the knife block evoked the image of blood oozing from her wrists; and she wondered where Hassoun had hidden the medications and contemplated going straight to a pharmacy in Beirut for a refill.

But Leila was working hard at suppressing those thoughts, and with each day, it became a little bit easier.

It wasn't that those thoughts were gone or fading away. It was that she had discovered something new within herself. Or, perhaps more accurately, she had rediscovered something within herself that she had forgotten. The optimism and expectation that had overtaken her the moment Maha told her of Nisreen's release - poor girl, whom Leila had abandoned on the other side of Viber at that very moment, leaving her to listen for God knows how long to God know's what - that feeling was something Leila immediately recognized as being an integral part of herself. She was a woman of vision and courage, resourceful and energetic and determined. She could despair at the way hope had been sucked out of her life, but instead she wanted to be that person who brought hope to the lives of others.

This was the Leila to which she aspired to be. This was the true Leila. The depressed, anxious, suicidal Leila was also a part of her, but she was learning to ignore those tiny demons and instead listen to the much truer voices of hope that had never fully been silenced. If they had, she would have been less frustrated, less disappointed with each turn of events.

She knew Hassoun didn't want her to go to Beirut. He didn't want to lose her the moment he had her back, of course, but more importantly, he was worried that she was still unstable. Also, money was already tight with all the other expenses they had taken on recently. But Leila knew she had to do this, even if it was risky, her ugly side still fighting a battle for her soul, because she also knew that it would win if she stayed. So she made sure to show Hassoun that she was fine, to do everything right so that he wouldn't worry about her. During the next day and a half, Leila spoiled her boys - all three of them - with as much love as she had to give. She cooked up a storm and went over housekeeping instructions with Mila. She wrote little notes to her friends in Kuwait, the ones who felt as far from her now as Timbuktu, apologizing for missing their assorted soirees and wedding parties and circumcision celebrations.

And not two full days after being released from the hospital, against doctor's order and against both her own and her husband's better judgment, once again wearing her blue travel *'abaya* with a red floral headscarf, Leila gave each little boy a hug and a kiss, embraced their father as tight as she could, then waved goodbye as they drove away from the airport drop-off area.

Chapter Twenty-Nine

Maha was waiting at Beirut International Airport, Samir by her side. Leila saw them standing together the moment she emerged from the automatic double doors. Maha looked completely different than she had when Leila last saw her as a university student. Her eyes had sunk, and her hair was prematurely gray. But she was positively glowing nonetheless. Her face was round and full, and she wore a cute yellow top that flaunted the contours of her utterly massive belly. Even so, the smile was the same, and the look of thrill in her eyes told Leila that Maha recognized her as well.

They ran toward each other and gripped one another tightly, tears flowing freely from the moment their bodies touched. Pressed up against her friend, Leila could feel flutters in Maha's belly, which made her cry even harder even as she struggled to hold back giggles.

Standing like that for an unknown amount of time, it was Samir's awkward clearing of the throat that pulled them apart.

Wiping her eyes, then smoothing her blouse, Maha stepped back and asked, "Leila, do you remember Samir?"

"Of course!" Leila exclaimed. "It has been too long, but it is wonderful to see you again. And congratulations." She stuck out her hand to shake his.

"It is good to see you again too. My lovely wife has not slept a wink since you told her you were coming."

They began wandering toward the door as Leila joked, "I don't know how she could sleep anyway; she's huge!"

Maha took Leila's arm in hers as they followed Samir and the cart of luggage. "Seriously. I'm not sure I can take this anymore."

"Don't worry, dear, the baby will be here soon. And it's going to be beautiful." Leila tapped Maha's belly softly.

They didn't speak again until they were in the car and headed out of the airport. The sun was setting, shooting a glorious array of color over the Mediterranean to their left.

Leila commented, "I've never been to Lebanon before. This is beautiful."

"It's not for nothing that they call Beirut the 'Pearl of the Mediterranean'," Samir commented.

"Just don't look to your right, then!" Maha added. "That's one of the worst slums in Beirut, the Bourj al-Barajneh camp."

Leila couldn't help but glance to her right, and saw a neighborhood, not unlike the one where her family was now lodged in Amman, but worse. She turned again in the direction of the sea to watch the last rays of sun blasting across the sky.

Maha then began talking about plans. "So, here's the big news. While you were in the air, Nisreen was officially released. Just about an hour ago, she was deposited at the German embassy. I haven't spoken to her yet, but received a text message from my contact there confirming that she was free."

Leila couldn't help but let out a little "Lalalalalala" cry like she would at a wedding celebration.

Samir offered, "It's amazing what Maha has achieved in these past few months. We're all in awe that it has worked."

Maha ignored the flattery of her husband, saying, "The agreement is that tomorrow morning an embassy car will bring her into Lebanon using the military road, no questions asked. She should arrive at the German embassy here by noon. Germany has offered her asylum, but she may choose to stay in Lebanon. She doesn't know anything at all yet, as far as I know. No one has had any contact with her since she's been in jail."

"Not even her family?" Leila asked, the vague possibility of encountering her old college boyfriend, Nisreen's older brother, making her a bit nervous even now after all these years.

"We were never able to contact them. As you know, we did find her brother – Ahmed, you know – in Canada. He encouraged us to do what we were doing because he was too far away. Seemed a little cold, if you ask me. I'm so glad he's there, and you're here. And her parents are gone in the wind. That's not true. We know that they're still in Syria. But whether they're in an area under siege, or hiding for their own self-preservation, or being careful because they could make her situation worse because they have done something – we don't know."

"So literally, we – well, you, it's not like I actually did anything in the end – have pulled her out of her country to exile, away from her family possibly forever, and she doesn't know anything at all."

"Yup!" Maha said with surprising gaiety in her voice. But then she added, "Before we started any of the backroom negotiations, we did confirm her situation. She was arrested because of the blog, and because of that, she was suspected of having ties to certain rebel groups. We don't know if she actually does have any ties, though we couldn't find any evidence of it so we argued that she wasn't."

"Who is 'we'?" Leila interrupted.

"There are three of us on the team here in Beirut now. Well, four really, but the fourth is too busy to do too much. But for Nisreen, I also started working closely with a British advocacy organization and someone here in Lebanon from the United Nations."

"Did you know anything about this kind of work before?" Leila asked.

"Nothing. I'm learning as I'm going. And I'm not stopping with Nisreen," Maha admitted proudly. "But back to tomorrow. So she has no idea you have been involved, nor me."

"Have you ever even met her?"

"Nope. I only know her from your stories. But they are expecting us at the embassy, to receive her. They will call us when the car crosses the border then we can head over. It's just a five-minute taxi ride from here. But we don't know what shape she will be in. She was probably tortured, maybe a lot, while in prison. It has been four months. A lot can happen in four months. So they warned us to be ready for anything."

"Sure, of course," Leila agreed, trying to imagine how one was to behave when receiving an estranged friend in a foreign country when that friend had been tortured in jail just the day before.

Samir then interjected, "Leila, are you hungry?"

Leila replied as noncommittally as she could. Her appetite was still not back from her own ordeal of the past few weeks, but she was forcing herself to eat as normally as she could, both for her own mental health and to reassure others that she was well.

Samir apparently chose to interpret her reticence as politeness, because he immediately suggested that they stop by a mezze restaurant overlooking the Mediterranean on their way home. He pointed out that his and Maha's days of spontaneity would be ending soon so they should celebrate not only Leila's arrival but also their own last days of childless freedom.

The restaurant was like nothing Leila had ever experienced. It was perched by the famed Pigeon Rocks on the top of a cliff overlooking the water and the rock formation below. The smell of the sea and the sound of the soft waves lapping against the rocks was idyllic. The food was like something from another world. It reminded Leila of what she might eat in an old Damascene restaurant: hommous, yogurt balls, a variety of olives and salads, chips, skewers of meat, and assorted other dishes. While she didn't find the flavor quite as appealing as it would have been in Syria, it was much better than the Lebanese restaurants in Kuwait, and the presentation was impeccable, with flowers carved out of radishes and drawings somehow sketched into each dip, using finely diced parsley.

As they ate, they caught up on the good bits of life. Plans for the baby's birth and arrangements for the baby room, news about Saleh and Hammoudi and their performance in school, Hassoun's job, Samir's workload at church. They easily steered away from any mention of Samir's imprisonment, Maha's mother who was still in mourning, Leila's family in Amman, her recent illness, or their mutual friend Huda who had now done the stupidest thing either Leila or Maha could imagine, though they had not yet admitted that to each other. They did speak of Roxy, though, and Maha shared about how Roxy had reappeared in her life at just the perfect moment, then disappeared again, but only after Maha was at a place where she could face life again. Maha still missed her, even though from all Roxy's correspondence it seemed that she couldn't be happier caring for her now-disabled husband in her parent's home back in their hometown of Sweida.

When they arrived home, Samir gave his apologies and withdrew to sleep. He said he had had an early prayer breakfast that morning and had planned another meeting with the church deacons the next morning.

Left alone, the women immediately ventured into more difficult conversational waters.

"So what happened, Leila, that you were in the hospital for over a week?" Maha started.

Leila was surprised to find how difficult it was to answer the question. She had been preparing herself for this and had made a solemn promise to Hassoun that she would tell Maha everything and ask her friend to keep her accountable. She had told Hassoun that she and Maha were like sisters, even closer than sisters, so of course she would tell her and, of course, Maha would be supportive. But now, sitting side by side on the same sofa, seeing each other face to face for the first time since university, Leila's mouth went dry. She made a little choking sound.

"What is it?" Maha asked, suddenly concerned. When Leila waved her off, gesturing with her hands that she was fine, Maha offered to make them some flower tea. Leila waited in the living room, building her courage.

The moment Maha returned, tray in hand, Leila said the words, to get them out of herself as quickly and as definitively as she could. "I tried to kill myself."

In the next second, Leila saw Maha's grip on the tray loosen, and it was as if in slow motion that she watched the tray with its two little glasses, pot of hot tea and sugar bowl begin to fall to the ground. But Maha recovered herself, and it fell not even an inch before she regained her grip and managed to drop the tray abruptly, but in one piece, on the coffee table.

Then, she turned to Leila, still standing with arms outspread, and asked, "You what?"

Ashamed, Leila said, "You heard me."

Maha sat back down on the sofa, her bulk falling heavily by Leila's side. "Leila, I have no idea what to say. I mean, I never imagined... But...but why?"

"The doctors said that that's not a helpful question to ask. I don't really have an answer."

Maha stared at her a bit, then asked, "So what should I ask you?"

"No, 'why' is a good question. Just the doctors, you know. But of course, I have thought about why a lot. And really, I don't have a good answer. It started when I got back to Kuwait. No, actually, it started when I was living with my mother in that godawful slum in Amman. They're still there, you know. I still can't believe that such a terrible little flat was all we could afford for them. I think I was miserable there on their behalf. So I didn't want to leave, but Hassoun insisted. He was right, of course, because it was a horrid place for my boys. That's part of why I left them in Kuwait this time. They need to be in a supportive environment. I'm not sure what took over me, but I was completely useless from the moment we landed back in Kuwait. Then, last week it was like something possessed me that I couldn't even tell you what it was. I overdosed on pills, and they had to pump my stomach."

"That was just two weeks ago?" Maha asked, laying her hands on Leila's knees.

"Yes."

"Girl, what are you doing here? Shouldn't you be recovering or something?"

"Probably. But I needed to come. This is my recovery. I'm sorry, I should have told you all this before I came instead of just dumping it on you now that I'm here. I needed to get away from family for a bit. And I needed to be with friends. But it wasn't just that. This is the first time I have felt alive in, well, months. The first time I felt even a little bit happy was when you told me Nisreen was being released. I honestly feel like a new person now compared to two days ago. So I knew I needed to see this through."

Maha was nodding enthusiastically now as if she understood. Maybe she did understand. Maybe she was nodding her head silly because she understood nothing at all and couldn't think of anything to do but nod her head.

But before Maha could change the subject, Leila delivered the letter from Hassoun with all the instructions. Poor Maha. Leila felt a twinge of regret. Coming to Lebanon was a stupid idea. The icky compote of emotions began to well up again in her heart and Leila found herself drawing her knees into her heart as tears came to her eyes. She wanted to disappear into the sofa and never come out again. She could catch a taxi back to the airport and fly back to Kuwait though that prospect was even more disheartening. She ducked her head into her knees and took a deep breath.

Then Maha said, "Well, I'm glad you came. These last few months have been insane. For all of us. We sisters need to keep together."

This brought the tears out in full flow, and Leila accepted Maha's embrace gratefully. A friend who was closer than a sister.

Leila was amazed how, after this and after reading Hassoun's instructions and informing Leila apologetically that she would need to share this with Samir but that she promised not to tell anyone else, Maha acted as if everything were normal again. She asked Leila about her family in Jordan and Leila shared, in intricate detail, the entire process of finding a home for them and how much they were paying in rent and the terrible school her nephews were attending and everything else she could think of to share about her family. She mentioned that she had two brothers who were still stuck in Lebanon, but that she hadn't told them she was coming to town. She wasn't sure if it would be good to see them or not. Then she showed Maha photos of Za'atari camp and of the flat in Jabal Hussein and received the appropriate words of sympathy.

Next, in a whisper, Leila asked Maha about Samir. Maha shared that Samir still had nightmares and too many days in which he awoke on the proverbial wrong side of the bed, and about how he had become a bit of a workaholic doing dozens of different projects at the church. But that he was still a good and kind husband, and Maha wished she could somehow just erase that memory from their lives. Since they had been able to put it behind themselves in all practical ways, it would be wonderful to put it behind themselves in emotional terms as well. But that would take time. The head pastor of the church was reminding Samir all the time that he had to take it one day at a time, and Samir passed that bit of wisdom on to Maha at least once a week. Maha, in turn, shared the message of patience to her mother back in Syria, who was unwell. She would not come to Lebanon, though, because she refused to run the risk of being exiled from her country. Maha could not visit her mother, either, after the warning she had received at the border. Her one living brother was now studying in Europe, and most of their other relatives were either stuck in Syria or making a new life somewhere, so Maha was quite orphaned in Lebanon. Her advocacy friends now formed her social circle, and she was enjoying them. They had planned a party tomorrow night for Nisreen's homecoming though they were ready to cancel depending on how the Mockingbird felt. They were quickly becoming her family. Maha shared about how her heart and Samir's were miles away and that she feared they would never come together again. They still loved each other, but there were just too many things they couldn't share.

Once both women had exhausted their personal stories, dreams, and hopes, Huda's name came up.

"I saw a few messages from Huda on Facebook last week," Leila admitted. "But I was in no state to reply. Plus I think maybe I got the messages too late."

"Really?" replied Maha. "That's too bad. Did you never talk to her, then?"

"I chatted with her once. I was still in Jordan. It was right when she added me on Facebook. I think she had just gone to Turkey."

"Probably." Maha poured out more tea for each of them. It was their third cup so far.

"Have you spoken with her?" asked Leila, as she stirred sugar into her tea.

Maha, who wasn't taking sugar, took a sip of the pale green concoction. Then, she said, "Yes, a few times. It sounds like I spoke with her right around the same time as you. It was a very strange conversation. She said that it was because of Roxy and me that she went to Turkey."

"*Kif ya'ani?*"

"Do you remember before, when Roxy tracked her down on Facebook? I told you that she and I skyped with her when she was still in Latakia. It was a very awkward, short conversation, because we didn't know what could be said and what couldn't. But also because Huda was kind of like someone from another planet."

"*Kif ya'ani?*" Leila repeated, now done stirring and putting the spoon down on the tray.

"Well, if nothing else, so boring. We weren't sure if it was because of her work or because she had to be careful what she was saying. But it sounded like she had no life at all. Miserable at work, living with a sister who never talked with her, not dating, no other activities. Just infernally dull. Apparently it wasn't just Roxy and me who thought that. Huda thought that, too, so that's why she picked up and went to Turkey. I didn't see the connection, really, but when we spoke, she was so grateful to me, like I had brought her back from the dead or something."

"Maybe you had," Leila commented thoughtfully. "Maybe her life was exactly like you described it and maybe she needed something to remind her that she was capable of so much more."

"But to join the FSA? Who does that?" Maha exclaimed, putting her half-drunk cup down on the table with a thud.

Leila shook her head. She certainly didn't know anyone who would do that.

"I mean, I don't like being blamed for her going crazy," commented Maha.

"So, is it for sure that she went?" Leila asked. "Joined the fighters, I mean?"

"Looks like it. I never actually talked to her again, but we chatted a few times on Facebook. She was in Turkey for a month, and it looks like she met someone there."

"Really?" Leila raised an eyebrow. "That would be great. She was always so lonely, and would be such a great companion for a good man."

"Not good," countered Maha. "This guy sounded like a real asshole. Apparently, he was just trying to get her into bed. Her and a dozen other girls."

"How could you tell that?"

"You can just tell. There are a lot of those guys here in Beirut, too. I meet them because they're all activists and revolutionaries and idealists. They do great work, mobilizing people or managing aid programs or producing beautiful art or all kinds of things. But they are a little bit too free love if you know what I mean."

"I'll take your word for it. Remember, I'm just a simple Muslim girl from the village," Leila laughed. But then, serious again. "So then what did he do to Huda?"

"That girl is solid. I'll give her that," declared Maha. "Apparently she didn't change her plans for him or even give him what he wanted. At least not that I know of. I had kind of hoped she would, just long enough to get her head straight and stay out of a war zone. But no. The last time we chatted was just over a week ago. She said she wouldn't have communications again for a while. I didn't ask her more and didn't really want to know. Plus, you know, the Lebanese government monitors things, too. Probably the Turkish government, too. So if she was going to join a rebel command, she couldn't tell me much about that."

"So she went."

"As far as I could tell. I haven't heard from her again."

"The last message she sent me was just over a week ago, too," observed Leila. "And it said about the same thing as what you just told me. It's too bad I didn't talk to her again. I hope that we can catch up with her soon and that she doesn't stay there too long."

"Me too," said Maha. "I just pray she comes back safely in one piece. You know, alive and with all her limbs. And soon would be good."

Leila took the last sip and lay the cup down on the tray. Maha picked her cup up and finished her tea in one gulp. Then she too lay her cup on the tray.

The friends sat pondering their friend Huda for a few minutes.

Then Maha put her arms back to push herself up off the sofa. She groaned from her weight as she stood, but once standing she walked cheerily over to where her computer sat on the lower shelf of the television stand. "I have been checking her Facebook profile from time to time to see if there is news," she said as she unplugged the computer and carried it back to the sofa. "But with all the excitement getting ready for your arrival, and then for Nisreen, it has been a couple of days."

Both Maha and Leila stared at the screen as Facebook loaded. Maha typed Huda's name into the search box and was immediately directed to her page.

She scrolled down to below the cover image and profile shot and 'About' icons. Then her hand froze.

Leila's jaw dropped.

Both women just stared at the screen, blinking and with mouths open.

What they saw was a photo of a pale-faced woman, black-and-white checkered scarf wrapped around her head. Blood was seeping from an obvious bullet hole, just above the cheek, the bright red contrasting with the white squares on her headdress.

The face was Huda's.

The caption, written by one "Adnan Karwaji," said: Rest in Peace, martyr for Freedom, taken from us on her first mission #HudaHouria.

The shock took a while to register for both Maha and Leila. Neither had any coherent thoughts. Instead, they just stared silently at the disfigured face of their old university mate.

Eventually, Maha slammed the laptop shut. Then Leila spoke. "I remember once, in our second year at university, Huda gave me a full three-hour lecture on the rights of women in the Syrian constitution. She said she planned on dedicating her life to making sure that the constitutional law was applied to perfection. I remember being in awe of how much she knew, her ability to cite, in detail, every little nuance of the canon and the words of several jurists who had commented on it. But it wasn't just rote memory, you know? It was the first time I had met someone who truly loved learning, who was passionate about the words she was memorizing. Huda would rather spend a day in the library memorizing some old law book that she thought was important than do just about anything else."

Maha considered this for a moment, then responded, "Now I wish Roxy and I had never called her. I wish we had just left her to her boring Latakia life."

"Don't say that," Leila said. "Huda was not created for a boring life."

Maha gave no response, just sat there, now leaning her head against the back of the sofa.

Leila, for her part, did not voice the guilt that she felt at having ignored her friend's messages during the past month, at having allowed herself to become so self-absorbed that she had not so much as spoken with someone who she would have previously called her 'best friend.' And now she had sent her to her death. Leila's words to Maha were true. She doubted that death was a worse fate than a workaday existence for Huda. But if Leila had reached out to her friend, maybe they could have found a third option? Leila remembered how she had not been there for Huda during her darkest days at the University of Damascus, and she realized she had failed her friend more than she had done right by her. Leila, all of a sudden, felt an urgent need to get out of this stifling flat. And to die. She was the worst friend who had ever walked the face of this earth. She could add that to her resume as bad wife, neglectful mother, and spoiled daughter.

But the shock of the moment kept Leila glued to the sofa long enough for Maha to sit up.

"I know what to do," Maha said. "Let's write her an obituary. Let's write all the great things about Huda that this idiot Adnan – yes, that's the guy – didn't know. Let's tell the world that she wasn't just a martyr, but that she stood for something. Let's make her death count."

Given a task, Leila's mind was brought back to the present. With little thought, as if by rote, she began to write down the qualities that best described Huda while Maha zapped a message to Roxy, the only one who was friends with Huda's old Latakia 'sterilized' Facebook profile. She delivered the news with a one-line message then asked Roxy to send her a good photo from Huda's old profile.

A minute later, Maha showed Leila her phone. It was a message from Roxy: My prayers with you and Leila and Nisreen. God bless that beautiful soul. When you write the obituary, don't forget to say that Huda was the purest heart ever to walk the face of the earth.

At reading those words, a tear came to Leila's eyes. She heard a soft sob next to her and realized that Maha, too, was crying. Leila reached an arm around Maha's shoulders, and Maha hugged her back, and they shared a good cry.

In loving memory of our dear friend Huda, a woman of conviction and honor. She believed in justice and in truth and strove for excellence in everything she did. A world that was not perfect was a world to be improved. The purest heart to ever walk the face of the earth gave her life willingly out of a desire to see a Syria where freedom, justice, and excellence could thrive.

They chose a photo that showed her silhouette facing a field of wildflowers with the sun setting in the background.

When Samir emerged from his room the next morning, Maha and Leila were still on the sofa, empty tea cups on the tray in front of them and the computer flickering to Maha's side. Leila's head was on Maha's shoulder, and Maha's head was on Leila's head.

The noise of the bathroom door closing woke Maha up. She lifted her head and looked around, then tried to gently sit up, leaving Leila's torso resting against the cushion, but Leila's eyes fluttered open.

"What time is it?" Leila asked, sleepily.

"I don't know. But I hear Samir in the bathroom. He'll want coffee before he leaves. Do you want coffee?"

"Sure."

Maha lifted herself off of the sofa and walked into the kitchen, oddly alert.

She wanted last night to be a bad dream, but she knew it wasn't. Huda really was gone. They had seen the photographic evidence. Maha and Leila had spent the night texting back and forth with Roxy to get the text of their brief memorial for their friend just perfect. Then Maha had begun her posting routine to all her pages and groups on Facebook, with a new, kinder hashtag, #weloveHuda. She set the wheels in motion to spread it all over Twitter, and to a few activist fora.

Then as they watched the story get shared across cyberspace, Maha and Leila had swapped memories of the good old days, their student years at the University of Damascus. They told stories of Huda and of each other, and of Roxy and other dormmates. They always came back to Huda, though, and relived countless moments with their dearly departed friend, devotedly dwelling on the good. At some point in their nostalgia, sleep had overtaken them.

Water heating on the stove, Maha reached into the cupboard for the coffee grounds.

Leila stumbled in as Maha was closing the cupboard door. "What a day," she said. "I came to Beirut to celebrate a life saved. And instead, we drink to a life lost."

"Today is a new day," commented Maha. "Yesterday we lost a friend. Today we get one back."

Leila's eyes were red and near to overflowing with tears. Maha felt her own eyes begin to grow moist.

She put the coffee into the pot and stirred. While she waited for it to boil, she went over to Leila and gave her a hug. As she held her friend, it felt like Leila was clinging to her for dear life.

The coffee made, Maha showed Leila into the guest room. Leila's scarf, still on from when she had left her own home in Kuwait the previous morning, was rumpled and crooked. So Maha left her alone to remove and reattach it and to settle in. Right at that moment, Samir emerged from the bathroom.

Maha followed him to the living room and poured his coffee.

"I see you two stayed up chatting all night," he said with a smile. "Just like two schoolgirls again."

But Maha returned his laugh with a scowl.

So Samir said, "I'm sorry. It's not a problem, really. I don't mind. I'm glad you can catch up with your friend."

"No, it's not that," Maha hesitated. "It's just that, well, we got some bad news last night."

"Did something happen to Nisreen?" Samir then asked, alarmed.

"No. Nisreen is still fine, thank God. She should be leaving Damascus soon. It is another friend of ours from university, Huda. I think I mentioned her."

"Is she the one who went to Turkey?"

"That's her," replied Maha. "Well, she left Turkey and went back to Syria. She went to somewhere near the Islamic Front and, well, she's dead."

That was all she said and all she wanted to say. She stood up and walked to the kitchen with the pretense of getting some water before Samir could try to comfort her.

She heard Samir standing up and his footsteps beginning to follow her, but just then the door to the guestroom – soon to be baby room – opened and Leila emerged.

"Good morning!" she said brightly to Samir.

Samir replied wishing her a good morning, but Maha could hear that his voice was a bit stunned.

"Did you sleep well?" Leila asked in that cheerful voice which blithely ignored the realities of life, instead focusing on the etiquette of a good houseguest.

Samir didn't answer immediately. Then, he stuttered a bit before saying, "Yes, well, thank you. And you? I hear you didn't sleep at all."

Leila chuckled. "Just a little bit. Thank you again for letting me visit."

Samir again didn't reply immediately, and listening from the kitchen Maha felt his confusion about the news he had just been delivered, mixed with awkwardness around their conservative Muslim houseguest in the intimate early hours of the morning.

She walked out to the living room, carrying a bottle of water.

But she didn't want to talk about Huda. Not now. So she announced, "Here's the water! Leila, come, let me pour your coffee for you. You know, I can't wait until this baby is out and I'm allowed to drink coffee again. The smell is pure torture when you can't have any." She handed Leila a cup and gestured for her friend to sit beside her on the sofa. Coffee in hand, Samir plunked himself on an armchair.

Maha kept talking. "So, today, Leila, you and I will go to the embassy as soon as they call saying that Nisreen has crossed the border. But before that, we should go out and get some things for tonight. For the party, if we do it. Yesterday I bought some Arabic sweets and some chocolates, but I want to go up to the market that has good fruit. Samir, can you pick up some beer and wine on your way home? You know these guys. They can drink."

Leila gasped slightly. Maha had suspected that this type of party might be a shock to her friend. Leila had never been to a party where alcohol was served in her entire life. Such parties happened in the homes of many expats living in Kuwait, but she and Hassoun had branded themselves as good Muslims, and so had only been invited to the more conservative parties. But now Leila was staying with a Christian family in Beirut, and Maha's friends were mostly ultra-liberals who had worked hard on

Nisreen's behalf. She would have to respect the ways of the Christians and the liberals.

But Maha stopped herself and asked, "Leila, I should have asked first. Do you mind? Will your husband mind? I just assumed... Samir doesn't actually like keeping alcohol in the house either, but our friends do like a good party."

Leila waved off her friend's concern, saying, "No, it's fine. I just forgot where we were for a minute." Then, she added, "It will be fun."

"Thank you. Samir, make sure there are some nice juices also, ok? Maybe Leila and I won't be the only people not drinking."

Samir nodded, studying Maha.

But Maha wouldn't let him change the subject. She continued, "Even though Nisreen will arrive around noon, I have no idea how long it will take at the embassy. They will probably want to have a few meetings. Maybe they'll want to eat with us, maybe not. I wonder if Nisreen will be hungry? Should I have cooked something for lunch? Oh well, I think it's too late now anyway. We can just order in some food."

Maha kept talking and planning and plotting, chattering away about the minute details of the day while Leila listened, trying to follow the various steps so that she would be ready to help as needed. Samir also listened, but Maha could tell he was not following very closely. He didn't like it when she glossed over major issues, making light of big things. Maha knew that, but she also knew that Samir had not been with them in the middle of the night when Maha had cried into Leila's arms and Leila into Maha's. She had mourned Huda and would continue to mourn in her own way. A trite prayer or scripture verse, or even Samir's strong kind arms, were not the comfort she wanted.

Eventually, it was time for Samir to leave for his early morning meeting. He promised to be home by 5 when the first guests might start to arrive. Maha promised to text him with updates throughout the day. He leaned down and gave her a peck on the cheek, then said farewell to Leila, and walked out the door. Maha sighed with relief and carried the dishes into the kitchen, leaving Leila on the sofa texting Hassoun and her boys.

Chapter Thirty

Nisreen made it. When the message came, Maha and Leila were just finishing their shopping at the market. When the phone buzzed, Maha took a quick look then extended it so Leila could read it as well. Both women began screaming, Leila jumping up and down and Maha – whose body didn't allow for jumping – waving her hands in the air. They hardly noticed that they were squeezed up between a pile of oranges and a display of lettuce and herbs. They didn't care at all that half a dozen other customers were staring at them. They just screamed and jumped and waved. Then Leila wrapped her arms around Maha's bulky torso and nearly shouted into her ears, "Thank you!"

A minute later, they were once again two composed married women finishing up their shopping for the day. They calmly walked to the cash register and had their apples, grapes, pomegranates and cherries weighed. Maha paid, Leila not yet having exchanged any money, and then they meandered out of the store.

But as soon as they were on the street, Maha grabbed Leila's arm and seethed through her teeth, "We're going to be late. We need to find a taxi, fast."

Leaving Maha on the sidewalk with the bags of fruits, Leila walked up to the street corner to try to flag a cab. Five cars drove past, all with other passengers, and Leila turned to look back at Maha, shrugging her shoulders as if to ask what to do. Maha bent down awkwardly and picked up the bags, starting to drag herself and the produce up the street, but when she glanced up, she saw that Leila had managed to stop a car.

The taxi drove down the block, and Leila helped Maha load the groceries into the backseat, then crawled in herself, allowing Maha to climb in last so she wouldn't have to inch across the seat. Maha gave her address to the driver, then asked him to wait just a minute while they dropped off their bags, and then take them to the German Embassy.

"Twenty thousand," said the driver.

"What?" Maha said, in well-rehearsed shock.

"It's a special route. A special route costs twenty thousand."

"The house is just on the way. Ten is plenty."

They settled on fifteen thousand, then Maha leaned back against the black velvet seat of the classic Mercedes. But at the end of the street, they hit traffic and Maha leaned forward nervously again.

"How long does it take to get from the border to the embassy?" Leila asked.

"Oh, it's at least an hour," Maha answered, sitting forward and peering past the headrest of the front passenger seat to study the flow of cars ahead.

"So we still have plenty of time, right?" Leila asked. "It won't take us an hour to get to the embassy."

"It shouldn't."

"So we're fine," Leila leaned back contentedly. Then she sighed dreamily. "She's here. Nisreen is safe and she's here."

Eyes still on the traffic, the taxi having just pulled off onto a street with cars moving at little more than a snail's pace, Maha replied, "It's amazing, isn't it? Maybe I should believe in miracles after all because that's what this is."

Leila just murmured and stared out her window at the Beiruti women and children and men and pet dogs that were wandering by. True to Lebanon's fame across the Arab world, everyone, even the dogs, was fashionably dressed.

Then Maha said, "It's really going to be tight, though. We need to be there before Nisreen to meet with some people."

"Really?" Leila asked. Maha had not mentioned this before.

"I told my contact there that we would meet with the deputy ambassador. And, I guess, there's someone from a German newspaper who might want to interview us, but we agreed that there would be no publicity specifically about Nisreen's release; that was part of the deal. So he might want to do the interview before she arrives."

"Maha, I didn't know that! Why didn't we go earlier?"

"This was what they suggested."

Leila now leaned forward as well and peered past the driver's head at the cars barely moving in front of them. She had heard tales of Beirut's famed traffic, logjams that could stall all movement on the streets in central neighborhoods for hours on end.

Now neither woman spoke. They just sat leaning forward in the back seat of the taxi, a pile of bags of fruit between them, allowing themselves to get nervous.

Fortunately, at the end of the block, whatever had been causing the logjam gave way and the rest of the trip was smooth. They ran – or Leila ran and Maha loped – into Maha's flat and dropped the bags of fruit on the dining room table, Maha taking a quick look around the room and stopping to re-arrange a pillow on the sofa and a doily by the TV and a pile of magazines in a corner, then they rushed back down to the taxi that whisked them quickly enough to the German embassy.

Once they were done with security and identity checks, a tall blonde woman wearing a smart black skirt suit came down a long white undecorated corridor to greet them.

"Maha, it is so good to see you. What an exciting day, isn't it?" The woman reached forward to shake Maha's hand.

Leila, in her nicest brown *'abaya* and pink-and-white headscarf, felt underdressed all of a sudden. Maha was pregnant and carried off a bohemian look brilliantly, baggy white linen tunic covering her maternity jeans that were folded off mid-calf. But Leila had no bump-sized excuse.

"Anja, how good it is to see you. Thank you again for all your help," Maha was saying, in better English than Leila had realized she knew.

"When are you due?" the embassy official named Anja asked Maha. "You must be getting close."

"End of the month, the doctors say," Maha patted her belly self-consciously. Then, turning to Leila, she said, "I'd like to introduce you to my friend Leila. Leila is my close friend from university days, and also was a very dear friend of Nisreen's. She was the one who inspired us to begin working for her release."

Anja turned to Leila and reached out a hand, which Leila shook heartily with a smile. "What a privilege to meet you, Leila," Anja then said. "I have heard a lot about you and about your friends. We pray together for a free and peaceful Syria where you can all be reunited."

To her great embarrassment, Leila felt tears coming to her eyes. She pushed them back, saying, in her most professional English, "It is I who am eternally grateful to you for all of your help. Thank you for fighting for our friend. She really is amazing. You'll see."

Anja laughed softly, then said, "I have no doubt. I have read all her works, and they are certainly quite impactful. She has a strong voice and vision."

"You read Arabic?" Leila asked, surprised.

"Unfortunately no. But we have had her blog translated into English. We actually want to help her publish it if she's interested."

"Wow!" Leila exclaimed. "That's really amazing." She felt awe and a surprising wave of gratitude well up inside her.

Now, turning again to Maha, Anja said, "Come back to my office where we can wait." Leila and Maha followed Anja down the hallway, as Anja continued. "The journalist I told you about is not coming. We decided it was too risky. So you're off the hook for that one. We'll just sit and drink tea while we wait. The ambassador wants to meet you, so he will probably stop by to say hi."

As it turned out, not only the ambassador wanted to meet them. Seated at a table in the corner of Anja's little office, Maha and Leila were brought their drinks - flower tea for Maha and Lipton for Leila - and held court for the next hour or so while different Germans stepped in to introduce themselves and shake their hands. The women felt like mild celebrities and wondered what the Germans were saying about these two young Syrian friends who just wanted their friend out of jail.

At one point when they were alone, Maha turned and whispered to Leila, "Roxy would love this. It's too bad she couldn't be here, too."

Leila nodded, then added, "Huda, too. I really, really wish Huda could be with us today."

Her eyes were still on the verge of spilling over. Indeed, they had been so since the moment they set foot in the embassy building. She was glad to see that Maha was looking a bit emotional herself.

Then the moment came. Anja, who had been taking care of some business of some sort with someone just outside the room, stepped in and announced, "The car just pulled in."

Maha and Leila were up in a second, moving to follow her out the door.

Maha gripped Leila's arm and said, "Thank you so much for coming. I don't know why I'm so nervous, but I don't think I could have done today without you."

Leila, unsure she could get as much as a single word out without blubbering, just lay her hand on Maha's. Hand-in-hand, they followed Anja's lead and walked into a big driveway.

A swanky black sedan in keeping with the reputation of embassies, with Syrian diplomatic plates, was just pulling in, the big automatic gate folding down behind it. Once the gate was closed, the car engine turned off and two men in suits emerged from the two front seats. Each one reached back to open the door behind him.

First, a German man emerged. Neither Leila nor Maha recognized him nor were they very interested. They kept watching.

Then, from the near side of the car, they saw a slight girl dressed in rolled-up jeans and a ragged oversized T-shirt that had been gathered into a knot around her waist, with very short spiky dark hair, step out. She was wearing dark sunglasses and cheap plastic sandals.

Leila hardly recognized her. There was nothing of the fashionable young lady from an upscale Damascene family remaining. She could see no hint of the clever, impish character that Leila had so admired. In fact, her height was all that Leila recognized of her old friend Nisreen. She stood there staring.

Maha stayed by Leila's side, gripping Leila's arm tightly.

It was Anja who walked forward and extended her professional hand to the girl, saying, "Welcome to Beirut, Nisreen. We are so pleased to have you here. We understand that you know little about why you are here, but now that you're here we can talk about everything. But first, some friends of yours want to say hi." Then, Anja turned back and gestured for Maha and Leila to join her.

Maha pushed Leila gently forward. Leila stumbled up to Nisreen and stared at her. She had not rehearsed for this moment.

But neither had Nisreen. After a moment facing each other, Nisreen removed her sunglasses and peered into Leila's eyes. "Leila?"

That was the last straw. Leila began to sob as she grabbed Nisreen, who was tiny and so frail that Leila hoped she wasn't breaking her though she couldn't resist holding her tight. Nisreen didn't respond, but accepted the hug, leaning her head on Leila's shoulder.

After a moment, Leila pulled herself together and said, "Honey, we have been following you from the beginning, and have been so, but so, worried about you. I don't think you ever met my friend Maha. She was my neighbor at the university, but I might have mentioned her. I know I told her all about you. She really is the one who has brought you here."

Nisreen slowly extended an arm to shake Maha's hand, but Maha instead wrapped her arms around Nisreen.

The initial reunion now past, Anja quickly stepped back into the circle and took control. "Now Nisreen, we know that you have many questions. We know that you didn't know who would be waiting to receive you today, and I understand that this is probably not who you might have been expecting. Maha tells me that all of you lost touch with each other after graduating from university. And I don't think you have had any news of your family, have you?"

Nisreen shook her head no.

"So there's that to sort out. And then we need to start talking about your plans. I know your friends here are very eager to spend some time with you. Maha has offered for you to stay with her. Is that ok? If not, we can arrange something here at the embassy."

Nisreen shrugged. "That's fine."

"Good, then, that's settled. How are you feeling? Can we order you some tea? Coffee? How about lunch? You must be hungry after your trip."

Nisreen didn't respond to that. Leila offered, "Yes, some lunch would be good, wouldn't it?" She turned to Maha, who agreed.

So they all walked back to Anja's office and sat down at her little table. Drinks refreshed and food ordered from a nearby sandwich shop, Anja asked Maha to tell Nisreen the entire story of how they had learned she was taken, what they had begun to do to advocate for her release, the response of Nisreen's loser brother Ahmed and the fact that they were not sure what had happened to the rest of her family, the conditions of her release, and the global interest that had been generated around the Mockingbird and her blog.

When Maha was done giving her summary, Anja added, in a crisp diplomatic voice, "But we need to be careful about publicity. We need to keep our deal to not discuss your imprisonment in a way that makes, ahem, certain people look bad. But also, it should be your decision, whether you continue writing and how you want your writing to be used."

Nisreen then spoke for the first time. "I had no idea anyone read that blog. I thought I was just keeping a journal. I knew that people in Syria might catch on, and I kind of wanted them to. I liked to think it might give people hope. So sure I knew I might be putting myself at risk. But I had no idea anyone outside of Syria would ever care."

Leila then spoke, "Your blog did give hope. I loved it. Your words expressed what we all want for Syria but don't know how to say ourselves. You have always inspired me. You know that, right?"

Maha looked like she was about to add something, but then her mouth dropped and her eyes opened wide. Everyone stared at her as she turned her head to look at the floor below her chair.

"Um," she said tentatively, looking apologetically at Anja. "I think my water just broke on your pretty white office chair."

New Life

Samir was just going to have to get used to the idea. Maha knew that he had been dreaming of the day Maha brought their baby home. His dreams had involved just the three of them, and occasionally one or the other of their mothers. They had included a completed baby room, with crib and Noah's arc figures painted on the wall. They had included taking turns rocking the baby to sleep and then many hours of quietly sitting side-by-side staring together at the human being he and Maha had created.

They had not included two houseguests, two Muslim 'aunties' taking over the cooking and cleaning in the flat, vying for babysitting privileges, and sleeping in the room that had been designated as baby room but which had never been painted or decorated with cute little baby things. They also had not included the endless chatter of three women. And they most certainly had not included a raucous party, attended by every Syrian expat living in downtown Beirut who had ever heard of the Mockingbird or done anything at all on behalf of Syria's political prisoners, on the very night when baby Huda was brought home.

But that is what Samir got, and Maha knew that he would not hold it against her. They had a healthy baby girl who they had not hesitated to name after the friend who had fallen in battle that very week.

They had friends, friends who were in some ways closer than family. With their own families struggling to survive Syria or exile somewhere else, both of their mothers still in Damascus and cautious not to leave the city, the presence of Leila and Nisreen during the first month of little Huda's life was more than welcome.

And, Maha joked to him one afternoon, if Samir wanted to be an evangelist, then he had a project waiting for him in his very own home. Then, a bit more serious, she reminded him not to make her friends uncomfortable but added that she might be ready to go back to church with him.

Maha's labor had been quick and smooth, or at least, that's what the doctors told her. As she remembered it, the most agonizing 6 hours of her life had followed the embarrassing spillage of bodily fluid in the German embassy. Anja had offered to drive Maha to the hospital, and Leila had begun to join them when she saw Nisreen still sitting at the table, gazing at her folded hands. Leila had gone back to ask Nisreen if she would be ok there, or if she wanted to join them. Nisreen had brightened immediately at the invitation and jumped up, showing the first sign of life. There would be many more signs of life in the coming days – interspersed with endless hours of silence and blank stares.

Anja had left the three women at the emergency entrance to the hospital, expressing concern and offering to stay on but clearly not wanting to do so. Before driving off, she had commented that she would call tomorrow to follow up on their meeting with Nisreen. Then Anja was gone, and Leila and Nisreen had each taken one of Maha's arms and helped her, mid-contraction as it were, into the vast maternity building.

Leila had called Samir from the car, and he had come quickly, but this particular hospital didn't really know what to do with men in the delivery room. And so it was that Leila and Nisreen had each held one of Maha's hands during the next hours, encouraging her to breathe, telling her she was acting like a pro, giving her updates and telling her that it would be over soon. When a baby girl was pulled out, all three women sighed with relief. Leila, who had experienced this before, could empathize. Nisreen, who had not, seemed to be in a bit of shock yet enjoying this bonding experience with the woman who had been her salvation.

The nurse went to beckon the father, so Leila and Nisreen withdrew. Too exhausted to talk, they had just waited in the hallway, holding each other's hands.

Only a few minutes had passed when Samir appeared at the door and asked them to come in. That's when Maha, grinning ear to ear, told them that they were naming their little one Huda. Leila let out a little yelp and ran over to give little Huda and her mommy several kisses on their foreheads. Nisreen watched on, but later that night when Leila explained the significance to Nisreen, more tears would be shed.

After that, Leila and Nisreen had returned to Maha's house, while Samir stayed at the hospital. Finally, Leila and her old friend had a chance to catch up. For hours and hours and hours, they spoke about life. Nisreen told her story and spared few details of the agonizing months she had spent behind bars. The most vivid imagination could not do justice to the torment Nisreen described. Leila's story and that of her family felt innocuous by comparison, but she shared them anyway. They sent messages to Nisreen's brother, and a few cousins who Nisreen knew were living outside of Syria, short messages just telling them that she was in Beirut. Nisreen seemed to know why her parents were incognito but wouldn't share.

They dozed for a few hours but were up early to prepare the house for the new family to arrive home. Samir opened the door, Maha and baby in tow, just a few minutes before noon.

And so it was that Leila and Nisreen took over the running of the house, leaving Samir stupefied, having to accept that his family looked nothing at all like what he might have thought.

Maha and baby were coddled over and pampered, given the sofa on which to snuggle. Leila and Nisreen took turns holding little Huda while Maha caught up on her social media. She insisted on rescheduling the party that had been scheduled the night before. For tonight – with Nisreen's permission, of course, which Nisreen gave readily.

As the afternoon hours waned, Leila took over the kitchen, making sure the teacups were never empty. Nisreen asked Maha if she had a cigarette and Maha decided that, pregnancy over, she could sneak a quick smoke herself. The three of them sat there sipping tea and smoking – Leila even tried a cigarette and decided she could learn to like it – and talking until the guests started to arrive in the evening. Every hour or so, Maha lifted up her shirt and happily tucked little Huda's mouth onto her nipple until the newborn began to catch on to the idea of feeding. Maha was a natural at this, it turned out, a master at being mommy and juggling the adventures of life at the same time.

That's when they decided to stay one month. Leila would call Hassoun and tell him she would be back in Kuwait in exactly one month. Considering her last foray had been for four months, she hoped he would be glad to hear it. During this month, Leila hoped to start the process of registering a legal foundation to receive donations for relief and for the bereaved.

Nisreen would decide in one month whether to accept the German offer of asylum or stay in Lebanon. Or attempt to go somewhere else. Still in a state of shock, Nisreen had now been free for two days and in Lebanon for one day. The luster that Leila had always admired was beginning to come back, and Nisreen was fascinated by the offer to publish her writings. Maha and Leila, of course, loved the idea and told her so.

In one month, Huda would hopefully be on a sleep schedule and so, with the help of her friends who were closer than sisters during this first month, Maha could continue with her projects without missing a beat.

The party began, Samir hovering over his wife and baby, looking for ways to be helpful but clearly concerned that this was too much noise for a newborn and for a woman who had just survived childbirth. Finally, Leila offered to take baby Huda to the back room so that Samir could receive his guests. Really, though, she wanted a moment alone with her new friend.

Snuggling the little one and walking back and forth in the guest room, Leila tickled little Huda's face with her pinky finger. She was so tiny and absolutely perfect. "Dearest little daughter of Syria, precious one, you have a powerful legacy to live up to," she whispered. "You were named after an amazing woman. Your mother is an amazing woman, too. You are blessed with role models. But no pressure. The important thing is that you dream your own dreams and find a way to achieve them. We won't rest until you live in a world that lets you do that."

Dear Mockingbird Readers,

Today the bird was set free. I spent four months behind bars, but today I breathe the air of freedom and begin to dream of my future.

Thank you to all who breathed a prayer for me, who sent me messages of hope, and who in some way or another contributed to making today happen.

I wish to write this, my first post back online, not in anger at the injustices I faced, though those are many. Nor describing the inside of a Syrian jail, though you would find it as horrifying a description as you might have guessed. Nor railing against the people who thought that a mere blogger deserved to have her freedom taken away.

No, I wish to write this post in honor of the women who are the reason I am free today. Two women who worked tirelessly for my release. They did this, not out of obligation or even out of frustration, but out of a conviction that it was simply the right thing to do. And out of a sisterly loyalty, something I am afraid I had forgotten about, but which I pledge never to forget again.

Many years ago, back when Syria was a peaceful and tame land, my brother started dating a girl. She was very sweet and very smart, and we became friends. We would meet up to discuss literature and art and the world in which we live. It was to her that I would rant and rail against the inequalities and unfairness that surrounded me. She would listen, nod her head in understanding, then remind me that we couldn't let anger get the best of us. Then she would change the subject to our studies, or to my brother. When she and my brother broke up, I'm afraid we lost touch.

Well, this amazing friend was a reader of The Mockingbird. She remembered my love for the novel of that name and my desire to be, just a little bit, like Atticus Finch. She saw my voice in what I wrote and remembered our friendship of years past.

When I disappeared, she noticed, and she called a friend of hers. This friend, who was a student in Damascus at the same time as me, was someone I had never met. Everyone has told me, though, that the moment she learned that a friend of a friend was in trouble, she dropped everything to start advocating for my release. She had no political motivations - neither do I, for that matter. She just knew a friend of a friend was in trouble. She is a woman of incredible wisdom and resourcefulness, clever and tireless. I don't know what she did, but I know that whatever she did worked, because I am here, alive and free and beginning to dream of a future once again. Four months of dreams suppressed was the worst fate you might imagine.

To these two friends, I owe my life. They lost another dear friend on the same day that I was released. I pray for her soul and wish to God that he had taken me and spared them their friend. But God does not work that way.

I dedicate this blog to these friends, and to the precious little daughter born to one of them hours after my release, a child who I had the honor of helping into the world. This new life is a symbol to me of the new life we can all build together if we will only seek out Good and Right. Sisters, I look forward to pursuing all these things together.

With a heart pouring over,
The Mockingbird

I remember my affliction and my wandering,
the bitterness and the gall.
I well remember them,
and my soul is downcast within me.
Yet this I call to mind
and therefore I have hope:
Because of the Lord's great love we are not consumed.

(Zabur Book of Lamentations)

Glossary of terms (variations in ())

'abaya – cloak worn by women

Ahlan wa Sahlan (Ahlan, Ahlein, Ya Hala) – Welcome, general greeting

Ahmeen – Amen

Aindak (Aindek) – Near you, often used to ask someone to stop or grab something

Alhamdulillah – Praise God

Alhamduilillah a-Salameh – Praise God you are well, often used when someone arrives from a long trip

Allah yesalamek – General reply to well-wishes

Aloh – Hello, typical greeting when answering the phone

Arguile – hookah, shisha

Daiemeh – May it last forever, used to indicate one is done eating

Eid – Holiday, Festival

Felahi(ye) – Country bumpkin

Galabeya – traditional Arab robe or housecoat, worn by women or men

Habibty (habiby) – Dear, darling

Haiati – My life, used as a term of endearment

Hajj(i) – Pilgrimage, or someone who has gone on the pilgrimage to Mecca

Houria - Freedom

Iftar – Feast to break the fast at the end of a day of fasting

Inshallah bitruhi bi-salama – May you go and arrive safely in peace

Islamu Edeik – A blessing on your hands, often used as an expression of gratitude

Istaghfar Allah – God forbid

Khalas – Enough, or Stop

Kif ya'ani – How so do you mean?

Koussa – squash or zucchini, courgette

Kul al-'am wa anti bikheir (with reply *wa anti bikheir*) – Happy Birthday or Happy Holiday

Mabrouk - Congratulations

Malish – No big deal

Masha'allah – What God has created!

Phalangist – Member of Lebanese Maronite Christian militia

Sabah al-Kheir (with replies *Sabah al-Nour* or *Sabah al-Ward*) – Good morning

Salamtek – May you feel better, or response to a sneeze or cough

Shahada – Islamic credal statement of faith

Taieb – Delicious, but used to mean ok or very well

Ya – Means of calling the attention of someone, used before a name or a relational term

Ya'ani – It means, or Sort of

Yallah (Yallah bye) – Come on, or Let's go

Zuhorat – Flower tea

Relational terms, often used as expressions of friendliness or affection: *Khale* (Auntie), *Teta* (Grandma), *'ami* (Uncle), *kheie* (Brother), *Mama* (Mother), *Baba* (Father)

Map of Syria and Neighboring countries

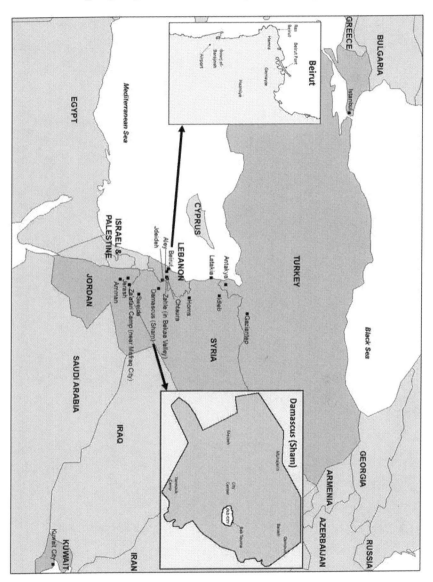

Made in the USA
Charleston, SC
17 May 2016